The Prophecy of Avalon

...a tale of Merlin

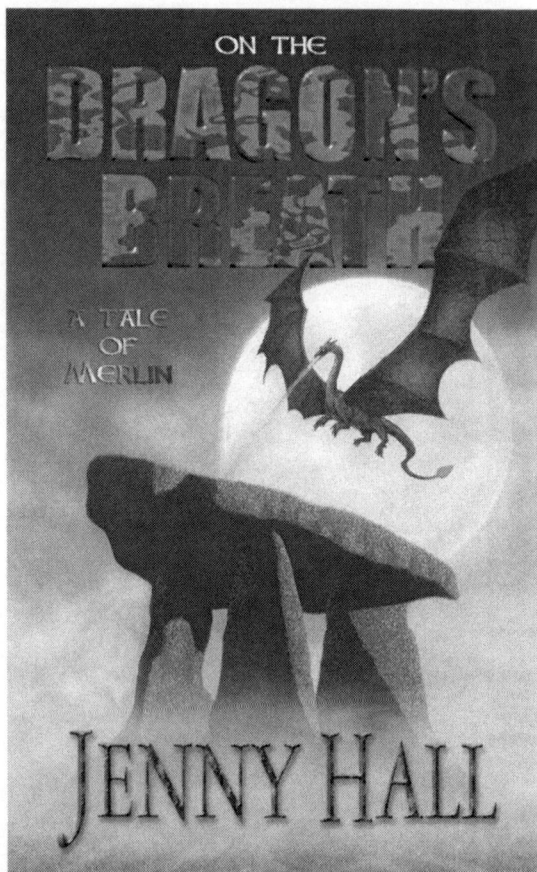

THE GLASTON GIANT
...A TALE OF MERLIN

Even though it's aimed at the young adult market, at 27, I thoroughly enjoyed this book and would recommend anyone to read it (Dragon's Breath). As for the Glaston Giant – a brilliant sequel! I love Merlin and the author has a wicked sense of humour! My skin crawls at the thought of the character Mordred but Mab just makes me chuckle! As for the giant himself – not what I expected – I always assume giants to be stupid lumbering idiots but he had a bit of intelligence – he was just lazy.

Claire Gardner – Wiltshire, UK

THE PLACE OF SHADES
...A TALE OF MERLIN

I have just finished The Place Of Shades and enjoyed it immensely. I must now admit that it could be my favourite book. I did wonder throughout the last few chapters of Shades why Merlin was quite so downcast but thought that the revelation at the end was brilliant and I am looking forward eagerly to the fourth book.

William Sharp – Briercliffe, UK

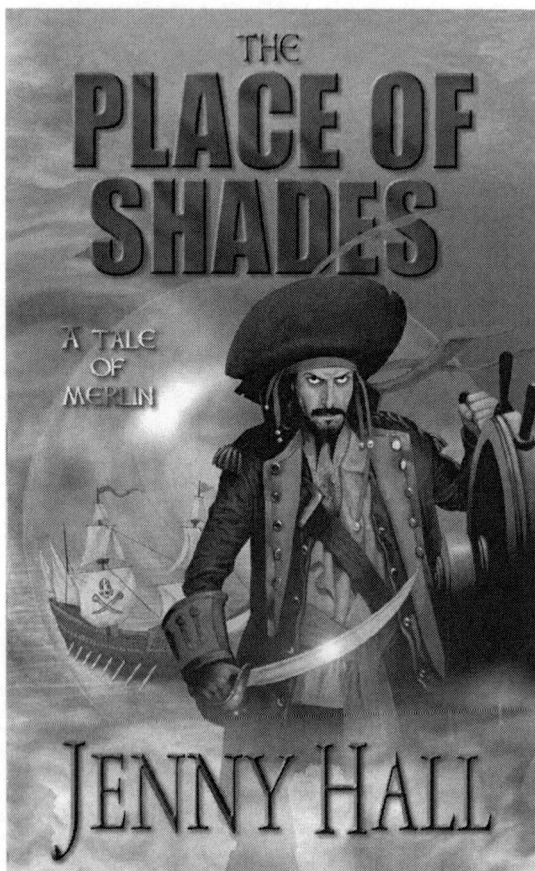

THE MASQUE OF ALL MYSTERIES
...A TALE OF MERLIN

The worst thing about this book was when I finished it.
I enjoyed it so much that I was upset to think I would
now have to wait months for the next one in the series.
Hurry up Jenny and write it quickly.

Joyce Tidd – East Sussex, UK

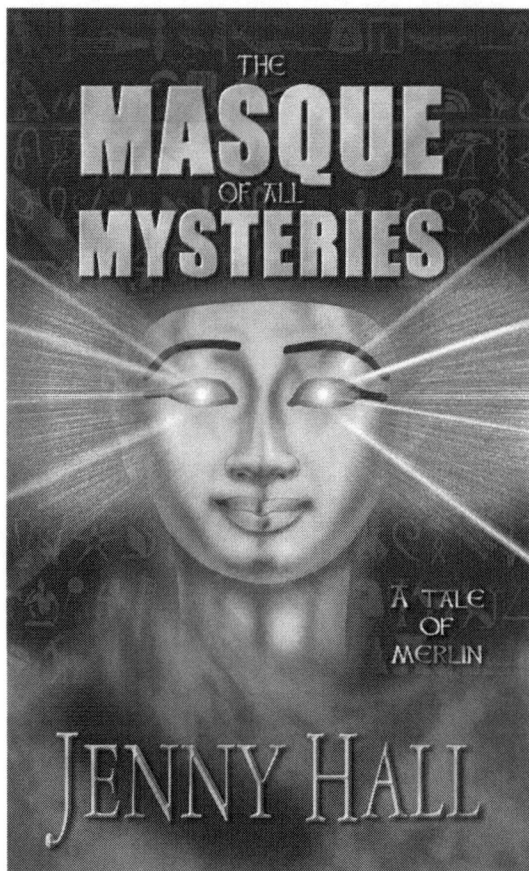

Jenny Hall was born at the end of WWII, spent her childhood in Essex and most of her adult life in London where she worked in a law firm. Her grandfather, having lost a leg in WWI, came to live with the family in his old age and delighted Jenny, her two sisters and other children with his prodigious storytelling, mainly about his life as a blacksmith in Walthamstow and Wickford and the "larks" he and his mates got up to in Victorian England. The storytelling rubbed off and Jenny, now a grandparent herself, has taken up his mantle and writes her tales by the sea on the beautiful south coast of England.

Other Tales of Merlin in this series

On the Dragon's Breath
The Glaston Giant
The Place of Shades
The Masque of all Mysteries

The Prophecy of Avalon

...a tale of Merlin

JENNY HALL

THEOPHILUS BOOKS

EAST SUSSEX

First published in 2012 by
THEOPHILUS BOOKS
13 Eastwood Road,
East Sussex TN39 3PR, England

A catalogue record for this book
is available from the British Library

ISBN 978-09545423-4-4

The famous short pieces that appear in this novel are
extracted, once again, from the works of that celebrated bard,
William Shakespeare, to whom I am very grateful.

Papers used by Theophilus Books are natural, renewable
and recyclable products, made from wood grown in sustainable
forests and certified in accordance with the rules of the
Forest Stewardship Council

Mixed Sources
Product group from well-managed
forests and other controlled sources
www.fsc.org Cert no. SGS-COC-2482
© 1996 Forest Stewardship Council
FSC

Produced and designed by members of
THE GUILD OF MASTER CRAFTSMEN
EVERGREEN GRAPHICS
11 The Drive, Aldwick, West Sussex PO21 4DU
Cover Illustration by Tony Masero
Design and Typesetting by Cecil Smith
Typeset in Minion

Printed and bound in the UK by
T.J. INTERNATIONAL LTD
Trecerus Industrial Estate, Padstow, Cornwall PL28 8RW

For my sisters Maureen and Eileen
– with love

ACKNOWLEDGMENTS

I am much indebted, once again, to Claudia Holness and Jill Barnes for all their hard work and patience in reading and re-reading my work and correcting those typos and errors that always seem to creep in unawares. I should also like to thank Mike Lynott of Bestsellers Books in Bexhill-on-Sea who has always been so supportive in being the first to request a book signing in his shop. I've once again drawn so much from the many fond memories I have of my old dog, Sandy – her character and sense of fun often appearing in my hero's hound Cabal.

JENNY HALL
East Sussex
2012

The Prophecy of Avalon

a tale of Merlin

Moon Song was dying!

There in the shadowy dawn that hangs between sleeping and waking she stood, looking for all the world to be lost within it, her expression confused – should she stay in the world of dreams or was it time (or even safe) to wake up? After a short while she settled down beside the silent pool and waited, searching its depths with an intensity that can only come from deep longing as she sought a movement – a sign that it would be today. The picture faded – night flew away on wings unseen, the trees and grass melted into an emerald river that flowed off into the distance and disappeared and finally she, too, was gone.

Jack shook his head and roused himself from the never-ending dream. How he longed for Rhianne. As he got older he wondered if he would ever see her again. Merlin, who'd begun to travel to the Twentieth Century quite regularly as it reached its end had lately not said if she was alive or dead; well he thought she must be dead because he'd left her back in the Dark Ages some fifteen hundred years ago, but then, again, Merlin could take him back to those days and of the very few times he had gone back she was, year for year, only as many months older than him as she had ever been; and he was sure that Merlin would have said something if she was dead. He'd seen her that last time when Kate and the boys (though they were asleep when she had seen them) had travelled back with him and Merlin from the stone table, so perhaps she was still alive. Then, again, perhaps Merlin would say anything so as not to upset him. Apart from that one time he hadn't seen her or held her in his arms for over forty years. His intake of breath shuddered before he let it out with a long, distressing sound. *'Oh, for goodness' sake, Percy, get a grip!'* Cabal licked the back of Jack's hand and wagged a slow and compassionate tail. 'Yes, I know, old friend, I'm getting maudlin again.'

1

Jack's grandsons were much older now and although Ben had decided to take on the work in the farmstead, something he'd always loved doing since he and his mother and brother had moved back to the village, he still felt the pang of loneliness, and even more so now that old age was continually tapping on his shoulder. He sometimes wondered just what he would have done if Kate and the boys had never come back. Recalling what a miserable person he'd become and how he had almost cut himself off from everyone in the village up to that time, he almost smiled as the last ten years or so ran in fast-forward before his eyes; yes, they had become a true blessing. Determined to shrug off the melancholy of the moment, he ran over in his mind the story he was about to start telling them when they visited later that day, which related to the sad fact that Moon Song was dying.

Moon Song was dying! Just the thought of it, or was it that particular thought, sent a cold shiver up his spine. This was really the last tale in the story; was it, indeed, the last story he would tell? Fear, always present in his life when he was a boy, whispered in his ear. 'Go away,' he almost yelled, making Cabal jump; though the sound was in Jack's head it still reverberated through the hound's brain like a gunshot.

'Sorry, Cab. I must stop allowing these thoughts intruding in my life!'

We stood at the edge of the silent forest and, along with those cold and menacing trees, faced the island, waiting – for what? It seemed as though even they were holding their breath, watching, watching. Between the hill and the place where we were standing arose a vast expanse of mist; it increased in size until it encircled the small hill and gyrated like a drunken serpent in the throes of a weird and mesmerising dance that was being stirred by an unseen ladle in the hands of an invisible and mad spectre.

We'd been there now for a week during which time we had hardly slept and I, for one, was beginning to get extremely twitchy – every time I got onto the subject of just how much longer we had to wait I was just told to hush – it wouldn't be for much longer. 'And it will be well worth the wait I can assure you; trust me!'

Now there was the type of "not much longer" that was like five minutes and then, again, there was another type of "not much longer" that was almost forever. Well, I wasn't happy. I'd spent the last few months – almost a year actually – in and out of a frenzy of "how much longer was I going to have to stay here before he called me back?" "Was he ever going to call me back?" "Would I ever see Rhianne again?" "Surely he hadn't allowed us to marry and then never ever see each other again!" "He'd forgotten me, hadn't he?" "He'd got what he wanted and now he didn't need me anymore, did he?" "He was too good; he could never do that to me, could he?" "He was never coming back, was he?" and then becoming so morose that my family had taken me to see a child psychologist. Child psychologist! I wasn't a child anymore! I was a man – and a married man at that! I could recall once almost letting that information slip. Can you imagine how they would have taken it? "Sorry Mum, Dad! I am not a child anymore; I am married to a lady who was born in the Fifth Century; the wedding took place in a place where the Faerie had prepared it all and fairies flew all around, sprinkling us with fairy dust." Can you see it? They would really have thought me more than one day short of a full year! And as for being hypnotised to see into my subconscious! Well, I certainly wasn't going to let that happen – it might all come out and then what? The psychologist would have had a field day. "Let's try electric shocks; perhaps a spell in a mental home? Might he be on drugs, Madam?"

Well, I knew I couldn't ever tell them anything about being married at 17; for a start it wasn't legal in this country without parental consent, or, more weirdly, not produce said wife and even more bizarrely, tell them she was over 1,500 years old! No, if that happened it definitely wouldn't just be the psychiatrist – it'd be the men in white coats and I'd be locked away.

So I'd had to keep quiet about it all and try and look and act sane just to keep them off my case – and now here I was again, back in time and standing beside Merlin, looking out over a mist that looked deceptively like a lake with an island in the middle of it – waiting – for what and for how much longer? He hadn't said and refused to say anything except "hush" and "not long now".

Though when we had first arrived and I'd asked him what we were waiting for he did go off into some sort of trance and tell me how he'd been here before.

'When the world was young,' he had begun, 'and still wasn't quite sure how to dress herself properly or act in public, I sat high on the peak of the hill opposite Avalon and called out through my mind into the swirling mists that surrounded it. I sat day after day enduring the biting winds of winter until spring's smile melted my icy bones; then those gentle, caressing mists came and went until the hugs of summer began to warm my bones; summer, welcomed at first, turned up the heat and threatened to burn me to a crisp as I searched the horizon from the light pink of early dawn to the deep crimson of evening's dusk, watching all the while as mountain ranges pushed their way up through faults in the earth's crust and snow, as deep and cold as a witch's heart, chilled my soul and then volcanoes, bursting open and ejecting heat so intense I believed the world would be cracked open before breaking up and disappearing into the heavens, shaped the earth. Yes, the world was young and I watched its formation, Percy, as the good and the bad fought for dominance. Then, as it grew older I saw what could happen and knew I had to do something. I then started searching, searching until autumn once again brought back those mists – and then this time she arose. I wanted to cry as she spoke to me. The beauty of this place was all she had seen for aeons. She was tired even then. She had no strength. She had to go. She couldn't tell me what I wanted to know. But,' he added in a more positive tone, 'one day I will know it is the right time and then I could return and she would give me aid. That time, Percy, is now. So we wait – she will come.'

'Well, Merlin, how is it that you actually know that that time is now?'

'Hush.'

And he wouldn't elaborate.

So we waited.

I asked him about Rhianne and he just smiled and said we'd soon be on our way but that this was much more important and 'things have to be done at the right time and in the right order or who knows what might happen!'

I knew that once he got onto that tack there'd be no turning him.

So we just stood there *again* and waited.

But today it happened! It actually happened!

Just out of arm's reach the mist, which had settled down to a silent, slow undulation, began to swirl – like water going down the plughole but in reverse. Merlin had seen it first and had drawn my attention to it by gripping my wrist and holding his finger to his lips for quiet as he stared toward it. I turned my face to see what he was looking at. The hair rose on the back of my neck.

We watched.

We waited.

And then she was there.

'Merlin. I see you.'

Her voice was like the tinkling of many waterfalls and though the words were soft they were clear, but we had to concentrate on them because they were whisked away by mysteries unfathomable as soon as they were spoken, as though, once said they had to be locked away before any evil ear had a chance to listen to or use them.

'I see you too Lady.'

'Why have you called me here?'

'I need your help.'

'How can *I* help you?' Her voice had taken on a sadness so deep that I thought she would disappear; she faded to almost nothing, but then rallied. She continued. 'My power is almost gone and I was sleeping the long sleep of dreams before your voice called me out of my reverie. I believed my waking days were over, that sleep was now my permanent companion and that all I had left were my dreams.'

I was staring at this vision and pulled up my jaw, as the realisation came that my mouth, true to its previous form, was hanging open.

She was beautiful. But I could see right through her. Her hair was long and drifted on a gentle almost non-existent breeze with the ends floating across the top of the mist as she looked around at her surroundings; she was clothed in what appeared to be the finest diaphanous silk that shimmered with all the colours of the rainbow as she hovered within the haze. I wanted to ask Merlin who she was but obviously could only just stand and wait as I watched this slow-motion drama played out in front of me.

'As long as people believe in you, as I do,' Merlin replied, 'you will always return. But I need you to tell me all you know about the prophecy.'

She was silent for so long and looked extremely perplexed that I began to think she had forgotten it or didn't know what Merlin was talking about.

Then she spoke again, 'My prophecy?'

'Yes, the one you shouted from the island all those years ago.'

'Ah, when the world and I were young! When I was strong. When I lived.'

Merlin sat, well his backside leaned really, on a huge boulder at the edge of the mist. I joined him.

We waited while the Lady gathered her thoughts, recounting all that led up to her recollection of the prophecy.

Then with a voice that sounded like many people whispering in harmony, she began.

'My sister and I played here, on this very island and over there in the forest and up there in the hills.' Her hand moved languorously and elegantly as she pointed from one place to the next. 'We were happy; she was kind and would do almost anything for me then. I was the weaker child and the younger of the two by twenty minutes so she was always fussing around, making sure I was comfortable, that she wasn't walking too fast for me; all the things a kind sister would do. Our parents were hardly ever at home as they worked for the king and were always off doing this and that, but when they were at home they were loving and would spend hours with us both, playing, telling us stories and being just the most wonderful parents a child could have. Those days were truly precious. But while they were away one of our tutors, a dour woman, would take her away at night – sometimes all night – and she would be unhappy and tired all next day.

'However, because I was the weaker of the two – now, don't get me wrong, by saying weaker I don't mean weak! We were both exceptionally strong, but she was stronger. So, to get back to what I was saying, because I was the weaker of the two, my parents started to give me special attention and I probably wouldn't have taken any notice but one day, as I looked up quickly, I saw something in my sister's countenance that caused me a little concern; there was a turn to her mouth and a glint in her eye that I had never seen there before. It was gone in a trice and I might have thought I'd been mistaken; I even tried to convince myself that I hadn't seen what I had, but I knew in my heart that I had.

'Our tutors eventually left. The sullen one just disappeared one night and never returned; the other one, who was quite nice, stayed on for a while longer but as my sister gradually got more and more unpredictable she became fearful and decided to go, saying that we were both now grown up and actually didn't need her anymore.

'It was years later when things really started to go wrong. My sister, once our parents had died, began to keep more and more to herself. We rarely went anywhere together any more – there were no walks in the forest or summer picnics up in the mountains; she only ever went there furtively, collecting herbs and leaves, toadstools and newts.

'I loved my sister and missed her so much but I was becoming scared, not of her but for her.

'She spent hours locked away in the west wing of our home; I got increasingly concerned by what I heard, smelled and saw – well, not exactly saw but could see that she was up all night at times by the fact that there was light from that upper window and she was beginning to look so unwell – that I knew I had to confront her.

'It was a clear calm October morning. This mist was thick and swirling around the island and because I'd been kept awake all night by clangs, screeches and smells I decided that I would go and see what was happening.

'But before I could go to her, she came to me.

'I was sitting on a bench outside the kitchen door eating my breakfast as I watched the sun lift herself up over the mists, when she strode round the corner and stood between me and the sunrise. The shadow cast by her blocking out of the sun was not the reason a sudden chill draped itself over me.'

'Well, sister, it's time to go our own separate ways!'

'What do you mean?' I asked, forgetting that it was I that was going to confront her.

'I mean one of us has to leave this place. It's too small for the both of us and your goodness is impeding my power. Also, as you have decided to ask me what I'm up to, I think it's time we said goodbye.'

'I don't understand!' I cried, recalling what I had been about to do at her comment and now extremely worried at the fact that she somehow already knew I was about to confront her.

'You don't have to understand,' she growled.

'I'd never seen her like this before and was beginning to get more than a little frightened. She still looked like my sister but it was as though she'd been taken over by some sort of evil being; she had obviously not washed for a very long time as could be seen by her filthy blue dress and grimy skin, let alone her hair, and she certainly didn't appear to smell too pleasant either.'

I gasped! Merlin dug me in the ribs with his elbow.

'Sorry, my Lady, please continue.'

'I said that I thought she should leave if she wanted us to separate; this was my home and I had no intention of leaving it.

'She narrowed her eyes as she looked at me and her mouth took on that same malevolence I'd seen all those years before, though now it was more pronounced. I suppose she'd had more time to practise.'

'No, my dear, we are both going to leave. I've made a new home far from here. I've furnished it and filled it with all I need to become the most powerful wizard of all time. Our parents were good – very good – and look where it got them! But they needed to be evil to be powerful – *and live!*' she shouted at me, narrowing her eyes as she watched my reaction. I went cold! Surely she hadn't – not our parents! But I couldn't finish the thought – it was too evil to contemplate. Though looking at the satisfied smirk on her face I could have cried.

'If you refuse, then I will use a spell that will shackle you and you will be bound to this place forever; you will not be able to leave, and though there is a power in this place, I've harnessed most of it so you will never be able to use its might!

'But I don't want you to stay here,' she continued, ignoring my unasked questions; 'We both have to leave this house! Today!'

'Where it came from I never knew, but then it happened.

'The mists thickened to an amazing degree and the voice spoke inside my head – it was a powerful and compelling voice and right then and there I knew I held a key that was more powerful than anything she could ever hold and as the voice spoke to me I spoke the words out to her – even my voice seemed to take on a timbre and resonance that was otherworldly. She was transfixed to the spot; she was completely unable to interrupt because the power that was holding both of us was too strong, even for her. She went very pale as I spoke and I thought, even then, that she might repent of her wickedness and come back to me as the dearly loved sister she had once been, but then when I had finished speaking she just squared her shoulders, turned on her heel and walked away. I haven't seen her since. Then again, she has not returned here and I have been unable to leave.'

'What did you say, my Lady?'

'Just what the voice told me to say – the prophecy –

'He will come
On a powerful charger with sword held high
He will come
Wearing the golden crown of the Once and Future King
He will come
Uniting all the kingdoms into one land
He will come
In the power of the Prince of Peace
He will come
He will rule in fairness and majesty
He will destroy every enemy
His most evil foe he must kill
And with the edge of Excalibur he will.

He will come.

But
If he turns from the True Path
If he looks to his own glory
Then she will come
And him she will destroy.'

We had been holding our breath, which we now let out as slowly and silently as we could as we mulled over those words; her voice had taken on a quality both powerful and as though all her strength had returned, echoing to and fro as those words ran across the mists in slippered feet before running up the trunks of trees and bouncing back, and not only that, but this time the words rose up and away out of her mouth as actual writing; the formed words floating out and around as lilac-coloured mist, finally disappearing into the ether as both Merlin and I tried to fathom the things the Lady has spoken – the prophecy.

'I shall have to go – the mists are disappearing.'

'One moment, my Lady – take this.' Merlin unwrapped the sword from the oiled cloth that had been strapped to the side of his horse and held it high. With the hint of sun about to break through the clouds, it glinted in the morning light and flashed as Merlin threw it into the sky; twisting and spinning a few times it finally landed, amazingly, hilt first, into the firm grip of the Lady, where it continued, for mere seconds, to point skywards. 'Take care of it my Lady. It will be needed soon but your sister is searching for it and you are one of the only people that can stand against her. And I know that once the mists take you away, no-one will be able to find you, so it will be safe.

'And help me with this. How can I save the dragon? She rescued Nimue by letting her live in her when Mab put a curse on her. Now that Nimue is safe the curse still has its power and appears to have taken root within Moon Song. She is dying!' Merlin's voiced choked as he made this pronouncement.

'That is what will have happened,' she replied, still holding the sword aloft. I stared at Excalibur and waited for her to continue. 'But I cannot help you,' she added, gripping the hilt more firmly as the morning sun began to flash all around from the tip of the blade almost blinding us as we stared at the scene before us.

Merlin's face dropped.

'You may need to go to my sister. The one who placed the curse is the one who can remove it. Unless you can find another way.'

'She would never do that!' Merlin wailed.

'There is a way,' the Lady spoke very quietly. 'Come here.'

Merlin drew near, wading into the 'water' up to his waist. The Lady whispered a few words and he returned to my side.

Her voice was fading as she stared sadly at Merlin; then, sword still pointing to the sky, she and it disappeared below the mists and within seconds even those vapours had vanished.

Where had she gone? There wasn't time for her to go anywhere in such a short time.

'The Lady of the Lake isn't like you or I or even like Mab any more. She's a thought, a dream, an imagination.'

'But she can't be! I saw her! She took the sword!'

'Ah yes. But who would believe you?'

'But the sword isn't imagination!'

'No, but it is now held within her spell.'

I considered all this for a short while before adding, 'and she's Mab's sister? I can't believe that! But then, in a peculiar way, they do look somewhat alike.

'Twins usually do, Percy, but it would seem that that is where their identities finish; it would seem that one has all the goodness and the other, well, you know what Mab is like.'

'But what is her name?'

'No-one knows. Mab certainly doesn't even accept her as her sister any more; she forgot her a long time ago. She is a mystery and I'm afraid will remain so to most. But to those who believe, she is known as the Lady of the Lake.'

'Lake? Where is the lake?'

'The lake that surrounds Avalon.'

I was starting to get annoyed at Merlin; he was on one of his "ask this question and I will answer it so obscurely that you will be forced to ask another one until finally you forget what you were talking about in the first place" hobby horses. I had to take the bull by the horns.

'OK Merlin – tell me, where is the lake and where is Avalon? And, what did she say to you?'

'You have seen the lake – it is the mist that rises around that hill over there, and that hill is Avalon.'

I stared. I knew the story. One day Arthur would be buried on that island and would remain there in a state of perpetual sleep until the time Britain was in dire peril and in need of a champion; then he would be raised from that sleep, take up the reins of kingship again and save the land – the Once and Future King. It made sense. But ...

'But this isn't a lake!'

'Do you think that we have to make it that simple? It would be like putting signposts to every archaeologist or grave robber or whatever and say, "come this way and dig up the bones of Arthur – make a name for yourself – become wealthy". No, Percy, it is only for the likes of you and I, people that love Arthur, that look to his welfare and well-being, to those of us that actually know the real reason; we have to make sure that when that time comes he will be safe. But that is looking well down through the avenues of the future and we must at this moment just look to the now.'

'But won't it be easy for those same archaeologists to find Arthur's burial place at some time or other because they won't need to cross the water to get to the island?'

'That's the beauty of it, Percy: they will be looking for an island, not a hill – they'll never find it!

'The lake – or should I say the mist – rises and completely covers the island at times and people will pass by and not even see Avalon – and he will be safe. The Lady you saw, though she, too, sleeps, is still the guardian of the island and as she sleeps she breathes out the mist – she keeps safe whatever is entrusted to her within those vapours – even when they have disappeared, like now. When the time comes she will awake and those mists will completely disappear; the time will then have come for Arthur to return.

'But,' he jumped up and brushed down his robes, 'that is well into the future. Now we have a task before us that I have not the foggiest idea how to tackle, let alone achieve. We have to confront the enemy if Moon Song is to be saved.' He gave a shrill whistle and Cabal, Arthur's huge wolfhound, came loping out of the trees to join us.

'And?' I asked.

'And what?' he replied.

'And what did she say to you when you went into the mists?'

'Oh, well,' he prevaricated, 'I must find a particular thing that Mab wants so as to exchange it for the removal of the curse.

'And you can't tell me what that is?'

'Not yet – if indeed there is anything. But there might still be another way, if only I can discover what that is!'

'So now I can go and see Rhianne?' It was more a statement than a question but Merlin would always have the last word!

'Er, yes, we will eventually get there but we have a slight detour first – a few hours – a couple of days at the most,' he hedged before striding out toward the trees.

'Merlin,' I grumbled.

'Oh come on man,' he called back over his shoulder, 'it could have been worse; you could still be over a millennia away. We'll get there.'

I almost stomped off after him, acting like a two-year-old, until he turned and looked at me.

'Come man,' he whispered, his eyes staring sadly into mine. 'Moon Song is dying.'

TWO

'Granddad, where is this Avalon? Is it near here?' Ben asked as they all strode in through the door of the cottage, shrugging off their coats and stoking up the fire.'

'Yes, and where did the Lady disappear to? She couldn't have just vanished – I mean, once the mist had gone she would have been found; that is, unless she had a secret door into a rock or something – even so and even if she was the vanishing sort of person, well the sword wasn't and it would have been seen, possibly just lying on the ground not far from where Merlin threw it; it couldn't be that magical! Maybe if we knew where the place was we could go and look for it. Is there a secret entrance?' Danny was almost ready to depart there and then.

Jack laughed. 'You are just about the same age as I was, Ben, when I stood beside Merlin that day and I, too, asked all those questions but as Merlin didn't respond with anything other than oblique answers I'm afraid I can't help you.' *'And even if I could,'* Jack thought, *'I most certainly wouldn't. I gave Merlin my word.'*

Cabal nudged Jack's elbow with his cold, wet nose as if to give him some comfort in the fact that he had secrets from his nearest and dearest. He was rewarded with the ruff of his neck being scratched.

'OK! So what happened then, granddad?'

We made our way back to the stone circle. It looked lifeless. In those days a lot of the stones were still in their original positions, not like you see them today – all thrown about or broken or, worse, graffiti having to be scrubbed off them. If only those idiots knew what they were doing when they do that! Do you know, Moon Song will one day arise again and I'm sure she'll have some scare or worse for those morons that have dared spray paint all over her! I'm certain she'll search them out! Whether in this world or the next!' Jack scowled before returning to his tale.

We arrived at dusk; Merlin and I had been gathering kindling and wood for a fire, knowing we had a long, cold night in front of us.

As we looked down the incline to the plain where the stones rose out of the ground, I couldn't help but catch my breath. They were glorious. I mean, you think they look magnificent today, but then, they really were.

Though still only boulders and stones, you could almost see where the head of the dragon rested on her front paws in sleep and to where the tail curled right round to almost reach her nose and those blue stones you see today were, in those days, much more of a deep shade of purple, while the sarsens glinted red – pulsating with life.

'We'll stay up here at the edge of the trees tonight,' Merlin spoke softly to me. 'Let's light the fire. We'll make our vigil here and not disturb her till morning.'

I hadn't said much on the journey – there were too many things going through my head and I thought that if I did start talking it would be so disjointed I'd end up rambling – or ranting. I always seemed to rant when Merlin appeared to be, to me anyway, deliberately obtuse. Though I understood how serious Moon Song's plight was and knew we would have to sort her problem out sooner or, most probably, later, I was still yearning to see Rhianne.

Then Merlin was shaking my shoulder. Somehow I had managed to drop off to sleep. The fire had been kept alight all night and was still burning quite brightly; Merlin had not slept! Did he ever?

He threw a few handfuls of soil over the flames and left a mound with half-hearted smoke struggling to climb through. It was still dark but dawn was sending some careful feelers over the horizon to see if it was safe to start pushing back the shadows.

'Come, Percy, let us go and see how she is.' He strode off so purposefully that I had almost to run to keep up with him. Cabal, as I turned to call him, sat doggedly in front of the dying fire and I could see, by the set of his head, that he would not be following us down to those stones.

We stood for quite some time staring at the sarsens and then past them to the smaller stones inside before we finally walked right round the outside of the stone circle; after completing a full circuit we moved inside and walked another full circuit along the corridor between the sarsens, the highest stones, and the bluestones. Finally, moving into the middle, Merlin climbed up onto the central altar stone and, holding his staff aloft, waited.

He'd already told me to stand in front of him but Cabal – well you know what he's like – he had followed us as far as his nerves would allow and was now pacing about outside the circle. He hated these stones. As you know, he'd almost been turned to one once and it didn't matter how many times we tried to reassure him – he wouldn't trust us to look after him inside.

'You aren't going to leave me to get turned to stone again,' he had argued. It didn't matter how much we tried to reassure him, he would not budge.

'You promised once before and look what happened then!' he had grumbled.

'That was then,' Merlin had tried to reassure him. 'I won't let it happen again.'

'That's what you promised the last time!'

It was no good; he wouldn't budge, so we just let him do his own thing.

We were staring at the lightening sky; it was a cloudless morning and there was no wind and no mist – the sky turned from a hint of indigo through orange, pink and red before any sort of daytime blue finally washed through it. We waited. Then, with a suddenness that almost made me jump, the sun fired her arrows of brightness unswervingly toward us through one of the stone archways and directly onto Merlin's staff. The ruby eyes set in the silver merlin's head attached to the staff flashed as he held it aloft and turning it hither and thither the silver head dazzled us as the midsummer's dawn sun bounced from it and onto the stones.

I had to squint so as not to be blinded.

That first initial anointing was sufficient.

Merlin, with the fire still burning and flashing from within the bird's eyes, spun, bouncing the reflected light over and through every stone in the circle; then finally jumping down and crashing the staff's head onto the central altar stone before holding it aloft again he waited.

I thought that the force of his strike must surely break his staff but it held not one dent. I then recalled the stories of how he fought against those with swords and other sharp instruments and amazingly it was his staff that had cut those other weapons in two.

The sun climbed slowly and majestically – her initial brilliant display quieting as she lit up the land – and seemed interested in what we were doing as she stared down directly upon the scene; she, too, waited, seemingly with anticipation, to watch what might happen next.

Those initial shards of reflected light were buzzing through the stones; at first they were frenetic but after a few minutes calmed down to the occasional spark or murmur.

Then an eye slowly cracked opened.

It was an eye wracked with pain.

A huge mouth – dried spittle looking like stalactites and stalagmites which had been gluing her jaws together – opened slowly and a dry tongue hung out one side; a small cough emitted a single foul-smelling puff of charcoal-coloured smoke. Yes, at best she was very ill. At worst? Well, we didn't want to think of that. In fact Merlin shot a warning through my mind to stop being negative – *it was not at all helpful and she might pick up on it!*

Merlin walked slowly over to her head and laid his whole body against her cheek. He was speaking to her in words that I could hear but not understand; a language that sounded as old as time itself – almost a language of love.

I knew he loved Nimue as his soul mate but I also knew that there was something between this dragon and him that tied them together in some mystical way.

I jumped.

A thought had dropped into my head from somewhere. Would Merlin die if Moon Song died? I didn't know. The thought scared me. It made sense. Was that why this mission was so important? I looked over at Cabal – he was still pacing. I looked back at Merlin, who was still speaking in this seemingly sacred language. It reminded me a little of when they both sang together, but this time only he made a sound – a dirge, not a symphony. Moon Song appeared to have no additional strength; she could hardly keep her eyes open, let alone sing.

I had made sure that when those thoughts were rushing through my head I had put my barriers in place; I didn't want Merlin or Cabal for that matter knowing them. I didn't even think at that time whether Moon Song was capable of mind speaking or listening. My thoughts at the time, though, were too frightening to be shared with anyone and, also, I did not want to interrupt what was obviously something of dire importance.

I looked back at Moon Song - her head had drooped onto her front paws again - well, what should have been paws but were still stone, as she hadn't completely changed from stone to flesh. Could she? Was there something that was inhibiting her transformation? Was it possible that there might not be a way to bring her back to the beautiful dragon that could take me up almost to the heavens? Oh I hoped there was something Merlin could do; there must be something!

Again, he warned me through his mind that maybe more than he might be picking up my thoughts. I looked across at him and though he was still lying against the dragon's cheek I could feel his rebuke. He finally pulled away from her and walked the few steps to the central stone.

Raising his staff he spoke more mysterious words, spun a full circle about two feet above that central altar and, coming back down to earth, watched as the dragon returned to stone. The sound was awful; it was a bit like one of the locks being opened or closed on the Norfolk Broads when it needed oiling. The creaking and cracking made me believe that she must surely break up. She did not but she didn't look at all good.

Taking my fingers out of my ears, I let out the breath that I had been unaware I was holding and returned my gaze to the sorcerer.

'Come, Percy, we have things to do.' He looked exceedingly grim; more so than I have ever seen him before and once again I had almost to run to keep up with him as he headed back to our campsite.

Cabal was more than pleased when we exited the circle and almost danced along in front of us as we headed up the slight incline.

'What are we going to do then?' I asked, finally plucking up my courage.

'Oh, I'll bring you up to speed just as soon as I've sorted it out in my own head.'

He can be extremely annoying at times!

'But I think it is now time for you to be returned to your wife.'

That changed everything and all other thoughts fled.

THREE

We had had to walk a long way before we were able to purchase a couple more horses. The man didn't really want to sell them to us so Merlin agreed to hire them while ours recovered and we were joined for the rest of the journey by a young man called Peter who would eventually take the horses back with him. We rode slowly on our fresh mounts, our own horses trotting along behind us on long reins but with not even a saddle on them to burden them. Peter was a pleasant enough lad but had the unfortunate habit of continual chatter. Merlin had tried to get the boy to stop talking but short of putting a spell on him it turned out to be a waste of time; he'd stop for a few minutes and then, off he'd go again, talking about anything and everything that popped into his head. Merlin was glad to see the back of him when he finally left us.

'Thank goodness for that,' Merlin sighed as we watched the large backsides of the three horses disappearing back through the trees. 'I always thought you were bad enough when you kept asking one question after another but at least you have a few times when you keep quiet for a decent length of time; then again, I wouldn't have chosen you if you hadn't been exactly what I was looking for, so I think I have done really well, don't you?'

'How does he do that? How does he turn virtually everything into patting himself on the back? How could a young lad who talks continuously end up being the means to an end of Merlin letting me know how magnificent the great sorcerer is?'

'Because I am!'

'Oops!'

After a good night's sleep in an inn we and our mounts were completely refreshed, so in the morning we mounted and sped off – it was now less than half a day to our destination. You just don't know how excited I was. At last, without any more detours, without Merlin saying we were going and then saying something like, 'well we have to do this first,' or 'only a little bit out of our way,' when that little bit out of our way was more than a week or even longer! Now, though, we actually were heading to Sir Ector's caer.

I'd already forgotten the boy and the headache that had

threatened by his continuous talking as we strode in through the gates at Sir Ector's and then felt quite guilty as I remembered that I had also almost forgotten Moon Song. But I had to put all that to one side; I was too excited now that I was about to see my beloved Rhianne and all thoughts of sorrow just had to be wiped from my face.

I looked up at the Hall, at the windows and the door, at the surrounding courtyard, stables and stallholders. It looked a happy place today and I suppose I expected Rhianne to be standing at one of the windows waiting for me – how conceited is that? Well, I mean, I had been gone a year! Who could stand on the steps waiting that long?

Merlin strode ahead of me through the central doorway, eventually turning into the main hall.

My heart stopped. Rhianne was sitting by early summer's empty hearth talking to Iris. She stopped suddenly when she realised, by Iris' expression, that they had guests. Turning she almost sobbed as she leapt out of her chair and rushed over to me.

'Where have you been? Why did you leave me? Have I done anything wrong?'

I held her close. Would this always have to happen? Would I always be taken away – back to the 20th Century – without any say in the matter? Invisible hands were crushing my heart as a premonition crept into my mind telling me to wait and see. I felt her tremble in my arms and with my tears mingling with hers pushed the awful thought away.

We finally drew apart, Rhianne waving Iris away as we sat down together on the seat near the hearth but I was holding her hand so tightly by now that she had to tell me to stop.

On the way here Merlin had already told me that I should tell Rhianne all about the real me as soon as the opportunity arose; now that you are married, he had said, you should keep no secrets from one another, though he did say it might be a hard job to get her to understand but that, because of the fact that I would always be coming and going, she needed to know.

'Come, Rhianne, let's go outside. I have so much to tell you.'

It took much longer than I thought. She didn't interrupt once but just stared at me with those beautiful violet eyes. Once or twice she almost cried but mostly she just watched my face as she held onto one of my hands with both of hers.

Of course, I had to keep Arthur out of the explanation – that was still a secret from everyone.

I finally finished with, 'and I thought I'd never come back. Merlin always called me back – well, almost always, as last time he said he didn't but I got here anyway – and it has been a year – a whole year and I thought I'd go mad.'

'Oh me, too! I really needed you with me and didn't know where you'd gone; I didn't even know if you were still alive! Or whether you'd ever come back. And Merlin hasn't been here either so I had no-one to ask.'

'Poor Rhianne. But now you know the reason why, and so now does Cabal,' I added looking down at the hound who had also been hanging on my every word.

'Hrmmph,' was all he had to say before sneezing several times.

'Come, Percy, there's something you have to see.'

How she had managed to keep herself from telling me for those two hours I'd been talking is beyond me, but she had and now I was in for the biggest shock of my life.

Holding my hand in hers (and her hand was trembling slightly – I'd put that down to my sudden appearance and my shocking explanation), we left the Hall and climbed the staircase. I tried to talk but placing a finger to my lips she whispered a "hush" and we continued up the stairs.

The door to our room was slightly ajar and Rhianne, pushing it open but keeping hold of the handle stood back, beckoning me to enter. I can remember turning my head to one side in silent question but when she just stood looking at me I walked through the door and entered the room.

Now you know I love Rhianne with all my heart and soul and had done so from the very first time I'd laid eyes on her at the ripe old age of nine, but it was right then and there at that very moment that I fell in love – a different kind of love, you understand – for the very first time in my life.

Iris stood in the centre of the room cradling a gurgling baby in her arms. I could see its face as it peeked out of the blanket – bright blue eyes stared back at me; serious eyes that suddenly screwed up as a sunny smile lit its face (or was that wind?); no, it was a smile as a gurgle followed it. It had no hair but dark, beautifully defined eyebrows showed that maybe, when the hair grew it, too, would also be dark.

I turned enquiringly to Rhianne.

'Your daughter, Percy.'

My heart melted. I was still very young and as there hadn't been any babies in our family since, well, forever, I had no idea what to do. I didn't want to hold her in case I dropped her and, I suppose, just stood there like an idiot.

'Don't you want to know what I've called her?'

I just nodded, not taking my eyes off that happy little face.

'Kathryn – but we all call her Kate.'

It was all too much for Danny.

'Granddad, this isn't funny. You keep telling us that these stories are just made up in your mind, well, you don't really tell us that either – you just smile and don't say anything – but then you go telling us things like you got married and now our mum is your daughter. Well, of course, I know she is your daughter but I can't believe you're telling us that Rhianne is really your wife and that our grandma is hundreds of years old.'

'And we've never met her! Well, I suppose we wouldn't, her being that old!' Ben added.

Jack burst out laughing.

'Danny, Danny, a good story has to be a little bit believable otherwise it isn't a good story, is it? And I never said that they were made up – I just said they were stories – they might be true or they might not! I know I've brought your mum into it and I'm sure she doesn't mind, and even if it is true …'

'Is it?'

'… and even if it is true, I don't think I'd tell you anyway! And in any event, she isn't just a few hundred years old, she's one-and-a-half millennia old!' Jack chuckled, watching the boys' confused faces.

They knew their granddad very well by now and, giving up, urged him to continue.

Things had got to a crossroads now, hadn't they? I'd been away from my beautiful Rhianne for almost a year, she had had our child and I wasn't there for when Rhianne would really have needed me (though what I could have done for her at that time was really beyond me as I couldn't have done much – I mean, I felt too clumsy right at this moment to even hold the child, but I was beginning to get angry now!) and also for what should have been one of the happiest times of my life. How could Merlin have done this to me? There would have to be a showdown.

I stayed until it was time for the baby to be fed and like any shy young man fled the room and left them to it.

With a plethora of emotions I went in search of Merlin.

I found him over the far side of the vegetable gardens talking with Sir Ector as the two men strolled in and out of the spring greens. I knew I couldn't have a showdown with him right then and there, and he knew it – looking over his shoulder at me and raising one eyebrow. Realising my mind was wide open to him I quickly raised my barriers and stomped off in the other direction, being caught up by Arthur some few minutes later.

'I heard you'd come back,' he grinned at me as he flung a friendly arm around a stiff shoulder as he led me out of the compound. 'Let's go for a stroll and catch up.' He ignored the scowl on my face, which eventually disappeared as my friend chatted and laughed. Bit of a turnaround, really, as it was usually he that was serious and me that had the sunny nature, though I was one of the only people I can recall that was blessed to know Arthur's real character and his sometimes completely mad sense of humour.

I didn't say much, waiting for him to tell me about the latest villain, disaster or battle, but there was nothing. Everything was serene and peaceful, there had been no sight of warships on the horizon, the Picts and Scots had kept to their borders, no-one was robbing his neighbour or declaring war, the cattle had produced more offspring than at any time anyone could remember, the crops hadn't failed and were growing as they should be and all was tranquil. It was quiet – and I had the uneasy feeling that perhaps it was too quiet.

But I shook off that thought as Arthur's happy chatter, which I had been only half concentrating on, continued.

'... and Merlin says he has found me a bride.'

I stopped dead in my tracks. Now I knew the reason for his

light heartedness. Mind you, I did feel a bit miffed that in all our time together over the last week or so Merlin hadn't deigned to inform me of this piece of information.

'What?' and after a pause, 'Are you happy with that? I mean, what is she like? Don't you want to find your own wife?' I wondered what she might look like. I mean she could be absolutely awful; then again, knowing Merlin, he wouldn't do that to anyone, would he? Um, would he? No! I shook those thoughts out of my head before I conjured up some of the most hideous faces and bodies that were waiting in the wings to mince in front of my imagination.

'Why should I want to do that?' Arthur brought my thoughts back to the present conversation.

I had forgotten that in those days most marriages were political; well, they were in my day, too, but not quite the same as this. Now that I remembered some of my history it became clear that Arthur, though obviously hoping that his future bride would be at least tolerable, was happy to do what his father wanted him to do. Then, I thought again, Sir Ector is not really his father so what was happening here? What exactly is Merlin up to?

He stared at my open mouth and slapping his leg burst out laughing.

'You are funny Percy. I know that you and Rhianne were just meant for each other and I can't understand why you left her for so long, and perhaps you will tell me at some time?' He raised his eyebrow questioningly at me. 'But I am made of different stock; I don't intend to be home much as I can just feel it in every part of my being that I am destined to be a warrior. So, I am happy that if Merlin and my father have chosen a wife for me, then I'm sure she must be someone who is the perfect choice: quiet and submissive, happy to stay here and help my mother, that is, if Kay lets us stay here – it will be his rightful home as lord one day, you know – and just be, well, just here,' he added lamely. 'But I don't see a problem; Kay'd probably be most happy to have my wife keep our mother company, and maybe his wife, also, should he ever marry. And, I hope that she will raise a large family for me – that will keep her busy and happy so she won't miss me at all when I go off on my adventures.

'I have been sitting with Smith some mornings as he is about to put some armour together for me; I have my sword already and he is … why am I going on about that?

'I am also going to design my own tabard – I thought it could be embroidered with a red dragon on a white background – what do you think? I am sure she will be happy to sit and sew it for me – it will take her ages and will thus keep her happily employed. So, no – I am happy for them to choose my bride.

'In fact, in a few weeks she will be here. Her family are bringing her, along with mother's family, to meet us all and to carry out the formalities of betrothal. We shall then marry the following spring.'

'Does she have a name?'

'Percy, of course she has a name,' he laughed, thumping me on the back. I thought that now I was grown enough to be a husband and a father that I was beyond the thumping, but no!

'She is called Gwenhwyfar. She is sixteen years old, almost five years younger than me, so she's young enough to be quite submissive and teachable.'

What! I couldn't believe the way Arthur was thinking. Did he really believe that this young woman could be treated so badly – almost like a slave, a chattel – not a person but a piece of personal property. I kept quiet; I had heard so many tales of Guinevere (and that was as near a name as the one Arthur had pronounced) and I couldn't remember one that said she was anything like the shy and retiring sort that Arthur had conjured up in his mind. Hmm, this was definitely going to be an interesting encounter.

'So, let me get this straight. You are going to marry a young woman that you have never met; she is shy and obedient, she will be happy to live here with your mother for most of the time, raise a huge family, cook and sew for you and she will dote on you when you are here?'

'That's about it Percy as I can't think of anything else she could do at this moment. Yes – I think you have hit the nail squarely on the head. Sounds good, eh?'

I groaned inwardly. Arthur wasn't a fool and he wasn't unkind but right at this moment he was positively annoying in his thoughtlessness. Then again, he was brought up in a different time and had really had no dealings with the opposite sex up to then, apart from Rhianne, that is; but sisters are different. Again, I was now married and knew the difference between actually having a wife and just thinking of what one would be like when one had absolutely no experience whatsoever. However, I was just going to let him get on with it. This was definitely going to be worth watching.

By now we had strolled around the woods adjoining the caer and were once again entering the grounds surrounding the Hall. Sir Ector, with time on his hands, had made several improvements to his home, adding extra stables, a larger granary and was now in the process of adding another floor above the kitchens. The workmen had finished for the day so, although everything looked chaotic, all was now quiet

I left Arthur and made my way back to Rhianne, Cabal at my heels. Poor Cabal – we hadn't had a chance to speak much while Merlin was around or while I'd been out with Arthur. It had just been too busy but now we were alone for the first time since I had returned to this time zone.

'*I'll need to catch up with you soon, Percy. I want to find out more about your "other life". I always knew there was something funny about you, you know!*'

'*Now, Cab, don't be unfair. If you know Merlin, as you surely do, you would also know that if he told me to keep something secret, then secret it would have to be.*'

'*Right!*' He didn't sound too convinced or even too happy with my explanation.

'*And another thing. Moon Song is dying.*'

'*I know. I gathered that much from our visit to the stones.*'

'*We have to try and save her. Merlin listened to the Lady of the Lake, as you know, and she has told him what he has to do but so far he hasn't told me what that is.*'

'*It has to be done when the leaves start falling.*'

With furrowed brow I looked at the hound.

'*How do you know?*

'*It is when she is about. Merlin says that unless he can find another way, we can only achieve this by getting her to do it.*'

'*Ah, yes. But isn't she locked up?*'

'*She was!*'

'*Why didn't I just know that she'd get away! She always gets away. Why did I think that this time it would be different? Why hadn't Merlin told me?*' I groaned inwardly.

'He would have told you when you needed to know; when the time was right. And she's worse! Her time spent in that awful place has played havoc with her mind. If you thought she was mad before, well, you should see her now.'

'Have you seen her then?'

'No, but the stories we have heard! Many have gone missing. Several search parties have been sent out to find them but sometimes even all of them have not come back so it is now virtually impossible to get volunteers; who can blame them? Whole areas of forest have turned into tangled wildernesses because no animal or bird will go there to keep the undergrowth down – she is there, you see, and she traps all the wildlife to use for her magic. People say they have seen eerie lights of dark hue creeping to the edge of the woods, like eyes staring – so they keep away.'

'Is that where her castle is Cab?'

'Rather where it once was. It is now just a pile of moss-covered ruins.'

I remembered what it had been like the last time I was there with Merlin.

'But what is it like underneath all that I wonder?'

'Apparently not too different to what it was before – just darker.'

'And do you know what it is that we have to do to save Moon Song?'

'No!'

'Great!'

'We have to trust Merlin. You know he always does everything right; he always knows the best thing; he will always let us know when we need to know.'

So I had to put up with that as I entered the courtyard; Griff joined Cabby as they went off to search for early evening game in the forest.

I spent the next few happy hours with Rhianne and Kate until Iris took our daughter away for her sleep.

'She sleeps right through the night now, Percy,' Rhianne told me proudly as we left the room to join the others for supper. 'And Iris just loves her – she'll do absolutely anything for her.'

It was a happy time round the table that evening. All the family were there. My mood had softened but I still wanted to speak to Merlin.

Two new young women that Old Molly was training up waited upon us; Abigail had left, now that she was married to Cal and Sir Ector only wanted females working for him that had no other ties. They were a little clumsy (but improving, so I was led to understand) but we didn't care; we were so happy to be together.

I was finally able to have a quick word with Merlin, first about him keeping me away from Rhianne and my new daughter for so long and then about what we had to do come the autumn and why he hadn't said anything about Arthur's coming marriage.

He said, quite rightly, that this wasn't the time to talk about it but that we should meet up in the morning and go for a long walk. So, I had to wait – again.

However, when I asked about Gwenhwyfar, and how Arthur had been given the impression that she was a shy and biddable young lady, he chuckled.

'Shy is something Arthur couldn't deal with, biddable is something that wouldn't lie happily with him and quiet would be something that would definitely drive him mad. No, he is definitely going to be challenged with this lively young thing.

I couldn't help but smile as well as I looked across at a serene and jovial future king who, misreading my amusement, merely smiled back.

FOUR

I was up at the crack of dawn, or should I say at the crack of a wailing child.

I left Rhianne and Iris to minister to an indignant and hungry Kate and went in search of my own breakfast.

Merlin was up early as well and the two of us ate in silence in the kitchens before wandering outside, through the main gate and off into the forest, with Cabal at our heels, already replete, having eaten whatever it was he had already chased through the forest and consumed.

'*Good sport too,*' he had added, unnecessarily!

'So, Merlin,' I asked, ignoring him, as we strode shoulder to shoulder through the dappled light with the morning sun winking merrily down at us as she played hide and seek in the trees, 'what now?'

He stopped and turned to face me. We were now of a height; two grown men at least six feet tall, though I was still a teenager with still time to grow and he a man of indeterminate age but looked about thirty-five years old at that time.

'You are now almost ready to learn as much as I am able, or willing, to teach you. You know much of the ways of the Druid and more of the Old Way than even some of them, but that was already inside you waiting to be winkled out, not something you have learned; no matter how much one might strain to get hold of that Gift it is not something that can be caught or taught, though it can be improved upon and I must admit I've done a particularly good job with you.'

Always, always, he took the credit! I kept an open face and a closed mind.

'So, this is what has to be done and we are the only ones that can do it. Well, Salazar could too, but he and Jasmine are recovering their powers elsewhere. Maybe they will get back to aid us – maybe not. Whatever else may be happening, we have to be prepared.

'Over the years, and there have been more years than you would know about, we have had many many confrontations with that mad witch.' He strode on and his face was grim but determined. 'But now it's time to stop pussyfooting around and deal with her once and for all. She's shown us exactly what she is like, what her aims are. I mean, you only have to look at her sister to see that if she will drain the life force out of even one of her own kin so as to grab what she wants, she won't think twice about doing it to anyone else. There is absolutely no goodness in her at all – not a spark. She is self-seeking, violent, ruthless, evil!

'And you heard the prophecy, Percy. She is out to kill Arthur. We've known that all along and she's got very close to it on more than one occasion. No, she has to be defeated once and for all. This time we will show no mercy!'

'Didn't you say to me once that it would be Arthur that would kill her?'

'I did, but I believe I also said that she knows that and also knows that it continues, "unless she kills him first", so it is not a definite. No prophecy is, Percy – there are nearly always provisos. So, I believe it is now up to us to do the honours, don't you? If Arthur does it, fine – all glory to him, but he must be king – he *will* be king, or the whole course of history will be wrenched out of time.

'Also, Moon Song needs to be saved.'

We had now been walking and talking for several hours and, as I digested all the information Merlin had divulged, carried on in silence for a good few minutes.

Cabal rejoining us after another forage through the undergrowth, broke into our thoughts with, *'Plenty of young hare about today; nice and tender,'* whilst licking his lips.

'Cab – shut up!

'So what's the plan then?' I asked Merlin, turning my attention away from the hound.

'Well, I reckon I'll have to spend the next month or so in my sky tower.'

'Just where is that Merlin?'

'Ah, it is a place known only to me. Sorry, Percy, it will remain that way; though I can tell you that it is in a place that will only allow me to pass through – I have made it that way for now so that it is safe. It is a place that has a doorway to another world that Nimue and I will one day disappear to so that we can be together at last – away from the wickedness of this world, but that world can also only be reached upon the wings of the dragon; only she can take us there. But I will go to my sky tower for now and meditate.'

'And where is Nimue and will you ever let us meet her?

Merlin laughed. 'She is recovering and is safe and maybe I will let you meet her one day. *Maybe!*'

'But – what about Arthur? What about when he returns when Britain needs him again? You and Nimue can't just leave! What if the time is now – I mean in my time – in the 20th Century?'

'Percy, Percy, calm down! I won't "just leave" as you put it. I can see you but, and this will be even more important, you will not be able to see me. Something like a two-way mirror.

'For now, though, I shall go to my tower.' He held up his hand to stop my imminent interruption, 'and will contemplate the stars through its open ceiling.'

'You can read things in the stars?' I asked incredulously. 'I thought that that was rubbish! Just a load of old mumbo jumbo so that someone can make a lot of money out of the gullible!'

'No! Don't be naive Percy – I stare at the heavens and my mind rests. The vastness of the universe tends to make me realise how small we are but in that smallness we all have a purpose. I can dream and daydream; my mind rests but my brain works. It takes on a life of its own and even though I don't realise what it is doing it somehow takes hold of the threads of every thought and knits them into an amazing pattern that eventually becomes a mural of wholeness at the front of my mind; I can almost see it playing out in front of me and then I'll know what I must do.'

'So, does that mean that right now, right at this very minute, at this exact moment in time …'

'Get to the point Percy.'

'… you have no idea how to go about it?'

'Correct!'

'Brilliant!'

'But I will have.'

'You can be sure of that, can you?'

'Absolutely!'

'Fine!'

Then he burst out laughing. 'Come, Percy, let's get back to the others. Your beautiful family is probably wondering if you've gone off again and I need to make my goodbyes.'

'You're going so soon?'

'I have to my boy. There is no time to waste and I need to get back to you again by the end of the summer, in readiness – you know that's when she gets active. Also, I want to be there when the lovely Gwenhwyfar arrives if I can.' At mention of her name he fell into almost uncontrollable laughter, the tears rolling down his face until a stitch, causing him to hold onto his side with a few, 'ooh ohs,' threatened to double him up with pain.

I almost felt like the adult in this scenario as I waited, straight faced, for him to get himself under control.

'So, what am I supposed to do in the meantime?' I asked when he finally quietened down.

'Do I need to spell it out? Enjoy yourself lad. You have a beautiful wife and daughter! Spend time with Rhianne and Kate – have fun getting to know your new family. Practise with the men – archery, fencing, wrestling – all the things you have to do to build up muscle, stamina and camaraderie. Who knows what might happen; who knows what might be needed? Who knows when *she* might come back! I'll have a word with Sir Ector and Arthur. They trust my instincts and will prepare for all we might need.

'You will not return to the 20th Century while I am away – I promise, so enjoy the next few months and if I need to contact you I'll send one of my little men.'

'But I've never been able to understand them; they speak in a language completely incomprehensible to me.'

'I'll write a note for them to bring. But don't worry about that now; when I need you to know something it will all become clear.

'Anyway, once I am in possession of all that is needed I shall send for you – you still need to be trained up.

Chuckling again, he allowed his laughter to run its course before heading back to Sir Ector's.

Then we were back at the caer and some time later that evening he was gone. I didn't see him go; in fact I don't think anyone did. We knew he was going and it seemed that one minute he was there – eating and drinking and laughing or discussing or just watching us. He'd said his goodbyes and didn't need to go through all that again – and then he was gone.

FIVE

Those three months were the happiest in my life up to that time. Little Kate got to know me and was a very good child. Mind you, when she got a bit miserable (teething and the like) she was taken away by Iris, so we only really saw her when she was good. As far as I know, she could have been a little monster. But we didn't see that side of her if there was a side like that. As I said, Iris took care of her and loved her like her own so if she was a little monster I expect we have to thank Iris for making her good again.

Time went quickly. Too quickly!

Arthur and I were now sparring partners as we were of a similar height. We spent much time together – especially hunting in the forests around the Hall. I had learned to ride quite creditably by now as well and it was great fun thundering across the plains, especially when other young men, the sons of visiting dignitaries, came to stay. I had to laugh, later, at this because when I came home to the 20th Century I amazed my father at my prowess with the horses when, to his understanding, I had only ever before had a ride on a donkey at the seaside! But back to this time.

Balmy days of sunshine, fun and happiness. What more could I want.

'She's coming, Percy – next week. She'll be here on St Ninian's Day! A little earlier than we thought, eh?'

'Eh? *Oh no! Not saints days again!*'

'Gwenhwyfar!' by way of explanation as he looked at my face of dismay. 'We've had a rider; they've left Wales and by now they might have disembarked and are on their way here. It's all hustle and bustle now to get the rooms ready. And have you seen the amount of food being brought in? Enough to feed an army!'

He was so excited I recalled Merlin's state of hilarity and found that I now, too, couldn't stop laughing. Usually dour in the presence of strangers – especially women – he was all animation. He kept on checking the rooms to make sure everything was coming along as it should. He gave orders for hundreds of flowers to be chosen and picked on the morning they were to arrive. The men were brought in from the fields; fortunately the harvest was at least a week away, so weather permitting, they were free to come along and help. It was a hive of activity; Cabal and Griff were nowhere to be found – it was much too much for them. But nothing was too much for Arthur – everything of the best was being brought in to impress his future bride.

I, on the other hand, couldn't believe that someone could be so excited about getting married to someone they'd never met, let alone to someone they weren't in love with. If it were me, I'd be in a right old sulk. I mean, what on earth would he do if she were a troll?

But, then, as I said before, things were different in those days. Or were they?

The day arrived.

We were all standing along the battlements watching the dust cloud getting ever closer. As we saw a couple of riders leave the main party we all rushed down to the courtyard to welcome them in. The two outriders thundered up to the caer to make sure we were ready to receive them. They were obviously important personages as they were dressed very finely and had gold torcs around their necks. We found out later they were the future bride's oldest brothers and they were not going to let their beloved sister marry into peasantry. I can remember Arthur bristling at this insult but after Sir Ector took him to one side and said that as they were happy to go ahead with the wedding, then they obviously thought that they were not peasants, he calmed down, though he had been ready to knock the man's block off.

His mind was taken off his annoyance as the rest of the party began to pass through those huge gates.

And then she was there!

Oh wow! You should have seen Arthur's face. You'll remember that I have this terrible habit of allowing my jaw to drop and thus look completely moronic with my mouth hanging open, and usually with my eyes staring out of their sockets like organ stops?

Well, it happened to him. Not for long, I have to admit, but his eyes were goggling as he stared at her and I almost burst out laughing. Fortunately I didn't.

He got himself under control and walked, very tall, up to the lady and offered her his hands to help her down from her extremely large horse. We would eventually discover that she was an excellent horsewoman, could have easily alighted without any help but had obviously been taken through the correct etiquette for this particular outing, and would certainly not be left behind with the women when it came to going out on the hunt.

But, back to the here and now.

She looked to be as light as a feather as he helped her down but we would also discover how deceptive those looks were; she was very strong. But I'll get to that later.

We waited till all the others had dismounted or alighted from the following coaches and then turned to enter the Hall, where by now the craziness of loading all the tables with food and drink was over.

Offering Gwenhwyfar his arm, Arthur led the procession inside.

After the welcoming ceremony Sir Ector and the bride's father spent the next few hours deep in conversation, a prelude to the almost week of marriage details they were negotiating; it was a long week.

I wondered, not for the first time, and with my barriers strictly held in place I must add, how Sir Ector had the authority to allow Arthur to marry. I mean, he wasn't his real father – that was the late King Uther Pendragon – and it might all go pear shaped if what was happening here was, to say the least, illegal. But, then, Merlin would have known about it so it must surely be all right. Then, again, Merlin wasn't really in his right mind at the moment, was he? Was he getting soft in the head because of the fact that Nimue was back on the scene? Also, he was very concerned about Moon Song and then, again, because Arthur was getting close to the time he'd be acknowledged as king, Mab was sure to make a stab – pun not intended here – at killing him before he killed her.

Even with my barriers up, I was sure I heard a disjointed and distant echo of a "tut tut" as I thought these thoughts. 'Barriers, Percy, barriers,' I told myself.

The bottom line was that the betrothal was presently taking place and at the end of that week there was a mighty cheer as Sir Ector shook Count Gwythyr's hands and gave him one of his famous bear hugs, before turning and shouting for a toast.

'It is agreed; it is agreed!' he shouted again and again, thumping as many people on the back as were around him; I kept my distance.

The Count merely smiled.

Arthur grinned.

Gwenhwyfar looked as though the declaration made not a slight bit of difference to her, though her eyes flashed.

'Just who is Count Gwythyr?' I had asked Rhianne on that first day.

'Count Gwythyr is a lord of Léon in Brittany who just happens to be married to a Welsh lady of Gwent.'

'A lord?'

'Yes, his father is still quite young and is expected to reign in that part of Brittany for many many years to come. So, Gwythyr enjoys the easy life in Gwent with his wife and six children – they have four sons and two daughters, one of whom is already married and has children of her own. Gwenhwyfar is their youngest child and a trifle spoilt I should think.'

'Why do you say that?'

'Oh, I have merely been observing!'

We both then turned to look at this young woman. She was tall – almost as tall as Arthur himself, with long, very long, softly waving deep red hair that had been interwoven for the occasion with dark green ribbons that matched her outfit; her colouring was possibly a mix between the bright red hair of the Celt and the dark hair of the French, though from what I could understand, they were distantly related, the Count's family having migrated to France several decades earlier. Her features were even but the most striking thing about her was her large, slightly upward slanting green eyes; she had extremely pale skin but it was of a healthy not sickly hue.

She had quite large hands with long fingers and on one occasion, when she was tucking in a wayward curl, I noticed how calloused that hand was. I can remember thinking that something was not quite right. Was she a lady or a lady's maid; were they trying to trick us?

Over the following days this crazy thought was put to rest. The lady was definitely not going to be the compliant stay-at-home wife Arthur had imagined; no, Rhianne most probably was right in her assumption that she was spoiled because she did whatever she wanted to do. She was her father's favourite and he gave in to her every plea – well, almost her every plea – I don't think this marriage was something she wanted but her father was adamant so far as it was concerned.

She hunted – she was a better horse rider than most men and refused to ride sidesaddle like the ladies, wearing almost dress-shaped pantaloons so as to achieve this; she used the bow and arrow, making her own shafts and flights a lot of the time; she could bring down the highest bird or shoot the farthest deer; and could use the sword as well as most of the men! Wow! No wonder those hands were rough!

A lot of people didn't like it and would whisper behind their hands, but Arthur was entranced. It would seem that this young wife-to-be would be more of a helpmeet than he had ever believed and not the stay-at-home, compliant spouse he had previously imagined.

All too soon the celebrations were over and the party left to return to Wales to do everything that was needed before the wedding, which was to take place on St. Mark's Day, 25th April the following spring.

'It's a good day to get married on, Percy,' Arthur had said (I groaned inwardly), 'because farmers don't plough on this day as it is feared their horses might die within the year, so that means everyone is free to come and celebrate with us on our special day.'

Phew, I thought he was going to go on and on about saints' days again and as he knew I didn't know much about any of them, once he got started he felt duty bound to educate me.

Arthur was sad to see them go as that week had been a happy and full time, with sport and entertainment galore, unlike the usual and sometimes boring life at the Hall, but he had not known the woman for long enough to be distraught; he was entranced by her, certainly, but, so far, I don't think the word "love" had entered the equation. Would it ever?

Things got back to normal for the next few weeks. Rhianne and I were very happy and little Kate was starting to grow, not only in stature but also in personality.

I'd warned Rhianne that Merlin would be calling for me soon and that although I would be gone for some short while I would still be here; well, here in the Dark Ages that is.

Rhianne had been so inquisitive about my past. I'd tried to explain a lot of what it was like living in the 20th Century. She accepted quite a lot of what I said but when I tried to explain what a tractor or an aeroplane were I not only got chided by her for embellishing it a bit too much but also got a jolt in the mind from Merlin. *'Keep it simple, boy – or you might get locked up – at best!'*

I laughed along with Rhianne and said that I was truly sorry and that I would not exaggerate reality in future.

The time came at the beginning of a very hot October when Merlin, himself, returned to take me off to be trained.

'We've got our work cut out for us this time, Percy,' Merlin's voice was deep and sombre as we rode out of Sir Ector's enclosure. 'We not only have to get that mad woman to somehow take the curse off Moon Song but we have also got to disable her as well. I really don't like all this killing off and the like; it goes against the grain to have to do it and, more importantly, it drains me of such a lot of power for so long that I think I'll not be able to return. But it is now getting desperately important to rid ourselves of her; Arthur will soon be king. Yes,' he looked across at me with a flash of his eyes, 'the time is nigh and if Britain isn't going to succumb at best to tyrants or at worst to Mab, it has to be soon.'

'Have you thought of a plan?'

'No!'

After several miles I mentioned that it was sad he had missed Arthur's betrothal to Gwenhwyfar.

'Ah, but I was there. I …'

'Where?' I interrupted him. 'I didn't see you; nobody did!'

'I didn't say I was seen, Percy, I said I was there. No-one saw me. I watched over the proceedings and should it have been necessary I would have been there in person. But I was there – it was too important not to be. It all went to plan, but I needed to stay in my sky tower for a little longer.'

I said no more and we rode in silence for quite some time before Merlin spoke again.

'I've left word for Salazar to join me if he returns to Sir Ector's. I suppose Arthur will bring him if he does go back there. I had the devil of a job stopping him coming this time; I managed to get him to stay because I told him that he needs all his clothes to be made for the wedding and how will they fit if he's not there to try them on? He cannot be seen to be going through the ceremony looking as though he's just fallen out of bed.'

I laughed.

Merlin stared at me, one eyebrow raised. I forgot that sometimes our different senses of humour were well off kilter.

'How are just you and I going to do whatever it is you think we can do?'

'I'll think of something.'

And that was all he said about it for the remainder of our journey to his cave.

Meanwhile.

'Look at those fools, Mordred.'

Mordred sidled up beside the witch and watched Merlin and me travelling through the forest.

She tried to tune into our thoughts but Merlin had already told me to put up my barriers, which I had, and as we weren't talking at the time she was unable to listen in to what we might have been saying.

'Well, we can get to his cave, as that is obviously where he's headed,' she snapped angrily, 'long before he gets there and we can, perhaps, cause some havoc. Come Mordred, get your boots on.'

They were gone within the hour but their travelling was not quite to plan or as quick as Mab had envisioned. It started to drizzle about an hour after they'd left and Mordred was forced to leave his horse tied behind hers and sit up behind her holding a canvas sheet over her head. After fifteen minutes his arms were aching like crazy.

'I can't hold this up for much longer Mab.'

'Well, you'll just have to. I can't hold it and hold the reins as well and I daren't get wet. I've lost enough power already, after being locked in that hell-hole; four months! Four months!' she screamed the last few words over her shoulder as she glowered back at the man.

'Well I got you out didn't I?'

'Not before time though!'

'I would have thought you'd be more grateful than this!'

'Shut up, shut up, SHUT UP!'

They rode on in silence for another ten minutes before Mordred dropped his arms and slid off the back of the horse. 'I can't hold up my arms for another second,' he complained, rubbing his shoulders and upper arms to get rid of the cramp that had taken hold.

The witch, screaming as the rain fell on top of her, grabbed the canvas and pulled it over her head before slipping sideways off the horse and landing, amazingly, on her extremely large backside which cushioned her fall quite effectively.

Grabbing a stick and jumping up, she started to whack the man over the head, all the time screeching insults at him, finally throwing the stick into the bushes and giving him a final kick.

'This is no good,' she finally grunted, pulling the sheet, which had slipped during her frantic assault, back over her head. 'We'll have to go back. Anyway I've thought of a much better plan.' With that she grabbed Mordred by the hair and climbing onto his stooped body got back on the horse; between them they somehow managed to tie the canvas sheet over her hunched body so that they could return to her castle on their own mounts.

They arrived – she mostly dry, he dripping wet and getting thumped again when he unthinkingly shook his cape out all over her.

'So what's the plan then?' he muttered, still rubbing his shoulder and battered head.

She finally calmed down and then, amazingly, even he experienced icy cold fingers climbing up and down his spine as he looked over at the witch's face.

Her eyes were narrowed and her mouth sneered long before she deigned to answer him. 'Oh, something lovely; I don't know why I didn't think of it before.'

SIX

Mab and Mordred had arrived back at what appeared to be the outwardly ruined castle as night fell. She was in an ill humour as she dragged her sodden hem through the grounds and into the kitchens. She was dry from the knees up and, kicking off her shoes, stood beside the remains of the fire screeching at Mordred to get it burning brighter. Mordred took not one bit of notice of the grimy feet and legs that were on display in front of flames that appeared to be pulling away from her.

Her mind was working overtime. She had had a half-cocked idea of getting to Merlin's cave before him but had still not refined a plan as to what she'd do once she got there. All she knew was that she wanted to grab him and me and disable us somehow but even how she was going to do that hadn't been worked out at that time.

But now!

Well, it was all coming together quite nicely – if one could ever use the word "nice" where she was concerned.

Merlin had a great deal to answer for. He'd locked her in that place when she was unable to resist. She had kicked herself on more than one occasion for not trusting herself to lay still; she'd therefore taken the powder that had made her unable to move so that the magic would do its work. Why had she done that? Why hadn't she trusted herself to keep still? All that pain and suffering because she wanted to make sure she was stock-still. Well, she'd make sure she trusted herself in future. He'd never get the upper hand with her again!

That place was just terrible. Where and what was it? Was it some sort of waiting room for hell? Well, if it was it was certainly not going to keep her; she was much too clever for that. But there was no handle on the inside of that door and try as she might, uttering one spell after another and even resorting to running at it to try and shoulder it open, she couldn't budge it. All she managed to achieve was a dislocated shoulder and dozens of bruises – not that one would have been able to tell the difference between a bruise amongst all that grime!

And those awful beings! Spectres! Demons! She couldn't believe it. She'd tried to grab one once to get it to listen to her and help her escape or give her a few hints about the place but they were either so ethereal that her hands just went straight through them or they were so greasy or slimy that they just slipped out of her grasp. And there were lots of them who were so much more wicked than she had ever been – was that possible?

But, he was now going to be sorry because she'd learned a lot in that place. Oh yes! Lots! And the goblins – well, they were one of the only beings in that place that she'd been able to grab hold of and she'd tamed them, hadn't she? And they were well up for what she had wanted them to do if only she could get them out of there and if she wasn't mistaken, they would, by now, have already done what she'd ordered. When she had finally escaped from that place she had wondered if the goblins would be able to leave as well, but she needn't have worried as they, too, like her hadn't yet been consigned to the deepest pit and they also had one great advantage – they were slug-goblins – slimy creatures that needed no other sustenance than grass and leaves. Oh, it was going to be so easy to keep them. She had promised them so much – that they would not return to the darkness, she would give them sway over all the land of Britain so far as greenery was concerned – well, she didn't like all that cabbagy stuff anyway, did she? She would also give them power over all insects, and other such trivial stuff that Mab never considered as important. Being almost manlike in form and stature they were able to walk, see, ride, fight and do almost anything humans could do and so, weaving one of her more potent spells, she gave them the ability to form a great army, kitting it out with all the armour and weaponry they would need. They needed something to enable them to sit upright and not keep sliding down – armour would do that. Or, what about if she were to get them to take over the bodies of some other evil being! Now who? Well, she would think on that and would be certain to come up with something.

They were already as evil as the witch, so were completely up to doing all she desired and pleased her no end in adding evils she hadn't even considered. And there were so many of them – if they couldn't overcome in craftiness (of which they had so much) they must surely overcome in sheer number.

On the day she had managed to escape, these weird beings shot through the doorway alongside her in a split second. Wow, they were fast! They'd be great warriors for what she needed them for, eh? People would get killed before they'd even seen their adversary. She laughed herself silly when thinking about this.

She had had a bit of a job getting enough horses for them – horses that baulked at the sheer smell of them – but after a little bit of magic and some very handy herbs that she was able to add to their feed, they became quite compliant. She had conjured up enough of them for the officers; the rest would have to march. But she still had a bit to do before all this would be ready.

Chuckling to herself, as her rancid clothing dried before the roaring fire, she took great pleasure in envisioning each and every awful thing that was a possibility now in overcoming Merlin and the rest of us. 'Possibility,' she thought. 'No! Inevitability!'

Yes, Merlin was going to pay – and pay mightily – for the months she'd had to spend in that abyss. Oh yes, he was going to pay dearly. She grinned.

Mab stood and counted off on her fingers just how she was going to make him pay. She soon ran out of fingers.

'Arthur, of course – and his hope for a united Britain; well, he isn't going to rule; in fact he isn't going to live much longer because this time it will work – I am determined to kill him off and it is I who will rule the land. All I need do is make things so awful for him that he will end up worrying so much that he won't be able to think straight; then he'll be so wrong-footed that I'll be able to pounce and then he will fall; on the other hand I could get him when he is in such a good mood that he won't see me coming, especially with those slug goblins.

'Rhianne – I know Mordred still wants her so I suppose, to keep him sweet at any rate, I shall have to let her live; though it really goes against the grain to do so. But if I get her, Arthur will follow; that has always been the way.

'And that dratted Percy – I reckon I'd better do away with him first because every time I think I have it all sorted – up he pops – somehow – but how does he do that?' She screwed up her face in confusion, 'I don't know how but he just does – so, yes, he's first!

'And now they have a child – well, it's so small it won't put up any resistance.'

Even Mordred shuddered as he listened to her mutterings.

'Then, to really put the final nail in the coffin … oh, that is really funny,' she laughed so loud and long that Mordred thought she'd have an apoplexy as she kept pointing at him and trying to repeat "nail in coffin".

She finally got herself back under control as she lifted herself up off the floor, from which position she had been lying and kicking up her legs, wiping the tears from her cheeks and revealing some of their pinkness beneath the grime, she continued. 'Nimue!' She had to say it a few times before her uncontrollable tongue managed to get around the word. Up to then Munniay, Niummee, and the like had edged their way around her tongue before she had finally been able to get it right.

'That would make him soooo mad – and I don't mean angry mad, I mean crazy mad – like a mindless idiot, that he'd never trouble me again. Ha! Wonderful!

'So now, Mordred, come. We have work – delicious work – to do.'

SEVEN

We arrived at Merlin's cave just as the sun was setting over the sea. The heavy rain clouds that had dogged us for most of the journey had parted just above the horizon and the red sunset burst through them to lift our spirits. It looked beautiful and peaceful. The tide was out and as I stared at the solitary rock in the middle of that small bay, I remembered the time I'd been there as a young boy and how the mist had made all the rocks seem like giants and monsters. I was older now but I expect there would always be that chill climbing up and down my spine every time I came here.

Merlin turned down his mouth on one side as he shook his head at me. 'You still don't trust me, do you?'

I blushed, and then got annoyed with myself for doing so. I really must remember to put up my barriers when Merlin was around, especially when thinking negatively.

'Come Percy, I have a lot to teach you – and you are ready. Quickly now, we have much to do and only a little time in which to do it.'

As the last of the sun's rays clambered up the rockface above us, we entered the dark and cold interior of the cave that nestles below the island of Tintagel.

We could hear the waves rolling against the far end of the tunnel as we entered and sometimes, when a strong wind was blowing in a certain direction, the water would penetrate as far as our end, but at the moment the elements were slumbering peacefully and so all was calm and serene, but still very cold.

'Let's light the fire Percy; you go out and get some driftwood; I'll find some logs – there're some in here somewhere,' he muttered as he disappeared down into the tunnels. I wandered back outside and in the quickly diminishing light found enough dry driftwood to get a fire started.

By midnight we were fed and warm. It was mid-autumn now and with the falling of the leaves came the niggle that this was the time when all was not quite right with the world – the land after the harvest was stark, with trees throwing off their summer clothes in order to blend in, the ones nearer the sea attempting to look as dead as the rocks around them; wickedness was just around the corner and you never knew when you might bump right into it, thus even nature was afraid to be noticed.

'Sleep Percy, tomorrow will be a busy day.

We awoke to the sound of seagulls. Their plaintive cry caused me to wake up feeling as though I had lost a loved one and it was as much as I could do not to groan.

Merlin, tuning in to my thoughts and knowing he had to pull me from them, began giving me orders.

'Today I will let you into some of the more profound secrets of the Druid. Those secrets are already within you, Percy, but need to be awoken; they lie dormant but I have the key. Today your schooling will formally begin; none of the little tricks that up to now have amused you – no, today you will be taken deep. Will you come out alive? I truly hope so.'

I shuddered. What on earth was going to happen to me? But it worked – I would think of nothing else but Merlin's instruction.

So from that moment on my mind was taken up with magic – magic, enchantments, spells, potions and the unexplained!

Time went quickly and it was only now and then that I would feel a little guilty that I hadn't even thought about Rhianne or Kate all day; some days were so full they blended into the nights so that I sometimes didn't even think about anything other than all that I was currently engrossed in.

Merlin, tuning into my guilt, told me that he had placed a curtain between them and my thoughts so that I wouldn't think about them too much, so that I could concentrate on the job in hand. It made me feel a little better – but not much.

I did ask him a question during a sunny afternoon that he'd decided we should take off to rest so as to regain our physical as well as mental strength; we had been very busy with him trying to get me to understand the art of disappearance and reappearance over short distances or longer distances or even over time, whether forward or backward. It had been extremely hard and I was still having difficulty in the coming back part – so Merlin suggested we took a day off.

I had asked if we could go back to the caer and see my family but he said it was not a good idea. We were nearly there and a week, two at best, should finish my education.

So we sat in the sun and dozed.

Dangerous!

I awoke with a start as a few drops of rain splattered onto my face. It had turned extremely dark and I wondered if we had slept too long.

'Merlin,' I called, noticing he wasn't beside me anymore.

There was no answer so I called again, much louder.

Fear began to creep up my spine as I dashed in through the cave's entrance. 'Merlin! Merlin!'

'Shhh,' he answered as, grabbing my arm, he pulled me to one side. 'There's someone inside,' he whispered into my ear. 'Don't know how they got past us but somehow they have; they must have enveloped themselves in invisibility. Maybe they came in through the seaward entrance. I have some naiad root ready. Tread carefully, be silent and hold onto my shoulder.'

I'd thought that creeping about was a bit late after all the shouting I'd done but Merlin, hopefully, knew best. Perhaps he had covered my noise so it wasn't heard.

We walked so slowly that it felt like we weren't moving at all. As we neared the room we noticed there were candles burning inside.

I jumped out of my skin as Merlin shouted. 'Show yourself!'

Salazar turned round at his call and bowed low. That was a weird experience I can tell you. First of all no-one was there and then, as he turned, he materialised. I'd never seen him do that before; he had, like Merlin, always preferred to walk into a room or out of the forest, or the like; perhaps he knew about my current training so thought it was all right to do it. But we didn't ask.

Phew!

Everything was all right!

Or was it?

Salazar's face was hard – serious. Well it nearly always was but usually, when we met up with him after a long absence, there was a softening, a glow, but now he looked solemn and grave.

We talked long into the night – thank goodness we'd had time to rest during the day or we might not have been alert enough to take it all in.

The African and his wife, Jasmine, had been travelling throughout Britain and Europe and had become more and more concerned at what was happening and being spoken of all over the places they had visited. They had visited Sir Ector's home, where Salazar had left his wife while he searched for Merlin – there was much to discuss as to what they should do.

There was trouble in Italy, where hoards of Gothic warriors were about to besiege Rome – they had apparently been stirred up by a sorcerer – a female from the west – who had promised them much if they won and then even more if they turned their army west to aid her in her fight. He had been able to listen in to a conversation by two of the Goths who were arguing with each other as to whether, once they had sacked Rome, they actually wanted to have their bodies taken over for a while. 'I mean,' one of them had said. 'Why don't we just take the loot and run? We could make ourselves emperors over a country that needed someone like us to look after them. We'd have enough!'

The other one had said that they had been promised so much more! 'Let's wait and see what's on offer; we only have to be joined to these goblins for a few weeks!'

Salazar said that it made his skin crawl as he listened to those two men. He believed he knew who was behind it all but as yet wasn't entirely sure what she was going to do.

Then, there were pirates in the Mediterranean who were attacking merchant ships and seizing all their goods, especially weapons, in readiness for war, their ships disappearing without a trace but Salazar was aware they always turned west.

And in Britain there were many lords and minor kings who were being stirred up, each one wanting to be the one to take over the whole of the nation as High King – as prophesied. There had been much in-fighting, even between close relatives, with each lord or king saying that it was his given right to take the role of King of all the Britons.

Merlin sat ruminating on what Salazar was telling him and waited for the man to finish.

'It's her! Mab! She's the one responsible for all of this!'

'Yes, Merlin, but that is not all.'

My blood turned cold. I'd taken no part in the conversation, still feeling extremely inadequate beside these two giants of both magic and experience – and age! I finally had to release the breath I had been holding.

'She's gathered up wickedness from all over Europe and, like those Goths mentioned, has taken charge of a hoard of goblins from that evil place in which you imprisoned her. Jasmine and I tracked them as she led them to a hiding place but lost them near the Iron Age burial ground in Carn Euny at Sancreed in the Duke of Cornwall's domain. We searched through the fogou but they had completely disappeared.

'What's a fogou?' I asked, repeating it again as the words didn't come out the first time – my mouth was just so dry.

'Underground passages,' Merlin explained.

'They are led by that awful hobgoblin from the place of shades. He knows Arthur, you see, and can therefore aid the witch in leading those hoards in trying to capture him.'

'Evil is building. We need to thwart it, counteract it, even counter-attack.' Merlin turned haunted eyes to me and I realised that this was going to be bad – our worst encounter ever with mad Mab and this time Arthur's life and all of ours and our loved ones would really be on the line.

'Right!' he turned toward Salazar. 'One more week with Percy. Help me, Salazar – we have to make him ready and he is nearly there.'

And so we set to, each of us with a will to succeed, to finish my education and bring me up to at least the level of junior Druid. I was determined to do all I could to succeed; I just had to keep my friend, the Once and Future King, safe from not only the witch (and I wondered if she really knew what she was dealing with) but from the hoards of hell itself.

However, somewhere in the back of my mind was the unbanishable thought that this important week of my education might be one week too far.

On my last day of training in that final week, we almost collapsed with relief as we sat down to relax; on the morrow we would be leaving for the caer. Merlin consulted the Glass. It was hung high on the wall of the cave and measured about the same size as the bird bath in my garden back home; it was frosted and looked for most of the time like a tiny frozen pond. However, when it was active it resembled a small television set, the difference being that if Merlin sprinkled some powder (and now I know what that powder is, but secrecy prevents me from telling you just what, as I would then have to kill you) over you, you would end up in the place that is being shown within the Glass. Great stuff! But sometimes you have to accept that you might end up somewhere completely different – but that didn't happen very often.

However, at the moment we were just searching. We got Salazar to concentrate on Rome and we saw the Goth general – Witigis – prancing about on his horse from a hill overlooking the city and could hear the groans from the people within its walls. There was another horse close by and it was obvious that the person sitting on it was a woman but she was completely covered in a cloak so we couldn't see who it might be, but each of us felt sure we knew just who she was, especially as no-one appeared to want to get very close to her.

Then memories none too pleasant returned to me as we watched another scene – pirates chasing, attacking and boarding a small Italian merchant vessel as a mighty storm tossed the two ships about.

The picture changed again and we saw two armies facing one another across a misty, boggy plain. Neither army moved but it was obvious that it wouldn't be long before one of them did.

I asked if it was Mab and Merlin merely nodded; Salazar, however, added that if it was Mab then she had become much more powerful than they had originally supposed, as he knew she was not in that place now – in fact none of them were; we were merely seeing what had already happened. I had already wondered if what we were actually watching was what the Glass had already seen and was now playing it back to us. Merlin said that I should now be able to tell what the Glass was showing me as either in the past, in the present or, and this was extremely rare, in the future. But I couldn't dwell on these thoughts for too long as things were now moving on uncomfortably swiftly, as you will hear.

For a most curious thing happened. The Glass frosted over for a few moments and then, when it cleared, showed a picture of a pair of sandals.

We looked at them, our faces showing our confusion; looked at one another for enlightenment (which wasn't forthcoming) and then back at the sandals again.

After a good ten minutes, during which time the picture didn't change, we turned away and sat down, Merlin telling me to light a few more candles; we had been concentrating so much on the Glass that evening had crept upon us unawares and night was fast wrapping her arms around us.

Salazar went in search of food and some half hour later we were sitting around the stone table, eating our supper and discussing what we had seen within the Glass, wondering whether we should have gone to those places to see what was happening and whether we could actually do anything about it, turning now and then to look back up at the Glass which still shone brightly down at us with the pair of sandals sitting visibly in the centre of its screen.

We talked for hours like this, every now and then one of us looking up, or over a shoulder: the picture was still there.

'Oh this is crazy. It's never done that before!'

'Perhaps it knows something we don't and that whatever it is it is too important to dismiss!'

'But – sandals! I mean, winter is on the way and sandals would be the last thing I'd want to wear.'

'Shouldn't we ask the Glass to try and explain it to us?' I asked.

Merlin glowered at me before, several seconds later, smiling, exclaimed, 'Now why didn't I think of that? Our efforts at your education have not gone amiss! Go over, then, and ask.'

'Me?' I squeaked. Why did my voice do that to me every now and then – making me sound like a two-year old?

Merlin just sat back and smiled, nodding and pointing to the Glass.

I walked over – slowly, stared up at the screen and, shaking my head to clear it, stared for what seemed an age; then, hearing a cough behind me, opened my mouth and asked the dreaded question – well, only dreaded because I felt so self-conscious; something that Merlin was trying to drive out of me. ("Druids are powerful and conscious – not weak and self-conscious"). Squaring my shoulders I asked, not expecting an answer you see, what the sandals meant?

The picture changed. Well, not changed exactly but moved. The picture drew back from the sandals, which could now be seen to be lying in an alcove inside a very small whitewashed room. There were two small oil lamps burning in front of but to each side of the alcove, lighting that which was inside. The house, we would eventually discover, was single storied and had straw and pots on its flat roof and as the picture moved it showed more of the house, then the village, then the countryside around, I gasped as we looked out through the window and over a town.

'That must be Rome,' I whispered, seeing Roman soldiers headed toward it.

'No, it is not Rome,' Salazar corrected me. 'It's Jerusalem.'

As we continued to watch we saw flames starting to flare up in various parts of the town. We saw a huge building on fire and parts of it – stone boulders – falling over. We heard screams and could see people running away, being chased by the soldiers on horseback. It was a terrible sight and I tried hard, so hard, to look away but either the Glass or something else wouldn't let me; I was mesmerised – it held my gaze.

'You have to go and get those sandals, Percy,' Merlin, who had come up behind me, spoke into my ear. 'Before those soldiers destroy that house as well. 'It is important you bring them back here.'

'But that burning – that sacking of Jerusalem by the Romans happened long, long ago,' I whispered. 'It's too late!'

'I brought you back here, Percy; was that too late too? Have you forgotten already how I've just trained you to disappear and reappear over time and space?'

I thought about it and began to shake. Was I now going to go back even further than the Dark Ages and, if I did, would I be able to get back?

Merlin, who'd been following my uncontrolled thoughts patted my arm and said that I didn't need the dragon's breath any more to travel; I had conquered that and now had my own ability to move from place to place and from time to time – 'and back again,' he added. 'But you mustn't allow fear to open the channels of your mind; you must conquer that. It is fear that seeks to destroy you! Besides, you will always have the dragon's droppings to throw over yourself to come back.'

'I'll go with him,' Salazar declared. I know the language of those people and should a Roman soldier try to stop us I can show him my Roman Citizenship, which my father attained for me when he gained his freedom so many years ago now.'

And so it was that my reuniting with Rhianne and Kate was to be delayed yet further as Salazar and I stood before the Glass while Merlin threw the dust over us. Before long we were standing in that small house and staring at the sandals that sat side by side in the lighted alcove. I had an old leather satchel slung over my shoulder in which to stash the footwear, a cord around my neck upon which hung a small twist of linen containing the dragons' droppings, and, apart from the clothes I stood up in, not much else.

I had taken one step forward to take hold of the sandals when Salazar gripped my shoulder. I looked, then, at what danger I had placed myself in; there was an old man and a boy sitting in the shadows and I had not seen them. The boy was about twelve years old and was aiming a spear at me. The old man was blind – we didn't know that at first, as we couldn't really see them clearly in the gloom.

I dropped my hand as Salazar started speaking. Amazingly, though I knew he was speaking in a different language, I could understand everything he said and, even more amazingly, I could understand the old man as well when he responded. And more than that, when I spoke they could also understand me, even though I was speaking in my own language.

A thought of many years ago whipped into and out of my brain in a split second as I recalled my very first meeting with Merlin – the time he tried to communicate with me from his little book and his obvious pleasure when he used the language I could understand. But that was a split-second remembrance and not at all really connected to what was happening here. Being a Druid, though, is an amazing experience – but very weird.

He started by wishing them peace and eventually explained just who we were and why we were there. He told them all about himself and me; about Merlin and Arthur and then, of course, about Mab and her evil plans. He told him about the Glass and the picture of the sandals that would not go away and then what was happening in Jerusalem, concluding with the fact that he wouldn't be surprised if it was Mab that had caused all the ills they were now suffering.

The man listened politely, while the boy stood beside him holding his spear, though now he rested it upon the floor with the spearhead pointing upward instead of at me; even so, he kept a wary eye on me nonetheless.

Eventually the man spoke.

'I cannot see things with my eyes as they no longer function but I can see things in here,' he pointed to his head, 'and in here,' he placed his hand over his heart. 'I can therefore see a lot more clearly than some others who still have their sight.

'I can see that you are a man with a straight tongue and a full heart. This boy here,' he pointed behind him, 'is my grandson and, from what you say, he needs to get away from here. My sight tells me that we are a people who are being hunted to be destroyed.

'I have been the keeper of the sandals for nearly forty years but now that we are being searched out I fear for them.

'You may take them and use them for the purpose you intend for them; in one way this is good because they will become disguised; I am merely the keeper of the sandals but one day they must return and be ready, once again, to be returned to their owner should he require them. Do you agree to this?'

Salazar said that he would do all in his power to make sure this happened.

'Then you have to take my grandson back with you. He must be the guardian of the sandals now. You have my blessing to make them into what you desire. I know he aimed his spear at you but he has, so far, never killed anyone or anything to his or my knowledge.

'Many have tried to take the sandals but have perished or gone mad. You cannot take that chance because you, too, might die.

'I shall pray over the sandals that they will only be used for good and not for evil; should they fall into the wrong hands, those hands will rue the day they were ever laid on them.'

The old man got up and made his way unerringly across the room to the sandals. He picked them up and with dry, gnarled hands lovingly caressing them held them to his heart as he prayed over them. His sightless eyes stared into space and tears ran down his cheeks as, speaking in a language unknown to either Salazar or I, he blessed the sandals. At least I was under the impression that he was blessing them.

We heard the hoofbeats first and then the yells as many soldiers crashed through the street outside and entered many of the little houses in the village. We dared not think of what they were doing as many screams filled the air.

'Quick,' the old man whispered. 'My time is now but you must away. I have prayed and the Lord God of Israel will be your shield.' He hugged the boy with great urgency as he thrust the sandals into his hands and with another language that we couldn't understand spoke to him for mere seconds before pushing him across at us. 'Now go, go, GO!'

As the first Roman soldier ran toward the house I threw the dust over the three of us and hoped that, as we disappeared, the young boy didn't see the awful things that were happening to the people outside his home.

Salazar admitted some time later that he, himself, most probably would not have had the time to explain his Roman Citizenship before also being struck down; those killers looked crazed enough to slay anyone who wasn't dressed in Roman garb.

I often wondered if they'd seen us at all and, if they had, whether they thought we were ghosts.

However, we had got away, and none too soon, but we didn't end up in Merlin's cave!

EIGHT

'Where on earth are we?' Looking around at the landscape I didn't have the foggiest idea where we were; we could even have been on the moon for all I knew but we were most certainly not in Merlin's cave.

The boy took me by the hand and led me up the side of the hill to a place he obviously knew but we didn't; well I didn't know if Salazar did but I certainly didn't.

My blood ran cold as we peered over the rim of the hill and watched what was going on below.

On a sandy plain at the bottom of the hill, set out on a slight incline facing east, was an amphitheatre.

The boy lay down on his stomach, urging us to do the same, and we stayed quite still for an hour or so just watching what was going on down there. Everyone was extremely busy for such a hot day.

Again there were Roman soldiers walking about and there were obviously wealthy citizens coming and going in their fine clothes; in the arena gladiators were practising, wild animals, somewhere out of sight were roaring and slaves were scurrying here and there.

I shivered, remembering what had happened when we were trying to rescue the mask. But in this case the animals looked familiar and not alien, albeit fierce.

'We should go,' the boy whispered.

I jumped. 'I thought you couldn't speak,' I said. 'I thought you were a mute, or that if you could I wouldn't be able to understand your language.'

He smiled; it was a sad smile. 'I can speak – if I need to.'

'What is your name?'

'My name is Androcles.'

'No!'

'What do you mean?'

'Oh, sorry, just that I hadn't heard that name before,' I blithered, lying. Well, Merlin had always told me not to let people know that I knew about them, especially before they did something they were supposed to do in the future, if that were the case here. 'But where can we go?' I asked him. 'We are in the middle of nowhere!'

How they managed to come up to us without us hearing them was beyond my understanding but the sudden shout made me jump out of my skin.

Turning, my blood ran cold, again; we were surrounded by a dozen Roman soldiers on horseback.

'*This is it!*' I thought. '*If they don't slaughter us here and now we're back in the arena again!*'

The leader of the men leapt from his horse and bowed low to Salazar. I had my eyes narrowed so that I could close them quickly if something was about to happen that I just didn't want to see! Androcles was standing tall beside me, holding the rough cotton satchel with the sandals in it tight to his side.

'Majesty!' the soldier made a curt bow to Salazar and my jaw dropped.

'*What was going on here?*' I asked myself.

'*Quiet!*' Salazar spoke into my mind.

'We have been searching for you for days; we thought you'd been spirited away.'

'I have been meditating, travelling and have acquired these two house slaves,' he pointed at us.

'*Eh?*'

'Please, use my horse,' the man offered his mount to Salazar.

'Perhaps you will lead the way; maybe one of your men could ride on ahead to prepare my quarters?'

The order was given and Androcles and I followed Salazar and the Romans down to the small desert oasis where Roman tents stood in military-precise rows on one side and eastern-style marquees littered the ground around the far side of the amphitheatre, close to the pools of water.

We were led to one of the more richly decorated marquees where a tall, dour servant held the silk curtain to one side to enable us to enter.

The Roman soldier, Gnaius, waited until Salazar turned and then told him he would be expected to dine with the Governor that evening, the Governor being the garrison commander.

Salazar nodded and entered through the curtains with us

following, asking Gnaius to send a squad of soldiers to escort him at the right time.

'Phew, I can't believe what's happening!' I croaked, my voice having nearly deserted me, as I flopped down on a pile of heavily decorated cushions.

'Who do they think you are?' I asked Salazar.

'I wish I knew,' he answered, looking, unusually for him, slightly mystified. 'They obviously take me for a king – but who? And from where?'

'We'll have to test the waters,' I suggested. Perhaps Androcles and I could go on an errand or something and see what we can pick up?'

'Yes, that's a good idea. Androcles,' he turned to the youth, 'I suggest you find a hiding place somewhere in here for your precious load. I will speak a word of concealment over it and it will be safe. Then go, both of you, and find out what you can, before I have to make my presence known to the governor and in the meantime I'll try to discover how we can get back to Merlin.'

It was all too easy really. I did get laughed at a lot by some of the Roman soldiers; my clothes were strange to them, even though I had replaced my 20th Century gear with that from the Fifth Century, but I just smiled back at them and hoped they might think me slightly loony and thus would leave us alone; well I had heard that many civilisations believed that someone who was possibly one card short of a full pack was someone who was blessed by the gods and should therefore be dealt kindly with. It was certainly working here!

We travelled around and through the soldiers' tents and on and through the places where servants or slaves were working – sewing, cooking, making weaponry and leatherwear or clothing. They didn't stop working when we talked to them; they were shifty and jittery – they probably thought we might be spies and were a little afraid, I think.

But we asked them if they could tell us a little about our new master. We said he had bought us in the markets and we wanted to know if he would be kind or if we should beware.

We spoke to several soldiers, merchants and slaves; they knew very little about Salazar except that he was a very important king from the east, an astrologer the son of an astrologer who had once seen a star rise over the land of Israel. It was supposed he could tell the governor the future.

'Well,' I thought, '*he could certainly do that as that was where he'd come from,*' but I kept my barriers well in place as I thought these thoughts; I mean, you never knew just who might be listening-in in this strange place; anyone here might have the gift of the Old Way – and just how old was the Old Way any way? Who knew?

We were gone for most of the afternoon and returned just as several slaves brought pots of clean water and perfumed oils to prepare Salazar, and us it turned out (the Romans did not want smelly slaves waiting on them) for the evening's appointment with the governor.

My stomach was starting to do somersaults, not only because I wasn't sure what might happen when we got to see this powerful man but also because we hadn't eaten for so long. There was a bowl of fruit on a small table within the marquee and I washed and dressed shoving grapes and dates down my throat as quickly as I could. Androcles did the same. Well I mean – we might just be there to wait on table and not eat – with all that temptation I'd pass out!

As it turned out, although we did have to wait on those important personages, we could also eat what we liked out of sight. And I did!

But, anyway, before we got to that point, I got Salazar up to date with what we had found out while the servants were preparing us. I used the special gift that Merlin had taught me which would only allow Salazar to hear what I had to say – just in case.

'*So, tell me what you've found out.*'

'*You were right! They think you are a famous astrologer – a descendant of Balthasar.*'

'*Balthasar?*'

'*Yes, I think he was one of the wise men from the east. Apparently you are named after him, as are all those descended from his line who have the gift. Anyway, so they tell me, you came here about six months ago with another wise man – sorry, but I don't know who he was – and just about saved yourselves from being used as bait in the arena. My blood ran cold when they told me that! You were said, when they came to take you away to the cells, to have looked up at the sky and*' raised your scimitar – immediately the sky started to turn dark in the middle of the day as, I reckon, a planet began to move slowly across the face of the sun.

'Everyone was running around screaming and calling out to whichever god they trusted in until in the end the Prefect himself came out to speak to you to ask you what you had done and to forgive him and to bring back the sun. After that they decided you were too powerful to risk in the arena!'

'It must have been an eclipse,' Salazar mused. 'What happened?'

'Well you stood for what seemed ages until you suddenly raised your scimitar high above your head and swung it round quite a few times, at the same time speaking slowly at the sky. No-one said they knew what you were saying, but immediately there was a small sliver of light and then, gradually, the sun returned. Now, one of them said that if you could do that then no-one but no-one should try to lay a hand on you.'

'Yes, definitely an eclipse!'

'That's what I thought but I kept quiet about that. We spoke to lots of people and most of them were happy to tell us as much as they knew but it was Gnaius who was the most informative. I suppose it is because he spends so much time with the Prefect.'

'What or who is a prefect?'

'He's the main man! The man in charge of this place – the Governor. Funny name for someone in charge of the whole lot isn't it? When I was at school a prefect was just one of the other kids who'd been put in charge of a few of us. But, anyway, he said that the Prefect is an extremely superstitious man and when you had made the day turn to night at noon he knew you were someone that had to be feared and honoured, if not worshipped.

'He almost fell on his knees, but just about stopped as that would have made him lose face in front of his men, to beg you to bring back the light and thus the life again.'

Salazar was almost smiling as I recounted this tale. Almost!

'And did I do that?'

'Oh yes! You stared at the Prefect for so long that everyone thought he was going to melt or burst into flames or even die, but then you looked up to the heavens, spoke quietly in a language that no-one understood and it was then that it reappeared. There was great cheering and sobbing as relief flooded through the area. You were

*declared a hero, a mighty sorcerer, if not a god and have been revered
and cherished ever since.*

*'Now, for some reason, you went missing and they have been
worried sick, so you need to be able to give them a good excuse.'*

*'Right. Give me some time to think up something. Probably the
best thing is just to stick to what we've already said – that I needed
some more slaves and so went and purchased you two. Yes, I think
we'll stick to that, so you'd better let Androcles know what we've
decided.*

*'But I wonder just who did all these things – it certainly wasn't
me!'*

Within the hour the guard of honour arrived and we crossed
the short distance to the Governor's magnificent tent as night fell
rapidly. It was extremely warm inside as the many lanterns let off a
lot of heat but there were also many slaves standing behind each
cushion and once Salazar had sat down with the half-dozen or so
other important people the slaves fanned them with giant palm
leaves to keep them cool.

The slaves themselves – all young men – were from all parts of
the globe, from pale-skinned and blond-haired through
Mediterranean brown to African black; none of them were over
about 20 years old, I thought, and all were dressed in white cotton
tunics – they had bare arms and bare legs from the knees down and
wore leather sandals. Each tunic was decorated with a wolf being
ridden by a woman in Roman costume and wearing a helmet with
eagle wings, the insignia embroidered back and front to match the
insignia on the Prefect's coat of arms.

Those slaves were needed for a short period only as the desert
night brought with it a chill that permeated even that well-lit tent.
The fires outside were now blazing until soon their warmth could
be felt by all of us.

We waited on those important personages and stuffed
ourselves whilst out of sight but only got snatches of the
conversations going on between them. So, I knew I would have to
wait until much later when Salazar would tell me what was going
on.

Androcles was a fairly quiet youth who, like he said, only really
spoke when it was necessary. He was serious and reminded me
somewhat of Arthur. He was tall, slim and had a mop of thick curly

black hair. His eyes, like Arthur's were brown with coloured glints of amber within them. His smile, which he was giving me now as he bit into a fruit I had never seen before, lit up his whole countenance.

We would be good friends. It's funny how you know when you meet someone whether they will be friend or foe and Androcles would definitely be friend.

He and I had been dressed in similar tunics to that of the other slaves but ours were plain white.

'The Prefect will send his seamstresses over to you to decorate your tunics, should your master so wish,' Gnaius had suggested earlier that evening as we arrived at the banquet.

'They are fine just as they are,' Salazar had responded. 'I don't want them getting big-headed!' he had added.

'*Thanks!*'

We arrived back at our tent by the light of a carpet of stars and a sickle moon; it was amazing – almost as bright as day with all that light in the sky. However, it was bitterly cold and we were only too pleased to step inside out of the chill.

I waited until the muffled crunch of sandals on sand disappeared as the soldiers marched back to their tents before I spoke, hoping to hear all that had happened at the Governor's table.

'I'll tell you what was said in the morning,' Salazar spoke to us after dismissing the grim servant. 'I am too tired now and I might even dream how to use the information while I sleep.'

I thought he might mind speak to me after we'd got into our beds but no, pretty soon I could hear the evenness of his breathing as he drifted off into sleep. So, turning over, I soon fell asleep myself; morning would come soon enough.

NINE

'They should have been back long before now,' Merlin muttered, staring at the Glass.

'*I knew you should have sent me as well*,' Cabal grumbled as he scratched energetically behind one ear.

'So you think being clever with your witty remark is going to help the situation?' Merlin didn't even turn and look at the dog as he snapped at him.

Cabal knew he should say sorry but he didn't feel it so kept silent.

Both of them stared up at a picture of a niche in a wall where once resided a pair of Mediterranean sandals but now held only a shadow. The two oil lamps had gone out leaving the place looking almost derelict. The house was very still and the old man was no longer there and as the picture panned back all that could be seen in the distance was a ruined city with burned buildings and stones piled one upon another. No life, apart from wild goats and a lone rock badger, could be seen; no civilians and no Roman soldiers! All had deserted the place as though it were cursed.

'And no Salazar or Percy either,' he added as he tried to get the picture to change. 'Where are they?'

'*I'm sure I could find them if you were to send me there.*'

'I'm sure you couldn't! They've used the dragon's droppings and have not come back here but have gone somewhere else! But where?'

'*Perhaps if you send me there and give me some of the dragon's droppings then I'd end up where they are as well.*'

Merlin stroked his chin in contemplation for long minutes until, grinning, he turned and ruffled the hound's head.

'I knew I was brilliant when I thought about giving you this gift.'

'*Phshaw!*' Cabal thought with his barriers up. '*He always takes the credit!*'

'Come, we'll both go! But we will both have to go in disguise.'

And so it was that in a very roundabout way the man and his dog arrived in a small, squat whitewashed house where they then proceeded to throw the obviously tainted dragon's droppings over themselves before Merlin landed in a silken tent in the desert where he took on the role of a miserable-looking servant and Cabal fell into a huge cage surrounded by several hungry-looking lions.

'Merlin! Help!'

'How's your roar Cab?'

'Eh?'

'Roar!'

And he did. As one of the beasts' curiosity got the better of it and it padded across to the hound he let out a huge roar and the beast backed off.

'That was weird!' he thought when he first heard his own noise and then, as he watched the lion retreat and as thirst got the better of him, he stared into a bowl of water and saw a lion's face staring back at him. At first he jumped back but on looking again realised that Merlin must have conjured up the beast in him – literally.

'Very good Merlin! How long will I stay like this? I'm scared to sleep in case I change back and they attack me before I'm awake enough to fight back. Not that I'd be able to fight back. I mean, if I end up as the real me, though I'm strong and fleet of foot, in this place I am merely a hound and these four walls will not let me run anywhere. There are five other lions in this cell. I'd be done for. And then how will you and Percy or Arthur cope if I'm not there to look after you? And how will you cope with all that guilt when I'm dead, knowing it was you that was the cause of it? I'm done for! I wish I hadn't suggested coming here. What have you done to me?'

'Cab – shut up! It's all an illusion. You are still you but the illusion won't change until I speak my special words over you. So sleep now and regain your strength. Just take each minute as it comes and remember – I'm always here!'

'Yeah, right! Until you're not, that is!' This said only to himself.

Morning came and with it the sun – within minutes the cold and the darkness of night were gone, whisked up and folded away with the stars to be held in a safe place until the following evening shook out their creases as it recalled them again.

Salazar was awoken by the severe-looking servant who, after pouring some sticky-sweet nectar into a golden goblet, held it out to him. Salazar took the drink and was about to bring it to his lips when I dived across the room and knocked it out of his hands. The sticky liquid splashed across the carpet and up the silken curtains that were draped inside the tent.

'What on earth are you doing?' Salazar half-shouted as he sat up, now fully awake.

'It could be poison!' I exclaimed.

'Poison?'

'Yes – we don't know him,' I pointed at the servant. 'He could be a murderer!' I knew the servant didn't speak; he might even be deaf as well, so apart from my actions, which were a bit extreme I have to admit, he couldn't be offended by my words, although I felt pretty sure he knew exactly what I must be saying.

Androcles had come running back into the tent at the commotion and just stood there watching us.

'He wouldn't dare. They'd execute him if he did anything to me!'

'And that would be a disaster, wouldn't it?'

'Merlin!' Salazar and I chorused.

'And a waste of such a lovely breakfast drink!' he tut-tutted.

'How? Where?'

'The same way as both of you and, I expect,' he turned around and looked at Androcles, 'this young man?'

Introductions were made and we told him how we'd come to Androcles and his grandfather's house, how we'd taken the sandals and how we'd then got lost and what had happened since.

Merlin explained how he had made the same journey with the obviously contaminated dragon's droppings and was surprised that he had actually managed to end up in the same place and, weirdly, well before they arrived. 'Well, I mean,' he had added, 'I could have ended up anywhere! Anyway, I've brought some new dragon's droppings with me, so I'm sure we can all get home now. You know, I think that I used the droppings that Moon Song deposited; I reckon that her sickness has affected them and that is why everything seems to have gone wrong. But I've brought some new dragon's droppings with me this time so all should be well.

'Cabal is in with the lions and …'

'Lions!' I exclaimed.

'You really shouldn't do that,' Merlin chided me. 'You know I'll finish what I am about to say and that it will all become clear; it's a sign of a bad education – at best or, at worst, impatience. Neither characteristic is one to be pursued.'

'Sorry!'

'Yes, well, now I've forgotten what I was about to say.'

'Cabal? Lions?'

'Right! Well, he has taken on the form of a lion.' (I just about bit my tongue in time – I was on the verge, once again, of repeating "lion".) Merlin knew – he stared at me for a split second long enough for me to know that he knew. 'I had a sneaky suspicion just before we travelled that he would need to be able to really take care of himself and, amazingly, a lion came into my head – so that is what he now looks like.

'We'll have to go and get him before I sprinkle this new stuff over us and then we can go back.'

'No, we can't go back yet, Merlin; they are having a gladiatorial display tomorrow and I have promised to be there.'

'Oh, you can break that promise!'

'No, I can't. I have never broken a promise in my life!'

I looked at both of the Druids – one looking affronted and the other looking irritated. We'd already told Merlin about the sandals and as far as he was concerned we had everything we needed and so we could go.

But now there would be delays!

'Apart from that,' Salazar added, 'there is a caravan coming from the east with spices and unguents and the like. We need some of those special lotions for the sandals; I know not for what reason but believe all will become clear.

'All right,' he conceded defeat. 'But, now that you know who I am I am determined to make everything ready for after the display … and it is a display, I hope, not a contest?'

'Yes. They said it is a show for our benefit. Apparently I saw them months ago when they were new and useless; the Prefect wants to show me just how much they've improved before they really fight.'

'*And not just each other*,' I grimaced, thinking of the wild beasts and hoping Cabal was safe.

'*He's safe.*'

I had let my barriers down.

'So, show me the sandals.'

Merlin had not been present when Androcles had taken the sandals out from the front of his tunic. Even so, they were wrapped in a cloth and could not be seen.

Salazar, mouthing the silent words of releasing, directed Androcles to their hiding place and waited until they were unwrapped and visible.

Merlin stood looking at them for quite some time; he had a very confused look on his face as if to say he didn't know what they actually were or even what they might be used for. I hadn't realised it myself but up to that moment no-one but Androcles had touched them.

Moving forward, Merlin stretched out his hand to take hold of them. Several things happened at once: Androcles tried to step back but was not fast enough, Merlin yelled as though he had been burned – he stuck a couple of fingers into his mouth to cool them (later we could see a tiny blister at the end of his forefinger), at the same time a sudden bright light filled the room – it lasted a split second and we couldn't tell what it was – it was as though there was lightning but with no crack or following thunder and finally Androcles fell backwards clutching his precious load.

'What happened?' Merlin was almost panting, once he'd removed his fingers from his mouth. Shaking his hand rapidly to dispel any lingering sensation he looked up at the youth with a quizzical expression and waited for his response.

'I do not know, lord,' he replied. 'But I do know that my grandfather told me that only those with a pure heart and good motives may touch these sandals – and live!' he added.

Well, Merlin had done that and was still alive so that answered at least one if not both parts of those points.

White faced at the best of times, Merlin turned even paler. 'Whose sandals are they?' he demanded.

'I only know they belonged to my grandfather's master.'

Stroking his chin, Merlin looked from the boy's face to the sandals he was clutching. They were nothing out of the ordinary. They were strappy, like most of the footwear of the time, made of leather and, apart from a few scratches and obvious dried blood splatters on them, nothing out of the ordinary; certainly not what any master would be proud of anyway. Shaking his head he decided that as they had, as yet, undetected powers, he would leave them with the boy.

'Wrap them up again, boy. Salazar,' he turned to his friend, 'hide them again.'

He watched as his orders were carried out, stroking his chin again until they had finished.

Taking on the role again of long-faced servant, he swathed himself from head to toe in black robes, wrapping the loose ends over his nose and around his head – only his eyes were visible – and took Androcles and I around the traders' stalls, pointing out various foodstuffs which we purchased and carried, all the time conversing secretly with me – sometimes telling me things about the place and sometimes asking me questions. Before long our sacks were full and we were on the way back to our tent.

Salazar, out of sight of anyone from the garrison who would have thought it odd, cooked supper for us all and with satisfied stomachs and no idea of what the morrow had in store we all drifted off into almost happy sleep. Sleep is a funny thing; I often thought about it. If I stayed up all night because I couldn't sleep it seemed like a week, but if I fell asleep straight away it seemed like I'd only just closed my eyes when it was time to get up again. Mad eh?

That night I dreamed about fortune-tellers. I've often wondered why people have their fortunes told and even if those fortune-tellers knew what was really in store for their clients did they only ever tell them of good things that might happen and keep the horrid ones to themselves? Did they make it all up just to get their palms crossed with silver? Pretty lucrative business I always thought. Silver? A bit more precious than coins, even though it was always coins that were passed. "Cross my palm with silver dearie," was what I'd always heard them say at fairs and in the movies. On the other hand, silver coins didn't really go a long way these days – perhaps it ought to be "cross my palm with a fiver or a tenner dearie". Then that was another thing – why was everyone called dearie? Someone who was dear was someone you knew and loved but these women – well some were old hags with warts on their noses, but I saw one once who was really pretty…

'Granddad – you're getting off track again.'

'Sorry! Where was I?'
'You'd drifted off into happy sleep!'

It seemed as though I'd only been asleep for a couple of minutes when we were woken up by the sound of clanging. It sounded as though anything and everything that was metal was being banged. We dressed hurriedly to find out what was going on.

Gnaius presented himself at our tent to escort us to the display. I'd been sound asleep one minute and because of the cacophony of noise wide awake the next thinking I was about to be murdered in my bed by an old hag of a fortuneteller who was advancing toward me with a hatchet in her hand and a wart on her nose.

'What time is it?' I tried to speak through my dry morning mouth.

'Early!' was the only response I got.

I listened while Salazar enquired as to the reason for this early start and heard that all contests were held in the mornings. As the amphitheatre seats faced west with its central arena, or stage, facing east; all contests, plays, concerts, etc had to be performed in the mornings because after noon the sun would begin to shine into the faces of the onlookers and they would not be able to see anything. Apart from that, it was always coolest before midday. 'Then, of course, if there was heavy gladiatorial fighting, well, they would need the daylight to see to clear away all the bodies and blood, wouldn't they?' the man had said matter-of-factly.

We had by now struggled into our clothes and were all, that is Salazar, Merlin as his servant, Androcles and I as his slaves, on our way to watch the display. Or were we?

TEN

'They shouldn't have gone!' she cackled, watching us as we walked across the sand toward the amphitheatre. Her crystal was very clear today as she and the man stared intently into it. 'I'll just finish what I was doing and then I think I'll take a little trip myself. Come, Mordred, let's get moving. We've the whole day ahead of us and I don't want a minute of it wasted.

'Here are the keys to the castle. There's no-one to protect her now, you know. That Ector fellow is too fond of his food and his beer. So if he's there, all we need do is make sure he has plenty of both and he'll sleep deep and long, especially with a little bit of this added.' Shaking the small container up before her nose, he watched a muscle in her cheek twitch as one side of her mouth turned up in mock smile. 'Then it will be easy. Oh it will be so so easy!

'Get the cart stacked with everything we need so we won't have to stop and then we're off to Cornwall to collect our men. And,' she croaked as she pointed a grimy finger at her crystal, 'I might even take a little trip out there. Oh this is going to be so much fun! With a little bit of precision we might be done sooner than we thought.' The laughter started to bubble from her belly upward and even Mordred had to cover his ears as she exploded with an even higher decibel screech than she'd ever managed before.

Another year had passed and she was looking worse than ever. She'd put on so much weight by now that it was getting harder and harder for her to walk properly. She couldn't sit a horse very well any more she realised, especially after the disaster of a few days ago, so the cart would have to be used; it was slower but it was better than finding herself in the middle of her journey with a clapped-out nag gasping out its last breath underneath her; she grimaced as she remembered trapping her leg beneath a dying mare during one trip which had caused her no end of misery (in fact she had limped intermittently ever since; and, of course, it had to be the same leg that the naiad had bitten all those years ago). Slapping the dead animal around its head with her hand for over a minute didn't help much either – it was past responding. Anyway, the cart was much more waterproof than any old nag had ever been; also, she'd be able to work her magic as she was travelling along – who knows what she might do or where she might go. So now, it was the cart, which also helped inasmuch as she could take so much more stuff with her – especially food – than her saddlebags ever could have held.

'And, of course, there will be room for our guests!' she grinned wickedly.

Setting off just as the sun started its descent she lay back upon a mountain of cushions and told Mordred, who was holding the reins, to go as fast as he could. 'We'll get to Sir Ector's by tomorrow noon if we hurry. I shall sleep now, so don't go over any ruts or rocks; I shall need to wake up early to put most of my potions together in readiness; they have to be fresh.' She settled herself more comfortably, mentally ticking off on all her fingers the things she would be doing the next day. The smile was a contented one as one evil part of her plan followed the next through her mind's eye until gentle snores and then those of a considerably higher decibel rent the air, which were soon accompanied by noises of a less acceptable quality.

Mordred had looked over his shoulder at her while she'd spoken; he, too, smiled but then he must have grown accustomed to Mab's extremely repulsive countenance. Her hair was, by now, virtually non-existent – what was left was stuck to her balding head with merely the odd wisps of frizzy ends floating on the current breeze as they swept along; her face was so grimy that only where her eyes had watered, her nose had run or where she had dribbled could one see pink flesh beneath and there were now, tops, only about seven teeth left in her mouth, and those were so discoloured or loose that they looked more like unswallowed pieces of cheese than teeth – so her smile to anyone other than him would have been grotesque.

But then again, she could disguise herself – so that was a blessing but realistically she wouldn't even be a blessing in disguise, if you see what I mean.

So her scheme, which she had gone to sleep dreaming about, was very much in readiness when she arrived at Sir Ector's. And that was, as she had planned, at mid-day the next day.

Checking through the goods they had on board the cart, Mab chuckled as she set out the pretty kerchiefs, shiny silver bangles and bed linen. 'This is going to be a piece of cake,' she muttered happily.

'This time it is going to work; I can feel it in my bones!'

Many had been lured to the cart by its beauty. It was decorated with ribbons and bells and had been painted with all the colours of the rainbow. There were now dozens of people looking at Mab's wares and others were being drawn by the crowd. She should have been a salesman – she had all the patter. She even told them she would take goods in exchange. The buying and selling was not the real reason she was there so she had no real interest in making money but some of the things she had on display were so beautiful and so rare (and thus so expensive) that the maids ran to their mistresses to tell them to come and see – as planned!

It was no surprise, therefore, when Mab peeped out of the side of her eyes and saw Rhianne and Lady Elise gliding down the steps toward her wagon. If only they had been able to see the wicked glint in her eye and the evil turn to her mouth they would definitely have turned and disappeared back into the Hall as fast as their feet could carry them, but their eyes had been drawn to the pretty things on display and the vendor held no interest for them at all. The men and women drew aside to let them through, knowing that they would never be able to afford those things that these two ladies would be buying. Somehow, Mab had managed to effect a disguise by clothing herself not only in the floaty silks of a gypsy but in a wonderful eastern perfume; for once she actually smelled nice! 'Come and see, come and see,' she chanted. Laces and silks from the Orient, spices from the East, perfumes mixed specially for the discerning ladies. Come and see.'

Lady Elise loved kerchiefs; she always seemed to have one clutched in her hand so as to be ready to dab at her eyes, which ever seemed to want to weep, and oohed and ahhd at several delicate wisps of lace; Rhianne was fascinated by an alabaster jar decorated with an even finer lid painted with roses and peacock feathers. Iris, accompanying them, couldn't take her eyes off the shiny baubles – each one more elaborate than the last.

'Smell them, smell them,' Mab urged them. 'They, too, are infused with perfumes from the East. You will never see their like again. And at such a small cost.'

Mab watched the three women lift the articles to their noses and it was with great control that she managed not to snigger.

As soon as payment was made for the goods purchased the witch packed up her wares, climbed on board the elaborately painted wagon and moved slowly out of the gates, Mordred looking to all the world like an Eastern prince's servant, leading the horse by its bridle.

Not even Griff, Cabal's brother, had a sniff of the evil that was passing by.

All who had stopped by the pretty wagon would have goggled at the way it transformed into a drab cart, along with its owners, as soon as it was out of sight but that is not really important to our story.

Thus it was that as midnight was reached, two women left their beds, dressed, and with sightless eyes left the Hall. They walked along to the nursery and wrapping up the baby placed her in her basket and ordered Iris to take her away. They watched with expressionless eyes as the nursemaid took the precious load through the main doors and down the steps outside and without even acknowledging her mistresses' existence moved trancelike out of the compound.

No-one saw them leave and no-one heard a thing; they were not missed until the next morning when Rhianne recalled what had happened in her dream. Grabbing her dressing robe, she sped across the bedroom and out through the door, telling herself that it was all a dream and she was being fanciful. Little did she know that the witch wanted her to recall what had happened; she was intent on causing as much distress as possible. Feeling the cold fingers of fear creeping up her spine she first of all began to increase her speed by walking very quickly before ending up running as fast as her legs would carry her to the nursery. It was empty! The baby's basket was gone as well! So, too, was Iris!

Rushing out of the room she went in search of them; finding her mother running along the hallway and seeing the paleness and worry on her face it became clear that she, also, was aware of what was going on and that the dream of the night was, in fact, reality.

Entering the kitchens they woke Old Molly from her ever-warm recess beside the fireplace and she, in turn, sent the maids scurrying to wake their lords; eventually Arthur rushed into the kitchens and with words tripping over one another they finally managed to get him to understand what was wrong.

A more thorough search was made, people were questioned and, finally, they had to admit that Kate and Iris were nowhere to be found.

'Iris wouldn't steal my baby,' Rhianne cried. 'She loves us all and is ever protective of little Kate.

'It must have been that merchant.' Rhianne concluded. 'What did she sell? Who bought stuff from her?'

There were only two or three other people – servants – who'd purchased some cheap brooches from her and once a search was made of the young women's rooms and their purchases found it was still a complete mystery as to whether the trader had caused the problem or not.

In fact it wasn't until Griff had padded up to the table in the kitchens in search of any unguarded food and had sniffed the alabaster box to find out if anything tasty might be contained within it but had then staggered off with vacant eyes that they had got any clue. Jasmine, who'd arrived a few weeks before with her husband Salazar, but who had stayed with the ladies when he had gone to rejoin Merlin and me, realised that the box had been enchanted and possibly the handkerchiefs too.

'Burn them,' she ordered. 'And the servants' brooches and anything else bought from her.'

They watched as all the items were thrown onto the fire and were all amazed at the horrific faces that formed in the smoke as it swirled out into the room seemingly to grab them before being sucked back up the chimney, and the creepy whispers and other noises that accompanied it.

Knowing that the witch was involved in this somehow, Jasmine determined to leave at once to find her husband and Merlin so as to rescue Kate and Iris. 'We'll all go,' Arthur cried. They knew it would be impossible trying to follow Mab; it might take days or they might never find her; Merlin was their only hope.

Swiftly discussing the matter, they immediately went their separate ways to make preparation to leave as early as they could that day, Arthur rounding up the men and some fresh horses to make the trip to Merlin's cave (hoping that it would be the right one but he was sure the magician had said he was going to the one at Tintagel). Jasmine took control of the provisions they would need for the journey; Rhianne and Lady Elise were too distraught to help. Arthur then went in search of Sir Ector. The big man almost went berserk when he heard what had happened to his granddaughter but agreed that he and Sir Kay would remain with Lady Elise and if they heard anything he would send word to Tintagel. In the meantime he would send out to the other lords round about to get them to beware and also to ready themselves for trouble.

'I'd be surprised if many of them will do anything you say, father; there is still a lot of discontent with many of them wanting to become High King of all the Britons.'

'Nevertheless, I shall try. Oh why did I sleep so soundly last night? I never sleep like that! I always wake at the slightest noise, especially if it is an unexpected one!'

'*Why indeed?*' thought Jasmine.

They left at two in the afternoon and would still have a good few hours before nightfall and so, even resting up overnight, they hoped to be at Tintagel by noon the next day. Rhianne accompanied them; there was no way she was going to be left at home to fret, though Lady Elise was in no fit state to do anything other than stay at home and wish her husband to "do something".

Sir Ector and several other lords had arranged a war council and were due to meet up soon; now he had the excuse to bring this forward. Things were happening – not only in the physical but now also in the mystical – they needed to be ready for every eventuality.

Arthur had been really looking forward to joining Sir Ector this time. Things were getting fraught in Britain. The Romans had gone, leaving a lot of wealthy Britons to take over where they had left off but without the military might and discipline of those Romans chaos had ensued. Many lords and minor kings had been murdered or chased away but the majority were still intact; the problem now was that many of them wanted and felt it safest to have one king over all the Britons. They had got so far as to agree that if Uther Pendragon still lived it would have been him; he was a great tactician, fearless and extremely strong; he knew how to command men and also command their respect, even though like many men he had his weaknesses, but as he was dead and had had no son and no-one else came anywhere near him, they all thought they had the right and the might to be this High King. Although all of them were arguing their corner they were getting absolutely nowhere fast and most of these meetings ended breaking up with sharp tongues or even sharper swords.

But now this had happened. Once again Arthur would be denied his place at the war council table. Then again, if he couldn't be trusted to look after his family he certainly wouldn't be put in charge of anyone else. So – it's off to Cornwall.

Iris had walked out through the gates of the Hall and looking neither to the left nor to the right moved straight toward the woods where the witch and the man waited.

Mab was grinning like a Cheshire cat as she watched them get nearer. Mordred only stared.

'Right my dears,' she cooed. 'Up you get.' She shoved Iris into the back of the wagon while Mordred held the basket. He hastily handed it to the woman as its contents started to squeal. 'Won't be long and you'll get breakfast. *Or you might even be breakfast!*' she chuckled.

'Climb up Mordred. Oh for pity's sake stop dragging your feet. Whip up the horse – let's get going.'

Mab had no fear that the woman would come out of her daze before they reached their destination; the fragrance she had inhaled would keep her well and truly under its influence for hours or until she provided her with the antidote, so it was with the accompaniment of a rather off-key tune they travelled west to Cornwall with the witch whistling happily through the ever increasing gaps in her teeth, though she was becoming slightly annoyed by the ever increasing volume from the hungry baby being rocked in her nurse's arms.

ELEVEN

The Prefect had arranged the platform with so many cushions that I had to watch the floor all the time in case I tripped over one of them as I helped carry in trays of food and pitchers of wine. Salazar and the other dignitaries eventually sat and only when they began to eat and converse could I take in more of our surroundings as I stood at the side in the shadows with Androcles and peeked through the drapes. The amphitheatre was almost deserted as this was supposed to be a very informal display, mainly for our benefit, though I had an uneasy feeling that it would be more to our disadvantage, but I tried to shake off those feelings.

There were only about a dozen sitting atop all those cushions with several youths, obviously slaves, standing around the sides and fanning them with giant palm branches. There were huge bowls of fruit, nuts and bread together with wine, sherbet and jugs of a very sweet and sticky nectar which were spread about, so although we had missed breakfast even we, out of sight most of the time and with several bowls at our disposal, would certainly not go hungry.

'They need the practice and get bored locked away. Look, here they come! See that brute there?' he pointed at a man who must have been at least seven feet tall. He wore a bronze-studded leather jerkin, a leather, loose-panelled short skirt and strappy sandals; on his head was a tight-fitting leather helmet that came down as far as his eyebrows at the front and with ear straps at the side. It tied under his chin and also had a flap that covered the back of his neck and another that came down over his nose. All that really could be seen of his head were his eyes and mouth. He had muscles that looked as though they were made of iron that rippled as he walked and even though the day's heat hadn't yet reached its peak, he and the others were glistening with oil and sweat. All the other gladiators had followed this huge man and it was only as they spread about that I got a look at them; mind you, I really didn't quite know where to put my eyes as all the others were completely naked – apparently all the combatants in those days fought that way. I expect the giant was too important and more than likely too fierce to be ordered to fight without his clothes. 'He's my champion! Killed dozens of gladiators and could use any weapon we gave him to do so; broke the necks of two lions with his bare hands! Impressive eh?'

Well, I was certainly impressed. I turned and looked at Merlin. His face was impassive as he stood at the back of our raised platform almost blending in with the dark silk curtains that hung there; I couldn't see his eyes but I knew he would be alert. Hopefully he'd have the dragon's droppings to hand, should things prove a bit hairy.

I turned back to the champion and watched as he and the others went through their paces. Well, I mean, as much as one knew there were dozens going through their paces but it was the champion that drew all eyes. They had drawn lots to see who would be fighting who and I bet all of them were hoping they didn't get the short straw; I certainly would not want to fight anyone of that size.

A man, obviously their trainer, was a stocky redheaded man of about forty – and I did wonder if yet again my redheaded enemy of all those years ago was still haunting me – but at least I wasn't one of the combatants I thought, only to have something creep up my spine on long hairy legs. He stood before them calling out instructions as they lunged or feinted, attacked or withdrew, swung or dropped to the floor as each command was called out to them. Not one of them was out of step with his neighbour; it was as if they moved by clockwork. It was extremely impressive, I must admit, but scary too. I was so glad I wasn't in their sandals – well, if they were wearing any, that is; also, my memories of the arena that Mab had conjured up were still too raw and I found that I kept looking at the Prefect and giving the occasional surreptitious sniff, just in case he wasn't a he at all! But all seemed normal; well, as normal as this abnormal place could be, that is; however, I couldn't get it out of my head that maybe he had been hypnotised and if that were so (another set of cold fingers slithered up my back) who exactly was it who might have done this? I searched the faces of all those sitting there but not one of them had any of the characteristics of that mad woman. I didn't know whether I was relieved or not; I mean, if she was about then at least we would be prepared.

Once they'd finished their show, they marched in unison back to their cells. I found I'd been holding my breath while I watched these events, as I was aware that just for a split second here and there the giant gladiator had risked a quick glance our way. Why? Was he looking to see if there was a way of escape or maybe he realised who we were and was seeing if he could somehow communicate with us. Well, it was too late right now as they had all gone back whence they had come.

Then they called for the wild animals to be brought out. I found I was chewing my lip in consternation; what animals would they be? I had visions of the conglomeration of beasts – normal and unnatural – that had been thrust at us not so long ago but I needn't have feared, as these were normal. What am I saying? They were fearsome – there's nothing normal in that! Lions – smaller than the ones I'd seen at the zoo – about ten of them, tigers, a jaguar, cheetahs and several warthogs. Thankfully they were all in strong cages that were being pulled along on carts by some magnificent horses and there was also one extremely large bear standing on its hind legs and hanging onto the bars with its front paws; it was in its own cage and being pulled along by a wild-eyed young elephant.

The roars and the smells were overpowering; I felt sorry for whoever was sent into this arena to fight them. I had this weird thought that if I was to be torn to shreds by any one of those lions, then I would have preferred it if they'd had a bath and cleaned their teeth first! How mad is that? I just didn't like the thought of those matted hairs and that foul breath catching me in the throat before the animal tore me to pieces. Just the thought of any of it made the hair on the back of my neck rise up. '*Nah*,' I thought, '*surely not! I shook my head to clear it of this ridiculous thought. Nah, not again!*'

The cages circled the arena twice and then I looked and looked again, almost bug eyed as one of the lions raised an eyebrow at me as it passed by in front of our dais.

'*Is that you?*'

'*Well, who else?*' Cabal answered.

'*Shhh,*' a disembodied sound tickled our ears.

We both closed our barriers.

'I wonder if you would like to donate your two young slaves to the games?' the Prefect asked Salazar.

I froze and desperately tried to tune in to Salazar or Merlin. I heard a quick exchange between the two sorcerers before both of their barriers crashed back into place and my heart fell into my sandals.

'Certainly! They need some training but they are young and strong enough I believe.'

'*Noooo!*' I almost screamed in my mind but was shocked into silence as Merlin threw his own barrier at me; I almost fell with the strength of it. I quickly got my mind back into a state of alertness – I didn't want to miss anything. Perhaps they would argue their way out of it; perhaps we might make a run for it – anything rather than go back into the arena again.

'What exactly is it that they would be doing?' Salazar asked politely.

'Oh, at first they would be trained up and then if they were skilled enough they would become gladiators. That one has quite a bit of fat on him so will need to be toned up!' He pointed at me.

'*Fat? Me?*' I was really affronted at that. Well I mean I had seen more fat on an apple!

'But, who knows,' he grinned, 'maybe one day they will be strong enough to fight Goliath!'

'Goliath?' Salazar queried.

'*Goliath?*' I almost fainted as I echoed the name. This was going from bad to worse.

'Oh that's what we call him. No-one knows his real name. In fact he doesn't even know it himself, I believe – he doesn't speak much so I'm told – I've never actually heard him say a thing. No-one's beaten him yet but who knows? Even Goliath might get bested by a younger and smaller man.' He chuckled to himself while in his mind he was obviously playing out this scene as he eyed me up and down. I cringed inside.

'I'll take them now and introduce them to the trainer. I shall send you two of my slaves to do your bidding.'

'I thank you for the courtesy,' Salazar responded. 'However, there are a few tasks I need them to perform for me that I've trained them to do. I should be most obliged if you would allow them to do this and then I will bring them to you first thing tomorrow morning. And do not concern yourself about sending me your slaves; I always choose my own and as I shall be leaving very soon I shall visit the slave markets and purchase some more.'

The Prefect looked a little put out but had to agree. 'First thing tomorrow then,' he replied as he stood to leave the amphitheatre.

They were dismissed.

I was relieved.

Merlin would now take us back to our tent where he would throw the droppings over us and we would return home.

Only two things were wrong with this decision of mine: one was that Cabal was still not with us and the other was that Merlin and Salazar had a completely different agenda.

TWELVE

The witch didn't travel far. Pulling up in front of a run down shack, she got Mordred to steer or carry each of the captives inside.

'Make sure they are secure. I don't want them escaping when I've gone to so much trouble.'

He sat Iris down along the back wall and manacled her left wrist with chains that he attached to a ring in the wall; she would be able to just about scratch her nose with it but that did not really matter as her other hand was free; it would be impossible to free herself. Plonking the baby into her lap he only half watched as Iris managed to absentmindedly cuddle the child with her one free arm before lapsing once again into semi consciousness.

'Oh, hurry up man!' the witch's voice grated against his nerves as she came back into the room, struggling across the floor with a large sack of stuff. 'Stop faffing around with those two and come here and help me.'

Taking a last look at the sleeping child he turned and helped drag the sack into the middle of the room.

'Get that bench and bring it here.'

Scrabbling about in the sack the woman finally pulled out what she'd been searching for and unwrapping it placed it in the middle of the bench.

The crystal ball just sat there – opaque and unyielding until the witch began her chanting. She started low at first but her noise increased until even Mordred covered his ears. Iris awoke with the clamour and with gradually focussing eyes realised her danger. Her first instinct was to cry out but her mouth was much too dry and she was afraid; her next was to cradle the child but only one arm obeyed her – the one that was still free. She bit her tongue in order to keep quiet, apprehending that both of her enemies were looking the other way. Without making any sound at all and squinting through her eyelashes she watched what was happening. Kate, who'd cried herself to sleep, amazingly did not wake up while all of this unholy racket was going on but it wouldn't be long before she would.

Mab's din stopped as suddenly as a slamming door. Iris

watched the crystal along with Mordred and Mab.

Mists swirled in the depths of the shiny orb, gradually clearing to show a meadow, then moving along to a forest and finally to Sir Ector's home's barricade. She watched along with them as the huge gateway opened, and felt a surge of relief as Arthur, Jasmine, Rhianne and some of the men cantered out on horseback; they were obviously on their way to save her and the baby. Griff was with them, sniffing the ground as their horses began to gallop, but it could be seen that even he had no idea where they were going.

'Ah, good,' the witch muttered. 'They are not coming this way – they must be going to Tintagel.'

'No!' Iris couldn't help it. The word slipped out before she could grab it.

'Ah, so you are awake at last,' the mad woman commented as her head turned slowly to look at her. 'Don't worry my dear; you won't be disturbed by Arthur. He's going the wrong way but my plan is that he will eventually try and rescue you – well, the baby really – and then,' she shouted. 'this time I *will* have him!'

There was then the most almighty sound that made even Mab jump.

Iris turned as it erupted and then tried as hard as she could to calm young Kate who was screaming again at the top of her lungs.

'She's hungry!' Iris commented. 'You have to take me back. The baby needs feeding.'

'But of course she does! I'll do something about that for you.' And she did. Grabbing Kate, she shoved her into Mordred's arms, at the same time slopping some porridge into a bowl. 'That should shut her up! Feed her.'

Iris strained at her bonds, the metal cutting into her wrist, but couldn't do a thing.

'Now,' Mab spoke to Iris once Kate was being fed. Well, by being fed one should envisage a man who had absolutely no knowledge of babies and who was desperately trying to hold onto a crying, wriggling child whose mouth was never in the place where the spoon was headed – it was initially but as soon as the spoon reached it the mouth spun around; then, when he eventually managed to get a little inside same mouth, it came out again, all down his jerkin or, worse, erupted and covered him from head to chest – and the smell! Regurgitated porridge or milk stank and still stank even after it was washed off. Mab, it seemed, had competition!

'Oh, for the sake of a warthog's uncle! Water it down or something – it's too thick for her.'

'Let me!' Iris almost begged the witch.

'OK. You carry on looking after the child while we pack up and then we won't take her away from you again; but if you try to escape you will fail and we will leave you here, manacled to the wall and you won't know what will happen to her; well, you won't know much at all after a while as you will either die of thirst or the wolves will get you,' she curled her lip as she nodded toward Iris, watching hungrily for the fear that would creep over her face; she wasn't disappointed. 'If you agree we'll be on our way.'

The poor woman just nodded.

Mab grinned. *'This was going to be so easy!'*

'Come Mordred, give her the child while we pack up all our stuff. Cornwall is a long way off with these burdens to carry but our friends will be waiting. And, who knows, we might just bump into Arthur on the way but I hope not – what I have in mind for him is so much better.' She sneered as she looked over at her captives but was not rewarded with any reaction; Iris was too busy trying to see to the baby, which was proving difficult with her arm still tied. Mab decided that now she knew the score she could be released and so gave the order.

'And you can look after them for a while – there is something I have to do. And make sure they are alive and unharmed when I come back,' she shouted at the man.

He merely nodded, though he didn't look at the witch – just continued staring at their captives.

Arthur and Shake Spear rode on ahead of the others, Shake Spear pointing out various flowers, trees, mountains or rivers and waxing lyrical on each subject to hand.

'Such stuff as dreams are made of,' he said more than once as he pointed out a butterfly or a robin; anything he'd possibly seen for the first time actually.

'What light through yonder window breaks,' woke up more than one of them as he watched the sun rise over the trees early one morning as they rested in a small inn.

After several miles of travelling the next day, and having not stopped talking once, several of the men began to tell him to shut up or they would have to gag him.

'How poor are they that have not patience!' he had responded; although he was not quite as noisy for the next couple of miles, he still had to point out things he'd thought that everyone else had never seen before.

After a few miles Arthur, who'd had the dubious pleasure of Shake Spear's company for the last twenty miles or so and also because no-one else would ride with him had had more than enough.

'Shake Spear, I should like you to go to the rear and keep Brosc company. He is looking a little scared – well, not scared exactly, but ill at ease. Your easy banter might lift his spirits. Perhaps you might ask Wite to join me for a while?'

'You are wise, young sir; you are every inch a leader!' he said as he rode back to do Arthur's bidding. Brosc sank lower on his pony as he watched Shake Spear heading his way; not the greatest conversationalist in the world, he also preferred to travel quietly. He was happiest with Wite because Wite didn't say much, and even when he did it was generally ridiculous and thus more amusing than anything else. He wasn't the sharpest knife in the drawer but then he had the kindest heart. And now he was having to swap him for the wordiest man in the world. Life was hard sometimes!

Arthur watched Shake Spear heading back down the line thinking he had been a little unfair; but since he'd been given those spectacles by Merlin and could now see as well as any man, he'd become almost unbearable – pointing out things that were obviously new to him but thinking they must also be new to everyone else as well. Never mind – Brosc could probably block out his chitter chatter as they rode along.

They camped that night under the stars. It was a warm night for October and with Griff on guard they felt it unnecessary for anyone else to do those honours. Baker and Tailor had made a fabulous supper – one grilling several hare over a roaring fire and the other making griddle and pancakes with jam and honey. So with that and some ripe cheese and a few apples they ate well and slept even better.

They might possibly have been a bit uneasy and maybe would

have had a nightmare or two if they had known that a certain mad woman and her party were camped on the other side of the same hill but to the west; a company of people that would be travelling almost parallel to them for part of the journey. Did either party know about the other's exact whereabouts? Wouldn't the witch have consulted her crystal whilst travelling to find out? Was she much too involved with Kate and the others to have the time? Well, we will just have to wait and see.

THIRTEEN

The two wizards had had their heads together for hours now. Androcles and I were given one task after another to perform, mainly, I believed, to keep us out of the way just so that they would not be overheard or, more possibly, to take our mind off our forthcoming departure to the cells.

'Make supper now,' Salazar spoke quietly over his shoulder as I re-entered the tent with a jug of sherbet.

I sighed heavily, partly because I was getting tired but also because I was miffed at not being in on the discussions. *'And,'* I thought, *'He was starting to believe I really was a slave!'*

'We have to put on a good show,' Merlin added, tuning in to my thoughts. 'If for one moment they thought we were not using you as we said, I'm sure someone would tell the Prefect and then they would come and take you. I'm not as sure as I was at first that they are quite as friendly as they've been making out. Instead of going to be trained as a gladiator, it might be that you would be bait for the lions!'

Without another word I did as I had been ordered and it was only about half an hour later that Salazar told me to go outside and collect Androcles, who had been polishing Salazar's scimitar, and join them for supper.

'Now,' Merlin began, 'Salazar and I have come up with a plan. For some reason that is not at all plain you were sent here – the droppings not having worked as expected; whether that is by design or accident we may never know – and now we have to see what is going to happen or what we have to do here before we can go back home. I believe it may be something to do with collecting herbs and spices from travelling merchants whom we believe should pass by here very soon; we do not have access to these herbs in Britain and I think they will be effective in the empowering of Excalibur.

'I will give you, Percy, this twist of paper with some dragons' droppings in it and also one for you, Androcles.' (He spent the next ten minutes instructing Androcles in the art of dragons' droppings' travel.) 'I know you've travelled this way before, young man, but this time you may need to activate it yourself, so tie it inside this leather pouch and string it round your neck. You can tell whoever might want to take it from you that it is either your family gods or some of the cremated remains of your father – anything like that will suffice as they are extremely superstitious people – they will not take it from you. Then you know what you can do if you get into a situation that you just can't get out of alive.'

My blood ran cold as I wondered what he thought might happen to us as gladiators, while I listened with half an ear to him explaining the use of the droppings to Androcles. What on earth were we going to have to endure? My mind gave me a swift panoramic view of our present location together with Romans, Goliath and lions – great! I was just about to embark on thinking of something far worse when a swift dig in the ribs made me pull myself together.

'Come, come, Percy, have I ever let you down?'

I put up my barriers – things had got very, very tight at times and although he had saved me – sometimes at the last minute – there was always the chance that he might just not make it in time.

He raised an eyebrow; I reckon he knew why I'd blocked him out.

'Right, now this is what we are going to do.'

The next morning Salazar, dressed in the bright and elaborate clothing of an eastern prince and followed by a sour-faced servant clothed from head to toe in black linen (only his resentful eyes could be seen), took Androcles and I to the door leading to the gladiators cells. The man who trained them – and he looked as fierce when he stared at us as he had the day before when he was taking those men through their paces – merely nodded to Salazar as he ushered us into the gloom. I looked over my shoulder as the door closed on the two sorcerers and hoped they had got it right.

Another thought crept into my mind – they called Salazar "majesty" but did they really think him that or was it all a ruse? Did they have plans for him as well? 'Come on, Percy,' I told myself, 'Get a grip!' That was a funny thought – when I was in the Dark Ages I really thought I was called Percy and when I spoke to myself called myself such; however, when I was back in the 20th Century, even when Merlin was around, I always called myself Jack – and another thought was that when I was back here I thought I was speaking in a language that was completely normal to that which I used in the 20th Century but had a vague notion that it was nothing like it – but this is just a funny thought which had to be inserted somewhere, so why not here!

But to get back to my troubles: It was a lot cooler in these semi-underground corridors, though the air was stuffy and mingled with stale sweat, old spilled blood and other more offensive odours.

We moved down a flight of steps before passing a dark room just off the lengthy corridor we were being taken along where two men could just about be detected as they lay on straw pallets – both wore bandages – one around his head and the other around his chest – and were either asleep or unconscious or worse. My skin crawled.

As the trainer moved along in front of us we found ourselves travelling around the circumference of the amphitheatre; we could look out of the grilles set into the walls that inside were at head height but outside were obviously at ground level. There were also iron gates set at intervals around the arena, which were reached by several steps leading up to and through them. I hadn't noticed it before; I suppose it was because I had only ever looked at the amphitheatre from above instead of here in this underground semi-dark corridor – but outside the arena was set down deeply so that the onlookers would not be harmed by the beasts or even the gladiators, should they wish to try and pounce. The arena, then, had walls surrounding it that were at least twelve or fifteen feet high, above which were the seating areas. All this I could observe as I passed each of the iron grilles set in and around the arena.

Passing over a wooden walkway we were able to look down underneath us through several metal grilles separating the animals and us; one or two roared and made a lunge up at us (I actually jumped away, which was ridiculous as they wouldn't have been able to reach through even if they could jump high enough). I tried to make out which one was Cabby but I don't think he was in that particular cage. I reached out to him with my mind and was soundly slapped down by Merlin. Remembering his orders to keep my mind-speaking skills in check I felt duly reprimanded.

We eventually came to a huge wooden door with strong metal fixtures including hasps and an unusually large lock. The trainer, who still hadn't spoken, made a great show in unlocking the door (I reckon he was telling us in his own way that it would be completely useless to try and break out) before pulling it open (and he had to really pull, flexing his muscles in the doing of it) and giving me, particularly, a mock bow, and inviting us in. Did we have a choice?

Once inside we had to adjust our eyes to even more gloom until we could make out the others sitting around within. Goliath was there but was sleeping. Some of the others were curious but mostly they ignored us. I wondered if they spoke a language we would understand.

Androcles pulled me down onto the chiselled-out seating that ran all the way around the edge of the fairly large room. There was a small grille near the very high ceiling that let in an extremely small amount of light – but enough for us to see now that our eyes had adjusted.

'I thought we were here just to learn!' Androcles whispered.

'Hmm, yes, so did I.'

'We seem to be prisoners.'

I didn't reply but felt a little uneasy. I would have felt much more uneasy if I didn't have the dragon's droppings around my neck.

Wondering what was going to happen next I thought I'd conserve as much strength as I could and so leaned back against the coolness of the rough stone-built wall and tried to doze. It was impossible, of course, because there was too much going on and it was still early in the morning and I'd had only just recently risen from a good night's sleep. Still, I made myself sit as motionless as I could and went over in my head all the points that Merlin had planned.

'While you and Androcles are with the gladiators, try and find out as much as you can. If it gets bad you will have to try and get to Cabby and all three of you will need to use the droppings and get back to my cave – if it works this time.

'Salazar and I are going back home. We need to find out what's happening there and also we'll take the sandals with us.'

It had been at this point that Androcles had jumped up and said that that couldn't happen. He had to stay with them. Anyone else, he had said, would perish if they touched them unless, of course, they were pure of heart.

Merlin had sat the young man down and had then gone through what he would do.

The sandals were enclosed in the leather satchel. They would stay in that satchel and only when Androcles came would they be taken out – by him or at his instruction, he had added quickly – and hopefully by then they would know what they were needed for.

Androcles, not really knowing Merlin but, after staring into his eyes for a very long time and seeing something in those eyes that made him believe that this man could be trusted, nodded his assent, hoping at the same time that he was making the right decision and not letting his grandfather down.

'*So now,*' I thought with my barriers up, '*we are in a right old state – we won't even have their protection and, as Androcles has said, it looks an awful lot more than a little bit of training – we look like prisoners and, thus, real life gladiators.*'

'Right you lot – on your feet. Jump to it!' I couldn't believe it – he sounded just like the auctioneer at our cattle sales! The trainer had somehow managed to open that huge, creaking door without any of us having heard the key turning or the door opening.

We jumped up and, along with the others in our cell and many more gladiators from other cells, were marched back along the gloomy corridor until we were thrust unceremoniously out into the glaring sunlight; I was not one of the only ones who raised his arms to shield his eyes. It took a while for them to adjust to the brilliant light but we weren't given too much longer before the trainer started to put us through our paces.

Today we would be practising with clubs. *Great!*

Androcles was a slight youth but agile and it was this agility that got him out of most of what should have been bone-crunching episodes. I, on the other hand, had had lots of practice with Sir Ector's men and more than enough with Arthur. I missed Cabby, as he would always be able to warn me when danger was near. I reached out to him but only got a quick, '*Quiet!*' and so didn't try again that day.

By the time we were marched back to our cells I was covered in bruises and was completely exhausted. Androcles was only slightly less so as apart from one whacking great blue-black mark on his thigh he had fared a lot better than I.

We drank as much water as we could; there was plenty of that at any rate, and ate whatever it was they had left for us. I was so tired I still can't remember much but just that as soon as I'd eaten I must have fallen asleep. And then, seconds later – well, it seemed like seconds – it was the next day and we were all being woken up again to go and train.

I groaned, as did many of the others, but within minutes we were all back out in the arena – this time with swords.

The routine was the same every day; only the weaponry was different. We must have been there for two weeks before something else happened, but before I get into that I'd like to tell you about some of the others.

Goliath never spoke – he grunted, especially when he was going through the training, which he took extremely seriously but he never spoke – not then anyway. No-one dared look him in the eye because they were scared that he would get up and crush them and almost everyone tried to keep away from him in the arena in case they had to spar with him – those that did got the most bruises and some got broken bones.

Crusher was one of them. He had been one of the first people to spar with Goliath when the giant had first arrived. He had been purchased at great price by one of the Prefect's aides especially to fight as a gladiator. When Crusher saw him he just had to fight him because up to then he was the number one gladiator and he needed to keep that position. Mistake! Bad, bad mistake! Goliath, once goaded by the champion, turned and planted an enormous smacker on his nose, which was completely crushed to one side – but he still kept the same name!

'Oh I thought it would have been changed now that his nose had been crushed!' I had exclaimed.

'Er, no!' had been the reply.

Then there was the Scribe. Now he was someone that could become really useful. I'd noticed some mornings, when I'd been able to wake up before the trainer did it for me, that he would be sitting quietly in the corner eating grapes or figs or something delectable instead of the oatmeal and hard bread that was our lot; sometimes he was swigging something sweet (I got a whiff of it once) from a very small goat's bladder that, once emptied, was secreted in a compartment in his belt.

I determined one night to try and stay awake to see how he got hold of this stuff. I tried hard to not let him see I'd noticed him and so it was, late one evening, I almost jumped out of my skin as I watched him take a small piece of chalk out of a hidden chamber in his leather belt, draw a door on the wall with a handle set in it and then just open it and walk through, closing it gently behind him.

I stepped across one or two sleeping bodies until I got to the wall but the door had disappeared; even the marks had gone.

'Right,' I'd thought; 'tomorrow I'm determined to get through there with him.'

And I did.

He wasn't too happy when he turned to close his doorway and I pushed through behind him but what could he do? I was there and that was that. He was in the act of sliding his piece of chalk into his belt and so was slightly off kilter to be able to stop me. Normally he would have been able to shove me back as he was one of the taller and stronger individuals in our group.

By then the doorway was gone and so he just shrugged. 'So, what do you mean by following me?'

'I had hoped to get hold of some of that delicious food I've seen you eating,' I said, following him down one of the weirdest tunnels I've ever seen. That would be good but I was much more interested in how the chalk worked and whether it was it or him that had this peculiar power.

'If that's all, that's easy,' he replied.

We came to the end of a tunnel – well, it wasn't really a tunnel because it had no actual real door leading to and from it but, like the chalk door, it was unreal; the only way I can describe it is like walking through cold sticky tarmac – and finally reached what must have been the end of it, when he took out the chalk, drew another door and we stepped through into the enormous kitchens. There were several people dotted round the edges of the room but they were all sound asleep. It must have been that part of the night when all the evening's meals had been dealt with, all the clearing up had been done and the morning's food was not yet ready to be prepared, and everyone was still in bed. They, I expected, like us would be exhausted at the end of each day, especially cooking hot meals in such a hot clime.

I started to gather up loads of stuff to take back with me for the others but was stopped by the Scribe.

'You can't do that; it would cause a riot.'

'Oh, surely we must share all these good things with the others; it's only fair.'

'I know it's not fair but then who said life was fair?

I saw the sense of this but still felt guilty that I would be getting fed better and the others wouldn't.

I took up some fruit and eating it as I walked around the kitchens, taking in all that they offered and the lie of the land in case we needed to escape through them, until the Scribe said it was time to go back.

I wondered that he didn't leave me there but he must have known what I was thinking as he said we both needed to be back because otherwise the Romans would go berserk if they thought something was up.

The chalk did its work on the way back and before long we were settling down for the rest of the night.

I might have lacked some sleep that first night out but I definitely felt much stronger after having eaten better than I had for weeks.

No-one had missed us.

FOURTEEN

The two wizards arrived back in Merlin's cave; after deciding that the matter had become critical spent the rest of that night preparing the new herbs, salves, liniments and unguents they had bought from the oriental caravan just before they had left us to come back to Britain.

'I'll make up the fire and perhaps you'll make an inventory of what we've bought and what actual stores we still have,' Merlin spoke crisply to the other Druid. 'If we want to be able to get one over on the witch we will need to be swift and accurate, otherwise who knows what will happen. In the meantime, I'll put this satchel in a safe place and create a spell of invisibility around it.'

Salazar left him, travelling further into the back of the cave and before long couldn't be seen or heard.

'We are still one ingredient short,' Merlin commented as all the other ingredients were spread out before them. 'We will have to see if we can get hold of it when we return.'

By now both of them were very tired, having worked for hours without taking a break. They had been preparing this and sorting that until the evening brought a weary Salazar back into the main chamber, when Merlin decided to call it a day.

Sitting over a tankard of beer and breaking pieces of bread and cheese they sat companionably and chatted about many of the things they had done together and separately over the months and years.

It was well on into the evening before Salazar's head tilted to one side, listening.

'What is it?' Merlin, who was straining to hear what the other man had heard, asked.

'Something is amiss. I know not what but the feeling is growing that it is so and is getting closer.'

'Let us consult the Glass!'

Standing in front of the huge Glass that hung from the wall they waited as they searched in the usual places.

First they concentrated on the amphitheatre where they found

Androcles fast asleep while I watched another gladiator. Nothing else was happening so, after finding Cabby also fast asleep, they next concentrated on Sir Ector's caer. People there, also, were fast asleep and they might have missed it if Merlin's observation hadn't been so acute; Rhianne's bed was empty! The Glass had actually moved on to other parts of the caer before the niggle inside Merlin's head became a concern and he told the Glass to go back to her room. 'Where is she?' They moved the vision to take in other parts of the building and found no baby in the nursery; the Lady Elise was sitting on a chair in that room and she had obviously been crying. Searching further he found that Arthur, too, was missing – though that wasn't unusual in itself as he often stayed at neighbours' houses.

'What is amiss there?' Salazar mused.

They tried to get the Glass to concentrate on other places but it couldn't, wouldn't or turned opaque and thus gave nothing away.

'It looks as though we have come back to trouble,' Merlin's face was grave. 'We will need to concentrate hard now; we need to see if we can find out just what is going on.

'First we shall sleep. We will not get anything done if we do it with no mental or physical strength and both of us have worked hard today to try and finish everything that needed to be done.'

Salazar agreed and both men then lay down where they were, close by the fire, closed their eyes and within minutes were sound asleep, but not before they had protected themselves from whoever or whatever might have been causing this problem. Anyone looking into their cave, either physically or by some supernatural means, would see no-one there, just an empty, cold, deserted cavern.

Thus it was that Arthur and the others almost jumped out of their skins after they'd entered the cave, first sitting down in despair at the obvious emptiness they found, only to see the two Druids materialise before their eyes when they awoke.

Merlin, quickly realising what had happened, threw something into the air so that no-one would remember that they hadn't been there when they'd first come in.

'Merlin, oh thank God you are here. We've travelled hard and fast to get to you,' Rhianne rushed into the sorcerer's arms.

'Whoa, Rhianne,' Merlin broke through this obviously troubled tirade. 'Come in first, sit down and refresh yourselves – all of you; come, come.'

He held up his hand, as Arthur was about to continue. 'It can wait five minutes! If you don't relax and get your breath back I shall not be able to understand a single word. Come! Come and sit,' more gently – he beckoned them over to the fire where Salazar, now joined by his wife, was coaxing it back into life.

The morning chill was soon chased away and after they'd all slaked their thirst they relaxed enough for two or three of them to start speaking at once.

Merlin held up his hand again and once silence had been achieved asked Arthur to speak first.

When he had finished speaking Jasmine added the little she had observed and then they all waited to see what the two sorcerers would do.

They looked grim.

They were silent.

Arthur couldn't stand it. He jumped up and with hands gripped behind his back walked over to Merlin. 'So what are you going to do?' he almost wailed.

'Now that isn't going to help is it?' Merlin spoke quietly so that only Arthur heard his response. 'Give me a moment; I shall search through my mind and try to grab all the information I need that I can recall until I can fit it all together and use it.'

They waited again.

For ages.

Until. 'Right!' He turned, all businesslike, and looking over to where Jasmine and Salazar were standing together beckoned them over and whispering a few words watched as they packed up a few things before they disappeared out of the cave's entrance.

'Where are they going?' Arthur asked.

'To do my bidding,' Merlin replied, raising one eyebrow and staring at the future king as if to say, "No more questions!"

'We have a lot to do now and little time in which to do it. If everyone only knows what *they* are to do and not what everyone else is to do, well, they shouldn't get in a muddle, should they? Arthur, come with me; we need some supplies. Shake Spear, Tailor, go and rub down the horses, water and feed them and make them comfortable. By nightfall we will have to be on our way so they need to be fully rested and ready to go.

'Baker, there are provisions over there,' he pointed to the shelves in a recess beside the fireplace. 'Make something for us all now that we can eat as and when we have a moment and pack up some food for all of us for the journey – nothing too messy, make some biscuits and bread and pack some oats, apples and cheese.

'Brosc, Wite, sort out some feed for the horses, there is some stuff over there,' he pointed, 'which you can pack into the saddlebags.

'Hurry now, all of you; there isn't much time.'

'Where are we going?'

'It's not so much where we are going but how we are going to get there and who is going with us!'

'Well,' Arthur waited a while but as Merlin didn't answer added, 'Just who is going with us?'

'We will have to wait and see, but it is imperative we are ready to go just as soon as they get here.'

Arthur turned with a strained expression on his face. He knew it was useless to ask just who "they" might be. Merlin never added information if he hadn't given it in the first place!

While Arthur and the others had been travelling toward Tintagel the witch and her party had turned due south toward Carn Euny at Sancreed, almost to the end of Britain itself. It was more by luck than judgment that the two parties had not collided as they continued on their journeys, especially as at one point they would have had to cross paths, literally. By some good fortune they missed each other by just under half an hour; Arthur's party crossing first, otherwise Griff would certainly have picked up their scent! If one could call it scent, that is – my mother always called perfume scent and Mab's was one she most certainly wouldn't have wanted bottled and placed in pride of place on her dressing table!

For some reason known only to herself at the time, the witch had not used any of her powers to transport everyone to the old Iron Age site but was taking the long route overland to get there. Was she conserving her powers? Had they diminished while she'd been incarcerated in that Awful Place? Did she need extra time to work on her plans or potions or spells? Maybe she had to collect stuff on the way? Perhaps she was afraid that in the time travel one or all of them might go missing. In any event, Iris' mind was in a whirl as she considered the reason for their abduction, each idea rushing into her head like a demented imp, chattering away sixteen to the dozen as it gabbled into her mind before being pushed out of the way by another imp with a more imaginative scheme, only to be replaced by yet another, *ad infinitum*.

Trying as hard as she could, she attempted to block out all these fanciful thoughts, for she knew that unless she could get her imagination under control she would not be able to work out how to escape if the opportunity arose. That would be extremely hard if it was a case of just herself but with the baby it would be nigh on impossible – but she wouldn't think too much about that because that would be admitting defeat before she started. Her spirits were lifted at one point when she espied the Faerie's chancellor sitting high in a tree and watching the little cavalcade pass underneath him. He smiled down at her whilst holding his finger to his lips. She said not a word but she felt better now that someone knew of their plight. How long now would it be before they were rescued? Did the Faerie know where they were headed? Would they follow them to where they were going? And, just where were they going?

It would take another two days to reach their destination and so she would still have to put up with the witch's threats, stories, rants and, of course, smell, but as most of those days would be spent travelling with her and Mordred both sitting up front to drive the horses (unless it started raining, that is) she was left to ponder their fate in the back of the wagon where the stench wasn't quite so overpowering.

'Only another night and a full day to go my dears,' she would say, making the time less and less as they got there, just so as to make the dreaded time get closer and closer and her fear more acute as the witch dropped sometimes not too subtle hints as to what might be waiting for them when they got there.

She had had to try to stop herself looking back to see if the Faerie had sent aid; the witch had noticed and had laughingly told her to stop wasting her time. 'No-one knows where you are! So stop wasting your energy. You are not going to be rescued! You will probably never be seen again. Everyone has to die at some time or other. Sometimes it's fast and sometimes it's slow. Sometimes it's painful and sometimes it's not! I wonder what will happen to you.'

Iris thought, just in case the witch really got wind of the fact that help might just be behind them, that she had better not keep looking back but she wished she'd be quiet – her threats were making her feel ill. She believed that the witch was doing it all just to make her feel scared and some of them were actually giving her a bad feeling. She was just glad that the baby had no idea what the witch was saying.

One thing, though, that brought the hair rising up at the back of Iris' neck was the obvious remark about goblins. She had heard of them and could remember some of the men telling stories about them to scare the children when she was no more than about ten years of age. She had been sitting by the window of her home at the time when old Carpenter, now deceased, had been rubbing down the replacement leg of a chair that had needed repairing and some of the other servants' children had been chanting, "Tell us a story, tell us a story," and he had told them the story of the Goblins of the Dark Forest, scaring them all witless when he explained that the Dark Forest was any forest at night, 'even that one over there,' he had pointed. Thus as they lived on the edge of the forest it stood to reason that none of them would dare venture out of their homes at night after that, sometimes incurring the wrath of parents who wanted them to do an errand.

Iris could almost recall the story word for word as it had had such an impact upon her. She learned never to go into the forest on her own because even at midday it could suddenly turn to night and then she would definitely be "got" never to be seen again or, if she was found, she would have no brain and would slobber dribble continually down her clothes, wet herself as well – or worse – and everyone would keep away from her; her teeth would grow like those of the warthog until they were so heavy that her head would fall forward and then she would end up with a hump like a camel on her back; she would snuffle out the rest of her days as a detested and grotesque sub-human, being unloved and rejected by everyone, even those awful goblins who'd gone to all the trouble to make her like this in the first place.

She had been so terrified that she had been unable to sleep for weeks and, when she did, she screamed at the nightmares that rushed into her mind every night until she was taken into her mother's bed and hugged until the spectres ran away.

Old Carpenter had been soundly rebuked by many a mother but he just laughed and took no notice, thinking up yet another grotesque story for the children when he was called into their homes to use his trade.

Even so, Iris couldn't shake off the thought that there must be some truth in old Carpenter's stories and now, now that the witch had dropped that quick bit of information, she was sure that probably most of it was true and that she was soon going to be turned into the monster of her nightmares.

The saving thought that permeated most of her mind to bring her back to some sort of normality, though, was that of the baby. *'I must get Kate back to her mother; oh God, please help me!'*

Salazar and Jasmine were back; well Salazar was back but this time Jasmine was with him and the Romans didn't appear to be at all surprised that Salazar had brought her with him.

In any case it was only just in time!

They may have been away what seemed like days to them but we had been here for over six months now.

The Prefect had turned nasty. He'd obviously got very bored being stuck out in this deserted place and now, for some reason he was determined to get us all to fight for real and, as I said, Salazar returned just in time.

We hadn't learned much while we were being trained. I had continued on my night forays with the Scribe together with Androcles who had caught us one evening just as we were about to step through the magical doorway and so had joined us. He wasn't very happy with me, however, as he said that I could have told him about what we were doing, 'I mean, what are friends for?' he grunted. But he was one of those really nice people and once he had had a taste of some of the fare from the kitchens he soon forgave me.

The Scribe got annoyed. 'I mean,' he grumbled, 'if this carries on there will be a great stream of people following me every night – then we'll get caught and I'll not have my full ration of food! You'd better keep quiet and not mention it to anyone.'

One night I asked him what else he thought he could use the chalk for. He reckoned that if everything really turned bad he would just draw as many doors as he needed one night until he could escape completely, but he'd have to have a plan because just getting out of this place wasn't enough – he'd need a camel or something to help him escape across the vastness of the desert.

I'd asked him once if he could draw a camel to do that for him but he said that although he'd tried the animal looked weird – like a child's drawing – and it didn't move. He said that he'd also tried to draw a bird and a cat but although they looked fine they, too, didn't move, so it seemed that he could only work with inanimate things like doors or windows; he'd added that he could draw clubs and spears and they worked.

And then the thought came to me one night.

'Can you draw a key to unlock the door? Well, I know that you could draw another door and we could get out that way, but if the others here saw that they might get the heebie-jeebies and go crazy. No, we need something they can understand and help us with – so, what about that key?

'If we could get out this way we could make our way round to the stables and grab some horses or whatever is there. I would think that perhaps some time in the middle of the night would be a good time when most people are asleep and those on guard are off guard!'

He looked up at me and grinned. He said that he'd give it a go and we'd try it out at noontime when everyone rested.

This was a great idea.

But why hadn't we thought about this before?

And why had we now only thought about it?

And why did we have to think about it on the day that everything was going to go pear shaped?

It took hours but finally the Scribe did it. The key was, as it had to be, very large and heavy. He had drawn it on the wall beside the lintel. At first it was too large and then the indentations for the lock were wrong. He drew his chalk lines on it, chiselling away until finally we heard the tumblers moving within the lock itself as the key turned full circle.

However we had made such a racket – well it was a quiet racket that could only be heard within our cell – that everyone else had woken up, including Goliath, and were all watching us intently.

The Scribe turned the key back again. We had a couple of hours to wait until the time when everyone rested.

Some of the men had asked questions but we just shushed them and added that if they wanted to get out they would have to be quiet and then they would have to do what they were told and follow us. I'd thought it was fortunate that they had only seen the Scribe chiselling the key and not opening doors in solid rock or even drawing a key on the wall and lifting it off, but that was only a fleeting thought. They had not thought to ask where he had got the rock from; funny that – it would have been one of the first questions I'd have asked. But, those were different times and, thus, different people.

We didn't really have a plan but obviously we would need to get to the compound where the horses and camels were so that we could make good our escape; I, on the other hand, would need to take Androcles with me to rescue Cabal and then we would use the dragon's droppings.

The time finally arrived. We waited and listened, though we had never heard anything before we felt it safest to try to hear anything – but it was all very quiet.

The Scribe inserted the key into the lock and everyone held their breath as the tumblers dropped when it was turned. Removing the key, which was merely dropped onto the floor, we pushed the door (which creaked badly – how hadn't we ever noticed that before?) and were met by the surprised look of about twenty Roman soldiers who were waiting outside, having been on their way to escort us into the arena!

Brilliant! Fantastic!

How had we not heard them?

The trainer, who was holding the duplicate key, stared hard at me and then screwed up his mouth in an evil grin that had me almost shaking. What on earth had he in store for me? In store for all of us?

We could hear the roars before we were halfway along the corridor.

Not the roar of the crowd because there wouldn't be much of one out here in the desert and especially at this time of day, although those that were there could be heard, but the roar of wild animals.

'*We haven't been fed for over a week!*' Cabal broke into my thoughts. *'There are ten lions, two leopards and a cheetah. They don't know about me and have kept their distance but I feel it will be difficult for me to protect you from any of them; my disguise is an illusion – I am still only a dog!'*

'Cabby, I want you to do something for me. Limp.'

'Limp?'

'Yes. If you limp I will know it's you and then Androcles and I will run over and use the dragons' droppings. We'll all escape together.'

We were then all ushered outside, each being handed one or other of the weapons we'd been training with for the past six months.

The lions and other cats were shuffling about on the far side of the arena and managing to give a fantastic display of their fangs. At that moment each animal was hobbled by a long chain that ran through a metal loop that had been fastened to one of its back legs but we could see that behind a secure grille a man stood ready to release that chain.

I could feel my bladder threatening.

Not only could I see these frightening beasts but I could also smell them; their breath and musky wild animal tang reached across to us from even that distance.

Silly thoughts jump into your head at ridiculous times – *'I bet Mab would love this!'* I wondered if she might even be in the crowd and I took a quick look up at the spectators but then things got too hairy to even think about that.

We heard the chains rattle as they were pulled through each animal's leg ring thus releasing them one by one and saw the lions shoot forward a few feet before checking to see what we would do.

Each of us stood our ground and waited. I scanned the heavily maned beasts for Cabby but at the moment they all looked the same until one moved, limping over to us with head to one side and jaws wide open.

Then it all went crazy.

Androcles and I rushed over to Cabal while some of the others ran to fight other lions. Out of the corner of my eye I watched as Goliath just about stopped one of the cats from grabbing my leg. He killed the beast with his sword and then picking up a spear that one of the others had dropped stabbed and chopped at each animal as it went for him or others close to him; not that many took the chance after seeing what he'd done to the cheetah – they kept their distance and circled us, obviously waiting for a better opportunity to strike without being killed in the process, though two had turned, obviously to find out just what the dead cheetah tasted like! My eyes were out on stalks!

I'd always thought that Goliath was someone that kept himself to himself and who had no thoughts for anyone or anything but here I had to change my mind as he fought like the warrior he'd been trained to be, defending himself and others alike. He was powerfully strong!

We got to Cabal and I was a bit disconcerted when he made a grab for me but then stood stock still before he turned suddenly and looked at and sniffed Androcles and then he did a weird thing – he rolled on his back exposing his belly.

Androcles stared for several moments before, grinning, he went down on one knee and gave the animal's tummy a rub and then hugged him round his neck. My eyes were bugging out of my head.

'*I'm over here, Percy,*' Cabal called from the other side of the arena.

I went cold. I had rushed into the virtually open mouth of a lion thinking it was my friend.

Before I could move, the trumpets sounded and the wide doors at the end of the arena opened to allow the elephant to enter. It had been painted with many bright colours and its head had been draped with a tasselled silken scarf. A brightly painted box had been strapped onto its back and inside were two soldiers and Salazar; they had whips and were leaning over the sides of the box to motivate the animals into action, obviously to make them mad and hopefully attack us. Pulled along behind the elephant was a large cage with an obviously crazed bear rattling the bars.

'*Salazar?*' I thought. '*Why is he up there doing this to us?*'

'*It's not me,*' he cut in. '*I'm over here but be encouraged, I am sorting it all out.*'

I turned and looked up at the platform and saw the Prefect sitting alongside Salazar and Jasmine. The Prefect looked very unpleasant as he sneered down at us and the wild beasts. He looked to be almost salivating at the gory outcome of this tournament as he turned his gaze to the occupants of the elephant's box and grinned. Salazar grinned back. Eh? This was crazy – two Salazars?

The Prefect then looked along the line of his guests and espied another Salazar. Confusion appeared suddenly on his face but he was helpless to do anything as things were now moving too fast, even for him.

'I'll say this quickly and then we must close our minds Percy. It's her! She's imitating me! That's where all this confusion as to who I am comes from. But look closely and you will see that it's her! Now – barriers in place!' Then it all went quiet – well, in my head it all went quiet. Outside it was another matter.

It was a nightmare! We could hear the crack of the whips, the howling of the animals, the shouts of the men and the roar of the blood rushing through our ears. Standing our ground, each man held his weapon in readiness for the imminent attack of the beasts – the bear had also been let out of its cage and was running at us with front paws, claws extended, in readiness to rip us to shreds – but nothing prepared us for what was going to happen next.

The noise gradually drowned out all the other noises and then we saw it. It had been a bizarre morning in any event; what with trying to escape and then seeing what we were going to have to try and fight our way out of (as if); however, the weirdest thing of all was the daylight – sunny but with a filter to it like an old fashioned sepia photo. The sun itself had lost a lot of its brilliance and there was a grittiness in the air that made my throat dry more quickly than the fear that was attacking it – I had thought it to be fear, but it was something far worse.

I had taken a quick look up at the dais where Salazar and Jasmine were seated with the Prefect (whose face had taken on a hungry look as he turned back to watch us out in the arena) and so quickly and directly that no-one else would ever have known, the sorcerer told me to get to Androcles and Cabby and use the droppings. He suddenly held up his arms and shouted words that no-one could understand and then, with the noise becoming a crescendo, the sand storm hit!

We all turned our heads toward the sound to see a yellow wall, at least a hundred feet high, racing toward us at a rate of knots that would engulf us within moments.

I called Cabby over to me – he'd somehow heard Salazar in any event and was already on the move – and at the same time turned to reach Androcles. The noise by now was so bad that even shouting would have no effect so I raced over to the youth, who was still crouched over the lion, and within seconds and only just in time – as the wall of sand had already knocked over the elephant, spilling all its occupants onto the floor alongside the bear – threw the dragon's droppings over us and waited to see where we would end up.

'Please, God, let it be in Merlin's cave!'

FIFTEEN

There was a flash and we all tumbled, literally, from about two feet above the floor down into the cave, alerting everyone to the fact with the thumps, ouches, grunts and yelps.

'Well, that was good timing!' Merlin grinned as I fell into a heap on the ground, quickly followed by Cabal who had now returned to his normal shape and who managed to land on all fours, Androcles and also the lion, and then, surprisingly, the Scribe and Goliath. Those three were a complete shock to everyone concerned, as they were not expected at all; I suppose the wind from the sandstorm had blown the droppings over them as well. I went cold – suppose it had missed me and only got them? I would most probably even now be choking my life out under tons of desert sand, never to be found again – maybe in centuries or even millennia from now – the mummified remains of "from a careful examination of his teeth and the fact that there doesn't appear to be any arthritis in any of his joints and his hair, which remains intact, I should imagine that this is the remains of a young man of no more than nineteen years". From cold to hot – the sweat began to run down between my shoulder blades.

'*Get a grip Percy!*' Merlin chided me.

I was brought back to the present; I'd clearly been watching too many archaeological programmes on TV.

All the others ran at the sight of the lion – well, I mean, you would wouldn't you? It stood there obviously completely confused and, I expect, not a little scared, as well as extremely hungry – so with all that going through its mind it did what lions did naturally – it opened its mouth and roared. Not for long, though, as the cavern merely echoed that dreadful sound back at him.

Androcles ran over to him, threw an arm around its neck and whispered something into its ear; it soon calmed down and sat against the wall with Androcles sitting beside it. Did both of them have the Gift? Apparently not, but maybe there was a gift of another sort that we didn't know about; thankfully, though, the lion eventually responded to Androcles' soothing words and lay down.

'If you have some food, sir,' the youth looked at Merlin, 'it would show him you are friends; he hasn't eaten for a week.'

Merlin provided the beast with the best part of a huge whole hog that he'd smoked over the fire for a good while. It was a shame because its meat was almost ready to be enjoyed but Merlin reckoned that it was probably better to forego the pleasure of a meal than to become, possibly, the meal itself! The lion set to with a will and peace seemed to be restored. Everyone left him to it; it was probably safest, even for Androcles, if the lion was left to enjoy it alone.

'*And is there anything for me?*' Cabal raised one sarcastic eyebrow.

I had to laugh as Merlin threw him a large shinbone still covered with a lot of meat.

In the meantime, while all this was going on, I had run across the cave the moment I saw Rhianne and we clung to each other. I had seen the horror on her face but had misjudged the reason why.

We now had to wait for Salazar and Jasmine.

I explained what had happened in the arena and then told them about the sand storm and hoped that he and Jasmine had been able to get away.

We waited – and waited while Merlin got us all up to speed with what had happened and up to that point I had no idea that the witch had abducted my daughter. Of course, once put in the picture I roared, completely at my wit's end.

I knew the witch had been knocked out of the box when the elephant had fallen over but didn't expect for one moment that she hadn't escaped. She always did. Well, unless she had been knocked out and then the sand would have done its work. No, that would be too much to hope for.

'We have to leave now! We can't wait! Who knows what that mad woman might have done to her? Iris might not be able to escape! She's getting old and wouldn't be able to run, not with the baby. Come on, Merlin, what are we waiting for?'

'We are waiting for Salazar. He managed to send the storm and he has his part to play. We have the sandals. But without Salazar we will fail!'

'Why?'

'You will see when he brings it back.'

I could feel my blood pressure rising. My face was hot and must surely be almost maroon in colour by now. I was gripping and uncurling my hands and was pacing up and down almost as good as Arthur would when troubled.

Then I woke up.

Somehow Merlin had done something to make me sleep. I could hear murmurings and then shot bolt upright as my memory started tapping at my brain for admittance. Kate! We have to go and save her.

Thank goodness Salazar and Jasmine had returned. They had only just thrown their dragon's droppings over themselves in time. The sand had swept the Prefect and the others from the dais as it shot through every nook and cranny to cover and suffocate everything it touched. Salazar told us that as they were whisked away they had a quick glimpse of where they had once been – nothing was left! The storm was advancing across the desert but had covered everything and everyone. The desert sands were ruthless and had no favourites – all had perished. I felt sorry for some of the other men I'd met in that cell where we had spent almost six months together; then, shaking those morbid thoughts away, I turned my thoughts back to my present predicament – I had to save Kate.

And why was everything so urgent in my life right now? I couldn't remember a time when I could just enjoy it. Well, there were those few months just gone but that was like one tiny oasis in a world of thirst – keep watch – dehydration is ready to shrivel you up!

While I had been asleep Merlin had retrieved the sandals from one of the cave's tunnels and had handed the satchel containing them to Androcles who now began telling them the history of those pieces of footwear.

Although I was extremely agitated I accepted that Jasmine had knowledge of up to a day and so, when she told me that all was still well, I relaxed and sat and listened.

'My grandfather had told me that, as a young man, he and my grandmother had been leather workers, mostly making drinking vessels from the bladders of sheep and goats. They also made footwear – sandals – as that was what was mainly worn in those days. They travelled around from Corinth to Jerusalem and back until, one day, they came across a holy man and, wanting to learn more from him, they set down their roots just outside Jerusalem itself so as to be near him. My grandmother, some few years earlier, had been struck dumb after falling one day when she was pregnant with my mother. She hit her head as she fell and the shock had almost killed her but she survived, only to lose the power of speech. The holy man touched her and after that she could speak. They went to listen to this man every time he came to Jerusalem because of this miracle and also he told such wonderful stories – he gave them hope where they had never had hope before.

'The Romans ruled in Jerusalem in those days and things were hard but this man told them about another kingdom – one where there was peace and goodness. When my mother was older and had married, my grandparents let them have their home and became followers of this man and would tell everyone they met about him.

'But because he told the wicked that they were wicked and had to turn away from their wickedness – whoever they were – some of the richer and more influential people got mad with him; he even told the priests that they were hypocrites – so they really had it in for him; it was they who plotted his death and one day he was arrested.

'The holy man was tried, whipped until his back ran with rivers of blood which stained the ground all around him and splashed those who stood too near; he was then forced to wear a crown that had been knitted together – the crown was made from a thorn bush and some of the thorns were as long as my thumb; they rammed it onto his head until more of his blood ran like streams down his face. Then they sentenced him to death – a man who had done no wrong. After that they forced him to carry a wooden crossbar all the way up the hill until they reached the top but he was falling so often that they made a man from the crowd carry the bar the rest of the way. There they nailed his hands to the crossbar and to an upright which they slotted into a hole in the ground; they nailed his feet to the bottom of the post and thus, on a cross, they left him until he died.

'The soldiers who were overseeing all of this had stripped him of his robe and threw dice to see who would own it. Clothes are very expensive, you see, and the robe would have been worth a lot of money.

'My grandfather had always thought that the man was a holy man and had often listened to his words of wisdom and so on that fateful day he followed him from when he was arrested. He didn't see the actual crucifixion himself but he heard later that they had nailed him to the cross.

'Before that, though, the man had been taken to the Procurator of Jerusalem who gave the order for his punishment. They had been dragging him to the whipping post where his sandals fell off and my grandfather picked them up and brought them home to our house, but not before the soldier, who had seen him following but who had obviously not seen him pick up the sandals or he would have taken them from him, lashed out at him with his whip. The whip slashed across my grandfather's eyes and blinded him. He managed to get home where my grandmother, who has since died, looked after him and I have cared for him ever since I can remember. I don't know what has happened to him now or how he will cope without anyone to help him.'

'I hope that when we have finished our work here that I will be able to return you to your home and your grandfather,' Merlin, with his hand upon the young man's shoulder, tried to reassure him. 'What happened then?'

'They took the man off the cross after he had died and they buried him in a cave somewhere but we've heard that when they went back there – so as to prepare him properly for burial – he had gone. We've heard that he is alive again and that anyone who believes this, when they die they will live again too. Yes, he was a holy man and now we have his sandals. But only someone who has a pure heart and pure motives can touch them. Anyone who touches them for wickedness will regret they did so.'

Arthur, who'd hung on his every word and who had wept openly as he listened now jumped up with joy adding that they must be the sandals of the Christ. 'Oh how Brother Geraint would love this!'

'Well, Brother Geraint or no Brother Geraint, we have things to do.' Night had now fallen and everything was ready. Merlin gave his orders – he'd found out about Carn Euny, where the witch was going and so had prepared men, mixtures and magic to thwart her.

'She might be dead.'

Merlin had listened to Salazar's account of Mab's exploits upon the elephant and both of them had since reached out with the Glass to see if she had been destroyed in the desert or was still alive. The Glass showed nothing but there were obvious signs in the atmosphere that she had somehow got back to Britain.

'The problem with Mab – well, it isn't a problem because most of us who have the ability to use the things of the unexplained can do it – is that we can move about in time. Sometimes I wish it was only us – those who wish the magic for good – that had this ability; I expect that there will always be those of the dark side who try to imitate – manipulate – magic for their own dark ends.'

He shook his head to clear it of the invading thought – there was much more to be done than dwell on the "what ifs".

'I want Salazar to take Arthur and the men, including Androcles and the lion, along with the Scribe and Goliath and head for the Iron Age works. We will meet up with them soon.'

As I've already said Goliath had never spoken up to that point but sitting round eating our supper one evening before we all headed off he did – in a very staccato way but, nevertheless, he actually spoke – and we found out that his real name for some reason or other was Buttox! He said he was given the name at a very young age when he head-butted his father's prize ox and it was the ox that was knocked out. I expect the name was given to him as a sign of honour! (We stuck with Goliath.) How we all managed to keep straight faces when he told us his name will always remain a mystery to me – I expect all of us thought that if we were to explode with laughter it might possibly be the last thing we would do on this earth! However, once we were out of earshot we exploded with what we'd been holding in and laughed so long and hard we thought we'd expire. My back ached for days!

He did ask us, later, the reason for our mirth; we just said Cabal was the cause of it.

'Thanks!'

I, not surprisingly, was to stay with Merlin! Jasmine and Rhianne would also stay with us and we would keep an eye on the Glass so as to instruct Salazar as to what was happening – if anything! Griff also stayed with us for a while, though I found myself trying to talk to him like I did with Cabal. They were so alike it was very difficult to tell the difference, except, of course, that he completely ignored me. Well, Cab sometimes ignored me but that was mainly when I'd had upset him and he was showing off. They'd had a right old rough and tumble when they first met up and had disappeared for a while on a hunting trip, returning only when their bellies were full. I sometimes wondered how they communicated with each other; I must ask Cabby one day. But, back to the present.

Oh how I hated not giving the orders some times – I mean, it was my daughter who had been abducted by the witch and therefore it should be me going to save her! But at least Merlin allowed Cabal to go! Hopefully he or Salazar would be able to get a message to me.

Merlin always knew best in any situation. Should I go, Rhianne would want to go; if she went she would probably be a handicap – I thought anyway. We were promised that once all was done that could be done, if Kate hadn't by then been rescued, we would all go. 'And we'll use the Glass,' Merlin had added.

'Why can't we use it now?'

'Because we can't! We have our part to play in all of this and we need to get that done.'

So for the moment we were to remain. We had to reshape the sandals; they were to be made into a sheath for the sword. A scabbard for Excalibur! It would take some time because the leather had to be soaked and re-soaked, left to soak for days more and then, guess what? – soaked again. This was going to take forever!

And that was the reason we had had to go to that awful desert place. Salazar had managed to grab the stuff and bring it back so that it could be used in the soaking and reshaping of the sandals – frankincense! It was the one thing the travelling caravan did not have on that visit. They had come from the wrong direction and said that on their return they would have it on board to take back whence they had come. So Salazar had to return. To westerners, it is also known as *olibanum*, an aromatic gum resin that needed to be rubbed into the sandals to make them work. We'd had to suffer that dreadful place for over six months in that awful, uncomfortable cell and then go through all the weaponry training and then, frightfully, face those animals just for that? I felt sure we could have used something else, but Merlin had said no! Why, oh why, couldn't we have just gone there, bought some frankincense and then left? Then, somehow, Balthasar had arrived back (well, Mab in disguise, if it was Mab) and now that Salazar had arrived there was obviously going to be trouble. So, the Prefect knowing that Salazar was a fraud (mind you, he wasn't clever enough to know that the real Balthasar was also a fraud) decided that we all had to be dealt with – Mab as well, I reckon; thus that awful arena was almost beckoning us with her semi-circular arms. Not only that...

'Percy, we don't have time to ruminate! You can enjoy your reminiscences another time!'

'*Enjoy?*'

'You know what I mean!'

Once the scabbard was finally made, Merlin told us that all would now be in place and we would be ready to retrieve the sword from the Lady; then, and only then, would Arthur be ready to claim his crown.

'But what about Kate?' I had whined.

'You still don't trust me do you Percy?'

The others had awoken long before dawn; hardly speaking as they got things together by the eerie light of the flickering fire and left during that unearthly quiet, when even pre-daybreak's slight breeze dared do no more than whisper. It was at the time when all the night foraging animals and insects were still creeping outside of the safety of their homes to feast until just before dawn warned them that if they didn't hurry home soon then the piercing gaze of the hawk would show them no mercy. We had had contact with the King of the Faerie, although I hadn't seen him on this occasion up to now, and he had said that the spiders were on Mab's case, that she had definitely returned, bruised and dusted with sand, and was headed toward Carn Euny at Sancreed. My blood ran cold when the diminutive king had added that that was where he had come across the slug-goblins.

'Slug-goblins?' I had croaked.

'A rare breed!' he had enlightened us. 'They are a mutant, being made up of part goblin and part slug and part Goth; maybe one of Mab's experiments or that of some other demented wizard that had gone wrong.'

'Maybe that's what they were meant to be like!' Merlin put in.

'Maybe. They look just like goblins but with slippery flesh and if they touch you they leave a silvery slime upon you which, if not washed off immediately, leaves a rash – an extremely itchy, burning rash. The spiders told us that Mab was seen bringing a large army of Goths through a crack that appeared at her castle – one minute there was nothing and then they were spilling through the crack until there were thousands of them encamped all around it. She then seemed to transport them to where the goblins were and somehow fuse them together; the general of the Goth army took it upon himself to argue that he didn't want or need to be fused within a goblin but after Mab stared at him for a few seconds he acquiesced – or it seemed he did – and then he, too, become one with the slug goblin. He is the one that has become the commander of that unholy army. So you now have, Goth, goblin and slug – all joined together as one creature – all have their own evil sides – apart from that, they are just as wicked as normal goblins.'

'Normal goblins? Are goblins normal?' I grunted.

'Well, I wonder what that old crone wants with them?' Merlin mused, ignoring my bad humour.

'Obviously nothing good! Probably aimed at Kate!' I exclaimed, starting to fret again about her.

'At least, now that we know where they are headed, we can see if the Glass can show us anything.'

We had looked as the mists within it swirled and faded until the old Iron Age works came into view and we could stare down the long tunnel and search the land around it; there was, so far, not even a footprint to disturb the long grass growing everywhere. So, they hadn't arrived yet.

'Couldn't we just go there? Through the Glass,' I added.

'Not this time, boy! We have too much to do at the moment and we don't want to warn anyone that we are on to them. The slug-goblins virtually live in that place and they might alert Mab to the fact that we know she is going there. If she changes her mind, which I doubt, knowing her overblown self-confidence, she just might end up somewhere where she can cover her tracks and then Kate and Iris would really be in trouble.'

I decided I just had to trust the sorcerer – well what other choice did I have?

After the others had gone we cleared the main chamber of the cave of everything unnecessary, brought in the pots, jars and phials of this and that that were required to be added to the water that at that time, with nothing having yet been added, was bubbling away in the cauldron over the fire.

Jasmine was in charge of the fire and kept rearranging the logs to be at just the right height so as to keep the water at a simmering level when Merlin required it. At the same time she and Rhianne kept themselves busy by making jams, pickles and chutneys with all the apples, blackberries, onions, mushrooms and the like that were profuse at this time of year. It fairly effectively kept their minds off what might be going on elsewhere, whereas I was going slightly mad with the fruit that was stewing in my brain! I tried to concentrate on all that Merlin was doing.

Moving his lips but not making a sound, he was right then and there adding a pinch of this and a handful of that, a drop of something else and a cupful of another liquid, all the time sniffing as the aroma changed from bitter to sweet and back again until he was finally satisfied that all was ready and as it should be. The final ingredient was added – the frankincense.

'Fetch the sandals,' he ordered me several hours later as he began stirring this concoction into the cauldron, and without looking round added, 'But don't touch them.'

'Eh?'

'Keep them in the satchel; just bring it here.'

I did as I was bid and stood finally in front of the Druid as he pulled on a pair of tough leather gloves. Opening the satchel he removed the sandals and with a look almost of awe on his face he placed each one gently into the cauldron. The sandals floated for a good five minutes on top of the water until the heat and the liquid began to penetrate the leather; they finally sank but could still be seen through the clear liquid as they bounced around slowly at the bottom.

'We must keep the temperature level and so will take it in turns to feed the fire; five days should be sufficient.'

'Five days?' I squawked.

'Percy! Just shut up!'

He looked down at me sitting beside the fire as I was about to add another log and his heart softened. 'I know you are worrying about Kate but we have to do things this way. Rush in and the witch might panic and who knows what she'd do then. You know how much she hates you and to watch you suffer would make her really happy; don't push her to do something that you will regret for the rest of your life. Trust me, Percy – this is the only way. Remember the prophecy!'

'All is still well,' Jasmine added softly, helping to make my suffering a little more bearable.

Merlin and I stared at each other for a long moment until I realised he just had to be right. His eyes, inscrutable to most people, held at that moment a softening with an undeniable love and compassion in them. Yes, he would do his utmost; all that had to be done to make sure that Kate was returned safely to us would be done.

But it still didn't help me to stop worrying in the meantime.

Those five days felt like five years. We took it in turns to rest, cook, eat, sleep and, of course, keep the fire burning. Merlin gave us a particular brew that helped us sleep so that we were wide-awake when we needed to take our turn.

Jasmine was fantastic – keeping us encouraged with her positive remarks that all was well and would be well for at least another day. She, like Salazar, was also a great cook and so we fared very well. Rhianne was much better than me; I only occasionally saw the heartbreaking look that covered her face when she thought no-one was watching but she didn't make the fuss I kept making. Hmm, it was at times like this that I really felt self-conscious and wondered if I was actually now a man or were the strands of youth still struggling to hold me back?

At the end of the fifth day (and Merlin had tested them at the end of each day up to then) he lifted the sandals out of the simmering liquid and placed them on the bench. I must say that by then they didn't look much like sandals at all – they were very misshapen and very slippery but Merlin was pleased with the result.

Between them Jasmine and Merlin, wearing thick leather gloves, pulled the softened leather this way and that, twisting the straps around them to secure them and moulding the whole thing together. They had used an old sword, which Merlin had given me the job of cleaning and I had spent time polishing and polishing it, taking out my frustration on it, I believe, until it was clean and shone like the sun. Merlin spent the next half hour greasing it with a candle's wax so as to wrap the leather around it but enable it to slide easily in and out until it fit as neat and snugly as did Merlin's cap upon his head.

Smoothing the now very pliable leather and stretching it over the sword, Merlin (and this, unsurprisingly to me, took an exceptionally long time) was eventually satisfied. Forming two loops out of the remaining straps to fit over a belt, he carried the whole creation over to the fireplace and, hanging the sword's hilt on a nail above the dying fire, left it there to dry out.

'Once it is dry it will need to be waxed and polished inside and out,' Merlin said as he stood back and nodded with satisfaction at their work, stripping off the thick leather gloves he had been wearing and slapping them against my chest for me to use to do this task. 'You can do that boy – should be ready to work on by this evening. I'll consult the Glass. By this time tomorrow we should be on our way.'

I would have grinned with relief if I hadn't still been feeling so wound up about my daughter. But at least tomorrow we'd be doing something other than making this sheath; I had kept wondering just why it was so important.

My mind was elsewhere as I listened with half an ear to what Merlin was telling the women; they were to stay in the cave until summoned. He gave them various jobs to do which Rhianne thought were merely to keep her occupied but Merlin told them that it was crucial that all the mixtures were ready for when he returned, so speed was of the essence.

'Are we going to go through the Glass?' I had finally interrupted.

'Oh yes; that's the quickest way and now that we are virtually ready there'll be no problem about using it.'

'Hadn't you better see if the others have arrived there already? We don't want to cause any problems with the witch or with those slug-goblins.'

And then my heart fell into my boots! Was I surprised? There was always a niggle in the back of my mind somewhere that things would always have to take the longest route where Merlin was concerned.

'Oh, we aren't going there, Percy; we're going to retrieve the sword.'

SIXTEEN

Arthur and Salazar had kept the pace at something a little more than fast but not quite manic.

'We'll probably not get there before her, but at least we won't be too far behind. I reckon she knows just what she's going to do but I should imagine it would take her some time to do it, whatever it is.' He tried to keep his mind from even beginning to dwell on what the witch wanted the baby for.

'Perhaps King Ogwin will be able to find out something and get back to us before we arrive,' Arthur broke in to his thoughts.

'Maybe, but he has said that it's quite dangerous for him and his people and even for the spiders because those slug-goblins are able to spit their slime over quite long distances and glue their adversaries; even if they aren't pasted to their webs, they get so sticky that it becomes extremely hard to move – some have drowned in all that spit. And, they believe, the slug-goblins eat not only leaves but also the spiders that live among them!

'The Faerie have also had their casualties – they lost two of their people about a hundred years or so ago and are now extremely wary. The king said he would try and glean this information from a distance and get back to us as soon as he could.'

'But we've not heard of these slug-goblins before now; and now you are saying that the king says they were here over a hundred years ago!'

'I believe they have in the past kept themselves to themselves and have always kept well out of sight – I mean, have you ever seen how that "owl's spit", as you call it, ever gets onto the plants in your garden? No! But that now that that wicked woman needs an army she has done something to them – put them under some sort of enchantment – they now do her bidding.'

'Why have you taken us captive? What is it you want from us?' Iris had finally plucked up enough courage to confront Mab who, after a whole day away, had returned in an extremely foul mood.

She had finally been left untied but it was obvious that she would not be able to escape. Two goblins, leering and slobbering as they stared unblinkingly at them, stood each side of the open doorway to this gloomy and sinister underground place where there were obviously no windows. Huge and many fluttering candles (the draughts that rushed through those corridors when the wind was in the east was bone-chilling) illuminated the room but couldn't quite penetrate the murk that sucked out their light from all sides and placed grotesque shadows that would dance manically around as the candles fluttered. Each sound echoed down and back through the gaping mouths of the many passages that beckoned careless explorers and Iris couldn't even bring herself to peer down one to see if it afforded some sort of escape route.

The mad woman looked over her shoulder as she continued to remove all the paraphernalia from her huge bag and merely shrugged. 'I don't want anything from you; though I shall let you live while you can see to that brat!' She looked across at the man. He was staring at the baby. 'He always wanted your mistress, you know, but he would even be content to wait for her offspring to grow up. Don't ask me why; I can't see what he sees in any of them!'

Iris, feeling Mordred's eyes move briefly up from the baby to her didn't give him the satisfaction of returning his stare but, holding the child more protectively, continued watching the witch. 'So why do you want her? And what do you mean by waiting for her to grow? Surely you don't intend to keep her that long?'

'Well, I would have thought that that was obvious. Now that Rhianne is married to that idiot boy Percy I have had to promise Mordred something of her and this,' she pointed a very grubby finger at the sleeping baby, 'is it. I've said that between us we can raise her into an extremely adept novice who can be used against Arthur and against her own mother as and when the time arrives – now that will be hilarious: Rhianne will be only too pleased to have her back but I will have worked on her to drive her mother mad.' She began one of her crazy cackles, but managed for once to get herself under control – there was too much to do to start laughing! 'Of course, Mordred will help because at the end of the day if he can't have Rhianne he will have her daughter instead – well, eventually!

'I have this exceptional spell that will work when I mix in some of the hair from the child.' In unison, they all looked down at the sleeping baby whose head, completely bald at this time, spoke volumes to the fact that now was not the time for that particular magic to work.

Mab shrugged. 'I can wait – and then, when I have that hair I will be able to cast a spell to make her grow. She will be an adult in less than two years – well, her body will but not her mind; that is all to the good, though, as we will be able to train that mind – which will be extremely pliable at that age – our way.' She looked so evil at the end of that awful piece of information that Iris couldn't stop herself from shuddering. 'They will pursue us here, you know. How do I know that? Well, I have left a really decent trail for them to follow. I haven't bothered to hide myself and it won't take them long to find me. Then I will have them.

'But, if they still manage to escape, which I doubt, I shall be able to get away with the baby and will eventually train her up to hate her mother and father and, much more importantly, because when she is rescued she will be on the inside, so to speak, she will be able to kill Arthur; well, when I say kill him, what I mean is she will clear the way for me to be able to do that delectable work myself. They, of course, will think that they've rescued her but, ha,' she shouted the last word as she clicked her fingers in the air, 'they will all be fooled.'

Iris, wondering just how Rhianne and I could possibly recognise a two-year-old that now looked to be about fifteen years of age, stated, 'You will never manage to make her do any of that because I reckon her father and mother, being who they are, will have produced a good person. She couldn't do any of that.'

'You, woman, won't be there to see it!'

Mab, beginning to mix her potions, looked almost pityingly over her shoulder at the servant as she shouted to Mordred to shut the door. 'Can't see a thing with all these candles flickering all over the place.

'But what they don't know,' she then continued chatting to Iris as though they were conspirators together, 'is how I am going to capture them. They believe they are stronger than me – especially that old rogue Myrddin – but I have a secret this time that will also capture him and this time for good.'

'Secret?'

'More than a secret, woman! I have an army! You have only seen a few of them but,' she chuckled, pointing at one of the slug-goblins, 'there are more than ten thousand of them – ready, willing and extremely able to do everything and anything I command them to do!'

Iris' blood ran cold.

'So,' she started cackling and, with her belly bouncing up and down as uncontrollably as her laughter, dribbling down all her chins as she continued, 'I shall have three birds with one stone! But, if I manage to kill Arthur this time I shall still keep the child – for Mordred, of course!' With eyes narrowing she looked over at her accomplice and was satisfied at the look of something a little more evil than greed that spread over his face. How simple he was! How easy it was to manipulate him with promises that she didn't care if she kept or not, just as long as she got what she wanted. She laughed then until her face was so red that Iris thought she'd explode.

It took some time for the witch to get herself under control again but she finally did and then, with a crafty look coming into her eyes at the knocking on the door, clicked her fingers and waited until one of the slug-goblins opened it.

Without taking her eyes off Iris she narrowed them and watched the effect it had on her as the hobgoblin entered.'

'This is all too easy,' Salazar whispered. 'She should have covered her tracks more than she has; I mean she has covered them but has left a few tantalising clues to the fact that she has been this way. She obviously wants us to follow her but I don't yet know whether it is because she wants us to believe that she doesn't know we've found her evidence and so might fall into a trap or because she does want us to know but she's too conceited to think we can do anything about it.'

Wite looked blank.

It took another few attempts at reorganising his thoughts out loud before Salazar could speak simply enough to get the others to realise what he was talking about.

'We will really need to be on our guard. It is obvious that the witch wants Arthur; she always has and always will.'

'I really don't know why!' Arthur exclaimed.

'Oh but we do now!' Salazar replied. 'The prophecy made that obvious.'

'Really? What is it?'

'It was given first to Mab by the Lady of the Lake; Mab just turned and walked away from the Lady and from the prophecy. That was many, many years ago, but the Lady only recently repeated it to Merlin and to Percy.'

'To Percy? Why to him?'

'Merlin had gone to find him to train him for this forthcoming fight against wickedness.'

'Yes, he had been gone for a long time. That in itself was weird seeing as how he'd only just got married! So, how was this prophecy given to him?'

'Merlin told Percy that terrible things were afoot and what was to happen would soon decide the greatness of Britain or its destruction. A king would be crowned who would unite all of the lords of the land and all the small kingdoms throughout the land would acknowledge him. This future majestic figure would be seated upon this royal throne of kings over this sceptred isle, and peace would reign and there would be prosperity.'

'Do you know the name of the king?'

'Only Merlin knows!'

'Merlin knows? Then why hasn't he said?'

'He cannot! Therefore he will not!'

'Then can you remember the prophecy Salazar?'

'Word for word Arthur!'

'Then please tell us.'

"He will come
On a powerful charger with sword held high
He will come
Wearing the golden crown of the Once and Future King
He will come
Uniting all the kingdoms into one land
He will come
In the power of the Prince of Peace
He will come
He will rule in fairness and majesty
He will destroy every enemy
His most evil foe he must kill
And with the edge of Excalibur he will.
He will come.

But
If he turns from the True Path
If he looks to his own glory
Then she will come
And him she will destroy."

'Say it again.'

And so Salazar repeated the prophecy until Arthur and the rest of them knew it by heart.

As they camped around the fire that evening enjoying the stillness and warmth of mid-autumn they discussed just what this could mean; who exactly was this Lady of the Lake? They began discussing the prophecy and suggesting and discounting one king or high lord after another as they wondered just who would wear the crown. It started off quite seriously, with the Duke of Cornwall being suggested or even Sir Ector, and ended up ridiculous as some of the more ludicrous characters they all knew were proposed.

Salazar, believing he knew who it was, kept his own counsel.

'But I still don't know why it is she wants me dead!' Arthur exclaimed. 'It's not as though I'm important.'

'You don't have to be important; you just have to be a danger!'

'Maybe, but there must be loads of people that are a danger to her and I don't hear about her going after them – just me and those of my friends!'

'It must have something to do with the fact that you are becoming a great warrior; perhaps the witch has seen something in her crystal – perhaps you are going to be the king's champion and protector. If that is the case, you would need to be taken out of the equation.

'Perhaps you have a more important part to play in all this, Arthur! Perhaps it is because your God is more powerful than the witch so she has to get you, and thus your God, out of the way. Who knows!'

'Who knows indeed?'

That aside, it was a contented band that eventually wrapped itself in their cloaks and, piling logs onto the fire to keep it going for most of the night, drifted off into their own dream worlds.

Brosc, with an almost straight face, had to advise them all the next morning that he had been visited in his dreams by a mighty golden warrior who had told him that he was the chosen one to wear the crown of Britain and so they had better start practising bowing to him and waiting on him hand and foot, whilst laughing and whacking away the apple cores and sticks the others threw at him.

However, Salazar had stayed awake all that night. He felt very troubled at the easy journey they were having. Wrapping his cloak about himself, he had sat with his back to a huge fallen tree and, with his chin on his knees, kept watch.

The others would not have slept so soundly if they had seen what he had seen during that night. The horses knew; they snickered and pawed the ground but didn't make too much noise so as to awaken the men, but Salazar and Cabby, who had crept up beside him, watched as the outline of shadowy figures stared down at them from the crest of a nearby hill. A gibbous moon was low in the sky behind and to the west of them and many stars were still twinkling in the sky whose glow outlined in sharp relief those distant and threatening beings as they moved along the skyline.

Salazar held Cabby close in the protective shadow of the gorse and mind-speaking directly and only to him told him to keep quiet until they had gone.

Those fearful beings had stayed looking down at the group believing they had not been seen until dawn threatened to give them away before they disappeared whence they had come.

Cabby eventually moved away and shook himself violently before turning back to the African.

'What were they? They looked like gargoyles with tin helmets on,' he asked whilst scratching his side as he stood on three legs.

'They were the slug-goblins Ogwin told us about.'

'But they were big!'

'Oh, they are! They are as big as a normal man because they've used the bodies of that Goth army – some are much bigger – and they do have heads like gargoyles with their hooked noses and pointed ears but where goblins are normally a charcoal colour, these are grey and slightly transparent, like slugs but their rubbery lips and eyes are Gothic black. They were also dressed for battle, by the look of things.'

They stopped talking about what they had seen when the others began to wake up but after Cabal had returned from his shortened morning run he managed to spend a few more moments with Salazar to tell him of the slimy trail he'd discovered. 'This time they'd tried to disguise it by raking over their footprints with some leafy branches but I found the odd shiny skid here and there and gobs of spit sprayed over some of the brambles. That made me think, you know, as I'd often seen spit on the brambles when I'd accompanied Percy and Rhianne blackberrying and had thought it was just owl's spit or something. Now I'm not so sure! Oh, and it stank! The smell was still fresh and with a nose like mine they wouldn't be able to disguise it. But I expect they didn't plan for me to be here trailing them.'

'Have you any idea how many there were?'

'Ten; twelve at most.'

'Which way were they headed?'

'Oh, they went back the way we are still headed – to Carn Euny.'

'Then we need to be alert. I fear there will be many more of these creatures waiting for us when we get there. Merlin has prepared a potion for us all but we will still need to be on our guard. Though they have already seen us, we must try to stay hidden; we must watch where we go and wait for Merlin.'

Androcles (and the lion which followed him around like Mary and her little lamb – though not so little!) came up to the sorcerer and asked if they were near their destination. He was happy to be with us and do what needed to be done but his heart was still in Israel with his grandfather.

SEVENTEEN

Have you ever got to the place where you know that everything is well out of your control? Merlin and I had saddled our ponies and with the scabbard wrapped securely within a sheep's skin and having an old sword that had been polished and cleaned until it was as pure as it could be placed within it to keep the sheath's shape and then placed inside the satchel, we set off for Avalon. I wanted to go south but just got "the look" from Merlin as I started to argue, wheedle and then whine.

'Come, boy! You're acting like a four-year-old!'

I stared at him, mouth agape; he sounded just like my dad!

I must have left my barriers down as he laughed like a drain. 'We have to do things the right way,' he was finally able to say.

'And what, if not rescuing Kate, is the right way?' I grumbled sarcastically.

'Well, to start off with, in order to rescue her we need power. First, the witch, as we have seen in the Glass, has a vast army; she probably doesn't know that we know, but as we do, we are aware and as such we need more power than we have at the moment. Oh I know I have the power of sorcery and magic but, as I have already said to you, most of the time it is just a trick, a sleight of hand. However, those of the dark arts use spells and wickedness from demons and other things that they don't really know what they are dealing with. I like to deal with things that aren't going to catch me unawares and jump up and bite me on the bu ... by the throat.

'So, first we need to go and get the sword and then we need to see what we can do about Moon Song.'

I felt a bit guilty then; I hadn't thought about the dragon for ages. Could anything be done for her and how on earth could the sword help her? And how would Merlin use her to help our current plight? And why was everything we knew and loved being attacked like this?

Merlin had followed my train of thought, even though I believed I had covered my mind.

'The sword has nothing to do with Moon Song. I've been

working on an antidote for her while you've been dealing with the scabbard and I believe I may have come up with something.'

Merlin proceeded to tell me how he had gone ghosting through the nights when Jasmine and I had been either sleeping or keeping an eye on the cauldron.

Now ghosting, as I've said before, is a bit like projecting either your thoughts or a spectre of yourself anywhere you needed to go. To me it had always seemed like the freedom we have in dreams – you know, you can go almost anywhere in your dreams; the only problem with dreams is that they take you – you don't take them. Ghosting was completely the opposite – you had complete control over where you went – even if it was over to the other side of the world or up into space! Merlin was an adept at making himself into an invisible spectre – well, I mean, he'd been doing it for, and this always amazed me, at least a hundred years! Just how old was this man?

I've always said I don't believe in ghosts but I expect that if they did exist, well, they were probably people that were not dead really but were just projections of themselves and couldn't hurt you. Well, they might be able to hurt you! Just think of Cabal and those two horrid boys all those years ago! So, I was now altering that train of thought as I thought on – could ghosts hurt you? No! Not possible (I think) because they aren't real – just shadows – but what hid in those shadows? I tried to shake off my train of thought – it was getting messy, not to say silly.

To get back to Merlin.

In this disembodied state he'd flown over the land toward Carn Euny at Sancreed at such a rate of knots that it would have been impossible for anyone or anything to see him even if he had been visible.

Arriving at the Iron Age works he floated in through its tunnels until he reached the one lit by many candles. He froze at one point as the witch sniffed the air – though how she could smell anything past her own rank odour always amazed him. She stared around slowly, sniffing as she peered into all the dark corners and down the passageway between the two slug-goblin guards and waited to see if she could detect the "something" that had alerted her but finally, after a good two minutes, shrugged, dismissing the thought as completely irrelevant anyway – she could overcome everything –

and got on with her preparations.

Merlin moved cautiously around the room, taking in Iris, the baby, the slug-goblins (one of which seemed to be following him around the cavern with his eyes), and Mordred. The baby slept while Iris rocked her. Mab was brewing some concoction or other, directing Mordred to fetch or carry something here or there. He, when not at her beck and call, merely stared at the child; it was chilling to watch his expression!

Knowing he could do nothing to help them then and there he merely stood and waited to see just what Mab was putting together. Nodding once or twice as the ingredients were added, he finally knew just what she was doing, noticing that she was using a potion that had been banned by the Circle of Druids and Sorcerers of all the known world, and thus what she had possibly done to Moon Song. So leaving her to it he slid through the rock wall and disappeared. Also, if she was using that liquid it was imperative she was stopped before she used it on the child, if that was her intention.

All this he told me as we moved toward Avalon.

I shuddered and said we just had to go to save Kate now!

'Not yet! I just had to see just what was outside,' he continued. 'It was all too quiet and the atmosphere was so dense you could almost touch it. And the smell! Well, I knew I'd been in the presence of what the Faerie always called the "Mighty Smell" but this was in its own way just as bad. Then I saw them. That was where this awful stench was coming from – each gob of spit stank to high heaven.'

Merlin carried on with his story of a dark camp of slime and waited until dawn approached so he could see them in all their splendour. Slug-goblins, which being cold-blooded needed no camp fires except for the few dotted here and there for night vision, were curled up in sleep all around as far as the eye could see: thousands of them! For every fifty men there was a sentinel keeping watch. He was sure that some of them, like the one inside, could see him, as they seemed to stare in his direction and move their eyes as he floated around. However, that could quite easily have been his own imagination.

But it was not his imagination as he stared at the rows and rows of crack troops, albeit unearthly, as they began to awake.

'I found Salazar with Arthur and the men. I'd told them to wait for me when they got there but now I have had to tell them to return – well some of them to return to me. It is a dangerous place in any event, what with Mab and Mordred on the prowl, and I need Cabby here with me.

I've told Salazar to stay there with Shake Spear and Tailor to keep an eye on things. Cabby is to lead the others back to the cave to meet me. We will have to do everything I've planned as speedily as we can. There is no time to waste.

'So now I've had to revise my plans a bit and come here first. You see, Percy, if we don't put things in place now, it will be in the wrong order and it will all go awry – then who will be saved? I mean, if you were making a cake and you mixed most of the ingredients and then found you didn't have any eggs, it would be a complete waste of time and there would be no cake.' He stared intently at me with one eyebrow raised, nodding and waiting for me look incredulously at him because of his great powers of deduction.

I was incredulous and not because I thought him clever but actually quite the opposite but I hid my thoughts – I sometimes wondered where his mind was; perhaps he was hungry right now! I mean, where did cake come into all this? This was also thought with my barriers in place.

We arrived at the Isle of Avalon at dusk; the shadows were lengthening in front of us as the sun sank slowly down behind the trees, before the moon rising behind us and growing in size nightly, shot our shadows in the opposite direction. The first chill of an early winter brought about an eerie mist that appeared to flow directly down from the island itself before settling in a ghostly fashion around it.

I'd wondered why we had to come this way on horseback as I felt sure that all could have been done so much quicker if we'd used the Glass but Merlin had mumbled something about things not travelling well that way at the moment and, when I'd asked him to explain, all I got was his usual pet phrase of, "I haven't really got time to go into that now", so I'd had to be content with the slow route.

Merlin now stood at the edge of those mists, raised his staff and called gently through his mind. Anyone around would have heard nothing.

We waited. He did not call again and he did not move but just stood with his staff raised high, the shafts of moonlight bouncing from one of the merlin's eyes set within it onto the "lake".

We waited. And waited.

I was just about to say something when Merlin grabbed my wrist and stopped me.

The mists swirled and then rippled outward like a lake that had had a pebble thrown into it.

Then she was there – diaphanous, mysterious, beautiful.

'You called me again Merlin. I was dreaming of you and my sister. It was a gentle dream of long ago.' Her voice was the sound of a tinkling stream.

'My lady, I need the sword.'

'Ah! Does that mean that the time is nigh?'

'My lady, I am sad for you but I promise you will not die. You will not be forgotten; the mysteries of the Dark Ages will keep you alive. One day, hundreds, maybe thousands of years from now you, like many, will return.'

'Maybe I will not want to return. Maybe I will want to stay in the gentle land of dreams.' Her voice, which I had remembered from those months before as a whisper, seemed to fade and then rally before fading again.

Before she vanished Merlin once again asked for the sword.

The lady held up an empty hand.

I was confused. Where had it gone?

Then, with eyes bulging, I watched as within her grasp Excalibur materialised and, as she turned it, flashed in the moon's light.

Merlin waded out toward the Lady of the Lake and, passing to me the old sword from within the sheep's skin that enveloped it, raised the sheath toward her. The lady turned the sword toward him and slid it easily into its new home.

'I cannot bear to know what will happen to my sister,' she whispered. 'If it is possible to keep her alive I shall be very happy but if that is not possible I really don't think you should tell me; but I know that I will know – that sort of thing pierces the heart even if one isn't told directly. But I shall sleep now, possibly for a thousand years, and dream, unless you call me back my friend, but I will only return if I hear your voice – none other.'

And then she was gone!

No ripple in the mist showed where once she floated. No sound, no sense she had ever been there.

Merlin turned; with a hard expression he bade me follow and so it was that we were mounted on our ponies and set off. I turned the pony's head as I twisted the reins so as to head south but …

'Where are you going?'

'To rescue Kate,' I answered.

'Oh, we aren't going there yet,' he stated, 'we're off to London!'

'London?'

'London!'

Groan.

EIGHTEEN

'I'd heard the stories and now find it completely true!' Gwenhwyfar exclaimed, dismounting from her still frisky mount. 'A cave – a marvellous cave by the edge of the sea. Is it really Merlin's cave?

Rhianne and Jasmine had rushed out of the cave at the sound of approaching horses.

'What are you doing here my lady,' Rhianne asked as she hurried across the beach to where a dozen or so horses and riders milled around on the rocks that surrounded the quiet bay.

Gwenhwyfar jumped down onto the sand from the rocks as light as a feather and strode almost manlike toward the other two women.

'First, please don't call me my lady – call me Gwenhwyfar or Gwen, and I hope I may call you by your given names too?' she asked.

'Of course.' Rhianne then suggested they step inside the cave and take some refreshment. 'And I'll send one of Merlin's little men out to your men.'

'My two brothers are also with me. Can they come in? And I also ran into Nell's son who was headed here. And Sir Kay – your father insisted he accompany us for protection.

'Oh is he here too?' Rhianne spun around, almost bumping into the man himself at the entrance to the cave and smiled as she greeted him. After welcoming both of Gwen's brothers – the older one called Edmyg (which means honour, Gwen had told them proudly) and the younger one called Bedwyr (which was to become known as the keeper of the sword), though both of these were older than Gwen, they were the youngest of all her brothers – and Nell's son, she waited until they had refreshed themselves before asking them why they had come and if they had any news.

'I think I should let Nell's son begin,' Gwen stated, 'and then, perhaps, Eddie …'

'Eddie?'

'My brother, Edmyg – sorry, that's what we all call him; oh, and we call Bedwyr Wirra, just so you don't get confused,' Gwen added as an afterthought.

135

Nell's son began to recount his adventures.

'For the best part of the last year I've been sailing around the west and southwest coasts. An exceptionally rich man hired me because he'd heard of my skill as a sailor and he offered me so much money I couldn't say no. He was a mapmaker and had sailed around almost the whole of Britain, including the land of the Picts and the Scots but his boat had sunk just south of Anglesey in a terrible storm which smashed them against the rocks at Trwyn Du. Before the shipwreck he was fortunate enough to save himself and his work as the captain of the vessel had bundled him and his portmanteau into one of the life boats with half a dozen others before his ship had sunk. He believed the captain and many of his men perished but the mapmaker and those with him, along with all his work, were washed up in a sandy cove nearby.

'I had been travelling between North Devon and South Wales taking merchandise back and forth when I was asked by an associate of the man if I would be interested in helping him finish his quest and, of course, for such a great remuneration I couldn't possibly refuse. I mean, my mother, Nell, is not getting any younger and as I see no future in working in an inn myself, I reckoned I'd be able to afford to keep her in a nice tidy little cottage somewhere in great comfort – that is, if I can persuade her to stop working, which I doubt, and I'll also be able to buy my own vessel and sail the seas. Captain Nell's son – my that sounds grand!' He stared into space for a short while until someone coughed.

'But to get back to my tale. As I was getting close to Cornwall I thought I'd take some time off to come and visit my old friend Merlin. The mapmaker said he had virtually finished his map-making and wanted to make an extended visit to his sister in Forrabury and to tidy up his maps, and as there were warnings of more storms and high seas he thought the safest thing to do would be to stay on land and winter with his sister till they pass. He paid me a handsome bonus and said that if I wanted to travel to other places in the world with him he suggested I return on St. Clement's day, and with that saint being the patron saint of anchor makers, he hoped to be blessed when he sails. I said that I would be there if I was happy that all was well here.

'I had only just left him when I had the pleasure of being visited in my hostelry by King Ogwin. Now that really was an honour, as I know he doesn't really like being seen by many, especially man. He was with his wife and chamberlain; the rest of his people were apparently keeping watch throughout the county, and he was just about being stopped from jumping up and down by Queen Gisele.

'I won't go into all that he said; just that the land in the south was covered by invaders such as had never been seen in quite such large numbers in Britain before. Even they were not the same as the ones that had been spotted on the odd occasion in the distant past; but these ones were huge – grey men with evil heads and slimy bodies, all encased in gleaming metal armour, were waiting around – for what? They had been alerted through their sensitive noses by the smell; it was overpoweringly bad and for some of the Faerie quite toxic – some of the younger of his subjects had almost passed out. "I mean, Jasper was only 92 and he really couldn't cope with it at all", he had said to me as an aside.'

Rhianne recalled that the Faerie lived for hundreds of years and so 92 was probably quite young.

'King Ogwin told me that he couldn't detect any sign of the magician thereabouts and the spiders had no knowledge either, so he would try to find Merlin and alert him to the danger of what was afoot. In the meantime I said I would come here to see if anyone was around. And here you are! I ran into these good people yesterday and we have shared what is going on. I'll leave it to them to add anything else.'

Eddie took up his part of the story and with his quiet but melodious voice told them how they had come to be visiting Merlin's cave.

'Gwen wanted to come and visit Lady Elise again. She said that her betrothal visit had been much too short and she wanted to get to know the ladies that she'd be sharing her life with from next spring. I thought that a peculiar request but as father and mother had no objection and things were a bit boring at home at the moment with nothing much going on, Wirra and I thought it might be a bit of an adventure.

'Imagine our surprise when we arrived at Sir Ector's home to find that all was in uproar.'

Wirra took up the tale and said how they had spent a long evening listening to Sir Ector and, on the odd occasion, his teary wife, recount the deeds of that fateful night.

They had taken it all in and since they didn't know where anyone was at this time decided that on the morrow they would set out for Tintagel to see what they could find out. They had slept badly but were up well before dawn to hopefully get to the cave as speedily as they could.

'Then we met Nell's son and told him all that was happening and he can think only that all this bodes ill.'

Rhianne and Jasmine got them up to speed with what had happened with them and also with where Arthur and his party were and where Merlin and I had gone. 'Though where any of them are right now, we know not – it has been too long.' Rhianne started wringing her hands.

No-one had interrupted and it was a good few minutes before anyone said anything more.

'Do you think we ought to go south?' Kay spoke for the first time.

'Could we fight that army that is supposed to be there?'

'Are they human? Monsters? Devils?'

'Shouldn't we wait for Merlin? He said to wait. He's given us things to do.'

'What do you have to do?' Gwen asked. 'Perhaps we could help you get it out of the way?'

'Well, I think we've completed the list so we actually don't really have anything else to do.'

'Then I suggest we leave,' Wirra said.

'Oh, but what if Merlin returns. He will be so angry.'

'I can stay here,' Jasmine put in. 'Just let me know what you intend to do and then when he returns he will be aware of everything and can sort things out accordingly.'

'I'll leave two of my men with you,' Wirra began to reassure her.'

'There is no need. I am capable of making myself scarce should it be necessary and I can take care of myself. You will need all the men you have,' she added.

'If you are sure?'

'I am sure.'

'Then we need a plan.'

'There is no time to waste; we will devise a plan as we ride. It will take us two days and one night to get there so let us make haste.'

Griff, twitchy with having been confined to the area for so long was only too happy to accompany them; his acute sense of smell would be a great help so they were more than pleased to have him along.

They had been gone but half a day when a weary Cabal, Arthur, Wite, Brosc, Androcles, a hungry lion, an even hungrier Goliath – if that could be possible – and the Scribe, walked into the cool interior of the cave.

'Brilliant! How can I get across what Merlin wants done when there is no-one here to understand me?'

Jasmine talked with Wite and Brosc, wondering how they had not seen the others who must have passed so closely by them.

'Terrific!' Brosc exclaimed.

'Perhaps they went a different way! Perhaps they were trying not to be seen?' Wite volunteered.

'Well, you had better tell me what you have come back here for,' Jasmine asked them as she dished out some food from the steaming cauldron that sat over the fire, throwing a huge bone, and I mean it was a very huge bone, over toward the far wall. Cabal's eyes popped out of his head as he considered the feast that this still well-endowed with meat bone beckoned him, before a crestfallen look descended upon him as the lion loped across the cave and started to gnaw at it.

The others laughed at him as Jasmine, taking pity, threw one – much smaller by comparison but still big enough for him – across to Cabal.

All was quiet, apart from the loud sounds of crunching and the more refined ones of chewing as everyone rebuilt their strength with food, for several minutes before they started to ask where Merlin was, where had I gone, what the others were thinking of trying to do by heading off to Carn Euny at Sancreed and then telling them why they had returned.

'And now he's not here!'

'This is crazy,' Wite added.

'Oh don't you start,' Brosc grumbled. 'Once you get going you scramble everyone's brains!'

'No I don't!' he exclaimed, being brave for once and standing up to his friend. 'I was just thinking that Salazar and Tailor are near those sluggies …'

'Sluggies?' Jasmine queried.

'Slug-goblins,' Brosc explained.

'Ah yes.'

'And then we are here,' Wite continued. 'Rhianne and Gwen and the others have gone back to where we came from.'

'And Merlin and Percy are nowhere to be found while the rest of us are charging back and forth all over the place,' Arthur concluded. 'What on earth is going on and what on earth are we to do now?'

NINETEEN

We arrived at the outskirts of London some five days later just as the heavy rains of the previous two days finally stopped. We had ridden fast and had hardly slept for the first part of our journey. Amazingly (or was it?), we'd managed to find fresh horses at every inn and for the last part of the journey had hired a cart which an old man of 42 had driven as fast as his nag (also old) could go, but we, at least, were able to finally keep dry and sleep, thus refreshing ourselves a little as we got near our destination late in the evening of the fifth day.

Standing on a hill we dismissed our driver and looking northward watched the smoke rise from the roofs of thousands of dwellings. The bright but waning moon kept winking back at us from the large river that snaked ever eastward, as fast-moving clouds took away the last of the rain and allowing her to keep lighting up the vista before us.

'Now are you going to tell me what we are doing here?'

'Patience!'

I almost laughed out loud; thinking of what I had had to endure with not knowing what was happening for the last five days, so how did he think I had no patience?

Although I had kept my barriers in place – I was actually getting really good at this now – he seemed to know instinctively what I was thinking.

'Percy.' He stopped for a while and then continued. 'This sword is not just any old sword, you know; it is one that has been used by the best of men in the civilised world throughout the ages. Theseus was the last to use it and before him his father – his immortal father, that is – as he had two – Poseidon; more recently it was lifted by Queen Bouddica before I travelled back in time to retrieve it once again from the past of Theseus and the Minotaur. There have been others in the past that have been honoured with the use of this sword but Arthur is to be the one to finally and eternally own it. Its previous life has been a training time for it; it has now reached its maturity and purpose.'

'And what is it to be used for now? What is its final purpose?' I enquired *patiently* as I waited for Merlin to eventually continue.

'Ah, now we return it to the water!'

'Eh?'

'We are going down there, to the Thames River, where there will be a boatman waiting for us. He will row us downstream till we reach the Eyot of Thorns or Thorney Island, as it is sometimes known. The island,' he went on to enlighten me, 'is fairly small, covered, as you will have probably guessed by its name, in thorns, so it is the perfect place for us.'

'And what do we need to visit this island for?' I tried to keep the sarcasm out of my voice but I believe I was quite unsuccessful this time.

'To place the sword,' he sounded exasperated, as though I should have known. 'Sometimes I really wonder if you are all the ticket, Percy. I mean, I've trained you up and then at times, like this, I wonder if you really do have the brains you were born with!'

'Merlin, I can only give out what has been put in, and you haven't told me anything!' Now it was my time to be annoyed.

He stared at me, eyebrows furrowed, eyes piercing; then he laughed. 'We are both tired and I was possibly thinking that because I knew what I was doing, you should too. Let's think no more of it.'

And that was as near an apology as I was likely to get, and no, he still hadn't told me anything! *Patience Percy!*

Finding the boatman, we clambered aboard his really quite rickety old tub that I seriously wondered would stay afloat. By the time I had followed Merlin into it, it sank so low in the water that there was barely an inch between the top of the boat and the river's water; it surely had to sink but, miraculously, it got us to our destination – almost dry.

Merlin spoke to the man who'd jumped out at the island and secured his boat and, while we wandered through the narrow path that meandered through the thorns, lay down upon a flattish slab of rock and nodded off to sleep.

The moon, three-quarters full and now floating gently in a cloudless sky, watched our progress, looking neither excited nor bored – just benign, as she lit the path before us. Nonetheless, we trod carefully, not wishing to trip and fall into those menacing thorns.

Then, without any warning, we stepped into a clearing and stopped in our tracks. King Ogwin, along with a party of his people, sat smiling down at us from the flat top of a huge grey rock positioned at the far side of the glade.

The formal greetings were observed; however, we had got to know one another so well over the years that even these observances were getting shorter and shorter.

The little king and his people skipped down from the rock and spread out in a semi-circle around Merlin as he drew near.

There was a lot to be said by the king as he got us up to date with what had been happening far and wide, all the while walking to the edge of the island.

'We will meet up later, your majesty, where we can talk more – right now I have to do something and time, you will understand, is of the essence.'

So, finally, when we had walked almost to the far side of the island quite near where the River Tyburn flows into the Thames, we all stopped and just stared out across them. The water at this edge eddies around quite violently as the two rivers meet but we were not so interested at what appeared to be happening on the top of the waters as what might be happening beneath.

Merlin turned his back to the rock and stood at the edge of the island, at the same time raising his staff. The moon glinted off the silver badge above his face and then from the ruby eyes within the silver merlin's face on his staff. They began to glow.

Everything was still. Even the river appeared to be holding its breath and seemed to have stopped flowing.

We waited.

The smoke from the myriad homes along the far bank of the river vanished along with the noise of dogs barking or the river lapping and every other sound was folded up and smothered and locked away as the mist rose from those waters.

We were secure on our island; no-one would see what would go on this evening, though we ourselves were not so shrouded.

We waited.

Merlin was still, staff raised. The rest of us, too, were almost mesmerised as we stared deep into the mists that were sliding up from the river and around our feet.

We waited.

The waters directly in front of Merlin moved as though an unexpected squally breeze had disturbed them; they were still for several more heartbeats before they suddenly moved again.

Then he arose.

Those waters parted as though cut by a knife as the man (and it was the form of a man) rose up from the deep.

His skin was as scaly as a dinosaur and as green as seaweed; well, most of him was covered in sea or river weed anyway but the skin that showed was definitely green and scaly.

The first thing to penetrate through those waters was a three-pronged spear, then the huge hand gripping its shaft and finally the rest of the man followed down to his waist. I wondered, and still do, whether he had legs or a tail like a merman, but he never rose above his waist.

'Merlin,' he spoke just like the Lady of the Lake, as he acknowledged the sorcerer, but with a male voice. It was as though spoken under the waters, even though he was now above them. 'Why have you called me? What do you want of me?'

'I have your son's sword, mighty god Poseidon, and I need you to use your powers to soak it.'

'What is the reason for this? I have to know if it is for good or if it is for evil.'

'The sword needs to be encased within this rock. The future king of this land, if his heart is true and he is to rule for good, is the only one who will be able to pull it out and then the land will have peace.'

'Then it is in accord with the will of the gods. Give the sword to me.'

It almost looked as though he was crying as he held the sword in his hand; the river water was still running off him as tears of it fell from his eyes. Thinking of what had happened to his son, I thought that if it had been me then my tears would also have been falling if I had taken hold of that sword.

Merlin watched as the man from the river lifted the sword high; it started to hum and then burned bright as day before returning to silence and grey steel.

'Quickly now,' he urged, returning the sword into Merlin's

hands, and at the same time cupping a large handful of water and throwing it over the stone. 'Or it will be too late!'

The rock hissed as the water hit it and Merlin, turning and taking the few steps up and onto it, held the hilt high before thrusting the sword downward at the stone.

I really thought the sword would snap; the force with which it came crashing down must surely break the sword in two. But it didn't and I must have stood there with my usual open-mouthed, bug-eyed expression as I watched the sword plunge into the stone and grind slowly to a halt some three-quarters of the way up to the hilt.

The sound it made must have reached to the centre of the earth, I thought. There was a crescendo – such a grating noise that I thought my eardrums would burst; there were also sparks and stars that lit up the whole clearing.

But we were encased in mist and I would have thought that the sound, rather than penetrate those mists and wake up everyone for miles around, would merely have bounced off them and back at us – hence that terrible, ear-shattering sound.

Then seconds later – silence! Not a sound. Even Poseidon slipping back under the eddying waters made no noise as he returned to his place of mythology and imaginings.

The Faerie were the first to move. They jumped up onto the rock and stepped gingerly toward the sword. I would have thought that it should have been red hot but the chamberlain touched it and it was cool, he told us.

Stepping up to it I stood upon the rock and slipping my hand through the hilt had a pull – solid! I grabbed hold of it with two hands and, with my heels giving purchase to my feet, yanked – even more solid – if that were possible.

'Well, you are most certainly not going to be king of all the Britons!' Merlin chuckled as he, too, gave it a go.

'And neither are you!'

'I don't intend to be, young Percy,' he said. 'I was just making sure that it really was secure, and it is. It will only be the one ordained to be king who will be able to pull out the sword – and pull it out easily, like it was greased with butter.'

'Yes, and when ...'

'*Percy!*' Merlin almost shouted at me, being aware that I was just about to let the cat out of the bag as to the name of that future king.

'Sorry.'

He smiled. 'Just be careful, man, we are nearly there.'

We left that place.

After telling King Ogwin where we were headed, we got back into our frighteningly fragile boat and returned, miraculously, safely to the mainland. Paying off the man, Merlin and I picked up our packs and headed down the hillside in search of our hostelry called, strangely, the Blue Pelican, where the Faerie once again awaited us.

'We've got so much news to tell you,' the pocket-sized king began as we sat down to enjoy a quite amazingly delicious meal.

TWENTY

'Well, what have you to tell me?'

Iris dug her heels into the rock floor of the cave and tried to push herself as far back and away from this evil smelling creature as she could, holding the still sleeping child close and hiding her within the quite inadequate blanket Mab had given them.

The hobgoblin, hoofed feet clattering on the floor as he trotted toward the centre of the room, peered craftily left and right before resting his eyes on the witch and grinning. Well, it looked as though he was trying to grin but anyone with any heart at all would believe it more a cross between a grimace, a sneer and a leer. His teeth were like short fangs, but powerful; they looked like they could tear flesh from limbs. The worst thing about him, though, Iris had thought, was his aura: it was a blackish-green and shrouded him like an enlarged shadow; when he moved it undulated around him seeming to be left behind and then trying to catch up with him. Iris dwelt on this for mere seconds – a memory from the past where she had believed she'd seen people as colours intruded into her mind as she watched this abnormal creature with its peculiar aura; shaking her head she mentally scolded herself for being fanciful – all those memories had probably been a dream.

Also he moved in a most peculiar fashion – sometimes looking as though he were going in slow motion and at other times as though he'd conquered time by missing out bits of it – one moment he was over here and the next over the other side. Iris shuddered and tried not to look at him; he was making her feel dizzy and sick.

'They are all running around like headless chickens!'

Iris shuddered again; his voice – well, really, it sounded like voices – seemed to be creeping up from the very ground they stood on – from hell itself!

'Most of them are on their way here – but they have no plan apart from trying to storm the place.'

Mab sneered. They had no hope of doing that with the army she had in place outside.

'Three of them are outside, about a mile away, on the hill overlooking this place.

'The women …'

Mordred interrupted, 'What women?'

'Ooh it speaks!' Mab was sarcastic as she turned her head toward the man.

Mordred, who'd been in a deep sulk for many months since he'd heard of Rhianne and my wedding, had hardly put two words together since and just obeyed orders as though he were in some sort of a trance. He'd tried just moping around and doing nothing, sometimes ignoring the witch for days, but after she'd put the itchy wart spell on him where he'd grown long stringy warts all over his face and had nearly torn his skin to pieces trying to scratch them off, he'd obeyed, though his eyes were glassy and his shoulders slouched. She always knew how to get her own way! Though she might have been just a bit uncomfortable if she had seen the look he sometimes gave her when her back was turned.

'So,' she gave him the cold shoulder as she turned back to the creature, 'the women?'

'Two women are on their way here with some of the men, not many but enough to guard them.'

'Do you know who they are?'

He curled his lip at her. Did she not know who he was? But apart from that action he decided he wouldn't, on this occasion, rebuke her. 'One is the Lady Rhianne and the other is called Gwen. She has two of her brothers with her, a sailor and some servants. Around ten people. And one dog,' he added as an afterthought.

'Ah!' Mab started pacing around the room with one hand holding her chin as she considered what she might do once she got her hands on all of them. 'And the others,' she turned and stared back at him. 'What about them?'

'Arthur and his men are also headed here but they are half a day behind the others. They will not catch them up. Well, not on the road at any event. They have taken a more northerly route.'

'Arthur,' her utterance of his name was almost a caress. 'Perhaps this time …' she left the sentence unfinished.

Quiet descended for two or three minutes as the witch paced up and down, sometimes stopping and grinning, nodding her head or shaking it as she spoke within her own mind before, stopping short, she turned once again to the hobgoblin.

'And Myrddin? Percy?'

'They are in London and have visited Thorney Island.'

'London? Thorney Island? What on earth for?' She looked completely bewildered – for once in her life. 'He knows what's going on here! Why has he gone so far away? This is not right! There's something fishy going on here.'

'He has called Poseidon and has embedded a sword into a rock.' The evil looking character didn't miss a thing – noticing how the witch turned sharply at the mention of the word "sword". He continued. 'That was when I last heard of him. Where he is at this present time, I have not been advised.'

And then the whispers of words from long, long ago began to speak softly into her ear. '*Sword held high ... powerful charger ... he will come!*' The hair – what there was of it – rose on the back of her neck and even through the dirt and grime that covered her face it could be seen that she had turned pale.

All thoughts of capturing and killing Arthur disappeared. He could wait. The prophecy mentioned that sword. If he didn't have it he couldn't kill her. She spun around and stared at the ugly creature.

'We have to get that sword. WE HAVE TO GET THAT SWORD!' Her voice had reached screeching proportions and even the hobgoblin had to place one or even two fingers into his pointed ears.

Mayhem!

Iris pushed herself even further back, if that were possible. With luck they might leave her and then she could attempt to escape. She'd try not to think about that just now, as she'd found in the past that if she did try to think about something, well, somehow that mad woman knew and then it all went wrong. So she just concentrated on gently rocking the child and looking as inconspicuous as she could.

'Mordred, get my bag. Nooo, not that one! Oh I might as well do it myself. No, why should I? Mordred ...' and so it went on.

In less than an hour, and that was something for the witch and all that great girth of fat she was now hauling around with her, they were ready.

Ushering them out through the door, Mab watched the

hobgoblin exit first – who seemed to float through; Mordred followed but was laden down with so much stuff it was difficult to actually see him. She had an overpowering urge to trip him up and watch as all the tins and things crashed hither and thither but she had to stop herself, realising the urgency of her quest. She was the last to leave, slamming the door behind her as she stomped through.

Iris held her breath. She couldn't believe it – they'd forgotten her. Letting it out with a silent sigh she was just about to try and stand up when CRASH – throwing the door back a red-faced woman wobbled back in.

'Thought I'd forgotten you, didn't you? Well, I didn't,' she lied as she pushed three slug-goblins into the room. 'Watch them!' she ordered. 'Don't dare move; don't leave them for one minute! Understand?' she thundered.

Iris could have cried at the disappointment but at least they wouldn't do anything to her so breathing deeply she sat down.

It wasn't long before the child awoke, wet and hungry again. With one eye on her captors she pushed herself up and walked over to where the cauldron bubbled over a dying fire. Adding some logs to keep it bright in the room for fear of what might happen if it turned completely dark (several of the candles were already guttering and she would need to find some more), she peeked inside to see if there was anything suitable for Kate to eat and found that the stew, if that is what it was, was thin enough for the baby to swallow. Hoping it would not upset her tummy she cooled an amount in a wooden bowl and, after tasting it herself, fed some to the hungry baby, all the time keeping her eyes on her guards. Nothing untoward happened and so for the next few days that was their unvaried activity. The slug-goblins fared far worse; however; in fact they ate not one thing and by the third day, one by one, had passed out through lack of sustenance.

Watching intently as those grotesque creatures slid one by one to the floor and then start to froth and bubble, Iris made her escape.

Some few days before this, however, Mab, exiting the fogue at Carn Euny at Sancreed, had stared around at the mighty army she'd amassed.

'Come here,' she ordered the commander.

He marched over and stopped, standing to attention at least two head and shoulders height above the witch.

Not liking it at all, as she always wanted to be above and looking down upon absolutely everyone and everything, she craned her neck and squinted up at him.

'You have how many horses?'

'Enough for each leader and a few more besides.'

'Good! You can spare a couple then! I shall need two hitched up to a wagon to carry me east. I shall also need at least half of your army to accompany me and the other half to follow in two days' time. I intend to capture my enemy by luring him after me and then he will be trapped. When he follows me we will be in front of him and the others will be coming up behind him and then he'll be captured. *Yes, Arthur, you will be captured and this time you will not get away! But I intend to get that sword before you can get your hands on it!* Get the wagon ready and instruct your men, er goblins.'

The commander stood to attention, turned and went to carry out her orders.

Mordred looked around at the devastated countryside. It hadn't rained for weeks now and dust was being kicked up everywhere by anything that moved. The ground was devoid of grass and the trees held no leaf – and it wasn't even the end of autumn yet!

Mab, catching sight of him staring at the nearest naked gorse bush, shrugged. 'They have to eat something, Mordred, and slugs eat greenery. They'll probably have to search further afield ...' she started laughing, 'further afield ... get it? Slugs eat greenery – a field!'

Mordred just stared woodenly at her.

'Oh I shall be glad when you go away,' she was eventually able to say. 'Should have changed your name to Morbid,' she muttered whilst directing some lower ranking soldiers to load her baggage.

'Now, you go up front with him,' she pointed to their driver. 'Don't want your miserable face putting me off my spells. We have a long way to go and I need to be able to free that sword. So, unless it is a matter of life or death, KEEP QUIET.'

It took four slug-goblins an age to somehow manage to push her incredible bulk into the wagon without pulling a muscle, and then, covering the wagon itself with cowhides and securing them, they were able to set off.

Even one or two of those smelly creatures were glad to see the back of her.

'And don't go over too many rocks. Make it a smooth ride!' she yelled at them.

Salazar and Shake Spear silently watched them depart until the dust cloud blocked them from view. It took a while – five thousand horses and riders and foot soldiers – all of whom ate grass and so were extremely hungry – moved slowly forward on the look out for greener fields than the ones they had just left. Salazar and the two other men quietly mounted their animals before they, too, left, taking a more circuitous route back to Tintagel.

Less than an hour later it started to rain.

Salazar almost smiled – that would bog her down a bit!

TWENTY-ONE

'Well, what have you to tell me?'

King Ogwin smiled. 'The spiders have been busy. At this time of the year they are out in force and every morning it becomes almost the crescendo at the end of a concert as they transmit their messages, the heavy dew upon their web effectively drum-rolling each communication before passing it along.'

He spent the next hour telling Merlin and me just what was happening all along the south-west of the country, where each of our friends were and what they appeared to be doing, and about the huge army at Carn Euny at Sancreed.

'How many slug-goblins do you suppose there are?' I asked.

'We understand there are around ten thousand.'

'Ten thousand!' I exclaimed, choking on a piece of bread and being roundly scolded by Merlin for putting so much food into my mouth at one time.

'Give or take a few,' he added. 'But half of that army is on its way here – to London – to the Isle of Thorns.'

'How are we going to defeat all of them?'

'Now, now, Percy,' Merlin shushed me. 'All we need is a plan.'

'OK, so what's the plan?'

'Don't hurry me; I don't want to have to make it up as I go along!'

'So you don't have a plan yet?' I grumbled.

'No! But I always get one, don't I? Anyway, how do you expect me to have devised any sort of plan when I have only had the information for two minutes?' He glared at me. 'And,' pointedly ignoring me as he turned back to the king, 'I don't know how she thinks she's going to get the sword out of that rock!' He chuckled as his mind's eye gave him a glimpse of what she might look like trying – if she could even get up onto that rock, that is.

'Now,' he said, jumping up, 'we need to go and see what we can do about Moon Song.'

I groaned. Was there going to be one thing after another before we could rescue Kate? Would we ever rescue her? What was Merlin playing at?

'Come, come, Percy, patience!' He'd followed my unguarded train of thought and was tender in his response. 'I know it seems so long but we will get there and she will be fine, I promise. After a good night's sleep all will seem different and we will be on our way. I've got some dust with me, and a portion of the Glass; we will just need to concentrate on the circle of stones and we'll be there before the birds wake up.'

Sighing, I got up and followed him up the stairway to our rooms. I felt very lonely; I missed Rhianne and Kate and, funnily, Cabal. I called out to him through my mind but I reckon he must have been too far away because he didn't answer, though my skin started to crawl as an echo bounced around in my head when a strange gravelly voice spoke to me in a completely incomprehensible language.

'Shut your mind now!' Merlin spun round and ordered me.

I crashed down my barriers, which I was doing in any event as the voice had scared me but now I was petrified when I saw the look on Merlin's face.

Like a worm, I felt that this disembodied voice had been attempting to crawl into my head – trying to find what?

'What was it?' I spoke audibly and could hardly get the words out; my spit had dried up and I had to manipulate my tongue a few times before it returned.

'It sounded like the hobgoblin.' He was almost whispering as though saying the name might conjure up the creature itself. 'You will have to try to make sure that when you are mind speaking in future you channel your words directly to the person you have in mind; you can do that, I know. I didn't spend all that time training you for nothing did I? Don't send out your words in the hope that someone, even Cabal, is around to pick them up. It has become too dangerous to do that now unless I am there and can have complete control over the situation. Do you understand, Percy? We are almost there! We have almost reached that time of prophecy! We can't let it all go to waste now, can we? So, we must be ready – that witch knows the score as well and things are almost certain to come to a head soon and I dread to think what she may have cooked up! So – take care – take very great care!'

After my meal I had felt myself relaxing and getting ready to have a wonderful sleep between clean white sheets in a soft, warm bed; now, I don't think I could have slept even if Merlin gave me a strong enough draught of something to help me. I tossed and turned all night, sometimes drifting into a light sleep where the hobgoblin was creeping up behind me to crawl into my ear so as to penetrate my whole being or hiding among the trees in the forest my dream was taking me through to jump out and destroy me, and once I thought he was behind me in the bed and breathing down my neck and stuff like that. It was a baggy-eyed young man that greeted, or didn't actually, Merlin before a merry fire where he was tucking in to a huge breakfast.

'I don't know how you can eat all that so early,' I complained, sounding amazingly like my dad. It's funny that isn't it, that sometimes you open your mouth and your father's voice comes out? Scary!

'Now, now, don't be so grumpy. You nearly always eat all this early – I've seen you. So don't give me all that nonsense! Eat – come on – or you'll pass out on the way.'

'On the way to where?' I asked, flopping down onto the bench and picking up a spoon that I merely played with.

'For goodness' sake, pull yourself together. Here, take this,' he handed me something that looked surprisingly like a boiled sweet, telling me to go sit by the fire and if I didn't want any breakfast to eat that instead and stop turning him off his food.

Well, it worked! Within five minutes the lethargy of a bad night's sleep had completely left me and energy, similar to Cabal's when he was straining to be off to catch whatever it was that was stupid enough to run across his path, was pulsing through my body.

Then the conversation of the night before jumped into my head and, thinking about Kate, I was urging Merlin to hurry up and eat his food – the quicker we went to see to Moon Song, the quicker we could go after my daughter.

'Before we go I need to tell you what happened last night.'

'Last night?' My heart fell into my boots.

'Yes, last night.'

I waited. He carried on eating. I could have screamed.

'What? What happened last night?' I could barely keep hold of my temper. Did he wind me up on purpose?

'I had a dream, though I don't think it was a dream – more a warning.' He popped some cheese into his mouth and chewed it for an interminable length of time.

'The dream?' I almost said the words through gritted teeth.

'Yes.' Before I could react I believe he managed to pull himself away from the vision that was playing across his mind and realise the effect his words were having upon me. 'Yes! It was the Lady of the Lake. She told me she had been floating around in her dream world, which, she told me, was a very happy place – a place of beauty, peace and safety, when a darkness and chill started to penetrate it. She hadn't experienced anything like this in a hundred years or more and it made her extremely uneasy. She told me she made herself as small as possible and began to explore her dream world, flying as high within it as it would allow and looking down upon it from that great height.

'She saw the witch, her sister, making her way across the land toward the east with a great retinue of ugly men – an army, glinting and rattling with armour; she saw another – something she believes from the very pit of the earth itself – goat-legged and hairy with the ugliest and wickedest face she had ever seen. It was moving quite rapidly away from her northward – alone. In her almost permanent dreamlike state she was able to move faster than this awful thing to see if she could find out where it was going and came across Arthur and his small band of men. Probably, by now, they will have met up!'

'Then why are we waiting?' I asked him, becoming quite agitated.

'Well, for one thing, if we are too late then what we can do will have to be after the event but, and this is more likely the case, it was a warning so we have time to do something about it!'

'So, let's go then!'

'Eat, Percy.' This said in such an authoritative tone that I was shocked into sitting down and doing as I had been told.

'It will be a long time before we can do so again and we will need all the energy this food provides. Anyway, how would you feel if you finally came up to the place where your family was held and instead of fighting your way in like a hero you dropped into a dead faint through lack of sustenance? Think of the tales sung by minstrels of the man who should have but didn't!' His voice was now softer but all in all it had the desired effect. I ate!

'I believe that the Lady of the Lake was warning me, too, as to what that creature was. It was the thing we thought it was last night when you tried to call Cabal. It is a wicked and terrifying being and we need to be extremely careful how we proceed from now on. Also, she wants her peace back and with all this wickedness going on it is disturbed and when that happens all the different elements around her isle are so agitated they send out ripples to the farthest ends of Britain – if not further.

'There is wickedness in this world, Percy, and, like the profusion of spiders that are able to communicate through their webs, this being has an excessive amount of evil beings at his command that can do the same. In fact,' he lowered his voice and staring into my eyes said, '*I think for the time being we will communicate anything important to one another through our minds – directly to one another so that no-one else can pick up on it.*

'Let's go,' he jumped up almost shouting as he grabbed me by the arm.

I stuffed the last piece of bacon into my mouth as he yanked me to my feet, put an arm round me and threw some dust over us as he stared at the circle of stones held within the small piece of Glass he was holding up with his other hand.

Then we were gone.

By now the baby was yelling her head off. They hadn't eaten for two days but had merely drunk from the streams that littered the countryside. Iris had been too frightened to approach anyone; the witch had scared her so much that she now trusted no-one. But things were getting desperate.

Coming across a run-down shack she waited, listened intently and searched until she was sure it was completely deserted and then, when she was absolutely certain, took the sobbing child inside and tried to rock her to sleep. It was impossible. Kate was drawing her little legs up to her stomach, which must have been cramping badly at its emptiness and staring up at Iris with eyes that seemed to plead for the food that she just could not provide. Iris felt terrible.

Even though she, too, wanted to weep she cradled the child in her arms and crooning a lullaby, held her as close as she could while she rocked her to sleep. Eventually she quietened and they both slept the sleep of exhaustion.

'Mooo, mooo.'

The sound finally penetrated their ears. Kate woke first, fidgeting in Iris' arms until she, too, woke up. She couldn't believe her eyes. Looking in through one of the windows was an extremely large black and white head with soft twitching ears.

'Mooooo.' Its sound became more insistent.

Sitting Kate onto the floor Iris jumped up and rushed out of the hut. The cow was crying for help. She had full udders and was in some distress. Rushing back into the hut Iris ran over to the far wall where, on her search for food, she had found an empty bucket. Sitting on a log she set the bucket underneath the cow and began to milk her. The "moos" became less and less until the animal began to relax.

Iris couldn't take the smile off her face. The cow's pain was eased and they would have food – only milk but that was probably the best thing for the baby at the moment. Porridge or anything heavier would certainly give her stomach more cramps than the empty stomach had.

Then she saw it. She had wondered why this cow was wandering around with full udders and no-one taking care of it. Her calf was caught up in the bracken and was trapped.

'Oh you poor thing,' Iris whispered as she moved over toward the young beast. Wrapping her arms in her petticoats she pulled and snapped until finally the animal was freed. It skipped over to its mother and Iris watched with satisfaction as it, too, started to feed from the still plentiful supply of milk.

The two animals somehow knew that they were safe and didn't even try to run away but stayed there for the next two days, supplying milk to Kate and Iris as well as the calf until Iris felt they were strong enough to try and move on. She had taken some of the milk and had stirred and stirred it until it had thickened. Wrapping these curds into several layers of her diminishing petticoats, she tied the ends and hoped it would not go bad and would last them at least a few more days.

The cows must have known they were leaving because when Iris woke up the next morning they were gone.

Tearing some more material from her skirts she made a sling and settled young Kate within it.

'Let's hope we can find help soon, my little one,' she smiled down at her. Violet blue eyes, so similar to those of her mother, crinkled back up at her trustingly, happy now that she was fed. 'Oh, dear,' Iris' tone belied her look, 'let's hope it isn't too long.' She settled the child more comfortably in the sling and with her bouncing and laughing at the movement they moved on in the hope that they were going the right way.

'There they are,' Merlin's quiet voice pointed down the hillside. I had thought that we were headed toward the stone circle; that is what I thought I had seen in the Glass when we left the inn but obviously I had not. It had all been so fast anyway and over the last couple of hours Merlin had put me straight.

'If that mad woman had left the fogue at Sancreed, and she was travelling with just Mordred and half the army, it stands to reason that Iris and the child would slow her down. She will have left them tied up within the Iron Age works.'

We had entered the cave where it was obvious they had been held had seen the three slug-goblins who looked dead and had then scoured the area to see if they were still around. Iris and Kate must have found somewhere to hide because the Glass gave us no indication as to where they were.

But now that they were on the move we had eventually spotted them.

Iris was sitting under a huge oak and Kate was in her lap. They both looked asleep but as we ran toward them Iris jumped up and clutching the child to her chest started running away as fast as her legs would carry her – panic giving her wings.

'Iris! Iris! 'Tis I, Merlin and Percy is with me,' he called before she finally came to a halt.

Almost weeping, she turned back and ran into the sorcerer's arms, making sure Kate wasn't squashed in the process.

I grabbed my daughter and held her close to me, rocking her in my arms and saying loads of really ridiculous things that only happy fathers say to their young and which would cause them a great deal of embarrassment should anyone overhear and repeat them at a later date.

She, for her part though, was yelling her head off and it was only when Merlin gave her a hard type of biscuit of I know not what for her to suck on that she quieted down.

'I tried to save some of the cow's milk, Iris sobbed, 'but it went off and there wasn't even a stream around here so we could have some water and ...'

'Now, now,' Merlin crooned. 'Let's take you home.'

And that was what he did.

Within moments the Glass came out, the caer came into view, the dust was thrown and we were standing in the courtyard at Sir Ector's.

Iris and Kate were handed over to a relieved but almost fainting Lady Elise before we, taking our leave and heading out of the compound, moved swiftly into the privacy of the trees whence we were whisked off to the Stones.

I've often thought, since those days, that I could have made an absolute fortune in this day and age – if only I had some of Merlin's dust and even a small piece of the Glass. People would be able to go on holiday without all the fuss of airports, passports, planes, boats and the like. 'Good morning sir, madam – Rome? By all means. Just stare into the Glass and imagine the Basilica. OK now, just stand still while I throw this dust over you.' Then, again, I wouldn't know how to bring them back – dragon's droppings being in such short supply in the 20th Century and, even if I did have some, they'd all probably end up inside Merlin's cave in Tintagel or one of the other caves. Probably get sued then eh? Think I'll have a word with Merlin to see if there might just be a possibility I could start up a business if there was enough dust and dragon's droppings so that I could ...

However, right now my mental wanderings were being interrupted as we had landed on the plain almost at the edge of the stones and Merlin was, even before we stopped walking, searching in his pockets for his potions.

'Percy, what I want you to do is stay outside the stone circle; let down your barriers but do not mind-speak – just listen, and then, if you hear anything untoward, run in and let me know. However, I really need time and quiet to do what I have to do to help Moon Song.

'If it works she will be restored to us and then we can round everybody up. There is going to be a battle my boy and we need as much strength and wile as is available to us.

So, stay alert – listen!

TWENTY-TWO

'There's someone coming,' Tailor pulled up his horse and spoke quietly to the other two men.

Shake Spear peered down through the avenue of trees and waited. His eyesight was still a wondrous thing to him now that he could see properly. Adjusting the spectacles he screwed up his nose and stared.

'It's the lion!' They watched – Shake Spear and Tailor were transfixed as this huge beast rushed headlong toward them.

A piercing whistle brought the animal to a screeching halt before several men on horseback came into view.

'It's Arthur!' Shake Spear exclaimed, forgetting his fear of the huge animal, which now lay in front of them. Androcles had dismounted and made his way over to the lion where he sat down, placing an arm around its neck. Tailor goggled. It still astonished him that one small boy could control such a huge, wild beast.

After they'd greeted each other Salazar took Arthur to one side and they caught up with what was going on.

'… and so I think we should storm the place and rescue my niece,' Arthur finally concluded.

'But there are at least five thousand soldiers in her unholy army; we'd never get through,' Salazar tried reasoning with the man. Also, he was aware that Merlin would never forgive him if anything happened to Arthur.

'We are a match for them,' he turned with a sweep of his arm as he looked across as his men. 'I mean, just look at the size of him,' pointing toward Goliath. 'He could fell a hundred men. And as for that lion …'

'The odds are one against five hundred; it cannot be done.'

Arthur's face fell. 'We have to do something!'

'We will do something. It is just over a day's journey to Tintagel. We will go back and see if Merlin has returned.'

'He hasn't – we've just come from there.' He started pacing up and down in the way he always did when he was trying to get his thoughts together.

Everyone just watched him and Salazar and waited. They were after all just followers and only ever did as they were told.

Cabal waited until Arthur stopped pacing before he went over and licked his hand, being rewarded by an absentminded pat on the head.

'*Nell's son, Rhianne and some others are not far behind,*' he cocked an eyebrow as he looked over at Salazar. '*And the Faerie are on their way here too! Perhaps we should wait before we journey back to the cave?*'

'*How do you know?*'

'*King Ogwin's chamberlain and some others were over there in the copse while you were talking to Arthur. He said the king had been with Merlin and was coming to tell you what had been going on.*'

'*What did you tell him?*'

'*Nothing!*'

'*Nothing?*'

'*No! I can understand him but he doesn't have the gift of the Old Way so he told me just so that I could come and tell you. He had to leave immediately as he had other things to do for the king. He just said to wait for the king and the others – they shouldn't be long.*'

'*We will wait.*'

They arrived at a place called Shooter's Hill, where the witch told the commander of the army to make camp. 'Keep south of the hill,' she ordered him. We don't want them to know we're here until we have to.

'When night comes you can light a few fires but keep them low. If they find we're here we will lose our advantage of surprise.'

Fortunately, after all that rain, which now seemed to have stopped, there was plenty of greenery around and had been for the last two days of their trip and so the slug-goblins were feeling fitter than they had for weeks; proof of which was that there were gobs of excess spit everywhere! Being thankful that the wind was in the right direction, Mab rubbed her hands together; '*They won't smell the slug-goblins,*' she thought, as if they were the only ones that smelled!

'I shall be travelling down to Thorney Island where I shall retrieve the sword. Should there be a problem on the way I shall send Mordred back to you and you will have to march back with him to help me. Not that I shall need any help!' she exclaimed, full of herself.

Taking it easy for the rest of the day she retired to her cart where, pulling the drapes securely around herself, she and Mordred sat and stared at the crystal to see just what was happening around and about and further afield.

They waited a very long time before anything other than swirls of mist came into view. Then slowly, oh so slowly, the mists parted and Sir Ector's caer showed up from deep within. She scowled. Taking absolutely no notice whatsoever of the amount of men that were amassing, or the reason for so many, she stared past them, over their heads and locked on to Iris – and the baby.

Grinding the few remaining teeth she still possessed she growled, 'I'll skin those slug-goblins alive when I get hold of them. How dare they disobey me! How dare they let them escape!'

She turned her attention to Carn Euny at Sancreed and was only slightly mollified as she looked around at the empty countryside; searching further she watched the second contingent of warriors on the march to join up with her and the others. Urging the crystal to look back inside the cavern she was just able to make out in the gloom the fact that the three guards were lying flat out on the floor; she ignored the foaming bubbles that were fizzing from their every orifice and the fact that apart from that they didn't appear to be breathing.

'They obviously don't know the punishment for sleeping on the job!' she grunted. 'Wait till I get hold of them!'

Just then a flaming torch was thrust into the room and two slug-goblins entered. They turned the first man over and, wow, he had almost completed melted away – there was just bubbling froth where once a terrible being had existed. She watched as they turned the two other slug-goblins over, saw that they, too, had suffered the same fate and so had shrugged their shoulders and left.

'Well, you won't have to punish them now, will you Mab?'

'Shut up, Mordred; you are really getting on my nerves now, you know. You either have the sulks and don't say anything or say something when you should be keeping your mouth shut! So, SHUT IT!'

Mordred made a weird croaking noise in his throat as he grimaced at the witch.

Things had deteriorated quite badly between these once bosom buddies.

Almost crowding him out by shifting her bulk so that she had her back to him and farting quite loudly in the process, Mab stared hard at the crystal once again and began chanting. The mists swirled, the witch's voice screeched like a banshee and the air grew thick! In more ways than one!

The mists didn't swirl away like they had before, they vanished in the blink of an eye and there, directly in front of them and slap bang in the centre of a clearing sat a huge stone – a boulder – encasing a sword, whose hilt gleamed, almost blinding her, in the sunlight. Only about one third of the sword stood out of the stone but Mab, staring hard, decided that that would be no problem to her. All she had to do was get to the island, pull out the sword, and Arthur would be history. Simple!

She waited to see if the crystal would show her any more but it wouldn't. She was a bit miffed as it would have been good to know where Myrddin might be and what he was up to. She shrugged. He wouldn't be able to stop her now and she knew he wasn't anywhere around here because she would have felt his presence. In any case, what could he do? He thought he'd done all that was needed by putting the sword into the stone in the first place but he really was the most big-headed person ever if he thought she wasn't able to use her much more powerful magic to counteract his.

She was aroused from her thoughts by a tapping on the footplate of the cart. Shoving the drapes to one side she almost felled the commander with the awful, condensed stench that shot out between those curtains. She watched him stagger backwards and for the shortest moment thought that perhaps they were under attack, but he recovered himself while her eyes scanned the area around and about.

'You asked me to wake you before twilight,' he gasped.

'Good man! Help me down. Mordred, get my bag and hitch the horses back to the wagon. I want to be away within the quarter hour. We should arrive an hour before midnight. Once I get everything set up it should be the witching hour and then the sword will be mine.'

The commander was to remain with his men at Shooter's Hill, while a small unit of two squads were to accompany the witch and

Mordred. If she needed help she would send a couple of them back.

The commander, with a sigh of relief, watched the wagon disappear into the gloom. He had got to the point where he was now not at all sure why he was accompanying this weird woman; he had, in the back of his mind, an idea that she had promised him so much to aid her and he had thus jumped at the opportunity to have what she had promised; now, though, he couldn't even remember what that was. So, in the hope of finally remembering, because it must have been such a lot for him to have agreed to in the first place, he carried on with her.

Reaching the riverside opposite Thorney Island, the witch suffered a twinge of unease. The river was flowing fast downstream and as far as she could see there was absolutely no way to cross it.

Sending two of the slug-goblins in one direction and two in the other she fumed and fussed as precious time slipped by. Eventually a very little man in what looked like an unbelievably small boat rowed his way along the river's edge.

'This is going to be fun!' Mordred thought.

Mab lashed out at the man and brought blood to the surface as she cuffed him round the ear. She then made the slug-goblins and Mordred drag the coracle up onto the bank while she inspected it. It was extremely light in weight and looked as though it would not hold more than one person. She could feel the blood rushing to her head as she looked at the impossibility of the situation.

'Calm, woman; keep calm!' Then the idea hit her. These river men were almost made of water. Grabbing the terrified boatman by the chin, she held his face up to hers and within seconds he would do anything she asked.

Thus it was that a tiny little man, with a thick rope between his teeth, fought the fast-flowing current as he pulled a small boat with a huge woman in it across to the island. He didn't hear her screams and shouts; he had been hypnotised too deeply for that and he didn't feel the whacks around his head as the demented and fairly wet woman laid into him when they arrived at their destination. He merely turned away and pulled the coracle back to the far shore and back again until Mordred and the slug-goblins were all safely across. Then he sat shivering and almost passing out with the exertion on the shingle beach until it would be time to take them all back again.

Finally calming down as she realised just how little time she now had, Mab made her way through the track between the thorns that led to the clearing on the far side of the island. There were no clouds and the moon was up – just half its size – and even before she reached the glade she kept getting flashes from the sword's hilt to urge her on.

She stood in front of the stone for several minutes before walking right the way around it many times. The top of the stone was flat enough for a man to sleep upon without hanging over the sides and the sword was thrust through directly in its centre. Once upon the boulder she gave the sword a pull. It wouldn't move but she knew that with the right spell the sword would come out like a hot knife in butter.

Grinning she turned and ordered Mordred to open up her bag. Time to start mixing.

TWENTY-THREE

I sat on the incline and looked down at the stones. The half-moon was so bright that it lit up the circle almost like day. The shadows were long and though Merlin was flitting about here and there, when he moved into shadow I could almost feel he'd gone.

Merlin had told me this would take some time and it might be morning or later before it would work. The witch's curse on Nimue all those years ago had been so powerful that it was a miracle that she had been saved albeit at the expense of that curse now being transferred to Moon Song.

I recalled our last visit when the dragon had only half animated and even that half had been so weak, almost splitting from that part of her that was still made of stone.

Opening up my mind, as Merlin had instructed, I tried to switch off all these thoughts and just listen to what might be happening around and about.

It was quiet! I thought perhaps it was possibly too quiet. I was alert to what was happening around me but also kept my eyes on the circle.

But so much had happened that day and now my mind drifted off. I was so glad that Kate was safely back home. Did Rhianne know? Was she still fretting about her? Oh, we needed to find her quickly and put her mind at ease. Did that witch now know that my child was safe? Was she doing anything else to try and snatch her? A cold feeling stole up my spine. We would need to get everything done as quickly as we could so that I could be reunited with my family. And so on!

Was I listening to the things that might be happening around and about? I thought I was! Did I think that whatever might be happening Merlin would know anyway and warn me to be vigilant? I'd hoped so! Did I wonder whether what he was doing was so important that he could not do other than concentrate on that? Was he relying on me to keep watch – trusting me to be faithful – be a man for once?

Did I hear anyone creep up behind me and knock me out? No! Not until I woke up slung across the back of a horse in front of an extremely smelly rider with long pointed ears, tied hand and foot and gagged and with an excruciatingly painful bump on the back of my head.

I looked around but didn't see Merlin. Surely they would have seen him and done the same to him! Perhaps Merlin was much better at keeping to the plan than I. Well, there was obviously no "perhaps" about it; he obviously was and I would be in for the biggest telling off of my life when he saw me again. Then I went cold! Perhaps I wouldn't see any of them again.

I was dug in the ribs by the knee of my captor and decided that the only thing I could do was try and relax, regain my strength and try and think of a way of escape as soon as these ropes were removed.

It was morning – late morning by the height of the sun on this chilly late autumn day and we were headed east. There were masses of men, um, slug-goblins, most atop large horses. The place smelt awful as these beings kept gobbing balls of spittle everywhere. We stopped often – when there was enough grass or leaves for both horse and rider and then, refreshed, they remounted and rode hard and fast until they reached the next place of plenty. No-one bothered to give me anything to either eat or drink. By the time night fell I was almost delirious and don't think I could have escaped if they'd paid me to. I was tied to a tree by a stream and just about managed to reach the water with one hand. It took a lot of palmfuls to quench my raging thirst. When my stomach, which was grumbling away like Old Jake's – my dad's old handyman who was as miserable as sin – used to do, allowed, I finally drifted off into a world of mad and crazy dreams where the slug-goblins had decided I was edible and had started to eat me. I could see Merlin flying around on the back of Moon Song but they didn't see me as I was being consumed. I tried to climb out of my dream but it wouldn't allow me and it was just as they got to my shoulders that I awoke, screaming like a banshee, to find that they were lifting me by said shoulders and were frog-marching me back over to the horse. Phew, my legs were actually moving under me – they had not been eaten and I was also relieved to find that my arms, though being gripped to my sides, were still intact.

The dream vanished behind me like a summer morning's mist as the logical part of my brain got a grip on reality.

I looked around as best I could. The stars (after the earlier evening's rain – from which I had also been able to grab a little moisture) gave enough light for me to see that there were only a few of us moving; the rest of the camp must have still been asleep.

The commander of this half of the slug-goblin army was giving instructions to his men and it was with relief that this time I was allowed to ride. My belly was bruised and sore from all the jolting I'd suffered whilst being carried face down across the horse's back.

'Don't try to escape,' the commander warned me. 'They have instructions to kill you if you try.' I just about understood all he said as his voice hissed through slack rubbery lips.

We left the camp at a cracking pace. I had a slug-goblin on either side of me, one of them holding the reins. Have you ever tried to ride a galloping horse without holding the reins? I had to weave my fingers into the hair on the back of my horse's head. We moved quite quickly but steadily down into the valley. Not many of the dwellings showed signs of life at this time of night and, actually, I wasn't even sure what that time might be in any event.

We had reached the water's edge and I was pulled swiftly across the fast flowing water by a glassy-eyed boatman before I realised where we were. I went cold! She was here wasn't she? And now I was here too!

And as if to confirm it, 'Ah there you are Percy!' She grinned down at me, holding a filthy arm forward to help me from the coracle. Funny how you notice things even in the direst of circumstances – she must have got a bit wet quite recently because her usually filthy arm was striped with pink as she held it down to me, streams of water had obviously poured down it washing away some of the grime and highlighting that which hadn't seen the light of day for years.

I pulled my arm out of her grasp as quickly as I could and tried to stop myself from shaking. Looking around I attempted to gauge how many goblins there were and if it was possible for me to escape. Surely the water wasn't too cold at this time of year! We'd had a wonderfully warm summer so it shouldn't be.

'Now, Percy – I know you were here when Myrddin encased the sword into that stone,' she chatted away as though we were about to take tea together with the vicar. I was wary; I knew what happened when she sounded so nice. 'And,' and she put great emphasis on that word, 'that he's been training you up with some urgency over the last few weeks, so I thought you'd be just the right person to let me know how he did it and then I can pull it out.'

She stared up at me, and that was something in itself; she had always looked down at me before. She'd always been an imposing figure, standing only a few inches shorter than Merlin, but now I reckon I must have grown much taller than her since the last time we'd met or that awful (and increasing by the day) amount of weight she was carrying was pulling her downward.

I stared over her head. I knew she had the power to hypnotise and there was no way I wanted to be drawn down deep into that crazy brain of hers. I said nothing.

'Oh well,' she seemed to be trying to penetrate my mind, 'let's go into the clearing and see what our friend is up to.'

Friend?

We wended our way through the path between the thorn bushes until, being prodded from behind by the witch, I stepped into the clearing. I knew what I would see and with the moon staring down with a somewhat interested look on her face I saw her reflection beaming back at me from that part of the highly polished blade that stuck out of the rock.

Then that creature stepped out from behind it. I had never seen the hobgoblin quite so close before and though he looked bad enough, he absolutely oozed evil.

I would have stepped back, except the witch shoved me forward and as she did so that creature moved just as quickly and in the blink of an eye was directly in front of me. He, too, smelled really bad – like rotting meat. My mind started going off into one of its over-imaginative moments when in just a few seconds I wondered whether the hobgoblin himself was rotting (but he didn't look as though he was) or whether he had rolled in something (my previous dog – not Cabal – used to roll in foxes poo and used to smell almost as bad) and it was that that was making him smell so bad or whether he was cannibalistic and what I could smell was rotting flesh being breathed all over me. Was I about to be eaten? *Get a grip Percy*, I told myself as I shook the thoughts away.

'You can come with me and show me how it was done,' Mab carried on "chatting" as the creature, talons on the end of its skinny arm extended, tried to grab me to pull me over to the stone but I kept it at bay as I voluntarily moved across the clearing. I just didn't want it touching me.

I walked around the rock trying desperately to think of something I could do or whether it was possible to escape. I glanced quickly at the edge of the water where Poseidon had risen. Was he still there? If I called to him would he help me? Would he even hear my call? All that in a split second as I realised that that was just not going to happen. After completing one circuit I stepped back and stared at the sword. I could feel everyone's eyes on me, waiting for me to come up with some solution as to how to get the sword out. I could feel myself getting hot – then cold.

Clearing my throat, which had constricted quite painfully, I asked, 'What have you already done?'

'What have I … ,' she started to boil.

Before she exploded, I re-jigged my question. 'I need to know what has already happened here,' I was desperately trying to recall all my training from the last couple of months. 'If I know, then I shall also know what magic is still hanging around and how to deal with it; if I don't, then it might end up worse.' I knew I was blithering and that she probably knew that anyway, but I was desperately playing for time. I mean I couldn't let her get the sword out of the stone, could I? I also didn't want to be murdered because I hadn't! I was fighting for my life here and I really didn't have anything close to a good feeling about the outcome.

She glared at me for well over a minute during which time I was searching all the cupboards in my brain. My first thought was dragon's droppings, but I didn't have any on me at that time. Why was that? Merlin always made sure I had some in a pouch around my neck. Naiad root? No! So I only had what was in my head and all those cupboards in my brain were not only closed at the moment but also seemed to be double-bolted.

I could hear her telling me what they'd tried already, ticking everything off on her fingers and, though I was listening with only half an ear – and that's a weird expression isn't it? Half an ear! How can you listen with half an ear? What does that mean? Does it mean that you would only hear half the story? Would you only have to give half an answer? The mind boggles! Sorry, I digress. Though I was hearing bits of what she was saying I was trying to figure out how to stop her, how to get away and how to warn Merlin and the others. I was searching the area for help, clues, a boat, while with my mind in a whirl looked for answers.

Then I saw her. She sat high in a tree just outside the edge of the clearing. I blinked twice before I realised it was her – she was sitting so still.

'Look away and don't speak to me, Percy, or she will hear. But delay her, I shall go and fetch Merlin. I shall ask you where he is and you just nod when I get the right place.' This was achieved within seconds. Queen Gisele spoke no more and was gone. I blinked and searched again but she wasn't there any more. Had I dreamed it? And was Merlin still where I'd last seen him?

Then I realised all was very quiet. The hobgoblin was staring at me and Mab was staring at where I was staring.

'What are you looking at? Why do you keep nodding?'

'Me?' I squeaked, coughed and then repeated, 'Me?' again in a more manly way.

'Well, who else?'

'Nothing! I was trying to concentrate on what you were saying.'

'Well, you've now heard what I've done and that it hasn't worked and now I want to know from you what Myrddin did and how it can be reversed.'

Then I had a bit of an inspiration. Oh, I just love it when that happens, don't you? However, Merlin says that I haven't got the wit to have inspirations and that it is he, even from a great distance, who puts these things into my head. Well, whether it is or isn't I am happy because I've either had the inspiration myself or Merlin knows where I am and is helping me, so I feel much better for it – a completely win win situation all round (hopefully).

'Well, we had Poseidon here,' I started.

'Yes, yes, I know that,' she interrupted.

'Please, let me say it my way,' I responded. Wow, I'm getting brave eh?

She stood there fuming – clenching and unclenching her hands but give it to her, for once she kept quiet.

'Merlin called Poseidon up from the deep as he stood on this stone and held the sword high.' I spoke slowly, loudly and clearly; no-one would be able to dispute that I had not been as clear as crystal. 'As he stood thus, he called up the god.' The next bit I spoke with great relish though hid my enjoyment of the disclosure. 'To enable the sword to be manipulated into the stone Poseidon had to saturate the whole area with water.'

I was staring at the witch as I spoke and watched as first she stepped back and then, even through all that grime, she blanched.

'Impossible!' she exclaimed.

'It is the only way!'

'There must be another way,' she was almost choking on the words as they struggled past her lips.

She slumped down onto the ground and leaned back against the trunk of a tree.

The hobgoblin clattered up beside her on his cloven feet. They sat for an extremely long time, heads together, discussing I know not what, but it gave me some more time to think and plan – well my plans were once again under the heading of "I'm making it up as I go along" which meant that if this happened I would do that, if that happened I would do this, and if nothing happened I would have to start again or hope I had yet another inspirational moment – and stuff like that.

I daren't think directly about Gisele or Merlin because I felt sure they would pick up on it, so I kept my mind only on what I might be able to do with the subject at hand.

Fortunately I was left alone for well over an hour, which I hoped would give everyone – by everyone I really mean Merlin in particular – enough time to know just what was going on in this place.

I was so carried away with what I had been thinking that I realised much later as I looked across to the tree that both Mab and the hobgoblin had gone. Was I free? I jumped up only to find that Mab was on the other side of the stone; she had set up a trestle and was mixing, pouring, bubbling this and that and looked, funnily, quite happy.

The hobgoblin was nowhere to be seen.

TWENTY-FOUR

Nell's son, not as used to riding as sailing, was having a little difficulty controlling the sprightly horse as he tried to get it to keep pace with Wirra. Gwen and Rhianne, obviously keeping themselves at a safe distance, followed some half length or more behind and Eddie was at the rear chatting with one of the half-dozen other men that accompanied them as they urged their mounts on to catch up with the rest of the party.

'*Rhianne – come over here. Make an excuse.*' Just moving her eyes, Rhianne looked over at the copse of trees they were passing and saw Queen Gisele balanced halfway up a spruce.

'You'll have to excuse me a moment,' she whispered to Gwen, blushing.

'We'll walk on slowly,' the young woman replied. 'But don't be too long.'

Rhianne turned her horse's head and moved over to the trees, making sure she was well hidden from her friends before she dismounted and looked up at the queen.

'Things are moving rapidly, Rhianne,' she spoke normally but in a whisper. 'Our chamberlain has gone to Sir Ector's home to speak to Iris, who has been saved along with your babe.'

Along with the overwhelming relief at knowing that our daughter was safe, receipt of which information almost made her collapse was the problem of letting the others know. '*Now how am I going to be able to tell the others this?*' she thought.

'Oh,' the tiny queen spoke again in whispers, 'you will have to tell them about me now, though they might not believe you and think your circumstances may be leading you to lose your mind. Well, you'll think of something no doubt. It's just that I don't really like showing myself to strangers, even if I know I can trust them. Anyway, let me finish, as I have to leave as quickly as I can.

'Sir Ector has sent riders far and wide to gather an army. He has apprised the lords and kings around of the serious threat to each of them; many have subsequently pledged their allegiance to him. He has amassed quite a few hundred men but that is not nearly enough and he needs to be on the march very soon. The slug-goblins are at least ten thousand in number and are dirty fighters. They are at Mab's beck and call; in fact I am not at all convinced that they are doing it voluntarily or, for that matter, are real beings! They may be her inventions. They may just be wicked. Whatever they are they are certainly not normal and seem only too happy to do Mab's bidding.

'That apart, once Sir Ector is ready – and he needs to be ready very soon, he will need to bring his army to London as swiftly as he can.

'London! Why London?'

'That is where it will all happen. The sword has been thrust into the boulder and only the true king of Britain will be able to pull it out! Word has gone out to everyone in the land that if they believe they are the one true king they will have to congregate in London and try to pull it out.

'Secondly, Arthur and the others think Kate is still at Carn Euny at Sancreed so my husband is on his way to stop them trying to fight their way in through five thousand slug-goblins on a wild goose chase; though they might meet up with them sooner as I understand they are on the march – Arthur will certainly perish if that were to happen.

'Merlin is at the stones trying to revive Moon Song and, lastly, the witch has captured Percy. Sorry Rhianne, there isn't a way of saying that other than the way it is.'

Rhianne, who had once more mounted her horse, almost fell off again. Recovering her emotions and straightening her back she held her head high before responding to the queen. 'And where has she taken him?' Her voice, even to her, was now softer than a whisper.

'Thorney Island in London – that is where the sword is. He appears to be all right at the moment as he is making it difficult for the witch to try and remove the sword from the stone but it won't be long before she loses patience – what she has of it – and he'll then be in a bit of a fix. My husband has gone to find Arthur and he should, even now, have told him where you are and he and they should be on their way back here. I think that once you've all met up you should head for Thorney Island at once; maybe you will meet up with your father on the way.

'Arthur is a great tactician, I know, and in the normal course of warfare would stand a good chance of winning, but the witch doesn't play by any rules other than her own so when I leave you I'll go and let Merlin know where you are and that you are on your way to London; I'll also let him know what is happening with regard to the slug-goblins and Mab; that is, if he doesn't already know.'

They quickly said their goodbyes and Rhianne soon rejoined the others and told them what had happened.

Wirra and Eddie were astounded and were extremely put out that they hadn't seen the Faerie queen – if she really existed.

'Oh, you should have called us over. I've never seen the Faerie before; in fact if you hadn't told us, well I, for one, wouldn't have believed you. But, just think, a tiny person!'

Wirra went off into a daydream while Eddie took over. 'Will she come back? Will we see her next time?'

Gwen told them to grow up! 'Rhianne has told us some news that is very disquieting and all you can think of is the Faerie. Come, let us with all speed try and meet up with Arthur; we need to combine our forces and make haste to London.'

Rhianne said no more. She was much in awe of the red-headed young woman who seemed so strong, where she was not quite as bold. *I suppose it's because she has been used to being brought up with older brothers.* She had forgotten Kay, but then again, Kay was so much older than her and had been away a lot; also, even though she could use the sword to a degree, she had no appetite for warfare, whereas this other young woman seemed eager for it.

They urged their horses into a gallop; Nell's Son believed they should be able to catch up with the others long before nightfall. Oh how the fates conspire some times and laugh at our futile attempts to succeed in our plans.

If Moon Song had been in flight at that time she would have looked down at the line of hills that separated the north from the south and would have seen one group of people pushing their horses to the limit riding east and another doing exactly the same going west – both groups separated by that mocking line of hills. Rhianne had put up her barriers so that the witch or anyone else would not be able to tune in to her thoughts but, unfortunately, obeying Merlin to the letter, Salazar and Cabal had done the same.

And Moon Song was not in flight so the two sets of friends continued on in opposite directions.

Merlin sat on the central rock inside the stone circle and stared at Moon Song. Her head turned; she looked at him with scarlet eyes wracked with pain as she moved this way and that and arched her back in an effort to rise – but her feet both fore and aft were still firmly in the grip of stone. There was now a very large crack where her animated body reached that which was still mineralised and Merlin was afraid she might break completely. Rising up and walking over to her, whilst speaking softly in that language that only the two of them understood, he got her to stop or the damage might be irreparable. Laying his whole body alongside her huge face he lifted one hand and stroked it.

He had tried so many spells and potions, even the one that he had known would heal her – but had not – that by now his sense of uselessness was beginning to take over the dragon's thoughts as well. Her warmth was diminishing; the redness of her scales was mostly ashen and her breath icy – she was turning back to stone.

Merlin's intake of breath was a shudder and the look in his eyes was one almost of horror. He had to find a way to make her well; she had to be as she once was – he couldn't contemplate life without Moon Song.

Something had to be done – fast.

But what?

And then it hit him! 'I have to place the magic in her at the time she was young – in the days of long ago; back through the mists of time. It had to be there in place before the witch ever had an opportunity to use her wickedness on her. If it was in place before anything was given her or any spell cast upon her she would be safe. Why oh why didn't I think of this before? Then she can fight this dread curse from the inside instead of me trying to remove it externally.

'Now, I need to go to Avebury and find the stone that is a doorway. And where is Percy?

'Percy! Percy!'

After searching fruitlessly for me he eventually gave up. Turning to Moon Song, he explained what he was going to do. She settled down, trustingly, and waited the long wait. It was almost a relief to be able to sleep; to turn from the agonising pain; to drift away again. Merlin, with eyes of compassion, watched her turn once more to stone and, packing his few belongings into the capacious pockets of his cloak, he picked up his staff and left.

He had another quick look around for me again until he found the disturbed ground and a few blood splattered blades of grass mingled with gobs of spittle; rightly discerning what had occurred he shrugged his shoulders with the thought that I could now look after myself and in any event he could return in moments to sort everything out. *'Well, I mean, don't I always have to do absolutely everything?*

'I only hope that my time away, though possibly a very long time, will only be minutes here,' he thought. However, he couldn't think too much about the troubles here; Moon Song and her role in saving Britain was much too important for that.

It's a good job I wasn't able to have linked in to his thoughts at that time or I would not only have been extremely miffed but very scared as well.

So, there they all were – every one of them ignorant of everyone else's movements; all thinking that they knew what was going on; all probably being laughed at by Mad Mab and her henchmen. Two groups of people were passing each other on each side of one of the groups of hills, another captured by a nutty female of horrendous proportions and even bigger stench on an island overlooking London, one more trying to raise an army – and now another one of their party moving out of time completely.

Was she watching? Did she have them in view in some infernal cauldron and was she stirring them all up.

No – don't let us give her credit for all of our problems.

TWENTY-FIVE

Sir Ector had mellowed a lot since the birth of his first grandchild. He had been worried sick when it had been discovered that she had been abducted. But now he was all grandfatherly protection and care as he cooed and clucked over Kate.

Lady Elise lifted her eyes and smiled at the scene. Having always been a very nervous and fragile being she was never so happy as when domestic bliss reigned. However, in the back of her mind she knew it wouldn't last – it never did, so the smile had a tinge of sadness shadowing it.

'Well, my dear,' he turned and looked at his wife. 'By the evening of St Canice's day we should be ready; however, St Luke's day may be more propitious, especially if the Duke of Cornwall is to be believed. He has grudgingly agreed to help us fight these monsters but is not sure how many warriors he can muster and how quickly. I've had to agree for him to lead, though as we all know he is a trifle unstable – *I would have put it more that he was deranged* – but he does have a very large army, so beggars cannot be choosers.

'Sir Philip from Mercia has agreed to stand with me to keep an eye on the man and he has over fifteen hundred foot soldiers and at least two hundred on horseback. And then there is Sir Malcolm, though he tends to like hacking off heads with that great heavy sword of his; mind you, because he is so famous for it, nearly everyone runs a mile when they see him coming; including his own men!'

Sir Ector continued bouncing his granddaughter on his knee and laughing at her as he informed Lady Elise of his plans; it made his wife's skin crawl as she heard him recount one bloodthirsty thing after another while at the same time, incongruously making it look like a fairy story as he played and laughed with Kate.

'My dear, you are making me feel very unwell,' she was at last able to say.

'Oh, how thoughtless of me,' he cried, stepping across the room and putting his other arm around her. 'I was so carried away with what is happening and playing with Kate that I completely forgot I was thinking out loud. Forgive me, my dear.' He placed the giggling Kate into his wife's arms before taking his leave, something that the child took exception to as she had been having such a great time with her grandfather.

'I'll send the maid in to you. Perhaps dinner is on the way eh?' he added hopefully, making his escape as the indignant youngster now started to scream.

Before long Kate had been whisked away by Iris and the lady was alone. Placing her embroidery on the chair beside her she stood up and walked across to the window. Outside the late autumn wind was swirling the leaves into rivers that seemed to run hither and thither across the courtyard. Evening was early now. The vendors had packed up their wares and had gone home long ago.

It had been a wonderful day – lots of stalls with the abundance of harvest spilling over them – rosy apples, freshly baked bread, cabbages and turnips galore. But then mid-afternoon had brought squally gusts and clouds that made everyone gather up their remaining goods and leave.

It was still cloudy so no moon or stars lit up the surrounding countryside. Even with the huge fire in the hearth, Lady Elise felt a sudden chill, a premonition, and a terrible fear taking shape and crushing her with cold, iron-clad hands. Was it because Sir Ector was going away? Was it because not only would there be no strong men to watch over them – and not only her husband's men but all of the warriors in the surrounding lands? Even Kay, who was not as strong as most men, would have made her feel better but he had also gone away.

She could feel the tears start in her eyes but then, angry with herself for allowing these fancies to frighten her, she shook them away and was determined to be brave – or at least try to look to be.

There was only Sir Ector with Lady Elise at dinner and they ate quietly – one because he loved his food and was too busy concentrating on it; the other because she was frightened to say anything in case her fear was to show. She ate hardly a thing!

'Well, I think I shall have an early night. Sir Philip will be here some time tomorrow and I need my rest. We will have a lot to talk about. Don't rush my dear if you wish to stay up longer; I shall be asleep as soon as I lie down. Tell Old Molly the meal was delicious. Eat up! Eat up my dear!'

Once more she was alone. She walked over to the chair near the dying fire, picked up her embroidery and silks. But her needlework went unheeded in her lap as she stared at the guttering flames. Was it her imagination or were imps dancing around the embers and spiralling up the chimney in an occasional mad frenzy? Not having had much imagination in her life up to now it was a surprise to her that she saw this little play being acted out in front of her.

'Did you want anything else m'lady,' one of the housemaids asked making her jump.

'No. You can ask my maid to go to my room and make preparation for me. I shall be up shortly.'

Once more alone, she jumped when a sudden gust of wind blew down the chimney, scattering sparks across the stone flags which danced over the floor until, going out one by one, the darkness they left behind was almost all consuming. Again that feeling of dread threatened to overcome her; however, wrapping her shawl more tightly around her shoulders she placed her embroidery on top of its box, hurried out of the hall and up to her room.

In one area of the hall, darker than all the others, a being moved forward into the light; goat-like feet clicked upon the stone floor a couple of times before it stepped back into the shadow.

Tapping a small container with one elongated claw he would wait until the whole house was aslumber before he would carry out the witch's orders.

TWENTY-SIX

The leaning man – at last Merlin found him. He had taken the almost direct route to Avebury and there he was – the stone that was shaped roughly like a man that was thinking as he leaned forward with hands behind his back.

Tapping the stone with the silver head of his staff he eventually found that for which he had been searching. Transferring his staff into his left hand he placed his right hand against the stone; it was warm.

Immediately the words, incomprehensible to everyone else – that would normally have been said as a song with the dragon – poured out of his mouth. If I had been there I would have had my hands over my ears; it only ever sounded wonderful when Moon Song joined in but on his own Merlin's singing, for that was what it was supposed to be, was ear-splittingly awful.

However, it worked! One moment he was there and the next, along with that dreadful noise, he was gone.

He later told me about his journey, which I shall tell you here, as here is when it happened.

Being dragged into and through stone, even the magical stones of the various henges, is not something to be desired. First, it is quite uncomfortable as you feel like you are being dragged through even though your whole being is trying to stay where it is, like a huge elastic band being pulled to its utmost extremity. Every time I do this, and I really try to do it as little as possible, I feel as though I might be pulled so greatly that I'll snap or, and this I am greatly afraid of, that just like an elastic band I might be pinged off into a dimension that because I didn't know where I was going I might never find my way back and be lost forever. One of the worst thoughts, though, is that when I am released it might just be to travel so fast that I'd be crushed against that stone instead of passing through it. However,' Merlin chuckled as he added, 'that hasn't happened otherwise I wouldn't be here talking to you would I?' Sometimes, however, one would travel so easily that it seemed completely normal, even though the journey would be over miles or time in a split second. I suppose that was the fun of it – one never knew which it would be. Merlin continued:

I was thrust into outer darkness where there was no moon; there were no stars or any other planets where I might be able to discern my position. I felt like I was swimming in the night-time sky but didn't know in which direction to swim. It was like swimming through mud! I held my staff aloft and set it to beam a light before me but it was a waste of time as the light was completely consumed by the darkness around it: it showed nothing before me, behind, below or above. I was suspended in space! It was a scary time, I can tell you.

It seemed like hours, or even days, or maybe years, who knows? But then, again, I was going a long way back to the beginning of Moon Song's life and she, like me, was born such a long, long time ago.

As I drifted I began to recall many things – how long ago it was that I was initiated into the ways of the Druid; all the kings and emperors I had met, helped or helped to defeat; the good, the wicked; my hates and my loves. It was when I came to my loves that I remembered Nimue. My heart melted within me. It was all for her, you know – everything was for her – and for me – one day!

She is the love of my life, you know. I nearly died because of her. Well, it wasn't really because of her it was because of what that mad witch had done to her that was the cause of it all.

Now, because I am always so busy and never really have time to do anything, let alone ruminate on times past, I generally don't think about what has happened in the past, but now, well it seemed I had all the time in the world, if not all eternity.

So, I recalled my time with Nimue.

She was so young, and, well, so was I at the time – when the world was young – and innocent – to a degree, that is – there always seemed to be some form of wickedness lurking behind a tree, within a still pond, or somewhere. Well, there we were – me being taught by Gaius, my mentor, and Nimue just a young woman among other young women in the hamlet.

But as soon as our eyes met we knew we were meant for each other. Gaius, who was one of the wisest Druids I had ever met, approved of our choice of each other but said that we would have to wait, as I needed to finish my education. Times were coming when he would not be here any more – and he did hint that when his time had come it would be a terrible end for him but he would not elaborate – and I would help lead Britain to victory and peace.

He asked me to choose but added that if I wasn't trained and ready, Britain would be in danger and then who would be able to help defend it – or any of their loved ones? If Britain was overcome by her enemies even Merlin would not be able to help – or help Nimue either, come to that!

So did I have a choice?

Thus, for years and years I was at the side of Gaius. I would sometimes see Nimue and maybe spend a few moments talking to her, but that was about it. It was painful but I knew my destiny. I wish that at that time I had also known hers!

She was beautiful; she waited for me. I sometimes think that Gaius kept her young (just as I never appeared to age – except when a spell made it necessary) just for me.

This went on for many a year until one day I realised I hadn't seen her for so long that I believed something must have happened to her. Had she died?

I asked Gaius but he said he had been too busy to notice; he tried to discern where she might be but said there was some sort of veil stopping him.

I became frantic and knowing it would be useless to try and teach me something in my present state of mind he told me to go and find her.

I don't know how long I searched or how long I would be away from my education but every time I asked anyone if they had seen her they always said they had and pointed me onward.

I went through many hot, dry summers and freezing winters before coming across that awful castle late one autumn day. She was singing a sad, melancholy song. I heard her before I saw her – she was sitting beside a quiet lake with the castle rising tall and sheer behind her.

I called and she turned; then, seeing it was I, ran as fast as she could into my arms. She wept, as did I as we held on to each other.

She was asking me how I had found her while I, talking at the same time, was asking why she had come here.

She eventually placed a finger over my lips and said that a wonderful lady had found her and had been looking after her. She had told her she had magical powers and had been teaching her to do amazing things.

'Come,' she had said, laughing, 'Let me take you to her.'

And that was when I first came into contact with the witch!

We entered the castle – the like of which I had never seen before. It was mighty, to put it mildly. Sheer grey, granite walls reached from all sides seemingly to the sky; one side swept straight down into the lake. There were round turrets at the top on each corner – and that was just the outside. Inside the courtyards were dusty and bare, with the keep to the right as we went through the small door that was let into the larger double-gated doors.

Inside the keep I was introduced to a seemingly homely woman of indeterminate age who was not too bad looking. She had a mop of curly blonde hair and pale blue eyes. Her smile, a little forced I thought, was welcoming. She was not slim but she was not fat either; she was just a normal looking woman. There was, though, a bit of a funny smell about the place.

I really cannot remember just how long I was at that castle; suffice to say that over the course of at least a week I was being steadily poisoned.

I happened upon the two women late one evening, when a bout of sickness and stomach pains had caused me to rise from my bedchamber and seek something to alleviate the problem. Halfway to the kitchen door I collapsed, my legs unable to carry me any further. With my head on my knees and trying desperately to keep down my bile, I wiped my forehead and then rested my head back against the coolness of the stone wall just underneath the kitchen window, hoping that my nausea would soon pass.

I was just beginning to feel a little better and was about to get up and move on when I heard them talking. Normally I would not eavesdrop but something in Nimue's voice made me stay where I was. I did think that if she was in some sort of trouble there was no way I could do anything about it in my current weak state, but even my health up to that point had not really concerned me; I really just thought I'd eaten something that had disagreed with me. So, listening, this is what I overheard.

'I really don't want to do this any more,' Nimue was saying.

'But if you don't, you know what I shall do to your family – first to your mother, then your father and then all of your brothers and sisters. Could you really live with yourself if you knew it was in your power to save them? Could you really live with yourself if you thought that you were the reason they had to suffer?'

'But I love him and this is killing me to do this!'

'I'll kill you if you don't!'

'Have mercy!'

'Hah! You don't know me at all do you? Look,' she continued, sounding like the most reasonable person in the world, 'at least I am putting you under my spell when you do it and so you cannot recall doing it; but it is so much fun when you have done it for me to bring you round and tell you just what you have done and to bring it all back into your memory! Well, I mean, it would be very unfair of me to keep it all from you, wouldn't it? You'd really want to know just what you had done, wouldn't you?'

The younger woman started weeping.

'Oh don't give me all that!'

'Why do you want to kill him?'

'Oh, I don't want to kill him,' she shouted. 'I want him under my spell.

'Look, there's a prophecy about a future king and apparently one day Myrddin is going to help him. If I can get him under my control I can use him to help me rid us of this king. The sooner he is in my power the better – mind you, I didn't realise how strong he is and if it doesn't happen soon it might kill him.'

I crept away.

The next morning I walked into the kitchens glassy eyed and stiff of limb.

I sat down and plonked both hands onto the table beside my plate and just gazed ahead.

The witch stared at me. She clicked her fingers in front of my face and flicked my ears to see if there was any reaction.

None!

She squeezed my earlobes until the blood came to the surface; I continued to stare ahead.

'Hah,' she exclaimed. 'Good! He's ready.'

I had felt really ill through the night but I had kept myself awake and had used all the enchantments I could recall to keep myself safe from whatever I had consumed already and from whatever else she might have in mind. In fact, I needn't have worried too much because in those days, although she was well on the road in her craft, she was still a novice, compared to me. She had been relying on her own wisdom but the greatest Druid of that time had taught me.

Using a lot of her chants and spells she believed she was overpowering me with her hypnotic magic and after two days of gyratings and enchantings she sent me on my way.

It was a struggle between her magic and my barrier and also my doggedness that I would only leave if Nimue went with me.

That was almost hysterical. As she opened the door and commanded me to leave I just stood there and said in as wooden a voice as I could muster, 'She comes!'

Mab pooh poohed me and said I was to go on my own.

I stood there almost to attention and just kept repeating 'She comes,' every time she ordered me to leave.

Eventually, after almost three hours, she had to agree.

Once we got out of sight of the castle and were well into the forest I collapsed with laughter. Poor Nimue had thought me really under her spell and after being a bit miffed that she had been taken in as well as the witch, joined in with me and we laughed on and off for quite a bit of our journey.

The spells Mab had used were to make me meet up one day with Arthur and in the course of our time put him in a position where he would be killed. Phew, I tell you, it was good to have this information from all that time ago – I've been able to be on my mettle ever since.

At that time the prophecy had only told us of a future king; it was much, much later that the realisation it was Arthur came to any of us – centuries, in fact.

For the time being though, it was important we got away from Mab. Nimue and I travelled as fast as we could and since that time I have tried to keep her safe, though that has been very difficult because since the witch initiated her into the arts she has been too interested in magic for her own good. On the odd occasion the witch has tried to get her claws into her again but so far my spell of protection has worked, well up to the time she was enchanted and had to live within Moon Song, that is.

Getting back to my dark journey. As I said, I really don't know how long I floated in space but I didn't waste my time. I went over and over all my training, spells, enchantments, powders, etc, and I believe came out stronger with the remembrance of them all. Till one day –

A whisper, a beckoning curl of a misty finger – and then the Lady of the Lake broke into my isolation.

'I have come to take you back to when Moon Song was young.'

She took my hand in her diaphanous one and we flew – out of that all-consuming darkness and over the green fields and forests of Britain, across the wild waters of the sea that lay between our Isle and that of the main land mass, sweeping low over sweet-smelling lemon trees, olive groves and warm vineyards, soaring high over freezing, snow-covered mountains, then low over sun dried deserts until we eventually descended into the gentle valley of dragons where beautiful waterfalls kept the land abounding in such lush vegetation that it enabled both bird, beast and butterfly to live in perfect harmony.

You should see such a place! Dragons and people living amicably side by side. The people worship them and spend all their time growing crops for them. Dragons are really vegetarian, you know; they only attack when they sense danger. The land is well watered and is lush with all sorts of plants and trees. The sun rises – a ball of red which lights up the skies with pinks, oranges and crimson, until it shines above the hills, glistening and glinting on the drops of dew that sparkle in the trees and fields. It's a wonderful place. But I could wax lyrical about this place for too long I think.

The Lady, continuing to hold my hand, took me to meet the keeper of this paradise – Hei Lei. I don't recall her leaving but suddenly I searched and she was gone.

Hei Lei and I spoke for hours. We spoke through our minds. He was sad as he told me that the day of the dragon was drawing to a close. I told him that I had come from the future and though what he told me was happening, there were some dragons that still walked the earth. I told him about Moon Song and he smiled. He said she was one of his best dragons. I also told him about Helion;

he frowned. He had been strong and he had been good once – till the witch stole him away. He dreaded to think what that awful woman had done to him; he must have suffered greatly at her hand. '*As we had at his*,' I thought – but this directly behind my barriers.

I explained as briefly as I could what had happened to Moon Song and what needed to be done so that she might survive.

'Come with me,' he spoke very softly, with a sad look to his face.

We were taken to the "nursery" into which he disappeared, finally returning with a very small – well eight feet long actually – red dragon at the end of a leash.

'This is Moon Song,' he said as I knelt down to look into her eyes.

She nuzzled against me and I knew it really was her. I murmured several inane things into her ear and almost jumped as she spoke into my mind.

'Yes, she is yours. They can all communicate – but only with the one destined to be their master – so she belongs to you. She is young but she can do that already,' Hei Lei chuckled. 'Whatever you have to do to her, tell her now; she will be acquiescent.

I explained to Moon Song what would happen in the future and that to enable me to release her from the terrible danger she would find herself in I needed to enchant her now so that when it happened I could effectively say the spell of releasing.

She said that that was good and whatever I needed to do I should do it.

So I did.

I gave her something really sour to drink but she swallowed it without complaining; she didn't even cough, though if she had it would have been all right because she hadn't yet acquired her flame throwing skills.

I was so overcome at her beauty and goodness that I started to sing.

(I can remember pulling a face when Merlin told me this but he ignored me.)

Anyway, as I started to sing, Moon Song joined in and the whole valley stood and listened to the beauty of it; a rainbow of colour emanated from where we stood and even when we stopped, nothing moved for so long you would have thought it a tableau.

Hei Lei eventually whispered that he had not seen this

manifestation of the supernatural in over a thousand years. Ours would truly be a mighty, powerful and lifelong bonding, when Moon Song was eventually full grown – but that wouldn't be for hundreds of years yet.

The man took us to his house where he had many beautiful things. I stayed there for several days – we had much to talk about and there was so much I needed to learn from him. Then it was time for me to leave.

Disappearing behind a screen he eventually returned with a large, pale green, almost white, jade glass. It was as big as the shield of the mightiest warrior but as light as a feather.

'Take this with you,' he commanded. 'When you want to see how Moon Song is getting on, just think of her and look into the depths of this Glass and you will see her; you can also think of whatever you like and you will see it.

'When you think of Moon Song, or anything, you can sprinkle this powder over you and you will be transported to where they are.' He handed me a small jar containing the powder – and, do you know what? It never runs out!

I made my goodbyes to Hei Lei and to Moon Song and the Lady of the Lake materialised and took me by the hand back to Avalon.

So, over the years I kept an eye on Moon Song through the Glass until one day she wasn't there any more. I had asked for the valley where she had grown up, so now I asked for her herself.

I saw her in all her adult glory flying high above a green plain until, ensuring that no-one was around to see, she circled and set herself down; once settled she lay her head upon her front paws and slept – the sleep of the ages; the slumber of stone, but one that can be re-awoken.

'But how can you have just done all this,' I had asked Merlin, 'when I know you have had the Glass all this time?'

'Ah, you still have so much to learn, Percy! Time and travel are not set in a consecutive procession; I went back along a time line, but it has offshoots and …'

He looked at my blank face and said that he would take up that part of my education when we had a lot more time. He went on with his tale:

Leaving the Lady to her mists, I returned to Moon Song. I

whispered to her until one pain-wracked eye opened. I stroked her head whilst telling her what I had done and then began speaking the enchantment, all the while dripping the bitter oil onto her tongue. Slowly, oh so slowly, the dark grey turned to ash, the ash turned to blue and the blue, with maroon glints appearing here and there, gradually turned to red from shining head to thrashing tail, all the while flashes and electrical impulses were running throughout her body – slowly and dimly at first, but picking up momentum and resonance as she grew stronger.

Then finally she trumpeted into the air before flying up and over the plain.

I stood there laughing and laughing until she settled back down into the ground, one fierce yellow eye staring straight at me.

'She will never ever be able to do anything like that to you again Moon Song – her spell over you is now completely broken.'

She thrashed her enormous tail about as she trumpeted while blasts of flame roared out of her mouth and then, climbing up behind her head and between her wings I told her where to go. She set off at a cracking pace. I only hoped I hadn't been away too long.

TWENTY-SEVEN

Encasing them both in an enchantment of invisibility and flying as high above the ground as he could without losing sight of man and beast, Merlin peered down through the night's gloom until morning's promise tinged the horizon with the faintest streak of red. He had reached the outskirts of London and, following the serpentine glints from the Thames, located the small island he had been searching for.

Percy sat with his back against a tree watching the witch. She, unaware that she was being seen by more than one pair of eyes, continued with her cutting and mixing.

'I'm back, Percy! Stop! Don't look for me; just keep still! Don't mind speak to me; just listen. She cannot hear me – I'm speaking directly and only to you. Moon Song is healthy, robust and vigorous again. We are going to find the men. Stay here and delay the witch for as long as you can. If you understand, scratch your nose.'

I scratched my nose.

'Good! I'll come back for you as soon as I know that the others are safe.'

You can have absolutely no idea how that short encounter raised my spirit and my hope. It was as much as I could do to keep the sullen look on my face and the hopeless slump to my shoulders.

'Something isn't right!' Salazar looked around at the countryside.

Shake Spear, who had ridden up beside the Druid, followed his glance but could not see anything untoward. 'There are no cattle around here – neither cow nor sheep. So why is the ground so bare? Why are there no leaves on the lower branches? It has been a mild autumn and the rest of the leaves have not yet fallen.'

Salazar looked again. Something had eaten all of the greenery.

Asking Arthur to stay with the rest of the party, Salazar and Shake Spear left the others to continue on their journey while they went to investigate.

'Look – there!' Shake Spear pointed to a spot near a copse of trees.

'An army has passed this way recently. Slugs! I think it is the witch's army of slug-goblins – there's spit everywhere. They've eaten all the grass and greenery,' he stood high in his stirrups, 'for miles!'

'They're marching east,' Shake Spear added. 'I think we should return. They're either headed to Sir Ector's or somewhere in that direction.

Salazar decided that he needed to try and contact Merlin or me and, opening up his mind, reached out.

Several things happened at once.

First, Rhianne answered, realising that they must have passed each other on the way, and told them where they were; secondly, I responded with what was happening to me on Thorney Island; thirdly Cabal replied that he was glad we were all OK, and, fourthly, Merlin cried out with:

'Danger! Danger! Close down! She might hear!'

Too late! She had!

To go back a week or so, Mab had arrived at the banks of the river near Thorney Island with half of her contingent of abnormal soldiers. In those days it was a quiet place, the main bulk of dwellings being further down and over the other side of the river. Her army set up camp and relaxed after its long march and began to systematically chomp its way through the lush grass that grew alongside the Thames; and waited for orders. She said she thought they'd only be there a day or so, so there should be enough provision for all of them until they moved off.

She had sent the hobgoblin off on a mission to scour the countryside and see what he could find and to also visit Sir Ector's and "make sure the thing did its work".

I never got to understand this creature (thank goodness really), how he travelled, where he came from, what he was made out of, etc, but I expect that he could travel great distances in a very short space of time. In fact, after what happened, I was sure he could get from A to B faster than modern day space travel.

Anyway, Mab managed to instruct him by what she had picked up from our not only careless but also reckless mind speaking conversations.

Arthur and the rest of the party had dismounted to give their ponies a rest and, leading them by the reins, moved slowly onward, all the while looking back to see where Salazar and Shake Spear had got to. The problem with looking back is that sometimes you forget to look forward, like now!

Without warning the ground, which had been rising for the last half hour, suddenly caved in and opened up before them and one by one they tumbled down the embankment, only stopping when they hit a low wall at the bottom – painful, not only to body but to pride as well. Before they could grasp a bridle or rein, the horses had galloped off.

Looking up, Arthur saw Salazar staring down at him from the top of the incline but that was to be the last he saw of him for some time, as the low wall they had fallen against began to grow around them, stone on stone, above and around them until within seconds it was more than fifty feet high; their prison was not there one minute and there the next. But Arthur took reassurance from the fact that Salazar had seen what had happened. But unfortunately, because of the spell, he hadn't! Salazar had arrived back on the scene seconds after the witch's spell had taken effect and had seen nothing except the land as it had been before the quake. Just as well Arthur didn't know that then, eh?

The lion roared, Cabal barked and the men shouted until Arthur, calling above all this noise, got them to stop. Baker and the Scribe had been knocked unconscious and though Baker recovered fairly swiftly, the Scribe was really out for the count. Androcles had placed an arm around the lion's neck and with soft words managed to pacify the beast.

'We cannot do anything or even think with all this noise going on. See to those men,' he pointed at the injured.

They finally looked around. Their prison was high – perhaps too high. Even if they stood one atop the other they would still be too low to grip the top and climb out. Arthur paced across the ground. 'It must be twenty feet in circumference,' he remarked. 'Just enough room for us all to be able to sit or lie down, should we not get out of here.

'Or die,' Wite added.

'Stop it; don't be so idiotic,' Brosc scolded his friend.

'At least the top is open so we can have light!'

'And air!' Wite breathed a sigh of relief.

Just then the light dimmed somewhat as an awful face stared down at them and grinned. Arthur turned pale as the remembrance of that face brought back the terror of several years before. It disappeared; none of the others had seen it. He thought it best not to mention it.

'Goliath,' Arthur, shaking the vision from his mind, turned to the man, 'Can you shove any of these stone slabs out? Perhaps we might be able to push together?'

But it was useless. No amount of pushing by hand, shoulder or buttocks by either Goliath or several of the men together was able to shift the stones even slightly.

Androcles voiced his concern on the second day that though he had befriended the lion in the past when he had removed the thorn from its paw, he could not be sure how the animal would react when it became overly hungry.

'Fantastic!' Brosc commented sarcastically as he and Wite looked at one another with bulging eyes!

Everyone else looked at the beast.

At least they were able to drink, it had rained, and rained, but who was complaining even though each one of them was wet through? Thirst is much worse than hunger! Well, you think so, until you get hungry that is!

Cabal had tried many times to mind speak to several of us, risking the wrath of Merlin in the doing of it, but his words just bounced right back at him.

Obviously the witch would be overjoyed at the fact that somehow she had captured a large contingent of her enemy. Had the hobgoblin told her yet? Was she, even now, planning Arthur's demise? Was she on her way?

TWENTY-EIGHT

Two whole days had passed and the lion was getting pretty twitchy. Cabal, also hungry, was wise enough to keep well away from this potentially ferocious animal.

The Scribe had been slightly delirious for most of the previous night but was now beginning to make sense. There was an enormous bump on the side of his temple, which looked red and angry but as Cabby had taken it into his head to keep licking it until it started to go down, he eventually became calm and finally slept quite peacefully. By dawn on the third morning the Scribe was lucid again and complaining of a raging thirst. There was a little water left, which everyone had been trying to capture when it rained, and giving him what they had he eventually drifted off to sleep again.

Night fell again but now no-one could stop the lion from roaring. Even Androcles, who had seemed to be able to keep it under control, was having difficulties in holding it down.

The Scribe, finally coming back to his senses, asked what on earth was going on; couldn't someone stop all that racket? Because he'd been out of it for so long, he had no idea as to where they were, how they'd got there, why they were there, why they didn't leave or why he was so hungry.

After explaining what had happened, Arthur slumped against the wall and could have wept. '... and so we've found it impossible to dig our way out, climb or break through the wall!'

'Oh, if that's all,' exclaimed the Scribe, annoying most of the people there, 'perhaps this might do it!'

At which he felt around in his belt, produced a small piece of chalk and started to draw a high rectangle upon the stone wall.

Arthur and Baker looked at each other as if to say, 'He's lost it again!' when, after drawing a handle, the Scribe turned it, pushed the "door" open and fresh air and moonlight flooded into their prison.

It took them ten seconds to realise that they were free before Arthur, taking control, ushered them all through and out into the cool evening air.

A few drops of rain were still falling but those came from the last of the clouds that were drifting away to the east and from the overhanging trees. The moon, staring benignly through those trees, lit their way, though right then and there they were not at all sure where they were going.

Cabal and the lion disappeared into the trees and no amount of calling brought them back. They were much too hungry and it would probably be better for them to eat game than any one of them – not that Cabal would eat a human; but then who knew what any animal would do if hungry enough?

'Collect some twigs and some small logs; let's build a fire.' Arthur sent some of the men off. 'Don't go too far though.'

'Won't we be discovered?'

'No – I think Mab is at the bottom of all this and she must think we are too firmly imprisoned to worry about us for the time being.'

It took ages to get the fire going; most of the area was soaked because of the rain, but once it started it wasn't long before they had quite a large bonfire blazing.

The Scribe had drawn some traps on the outside of their former prison and had caught several hare in them, so Baker cooked them over the fire and after a very short time they fed and felt a lot better; he also drew a couple of buckets by scooping out some hollows in the tree trunks so that they could fetch some water from the stream.

'Let's try and sleep; the morning might bring some inspiration,' Arthur told the men.

So, wrapped in their almost dry garments and as near to the fire as was safe, they slept as best they could.

Morning came and Arthur was awoken by an extremely wet nose being shoved into his face.

'Cab, stop it!'

Arthur's sleep had been invaded by dreams – terrible dreams of armies being slaughtered, his family disappearing, even Gwenhwyfar being abducted by the witch, hypnotised to hate him and driving a long spike through his chest, and the like. He looked haggard and in need of fresh clothes, a shave and definitely a wash, as did most of the others.

Androcles, who was still too young to shave, was sitting against the stone tower with one arm around a satisfied-looking lion. The lion had obviously eaten well during the night but, then again, he was still a lion and lions do not hunt for anyone other than themselves, so the rest of them were still hungry – a few skinny hare don't really satisfy.

'Right, we know near enough where we are,' he stated as he looked around at the hills, 'but as we now don't know what is happening, I think it best we return home. Perhaps everything has turned out for good by now.'

He didn't believe this for one moment but going round in circles, as they obviously would have been, and without a plan was definitely not going to help.

TWENTY-NINE

I awoke with a hollow feeling in my stomach, and it wasn't all due to the fact that I hadn't eaten for at least twenty-four hours. Mab was still mixing and stirring, singing and chanting and the hair started to rise at the back of my neck with the thickness of the atmosphere all around. I almost expected to see some awful apparition as the weight of wickedness pushed down upon my head. *What on earth was she up to?*

The hobgoblin returned and spent the next half hour or so whispering to the witch. The heaviness increased; I was finding it extremely difficult to breathe while a cold sweat broke out all over me.

They finally both turned and looked at me. I went suddenly light headed. He just stared – the evil look on his face was invariably the same; she, however, grinned (was I right in thinking yet another tooth had disappeared? Funny how even in the direst of situations sometimes the ridiculous dances in before you) and then threw back her head and laughed like a drain as she pointed at me.

I thought I would scream; she had obviously done, or got that devilish fiend to do it for her, something terrible.

But what? I wasn't going to ask her because I knew she'd tell me eventually; I also knew that if I tried she would draw it out so long that I might go mad – if I didn't go mad right now, that is!

She left me to my thoughts for the rest of the morning and as you can imagine I had almost written a book on the subject of what she might have done but little did I know how far even her wickedness would go.

I can recall my Uncle John telling me some of the wicked things that had taken place in the Second World War and how sick it had made him feel (and how sick it had made me feel when he told me some of them) and I think even he would have been surprised at some of the evil things this mad woman could cook up.

'So, how are you enjoying being a father?' she asked as she swayed across the clearing toward me. 'Is it fun? I expect you are able to play with her quite well, seeing as you are still a child yourself!'

I could feel the hobnailed boots of fear creeping up my spine but I kept my own counsel.

She waited for a while, peering intently at me before continuing. 'Perhaps you would have more freedom if you were rid of her eh?'

This time she got the satisfaction of my reaction.

'Ha! So I can still get to you!'

She danced around the clearing, wafting her stench around as she did so, before coming back to stand in front of me, hands on hips.

'She will die, Percy! Even now the disease has started to eat away at her! She has a raging temperature most of the time and now that she is finding it difficult to eat or drink I think it is only a matter of time before … well, you think of what comes after before!'

'What have you done, you evil monster?' I screamed at her. I couldn't help it! She had reached the core of my being. One part of me was saying that it wasn't true; that she was saying this just to get a reaction from me. The other part of me was saying that it was; she had always loathed me and now she was using her best efforts of getting back at me in a way that was worse than actually killing me.

I hated the look of satisfaction that spread across her face - distorted as it was through the tears that had sprung into my eyes – and if I hadn't been tied down I reckon I would have taken the chance and sprung at her, hoping to do some damage before she could have thrown her magic at me; as it was I strained at the rope and made my wrists bleed, which brought even more hysterical joy to the witch. The hobgoblin merely grimaced.

Flopping back against the tree I fought within myself to not call out to Merlin, to try and find a way of escaping, to search and see if there was something – anything I had learned from Merlin to counter-attack. I could feel my face first go red hot and then a cold sweat began to drape itself across my brow. My mind was going nowhere; I was much too distraught to even begin to think straight. I even called out to Arthur's God. Perhaps he might find it in his heart to do something.

All of this seemed to amuse the witch for a good few minutes before she turned and made her way back to her mixture.

'You can wait! Perhaps you will receive news of Kate's demise – some way or another!' she added as her huge backside, swaying from left to right and back again blocked out the light from the fire under the cauldron.

Then it started to rain! Was my prayer heard?

I would have laughed if my situation had been different.

Mab just screamed and took shelter, forcing the hobgoblin and Mordred to stand with a cover over either side of her bubbling mixture so it could continue to boil.

The rain became a deluge as the morning progressed until even the fire underneath the cauldron, attacked from each side by small rivers, spluttered, gave a final cough and went out. Mordred shook the cover and threw it to one side, finally taking shelter beside Mab who was so mad that it took all Mordred's strength to grab her hands and stop her beating him so hard around his head. The hobgoblin was nowhere to be seen.

I had been partially protected by the tree to which I had been tied and was getting a little excited by the fact that the ropes, now wet, were slackening. Hopefully, before too long, I might be free. I knew it would still be a problem getting off the island, let alone away from Mab, but I would cross each bridge – and I really wished there had been one to the mainland – when I came to it.

THIRTY

Arthur almost ran into Gwen and her party about three miles west of Sir Ector's caer; after taking everyone up behind them on their ponies they headed back to the hall. Rhianne would have rushed up to her brother if she hadn't still been afraid of the lion – who knew what it might do if one ran?

'We've all been going round in circles,' Arthur exclaimed, 'and have wasted so much time, it's impossible to think of what might be happening. It must have been that witch! If it hadn't been for the Scribe we would still all be incarcerated in that prison; I'm sure Mab is at the bottom of all this.'

'And we've been out searching for you since some of the ponies came back without you.'

Gwen waited until Arthur had jumped down from behind her and laid a hand on his arm before telling him what had been happening. 'We've seen how things have appeared to go wrong but we can't dwell on this. Kate has been rescued, though it has all been too much for her; over the last few days she has been quite unwell but is being looked after by the women, so all we have to do now is fight this unholy army and its evil commander.'

'*All we have to do,*' Arthur thought. '*Does she know how large this army is? Is she that brave?*' He looked at her with new eyes.

'You say that Merlin will lead us; but as he is not here we will have to devise our own plan,' she continued.

Arthur continued watching her face as she spoke and for the first time took proper notice; his mind was doing a double-take at the "acquiescent" fiancée he had expected. His interest in her was aroused; she definitely would make a great wife and undoubtedly a great captain. He mentally shook his head to clear it; how could a woman lead an army. '*No, that will never happen!*'

He had a lot to learn about his future wife!

Salazar, after returning to the cave to see if Arthur had gone back there, had returned to Sir Ector's with Jasmine and then met up with Gwen's party some half a day earlier. Taking Arthur to one side, he beckoned Sir Kay and Gwen and her two brothers over. 'We cannot move without Merlin. He will be at the caer by dawn.'

Arthur didn't ask how Salazar knew this; experience of past events, where everything happened as one of the sorcerers had predicted, made this a foregone conclusion.

'We will rest at my father's, then, and wait for him.

So, this large party entered the gates of Sir Ector's just as darkness began to wrap her cloak over the fields and around the caer and chaos ensued as the kitchens were sent into overdrive to feed everyone.

Sir Ector sat long into the night with Arthur, Gwen and Salazar. Everyone else had gradually left the hall to find their beds. Rhianne, sought out by Iris as soon as they had arrived, was tending her sick child along with Lady Elise; each of them worried out of their wits by the unhealthy baby.

'Oh I wish Percy was here. And Merlin,' she added. 'They would know what to do!'

Sir Ector got everyone up to speed with the army he had amassed. 'All is in readiness and we can be on the move within three days.'

'Perhaps you ought to send the runners now,' Arthur stated. 'It wouldn't do any harm to have them here.'

'First, I think Merlin should give that order; he knows what is happening all around and as he will be here tomorrow,' Salazar responded. 'One night more will not hurt.'

Eventually the good food and wine did their job and even they finally sought their beds.

Early the next morning, Merlin was sitting in the Hall at Sir Ector's as one of the servants entered to light the fire, making the poor man jump and drop all his wood.

'It's all right,' he soothed him. 'I'm just waiting for the others to awaken; do your duty, man. I make no demands on you.'

The man set to, clearing out the still warm ashes, before adding straw and shavings, kindling and sticks and stacking up the slightly larger pieces of wood before lighting the fire. He was exceptionally good at his job and Merlin watched him with pleasure. Before long a roaring, happy fire was dancing in the huge fireplace. Merlin had been mesmerised by the man's efforts and almost clapped him when he had finished, stopping short in the belief he might think him mad.

One by one the others entered and greeted the Druid, asking question after question as to what on earth was going on, where and who was this great army of alien beings, and the like. Merlin shushed them all with a, 'Wait till everyone is here; I only want to recount it once. Until then, let us repair to the kitchens to see what delights await us there; I'm famished after my journey.'

'How did you get here? Where did you come from?'

'Oh, that isn't important, suffice to say that I had to fly here as fast as I could!'

They ate in silence; each newcomer shushed into silence by the one who'd been shushed before until everyone had been fed. They eventually all returned to the Hall and settled themselves around the blazing fire – Merlin sitting just below the main window where the light would play over all of their faces but his would remain in shadow; Sir Ector took up his usual place in front of the fire, warming his backside.

However, before Merlin could begin, Rhianne, who had not been at breakfast, rushed up to the sorcerer and asked him to come and see her daughter.

What could he do? Her plea was urgent; her face was grave.

He was gone for nearly an hour, returning to the others with a face of thunder.

'That evil woman has done something to the child! At the moment I am not sure what. It is not a spell; it is not poison; it is definitely the witch's doing, however.' Turning he asked Jasmine to go and see if she could discover anything.

After sitting himself back underneath the window he stared out over all their heads for several moments to get his anger in check before he began to recount all that had happened since he had left them.

'Percy is in the hands of Mab!'

There were several intakes of breath before he continued. 'She is concocting a brew that she believes will remove the sword from the stone. That will not happen. I have been going about and even the weather is on our side; there is an almighty rainstorm headed her way. She will be incapacitated for at least half a day and it will take another three or four days for her to replace that which will be spoiled by the rain. Though she is only wasting her time – she can produce nothing to move that sword.

'The hobgoblin's time on earth is almost over. He has done bad things but he now has to return whence he came. It will be many moons before he is able, or even allowed, to return.

'However, the rest of her unholy army is on its way to her and she will be hoping to lead them against us. She still hopes to get the sword. She will either try to destroy it because she firmly believes it is the sword of the prophecy, or she will try and use it herself if she believes it is powerful only to the one who wields it.

'Sir Ector – summon your army! We are soon to be on the march. This could possibly be the final assault against her. Let us hope so.

'Then, when all the minor kings and lords meet up at Thorney Island, we will discover at last just who this prophecy relates to; just who it is who had been chosen as King of all the Britons.'

Final preparations were made and all the cavalry, bowmen, foot soldiers, pack ponies and goods wagons were prepared. On the third day Sir Philip arrived side by side with the Duke of Cornwall, followed by Sir Malcolm and all their men; by mid-afternoon every other lord had arrived or had advised that they would be joining the party as they travelled; all were kitted out as warriors and ready to fight. There were over five thousand men on horseback and on foot; swords were as sharp as they possibly could be, bows and arrows a-plenty were beside each bowman, horses were freshly shod and shields gleamed; there was a fresh wind and it looked an almost joyous party with all of those colourful pennants fluttering in the breeze – perhaps the enemy could be blinded if the sun happened to be in the right position. It would still be much more than two to one but each man was ready for the fight.

That evening was a merry one. Each tent had in front of it a blazing fire where men sat around eating, drinking, singing and telling tales of derring-do – building themselves up physically and mentally for the fight to come.

For the first time in his life Arthur didn't have to argue with Merlin to be able to join in this battle; in fact Merlin encouraged him. 'Your time has come, Arthur! Take up your sword and fight. Show everyone what a mighty warrior and leader you are. And here – wear this!'

Arthur was amazed. Where had Merlin found this? He thought he'd lost it many moons ago.

Taking the golden arm bracelet from the sorcerer he looked carefully at it before attaching it to his upper arm. Arthur had had the red-gold dragon made when he was around twelve years of age and had worn it occasionally until one day he just couldn't find it any more; searching high and low and stopping just short of accusing anyone of stealing it, he eventually gave up and it went right out of his mind – until now.

What had Merlin done to it? If, indeed, it was Merlin that had done it! But who else? Arthur had had it made entirely of red coloured Welsh gold but now it had emeralds for eyes and in one or two places it had real scales – of what? They caught the light in a myriad rainbow of colours that flashed this way and that and, when Merlin fastened it to Arthur's arm, it hummed – not audibly but throughout his being.

'Have you enchanted this, Merlin?'

'It will keep you safe, Arthur. It is the protection of the dragon. She might not always be around but she will always be with you. Never take it off.'

'Thank you Merlin. It shall remain there forever,' he said as he clasped his hand around it before clasping the hand of the sorcerer in both of his.

'And there is something of much more import that you need. It is a holy relic – made from the sandals ...'

'Christ's sandals?' Arthur asked, almost shouting the words in his excitement.

'As you say,' Merlin replied. 'They have been reshaped into a scabbard for your sword,' he told him. *The sword in the stone!*'

Merlin reached behind and laid the satchel on his lap, opening it carefully so as not to touch it but to reveal what was inside. However, before he could warn Arthur about just what could happen, the young man reached inside, pulled the sacred leather out and lifting it up gave thanks to God for the wonder of what he held in his hands. Arthur was not harmed as he handled it!

'*I didn't see this!*' Merlin thought in amazement. 'It has to be yours,' he told the young man. 'I had no time to warn you that possible death awaited anyone other than the one for whom it was meant. It was meant for you Arthur; truly it was meant for you. And now, you are ready. You will go with the others and this time you will fight; you will be the true warrior you were meant to be!

You will be the true warrior king you were destined to be!'

Merlin sat and watched as Arthur studied the scabbard and smiled at the young man as he fitted his sword into it – it almost fit but Merlin knew of the true sword that would fit it perfectly!

Just as the sun winked through the branches of the trees on the far side of the meadow, they left for Thorney Island; harnesses were jangling, boots were stamping, ponies were making sparks on the cobblestones as this great army left – great, but still far, far short of the huge army they would be facing.

Lady Elise stood at the top of the steps either dabbing her eyes with one of the flimsy handkerchiefs she always carried or waving them goodbye with it.

Rhianne and Iris were still beside the semi-conscious child, with Jasmine ministering to her as best she could. Queen Giselle had joined them within the last few minutes but, as yet, no-one had any idea what was wrong with her.

Merlin had promised to send the help that was needed as soon as he could find out from the mad woman just what she had done.

Lady Elise stood and watched as the army rode or marched away. The breeze brought back snatches of sound long after they had disappeared from view but she stayed there for at least a half hour more before a sudden gust of wind that sent chills down her spine forced her indoors.

Then all around outside the caer was quiet.

THIRTY-ONE

'But before I rejoin you I have to return to my sky tower,' Merlin had told the men as they took their leave that morning. 'There are things I keep there – celestial maps, histories, prophecies and the like that I need to consider; also I need to just be still and look up at the stars and the universe. I need to be strengthened in every aspect of my being. We have a work to do that is dangerous at best and deathly at worst.'

'We can't fight without you, Merlin!' many a voice cried out to him.

'And you won't have to. I will be there; before you arrive I will have explored all around and then we can plan our moves. Trust me. I will be there!'

They had spent the previous two days sharpening their swords and other battle equipment, feeding and grooming their horses and pack ponies, practising, when they had the time, and doing a hundred other things. It kept their minds off what was coming.

They were excited but concerned because it wasn't as though they would be experiencing the usual type of battle; this time they would be coming up against something that was, basically, unpredictable and unfamiliar, if not evil.

This apart, there was one real concern that seemed to niggle at everyone's sub-conscious – Kate was sick. Even Merlin was unsure what was wrong with her and though she wasn't really getting any worse, she certainly wasn't getting better either.

Rhianne, Jasmine and Iris would take it in turns to stay with her but as the days went by she had begun to eat less and less and sleep more and more, all the while beset by a fever that would burn her up one moment and send her shivering uncontrollably the next.

It was a good job I wasn't there at the time or I would have been beside myself. It was bad enough that the witch had told me about her symptoms, let alone what had caused them; my imagination showed me how ill she was but because I wasn't actually there I couldn't see just how bad everything really was.

Merlin told me much, much later that he was convinced that

the witch had done something to her but wasn't completely sure; however, as it was, it was about that time that the witch, herself, told me just what she had done. I passed on all this information to Merlin and he finally answered, grim of face, that he would see what could be done. He had assured me that there had to be something and not to worry.

It's maddening when people say not to worry, because when they say that it is obviously because there is actually really something to worry about. I must make a mental note never to ever say it to anyone.

As you must have realised, therefore, I was worrying myself sick.

The rain had finally stopped; it had been incessant for the last two days and everyone's spirits were as damp as the ground around them, but it was good that all of them were now together and that they would have a few days in which to catch up with all that had gone on while they'd been travelling around in their different parts of the country. Who knows, when all the information was collated they might make some sense of all that was going on.

Some of the soldiers kept their distance from Androcles and his fierce travelling companion en route but almost fought with one another to befriend Goliath, though the giant himself was very sparse with his conversation and before long they realised he would rather be alone. He was happy to talk with Androcles, though, as he had got to know the youth very well, and he seemed not one bit bothered about the lion. The scribe, too, didn't say much but was happy to just ride along with the others that he had also got to know over the last few months.

Salazar took his place at the head of this great army alongside Sir Philip, the Duke of Cornwall and Sir Ector. They spoke in soft tones, listening to Salazar for the most part and wondering if Merlin would return in time for the battle. 'He must be there,' Sir Ector repeated on more than one occasion, making everyone feel a little uneasy, as if to think that if he wasn't there then everything would go wrong.

'Did he say he would be?' Salazar eventually chided the man when he could see the adverse effect it was having on the men. When Sir Ector nodded he declared loudly, 'Then he will be there!'

Arthur joined them on and off throughout the day but because the conversation differed little from that of the time before decided that he would rather be with Gwen.

Most of the other men, Shake Spear included, had had to give up their ponies, which had been commandeered to carry baggage or pull wagons, so they fell back with the bowmen who were only too happy to teach them to shoot. Shake Spear had a great time – it had been so long since he had seen properly that he almost begged them to let him fire at anything that moved.

'It was a good job,' Arthur said to Gwen much later, 'that the bowmen jealously guard their own weaponry, which one of them told me almost grew to fit their hands like gloves, or who knows whom he might kill.'

'But one or two of them have spare shafts that they have been working on and now several of our men are practising daily on any stray deer or hare that happens to be in the vicinity.'

'Well, there won't be too many of them with the noise we're making, though my father has sent men ahead to try and bag some fresh meat. However, let's hope someone doesn't give Shake Spear his own bow,' he replied. 'But it is good my father's men are having a go; who knows what we might face – we need all the fighters we can get.'

Even Gwen, who had a short bow, surprised the men with her expertise, but she only joined in with them on a couple of occasions after they had set up camp for the night.

For the most part she rode alongside Arthur; they would have the following three days to get to know one another and it wasn't long before both of them started changing their ideas about the other. Gwen had been extremely annoyed with her father that he was, in effect, giving her away without consulting her at all – something he had never done before; she was still and had always known that she was his favourite but no amount of cajoling or sweet talking on her part would get him to change his mind. She had therefore been in a great sulk ever since.

Arthur, on the other hand, was getting to know a forceful, intelligent and almost warrior like girl – no, not a girl – a woman – who, even though she had only clocked up seventeen summers, was completely different to what he had expected.

Those few days went quickly for everyone but one thing was for sure – Gwenhwyfar and Arthur thought that those days had gone much too quickly for them – and not because of what was in front of them.

It was late in the afternoon of the third day, after they had started to sniff the breeze and wrinkle their noses at the wafts of fetid air that travelled toward them, that they breasted a short incline and stared down at the unholy army that stretched out for miles before them; it was impossible even to see the horizon as the slug goblins covered the ground even that far.

Salazar and the other lords, along with Arthur and Gwen kept themselves concealed among a copse of hawthorn and just stared.

'What on earth are we going to do?' Sir Philip whispered. 'There are just too many!'

Salazar, who had been staring hard, advised that the whole slug goblin army was now amassed. He had a quick thought that now all of them were in one place it wouldn't please the witch – she had wanted them in two halves to trap them; however, it would still also make it difficult for our army – there were just too many of them.

He had been looking at the ground since the morning, noticing that most of the greenery was missing from both tree and earth, and it wasn't just because autumn was coming to an end. He had seen the gobs of spit, that he'd heard one of the men call "owl's spit", which were increasing as they moved east – and the smell was getting much worse. It might be possible to make the slug goblin army wait; without food they might become weak; there is still a chance we could win if we had to fight them.

A sudden movement seen out of the corner of his right eye caused him to move his head quickly and he alone caught sight of the end of a red forked tail and the glint of a merlin's eye before both disappeared from sight above the clouds.

'Let us return to the men and make camp. Set guards. We will go over our battle plans while we wait.

'Merlin will come.'

THIRTY-TWO

The rain stopped eventually and the mad woman decided that as it was impossible for me to get off the island she would release me, but only to join Mordred in collecting as much tinder as possible to try and get another fire going. It was going to take days to remix the potion to try and release the sword.

Mordred's eyes never left me the whole of the time we gathered those twigs and small pieces of timber. I found, after a short while though, that if I was careful I could find a way, more or less, through the thorn bushes and not get snagged too much and thus got quite a bit of satisfaction at the ouches and curses from Mordred who, because he was watching me more than where he was going, was being scratched to bits. Again I would have laughed if my situation hadn't been so dire. Dare I try and call out to Merlin? No! He would know soon enough. The last time Salazar had done that he was heard and Mab had spent the next couple of hours figuring out where everyone was through her crystal. She had got in touch with the commander of the second half of the slug goblin army some days before, by the hobgoblin and even now they must have been positioning themselves for the assault against Arthur.

Anyway, even though the Faerie would have told him by now, Merlin was more than likely completely aware of everything that was going on anyway. I would just have to be patient.

'Pick me up, Percy,' a whispered command from a small log to my right. I reached down and picked up the piece of wood he had been standing on and held it close to my chest on top of all the other kindling I had collected. With a quick look around I was satisfied to find that Mordred was busily occupied in picking out thorns from his legs.

King Ogwin had come to let me know what was going on but spoke so softly that even I was finding it very difficult to hear; telling me to listen only. He let me know that Kate lived, though was very ill, that Sir Ector and several lords and their men were on their way here and that if I could possibly find out just what the witch had done to my daughter he would return at dusk that evening for me to tell him, if I could. He said he would come to me, so just to wait and look out for him wherever I happened to be.

'Why have you stopped?' Mordred poked me in the back with a stick.

I jumped, realising that I had completely forgotten my surroundings, concentrating only on what the little king was saying to me.

Looking down in fear that he would be discovered at any moment I was taken aback by the fact that he wasn't there any more. How did these little people manage to do that? Speed, I reckoned, remembering the battle outside the Blue Pelican and how dizzy I had become when trying to keep up with what they were doing.

Responding to Mordred I muttered something along the lines that I had snagged my trousers on a thorn.

'Well hurry up and get yourself unsnagged or there will be hell to pay!'

Of that I was sure!

We returned to the clearing and built the fire; the wood was still very wet but Mab managed, as always, to light it – using magic.

She set to with a will and, knowing just how she had put the brew together in the first place, it took only one day to finish. She looked over at me and smiled, then laughed, then collapsed with tears of malevolent joy running down her cheeks – which actually were quite clean for a change after all that rain.

After her hysterical laughter had subsided, and I had no idea why she had laughed like that, though thought it must obviously have something to do with me, the witch spent the rest of that day finalising what it was she was brewing.

'Now we are ready!' Mab gave a great sigh before giving orders for the work to begin.

'Get to it! Time is of the essence now. And don't you dare drop it!'

Lifting the huge, bubbling glass bowl that had rested on a plank of wood the hobgoblin and Mordred, between them, struggled to ascend the rock; it was slimy and on more than one occasion one or other of them slipped and it looked like all would crash to the ground and come to nought. I even thought I might laugh at one point. Mab was screeching at the top of her lungs with threats and promises if they dare drop it.

I felt sure that some of the things she threatened them with might possibly make them so nervous that they would inevitably drop it.

I often wondered since that day what would have happened should that broiling liquid have splashed all over them!

But it didn't.

They eventually reached the top of the large boulder and settled the plank onto the flattest part of it.

Mordred stood there sweating like a pig; the hobgoblin merely stood.

Mab started chanting again, at which her evil companion danced around the sword like an outsized pipe cleaner – manic and frenzied for the whole time Mab screeched. Then it all went quiet – even the drips from the trees seemed to stop – some even in mid air!

I was as still as I could be and held my breath; I sat propped up and tied once again to the trunk of a tree, all hunger forgotten watching bug-eyed at what might happen next.

Mab, after struggling up the incline to the top of the rock, yelling at Mordred to stop looking completely inept and come and help her, took a metal beaker by its handle and carefully scooped up almost a full cup of the bubbling liquid. Holding it extremely carefully and making sure none of the steaming brew splashed on her, she poured it into the place where the sword met the rock and then stood back.

She and I, as well as the whole of the clearing it seemed, held our breath. The mixture fizzed and sparked for a full minute before it all went quiet again. Mab moved forward gingerly to make sure there was no more danger from the toxic mixture she had poured and when quite sure, she turned and leered at me, grabbed the sword's hilt with both hands and, expecting the sword to slide out as it had in her imagination, almost fell backwards when it didn't move. Her legs slipped underneath her and she fell; holding onto the hilt for dear life and with her backside bouncing heavily down upon the rock each leg skidded forward and eventually stopped either side of the sword, it was amazing she didn't split herself in half. Now wouldn't that have been grand!

It wasn't long before the relief that that hadn't happened gave way to the complete and absolute anger that all her schemes appeared to have come to naught.

It is at a time like this that I have to excuse myself from repeating the language that filled the air for what must have been miles around. They were really old-fashioned, Dark Ages words but even if I mentioned them here you would soon realise what they meant and we would all blush; suffice to say she was as mad as a hare on a cold March day in a high wind!

Eventually getting herself under control she tried twice more before almost crying with frustration. I must have moved because her head swivelled in my direction and she shouted at Mordred to release me and bring me up to her.

It was as I was walking across the clearing that I saw the hobgoblin slowly fade and disappear in a hole that opened up beneath him.

Well, at least one wicked thing was now gone!

My journey across the clearing was achieved much quicker than I would have liked but before long I, too, was being instructed as to how I should, like her, try and release the sword from the stone.

I had often wondered before, and it still amazes me that she should think I might succeed where she had failed, how she thought I might be able to do it, but, hoping that she wouldn't be as violent to me as she had always seemed to be toward Mordred, I went through the motions.

'There must be something else you can try,' she eventually said after I had twice failed. 'Myrddin has been training you! DO SOMETHING!'

'There's nothing I can do. It is stuck fast!'

A crafty look came over her face. A chill came over me.

'If you can help me release this sword …' She let these words sink into my brain. 'I will tell you what I have done to your daughter. Who knows – you just might be able to save her.'

There was so much I wanted to do right there and then – scream abuse at her was one of them, but my mind told me that would just amuse her. Beat her to a pulp was another but, apart from the fact that she would be ready and would counterattack with some awful enchantment or other, she was so large now that trying to beat all of that blubber to a pulp would take me weeks. I didn't have weeks! Did Kate?

She was obviously following my train of thought but she, like me, didn't have time to dwell on any of this.

'So?'

'So I cannot help you. I do not know how to release it.'

She went wild. She lashed out at me with a fist but I dodged it, sliding down the uneven steps of the stone face; she kicked Mordred who lost his balance and fell off the side of the rock. I'm still not sure if he broke any bones, as he was knocked unconscious in the fall.

Finally getting herself under control Mab turned and stared down at me. 'I travelled to Rome and met a really evil general. I learned a lot from him about warfare and torture and have become quite adept at both. You might meet up with them soon; they've had a bit of modification but I can only say that I believe that that is for the better.' She stared at me for what seemed ages. Was she going to torture me? It wouldn't help. I knew that that sword was stuck fast and I also remembered the prophecy. Should I mention that to her? No! It might send her completely over the edge and then she wouldn't care what she did to me. I had made sure I had put all my barriers in place; she was watching me intently.

'I also spent several weeks in the Mediterranean where a wonderful pirate showed me all the treasure he had amassed. I told him how I could double and treble all that treasure if he were to help me. And he and a fleet of pirates are on their way here right now. So all your friends are in for a great shock when they arrive here – not only do they have my slug goblin army to contend with but hundreds and hundreds of tough, well-trained pirates. Now, what do you think of that?'

I kept my face straight but made a mental note to let King Ogwin know, if I could.

'But the best thing of all was something that happened while we were docked in a port in North Africa.' She watched me and waited.

'Don't you want to know what that is?'

I just looked at her – well, over her head really; I didn't want to take the chance of being sucked into the depths of those eyes.

She got a bit annoyed, as could be seen by the set of her mouth as I watched her out of the corner of my eyes but she went on evenly enough. 'Several of the men took sick. Some died and some, after a long time, recovered. The pirate captain told me the cause.

'Come with me, Percy. Come!' She clambered down the rockface and made me follow her across to her bag where she removed a fairly small bottle, which had a cork top with small holes in it. Inside was an insect which I could just about hear buzzing at it moved lethargically around inside.

'Its bite can cause severe illness or death!' She stared at me for what seemed like eternity, then: 'Kate has been bitten!'

Waiting for my reaction, she replaced the bottle in her bag and looked over at me.

'You …,' I started to growl and then took control of myself. I mean, I would just explode and she would merely laugh. Swallowing a few times I finally asked, through gritted teeth, what the antidote might be.

'Oh, there isn't one,' she replied airily. 'But I have a mixture that might keep her alive – if you help me.' She turned away and started to pack up her stuff.

'There's nothing I can do!' I stated through gritted teeth.

'Oh, but there is.'

My eyes rolled up in my head; what could I do? And then I saw King Ogwin sitting high in a tree. He gave me the thumbs up sign to let me know he had heard everything and then he was gone.

'*Oh, Merlin,*' I thought, '*I really need you right now.*'

The witch merely laughed.

THIRTY-THREE

Arthur took Gwen over to the fire that Baker had got going and sat her down beside her two brothers. Cabal and Griff were already sitting as close to the fire as they possibly could to keep warm now that a stiff, cold wind had blown up but also to make sure that if any food should fall to the ground one of them would be first to retrieve it as they watched Baker begin to prepare a stew.

'I am going to join my father to see what their plans are. I shall return as soon as I can.'

'Well, you aren't going without me,' Gwen replied, rising to join him. He looked at the determination in her face as her green eyes flashed at him and, realising that he was not going to win this argument, nodded his assent and offered her his arm; somewhere in the back of his mind was the thought that he had somehow to assert a little bit of authority when they were wed. Both of her brothers accompanied them. They walked over to where those older warriors were bent over their parchments and stood by to see what they were planning, all four of them respectful of the older men's years.

'Merlin will meet up with us when we get to the Thames. He will know what needs to be done. All we can do now is to prepare ourselves and our men and sort out where we can position ourselves in our ranks,' Arthur said as some of the lords started arguing when they got to the point where they could agree as to which one of them should be in control.

'We have agreed what is to be done and so now we should return to our own men and lead them!' the Duke added, cutting through their arguments with a voice that, though not loud, was controlled and forceful.

'Arthur and his Lordship are right,' Sir Ector added, realising, probably for the first time since he had fostered the boy, that this young man that Merlin had brought to him all those many years ago when he was a baby, had grown wise, was growing into a leader of men and someone really special.

He had taken him in at Merlin's request, not knowing then or right at that moment, come to that, just who he was and where he had come from. Would he have raised him any differently if he had known then that he was the son of Uther Pendragon and Igraine, the wife of the then Duke of Cornwall? Probably not! He had always treated most people the same and seemed to treat all people well.

They dispersed – each to his own troops to make ready to fight at first light – Arthur joining Sir Ector and Sir Kay and asking what plans they had decided upon before he had joined them.

'We'll obviously wait for Merlin to give us his consent, but our plans in the meantime are to attack at dawn and, when we realise how large an army they are, sound the retreat.'

'What? You are going to give up before you fight? I can't believe it!'

'No, Arthur; it is a tactical move and just in case that woman might be listening in we shall say no more, save to say that it is all part of the plan to defeat them. We had word from Merlin and from the king of the Faerie and we have since been putting it all together.

Once she and they are out of the way we shall go and see just who can pull the sword from the stone. Then there will be peace in the land.'

'Do you think that we'll defeat them so swiftly; so easily?'

'Oh yes; I'm sure; with Merlin we will have the victory!'

'Oh no, father, Merlin knows many things but it is with God's help we will win!'

King Ogwin returned while the witch and Mordred, who had now recovered sufficiently to help, though he had an enormous bump on his head, were busy pouring the rest of the mixture onto the rock. She was getting madder by the minute and Mordred was on the verge of rebelling. Each time it didn't work she would hit the nearest thing in her frustration. She had kicked the huge glass phial a few times and now even that had finally decided that enough was enough and had fallen off the rock and shattered, spilling the rest of Mab's concoction onto the ground where it burned through the grass as it sank into the soil; Mordred, therefore, was the only other thing, apart from the sword, upon which she could take out her anger.

The little king settled in a cleft in the tree behind me and said, 'I've spoken to Merlin. He will be here by morning. Our army is four miles away on the other side of the hill and is making itself ready for the assault. The slug goblins are between them and you – but they are running out of food! Merlin has a plan. Hold tight, young Percival; you will soon be free.'

'Does he know about Kate?'

'Yes, but trust him; he is doing everything he can.'

'Who are you talking to?' She stared across at me.

'No-one,' I replied.

'Yes you were! I saw your lips move.'

I said the first thing that came into my head: 'I was praying!'

'You what?' She burst out laughing. 'Think your prayers can help you? Well go on then – pray! Pray your head off Percival and see what good it will do you.'

I stared at her.

'Pray! Go on!'

So I did. I can't recall doing that for such a long time. I used to go to the village church with my family and, well, everyone in the village really, except old Mr Fellowes, that is, who was extremely odd and possibly didn't know what day of the week it was, let alone the time, and we all knew the service by heart, praying our prayers in unison until the end of the service, when we would all go into the church hall for tea and biscuits and sometimes cake, where the grown ups would chat and we kids would run amok.

Well, I don't know whether it was my prayers or not, but they worked!

Realising that she just wasn't going to be able to release the sword, Mab climbed down and, grabbing Mordred by the collar, dragged him over to her bag where, urging him on with the odd slap around the head or boot up the backside, they loaded it up and disappeared through the trees.

She didn't even give me a second look.

I managed, eventually, to free myself from my bonds, got up and walked over to the stone, climbing up the ragged steps to see what damage she had done. The stone itself seemed to be charred as though by some great heat but it stood firm and the sword, which I tried once more to pull out, did not budge one iota. Well, I didn't think I would be able to pull it out – I knew all that happened to the sword – but it didn't hurt to give it one more try, did it?

Climbing down I walked back along the pathway through the thorns until I reached the water's edge. I had given myself time so that the witch would not, hopefully, be anywhere on that path, then maybe I could swim across the river and escape.

What now? On the other side I could see Mab being hauled, with much indignity, from the coracle, which had been dragged across by a seemingly willing, but glassy-eyed Mordred, onto the bank where the commander of the slug goblins was waiting to meet her. That army stretched as far as the eye could see and I didn't see any way in which I could get through them. I felt an awful dread as I looked across those helmeted but otherworldly beings. I tried to make the spell of invisibility but I think I was so scared of everything I could see, distraught about Kate and I know not what, that it just didn't happen.

Well, King Ogwin had told me that Merlin would arrive by morning so I made my way back to the clearing, leaned back against the stone and tried to sleep. I would need my wits about me soon, I felt sure, so sleep would reinvigorate me – but my sleep was not restful: slug goblins were feasting off me, even though in the recesses of my mind I knew they were vegetarian – but you never knew what they might resort to if they were hungry enough. Rhianne also was there; she'd been turned into a beautiful palm tree that was slowly being consumed by several slug goblins that were fighting over her, each one shouting at the other with weird voices through their rubbery lips that the face was theirs. 'Noooo,' I could feel my mind screaming at them as I looked around my mad dream world for aid. Moon Song would have helped if she could but the stonemasons had sent in an army of trainees to the stone circle and they were chipping away at her to make vases and pots to sell in the gift shops round and about. Merlin had managed to land in a parallel universe and though he could see all that was happening to us couldn't get back. I stared helplessly at him, trying to decipher the soundless words he was shouting at me. Rhianne had been pulled out of the ground and was now slung over a horse in front of Mordred who was sneering at me and saying that this time I would not get her back, though I couldn't help but wonder what he could possibly want with a palm tree! Mab had managed to pull out the sword and was chasing Arthur round and round the stone where I rested (and rested was not the right word, was it?), and where I tried to trip her up each time she passed I found that that particular leg had already been eaten by the slug goblins so she just ran on. I stood staring at where my leg should have been and wondered how it was I could still feel it! I stared, bug-eyed at all these events until only my eyes were left (which would of course have looked bug-eyed as they now had no surrounding flesh) as I watched the slug goblins with lips suckered to them tear the last of the flesh from my bones and then toss those bones into the fire. I could feel the flames licking around me and wondered how I would scream now that I had no lips, but scream I did as I awoke in a cold sweat. I almost expected to see my enemies creeping stealthily toward me or even away from me as they carried bits of me off through the thorn bushes; then sanity finally returned. Shivering, not just from my nightmare but also from the sudden chill that was invading that place, I jumped up and started to rub my hands together and jump up and down on the spot to get the blood moving through those legs that I was thankful I still possessed.

It was now full night and I decided to go back to the river's edge and see what was happening. Beacons had been lit and the slug goblins had posted their sentries. All was quiet, almost peaceful if one forgot just what was going on.

I watched as the mist began to creep warily along on top of the river. It was that time when the river was still, had gone as far as it could go before the tide changed and it began to flow back again. It was still – there was no sound, no lapping against the banks of the island, no gurgling, nothing! The mist, tiptoeing on silent feet, seemed to spread down the centre before adventuring outwards to slide up the banks and over the ground. Before too long I could hardly see a thing.

'Beautiful, isn't it?'

I almost screamed as I spun around to stare into Merlin's face. 'Don't do that?'

'Oh, sorry, I thought you knew I was here! Have you lost all your powers? Surely you haven't let fear diminish them?'

'No! But I was concentrating on something else!'

'What?'

'Oh I've forgotten,' I lied, digging a bigger hole for myself.

Merlin stared at me for a long few seconds, obviously being able to read me like a book, before, shrugging his shoulders, he turned and beckoned me to follow.

'Come – we have a lot to do.'

He didn't look too pleased with me and I knew that within the next ten minutes or so I would be apologising to him left, right and centre. Why didn't I ever do it straight away? He always forgave me and smiled, very often patting me on the shoulder as he added that I was always a quick learner.

I spent the next half hour or so getting Merlin up to speed with what the witch had done, especially to Kate. He asked me lots of questions about the creature inside the glass bottle adding that he had heard of these things before – mosquitoes he called them. My blood ran cold because I knew about them and had heard how dangerous these things were and that if they didn't kill you, you would obviously need medication on and off for the rest of your life. Quinine was, I believe, used to aid a sufferer and quinine was not something easily found, if at all, in the Dark Ages.

I went on to tell him that some of the pirates in the Mediterranean had suffered and died because of these insects and that, thinking of them, Mab had said she had promised them much if they came to her aid and Merlin said that even now he thought they were on their way.

As I told him everything I could recall Merlin nodded here and there and then sat staring into space as I added each bit of information. He finally jumped up and, after inspecting the sword, told me that we needed to be on our way.

Where? How?

'Don't you still trust me?' He looked quite sad as he asked me the age-old question.

I looked at him for a while before nodding. 'Merlin, I think I have always trusted you.'

Then he called the dragon.

THIRTY-FOUR

I didn't see the battle but it was bloody, so I'm told.

I had met up with Arthur at Sir Ector's some three weeks later and this is what he told me had happened.

Merlin had walked into the final meeting of all the leaders and warriors as they made their last minute preparations. He took Sir Ector and the Duke of Cornwall to one side and spoke to them for mere minutes before striding off again into the dark.

Sir Ector explained what Merlin had told him and within the next half hour we were on the march.

As you already know, the two slug goblin armies had met up and so ten thousand of these unholy hoards were now about to press hard upon our heroes.

Arthur continued –

'The battle was intense. They first sent in their foot soldiers who were trained in all sorts of armed combat; we did the same. Their commander would instruct one of his men to blow a horn and their men would retreat – so again we did the same.

'Then their bowmen moved forward and knelt down in front of their cavalry, letting loose so many arrows we thought we would surely perish but Sir Philip had been instructed to call our bowmen forward and they, too, let loose their arrows.

'Finally the cavalry were sent and you could hardly hear your own breathing as their horses thundered over the ground.

'That was when Sir Malcolm sounded the retreat.

'Each of our cavalrymen scooped up a foot soldier and with those men almost skipping alongside each horse we headed west.

'The slug goblins were fierce fighters and had ridden down on us from the northern borders of Kent and along the edge of the Thames. With the fighting about to become its fiercest we retreated as far as Gravesend where many pirate ships were moored. At first we had wondered why they were there and then we saw the pirates swarming over the sides, screaming like banshees and triggering the traps they'd already set for a retreating army. Mab stood at the side of one of the ships directing this assault.

'There was only one thing to do, and that was to head further inland – toward an area that could be dangerous in that it was made up of mud flats and marshes – high tides could cause havoc at best, death by drowning at worst, but we were being pressed on two sides now and things were not going our way. So inland we had to go.

'But all was not lost for several reasons.

'There were several minor lords in Kent and the one who had sway over the area near the sea enjoyed the service of not just fishermen but marshmen. He had brought these men with him and it was they who knew the walkways through the marshes and so led the troops on. The men on horseback fared better than those on foot, but even they got bogged down and kept having to dismount to free their horses from the encompassing mud. The foot soldiers and bowmen could at times only travel single file along the walkways which, when the tide came in, were hardly discernable.

'There was a place some two miles through the marshes that was higher and flatter than much of the area but because it had taken so long to penetrate the area it was here that some of the fiercest fighting took place.

'The slug-goblins had enjoyed the last of the fresh grass and leaves some few days ago, thus they were now hungry and getting weak – they had warned Mab but did she ever listen? She had, however, tempted them with the information that there was much foliage to be had in the marshes, so they straightened themselves and made ready for the fight.

'And it was bad.

'The stragglers were the first to be attacked and the slug goblins gave no quarter. Many of those on foot were lost on those walkways, being cut down by the slug goblins on their powerful chargers.

'Sir Ector and I were standing high in our stirrups and calling out to the men to hurry or turn and fire but things really did not appear to be going our way. As we watched it seemed as though a mass of men and horses a mile wide and at least ten deep were now advancing on us.

'It was a hopeless cause. We were desperately outnumbered and it would not be long now before we would be completely overpowered.

'Then the tide turned – literally – the tide of the sea and the tide of our fortune. The sea began once again to lap at the marshes. Most of the cattle we had ridden were little ponies who were well up to all types of going and seemed to have feet like ducks – they just went on and on almost without faltering. But these animals were not up to the amount of men that needed them; so many of us were on foot but the enemy were on powerful horses that seemed to be able to move through any terrain whether dry or boggy.

'There was a hill – well a mound really – some five miles further into the marshes where the slug-goblins caught up with the main thrust of our men and where quite a lot of fierce fighting took place. Eddie was wounded in the leg and had to be surrounded by several of our warriors so that Gwen could see to his wound.

'Gwen?' I had asked.

'Yes,' Arthur smiled. 'She's as good a soldier as any man and not at all squeamish – she tore the leggings in two to get at his wound and not only stitched it up but bound it up as well. She was covered in blood by the time she finished but it seemed to energise her. What with her red hair and blood on her face and hands, she scared us, let alone the enemy – she looked like one of those Greek sirens you hear about. I tell you, I was glad she was on our side!

'The fighting was fiercest there. We seemed to get rid of one wave of slug goblins that were then replaced by another one – one assault after another seemingly endlessly. As one line fell back they were replaced by the next line and so were fresh, while we were fighting continuously and were getting really tired, though Goliath appeared to go on and on without the least sign of fatigue.

'Although we had been fighting as we fled, Sir Ector called the retreat again. I don't know how he does it but my father has one of the loudest voices I have ever heard. He had a boy sitting on his horse in front of him that then sounded the bugle but, to be honest, he wasn't really needed. Anyway, we grouped together and began to turn.

'A lot of the enemy gave chase but we did notice that several of their horses – about half, I think – were beginning to get clogged in the mud. Our little ponies, though, seemed to be made for the conditions. We gradually pulled away – even the foot soldiers kept up – and before long we thought we were safe.

'Do you know, Percy, I believe I heard that mad witch scream at one point. I tried to think that maybe it could have been some other noise but, no, I really believe it was her.'

'What do you mean, Arthur?'

'Well, we had got some long distance from the slug goblins and had slowed to give our ponies some respite, when I heard this scream. I had stayed at the back of our men to make sure all were safe and so had a grand view of the marshes.

'The sea had come in quite some way by now and it looked more like a lake than mud flats but you will never guess what had happened.'

He waited for me to guess.

I said that I could not.

'Salt! The sea contains salt and you know what happens with salt? Bad effect on slugs, let alone slug-goblins!

'They had had to dismount to try and pull their horses' legs out of the mud and once they had done that they started to froth; their foot soldiers fared far worse because they were attacked by the sea first. Not long after that all that could be seen was a lot of discarded armour with bubbles foaming out of it, just like the surf from the sea on a really windy day. Then there were riderless horses jumping and swimming about everywhere – through layers and layers of foam.

'Our men started cheering and once the survivors heard that they stopped to find out what all the noise was about; when they saw what was happening to their comrades they made sure they stayed on their horses and rode off as fast as their mounts could take them.

You should have heard the cheering then; our men were ecstatic! With the last of the slug goblins melting in the salt flats, their horses were rounded up and distributed between the lords; rich pickings – they will come in very useful. We went through the marshes and gathered up as much armour as we could; most of us now are extremely rich, Percy.'

'What about the pirates?'

'Well, as I said, I heard her scream – the witch! We left all our loot and those that had been wounded with a dozen or so men.

'Oh, I should have told you; Wite was killed.'

'Oh no!' I felt the tears spring to my eyes.

'He fought well but tripped as he tried to defend Brosc and one of those unholy beings thrust him through. Brosc is inconsolable. They have been friends since infancy. We keep trying to tell him that Wite is a hero and that he has been buried with the full honours of a warrior but it isn't helping Brosc deal with the shock of it. Well, none of us really as it is the first time that anything bad has happened to any one of our friends.'

Arthur waited until I got myself under control.

'Yes, we gave him a warrior's burial only two days ago, Percy. I know he was just a farmer but he was a faithful tenant to my father and proved to be a loyal soldier too. His brother, Cal, and Abigail have taken Brosc back with them and are treating him almost as a brother – they knew how close those two friends were and he didn't have any other family.

'Well,' Arthur continued after I had got myself under control, 'we rode back across the marshes toward the pirate ships. Most of those cunning scoundrels had seen what had happened and had decided that the sea would be a safer place than facing us. Our blood was up and we were ready for another fight.

'Those seamen were a very superstitious lot – red sky at night, etc – so that watching a lot of slug goblins froth and disappear did not bode well for them.

'Mab went mad. She was standing on the upper deck of one of the ships and as the sailors began to board she screamed at them – "Fight! Kill them! Go back! Go back!" She didn't give them long to change their minds and because they didn't they died. I really don't know what she did but she pointed at each one in turn and they just exploded. I must admit that the colours of each of them were quite spectacular, though quite troubling – each colour different as they detonated, turning to bright dust, though each colour was fairly dark – greens, purples, indigos.

'She did keep one or two of them and forced them to steer the ship out to sea and Nell's son, who was closest, along with Salazar, managed to climb aboard just as it was leaving.

Mab was soon out on the open sea! I reckon she must have felt safe in that little ship because everyone knows what Mab is like with water. Fortunately she had not seen Nell's son or Salazar climb aboard her ship or feel the spell that Merlin, who was flying invisibly overhead apparently, had placed around her to keep her frozen to the spot until it was safe for Nell's son to leave.

Climbing around the side of the boat, Nell's son eventually got to the bow. He lowered himself down and with as much netting as he could find at the rear of the ship, completely snarled up the rudder. Her boat would now drift for weeks if not forever.

Salazar hauled Nell's son back on board and, throwing that special dust over them both, returned to Merlin's cave where they spent time before the Glass and, much to Nell's son's increasing incredulity, landed just south of the Isle of Thorns on one of the now deserted ships. He's currently searching for the right men to help man the ship.

'Yes, Percy, he is a captain at last!

'All of that took several weeks, what with carrying back all the spoils and the injured *and the dead*,' he added, but Percy heard the unsaid words and felt an ache for his friend.

'Well, I mean,' Arthur concluded with forced brightness, 'with all the injured and all the spoils it actually took that long.'

But not one of them had seen Merlin or me on the back of Moon Song. I had sat between her wings and held on tightly to her neck whilst watching a master magician at work.

Was the tide due to come in at that time? Was the sea actually saltier than it normally was? Was Mab manoeuvred onto that ship? Well, I will leave the guessing up to you. Suffice to say I enjoyed every minute on Moon Song's back; I always had done but now I actually revelled in it.

THIRTY-FIVE

Merlin and I arrived at the caer within a quarter hour of Mab's defeat. Rhianne was beside herself with grief. My poor daughter was now unconscious. I sat for ages with Rhianne telling her that I should take her back to the 20th Century where I was sure she would be healed. She eventually agreed but only if she could go with me.

I have no idea what Merlin did but he must have been just as concerned about Kate's welfare as us – we left two hours later – time was now of the essence. Merlin agreed that he had tried all he could and nothing worked. He had done his best but Mab had done her worst.

We left, after Merlin had sprinkled a powder over us. I had one arm around Rhianne and the other round my daughter. We arrived, madly, in the middle of mum's kitchen. She wasn't there, thank goodness, or I don't know what would have happened if a sudden flash brought us to light in front of her; as it was she walked in a few seconds later and still looked as though she'd had the shock of her life. Phew! Well, phew of a sort – now I had a lot of explaining to do. Well, in for a penny ...

Taking in the scene before her – and that was something; we were all dressed as though we were headed for a fancy dress ball – she almost passed out when I introduced my wife and child.

I didn't even try to explain how one moment I was a carefree, if sullen and unhelpful at times, youth of nineteen summers and the next a husband and, even more bizarrely, a father.

But when she saw how sick Kate was she took control. Sending my older brother James, who for once was at home, to fetch the doctor, she took the baby in her arms and, ignoring the peculiar clothing, undressed her and started to bathe her burning skin with cooling cloths, all the while ordering Rhianne to do this or fetch that, pointing to here or there, wherever the items were located and, occasionally taking her eyes off the child to look at her new daughter-in-law (and that Jack is going to get the third degree when I get him alone!), wondered just what was happening.

If things hadn't been quite so serious with the baby being as ill as she was, she had told me later, she would have thought she was being taken for a right royal ride.

The doctor arrived in his car, closely followed by James on his bike, only to whisk Kate off to the local hospital without waiting for an ambulance. I went with him and wanted to leave Rhianne with my mother but she wouldn't hear of it. In any event I would have been worried sick at what might happen between those two women if I had left them together, had I not been so concerned about Kate. As it was I saw the look of complete horror on Rhianne's face as we and our baby got into a large piece of tinned armour – possibly even a dragon, and which had two enormous beams for eyes and spouted smoke at the back and, with a roar, carried us at great speed down the road.

We were gone for the rest of that day and returned home without Kate late the following afternoon.

'She's fine,' I said as we stepped wearily through the door, just in case my mother thought the worst. 'We can both go back to the hospital tonight to visit but they want to keep her in for two or three days just to be sure. They said we could stay with her all day but not at night, so tonight's trip will be a short one.'

'But not in those clothes! Come with me and I'll find something for you.'

Rhianne had had so many questions after we had left with Kate to go to the hospital and mum, when we returned had as many, if not more of her own. We sat down and tried to eat the meal mum had made for us during which we all helped answer them. For a start mum thought that I had met up with someone from a mental asylum because although they could understand each other, their languages were so different. Rhianne, on the other hand, thought my mum was very brusque and manly. Eventually we all had to laugh at our differences.

So, mum told her about everything that was alien to her, starting with the car, then the hospital, then the electric lights and log burner, dad's pipe and her knitting patterns, the clock and the tractor in the field, the vacuum cleaner, ironing board, and so on. On one occasion she had to stop Rhianne from diving to the ground when a biplane from the local airfield shot overhead.

She, in her turn, told mum about witches and dragons, the caer where she lived, sword fights and knights, saints and sinners. She, like me, did not mention the witch.

Each woman was as incredulous at what they were hearing as the other.

So it was, when I came downstairs at one point that I found two women laughing and trying to outdo one another with the things of their time. James was also joining in, obviously overawed by this beautiful woman who had come to their home and desperately trying to impress her with one amazing thing after another. But all stopped and all was concern as the doctor stepped through the door.

'It is as we thought – she has malaria but the doctors have given her an injection ...'

'Injection?' Another new word!

'Yes,' I answered. 'It is a medicine that is put inside a needle and inserted just under the skin, usually in the arm. It is effective and recovery is very quick if administered in time. Once she settles down the medication is much more simple – she will be able to drink it; when she gets older she will be able to take a small pill.

'What is malaria?'

'It is a parasite from a mosquito that invades the body. Not all people are affected, apparently, but those that are can become quite ill and some die.'

'Oh Kate isn't going to die, is she?'

'No, but there may be a problem!'

'What?'

'We won't know until they have done some more tests.'

'Tests?'

'Investigations – to find out how seriously she has been affected. She may have to stay in the hospital for a bit longer.'

'She may need medication for the rest of her life; well, not all the time, but the malaria could recur at any time and if it does it could kill her if she is not treated. Sorry to be so blunt, but I thought you would want to know.'

We thanked the doctor and he left, saying that he would drop in at the hospital that evening when we visited.

I waited until everyone except Rhianne and I had left the room and taking her hand filled in the blanks that the doctor had left.

'We won't be able to go back.'

'What do you mean?'

'We will have to stay here. If we take Kate back and she has another attack she might die.'

'Can't we take the medication back with us?' She asked if she had used the correct word and I just nodded.

'I asked the registrar at the hospital how long the medication kept before it was of no more use and he told me it had a very short life. I've been thinking of this all afternoon but can find no solution. It isn't so bad here, Rhianne. And Kate is too young to know any difference.'

'Then we will have to stay,' she stated quietly. 'Would we ever be able to go back?'

'We don't know yet how badly she has the infection. It could be that we might all go back. Merlin will know!'

'I'll go and make a bed up for you both,' mum said as she came back into the room. James can sleep on the floor. He's used to that anyway when your Uncle John comes to stay.

We didn't speak for ages after we'd gone up to our room and then Rhianne held my hand and just wept. It had all been too much for her, and me, come to that, but we were all fairly adrift until we knew what was going to happen to Kate.

Two days later we got the news that Kate had turned the corner and I could go and collect her.

Mrs Ambrose brought the news, arriving in a London taxi and urging us to get in and hurry, as she was just as eager to see the child as we were.

You should have seen Rhianne's face and her white knuckles as we sped off on the twenty-minute journey to the hospital. Mrs Ambrose just loved it though and urged the driver to go as fast as he could.

When we arrived Kate was shouting as loud as she could; she was wide-awake, in a strange place, and wanting her mother or Iris.

'Isis,' she'd been repeating over and over and threw the plate of ice cream that the nurse brought her onto the floor.

We explained to the confused nurse that that was the name of her nanny.

Completely misunderstanding, the nurse responded with, 'Well, my grandmother would have brought her up a bit better than that!'

When we arrived we were taken into a side room where a doctor asked us to sit down before he told us his findings. He looked at Rhianne in a peculiar way – although my mother had dressed her in more modern clothes, she still exuded an otherworldly air. She looked fairly up to date except that she insisted on wearing a long skirt that had been part of my gran's wardrobe. Anything shorter, she had said, would look indecent!

'I'm afraid that your daughter was ill for too long for us to be able to dispense an effective cure.'

'What does that mean?' Rhianne asked.

'She has had the parasite within her and because it has obviously made her so ill it could flare up again at any time. She will need to have the medication to hand at all times just in case she has another bout of malaria. I would advise against going to places where the mosquito thrives; it could be disastrous.'

Rhianne and I looked at each other – our eyes spoke volumes at this catastrophic news.

Mrs Ambrose, who unfortunately was not allowed to enter the ward (she was extremely miffed I can tell you), read the bad news in our faces as we left, even though we were laughing with Kate as we left the hospital. We all got back into the waiting taxi and went home.

Mum was overjoyed as she took the wriggling infant from her mother. 'Well, it's not every day that you become a grandmother, is it?' she grinned. There was an instant bond – little did we know, there and then, that mum was about to play a huge part in Kate's upbringing.

Mrs Ambrose disappeared almost as swiftly as she had appeared. She took me to one side out in the barnyard and told me what was happening elsewhere.

The fight was now well and truly over, though on a search across the seas he found that nearly all the pirate ships had been commandeered by who knows and sailed away but the one in which Mab had been cast adrift had beached on an island just north of the Thames estuary – Mab was nowhere to be seen.

'I have to get back. The lords are gathering. Soon the sword will be pulled from the stone. I have to be there for that – and so do you. So sort yourself out, and your family, and come back as soon as you can. Here is some dust. Come soon!'

Then Mrs Ambrose was gone.

I explained as best I could to both of my parents as much of my past as I could sensibly put together; I found it very difficult to get them to understand. I think that if Rhianne hadn't been there to back me up they would have taken me to see yet another psychiatrist! As it was, dad didn't say much – just puffed more vigorously on his pipe, but mum asked quite a lot of sensible questions, though she had to admit it seemed extremely far-fetched. I also told them that Kate would never be able to return to the Dark Ages because she just wouldn't be able to get the medication she needed there in order to stay alive. So we would all be staying here. Mum was very happy with that.

We had a lovely week at the cottage. It was one of those glorious Indian summers that rarely appears as late as November; the leaves had stayed on the trees for a long time this autumn and now, with the frosty nights and beautiful days they had divested themselves of their clothing so that the low sun could send dancing rays through their branches and light up the woods all around. We took Kate out in an old pram mum had discovered at the back of one of the barns and enjoyed our walks together as we pushed her around. She appeared to have no ill effects after her sickness and loved every part of our time that week.

Little did any of us know that that was going to be the last week the three of us would ever enjoy being together again!

At the end of that week, however, I had to tell my parents that Rhianne and I would need to return to the Dark Ages or history, as we now know it, might be changed forever. Would they look after Kate?

Of course they would. Mum was delighted. It had been a long time since there had been a baby in the house and she had always wanted a daughter and you know what children and their grandparents are like – Kate had taken an immediate liking to mum and, well, she was as completely soppy with dad as he was with her. 'And I have such a lot of new wool; she's going to look lovely in all her new knitted outfits!' mum added, searching through the cupboard beside the fireplace.

We enjoyed a wonderful evening with mum and dad and James

stayed with us till nearly midnight. He insisted on showing Rhianne how to play draughts but was slightly miffed when she showed a better aptitude than she ought. He left, having lost five games to three.

'I insist on a rematch when I come back,' he said as he took his leave of us.

When he left we all went to bed; I told mum we would be gone before she got up next morning, so it was a tearful Rhianne that had held onto her baby for as long as she could that evening, leaving her with mum so that she wasn't woken up when we left.

So it was that we arrived back where news of our problems had already been spread abroad by Merlin.

Lady Elise and Iris were crestfallen. How could they survive without the child? It took a lot of care and hugs to get them to understand that where she had been taken was the best place for her and that it would be impossible for any of them to see her again, or she might die. Merlin had gone so far as to say that they had had to take her to a place of healing but hadn't said anything about another century; would they have understood? He didn't think so.

I stayed with the family for several days before a disembodied voice called for me.

Thus it was that after using the piece of Glass that Merlin had given me I arrived back on Thorney Island at the banks of the Thames just as several of the lords, led by Merlin, were ferried across the water.

THIRTY-SIX

'Ah, you're here!' he exclaimed as, refusing my assistance, he jumped from the little boat onto the island.

'*Of course I'm here*,' I thought. '*It's completely obvious!*'

'Now, now Percy,' he tutted, making me jump. I expect my barriers were down because of all that was going on in my head at the moment.

'You can help them, though,' he added, pointing. 'It's a wonder they don't sink with all that armour!'

Salazar arrived halfway through the ferrying. He'd found a small lifeboat that had either come adrift from one of the pirate ships or he had helped its release. Arthur and Nell's son were with him, along with four or five others, one of which returned to ferry some more over.

Before long the island was buzzing with noise. Everyone was still excited at their victory, praising one another and expecting praise in turn.

Funny that! I never ever got used to the way they loved being praised, especially when the minstrels sang songs of their exploits. It had happened to me once and I felt like cringing with embarrassment but had to smile (it felt like one of those smiles you give when a photographer is taking too long to take the picture and your lips or cheeks start to twitch!) throughout and accept the cheers at the end gracefully.

It took ages before everyone had assembled in the clearing around the stone but it was strange to watch each person go silent, as though by magic, as they stepped through the trees and saw the sword gleaming red like fire in the late afternoon sun.

It was eventually as still as death as the last person stopped speaking; one full minute passed before each man started to whisper to his neighbour until the full import of the prophecy that each one of them had learned at his mother's knee broke in upon their thoughts.

Then there were loud shouts and demands after they reached the stone; each one of them started promoting himself, believing that he was the rightful king.

A fight broke out between two minor lords as they tried to elbow themselves into a better position to enable them to have a go at the sword and things looked like they might get out of hand when, speaking low but clearly, Merlin called for silence.

Everything stopped.

He stood on the rock beside the sword, his staff held high, and asked for them all to get in line.

The Duke of Cornwall shouldered his way through the crowd and stepped up first; then there were scuffles as to who was of next highest rank and should follow.

'No-one has the right to go first!' Merlin exclaimed. 'You will be chosen by lot.'

As you can imagine, the duke was quite miffed but there was no argument. It turned out that the duke ended up first anyway and then everyone else took his place.

The duke insisted he have several goes after the first pull failed but, eventually, he had to accept defeat and, red faced more by effort than embarrassment, climbed down.

Arthur and Gwen stood at the edge of the forest watching all this – Arthur extremely keenly as he wanted to know who would be the king he was about to swear allegiance to; Gwen with wry amusement at all of these puffed up lords making themselves look ridiculous. She leaned over toward Arthur and whispered, 'Might it be a queen instead?'

His eyebrows shot up as he considered the idiocy of her comment, but then, again, he recalled she was more than a match for most men.

I stood with Cabby on one side of me and Griff on the other, abstractedly scratching their necks as I watched what would happen next.

They all tried, one by one, to pull the sword, including Kay, but it would not move.

At a swift mental prod from Merlin I moved over to stand beside Arthur with my heart all the while thumping inside my chest.

He just stood. He was a nobody, so he said.

Even when I suggested he try, he ignored me. 'Who am I?' he asked, shrugging his shoulders.

'Well, everyone else is having a go!'

'Who else is there to pull this sword from the stone?' Merlin cried.

Sir Ector, after it had all gone quiet, came over to him and said he might as well try, as everyone else had.

He knew, didn't he?

Arthur, reluctantly it has to be said, walked across the grass and round to the side that had enough rough edges so as to be climbed. He stood at the base of those steps and stared up at Merlin.

'Come on Arthur, let's see if the prophecy might have been all about you.'

Funnily it had all gone quiet. Gwen had moved across to me and gripped my hand in hers as Arthur, who had climbed to the top of the stone, stood staring at the sword.

'Go on boy!' Sir Ector shouted.

'You might as well have a go,' another urged him.

And then Merlin, standing tall, commanded him, 'Arise, Arthur, son of Uther Pendragon, take hold of your destiny!'

If it was quiet before, there was deathly silence now.

Arthur stared at Merlin. 'What did you call me?'

But Merlin said no more – merely held his staff aloft.

So Arthur, face like granite, grabbed the sword and it came out like a hot knife in butter.

No-one there was as surprised as he. He held the sword aloft, more because that is where it ended when he pulled it out than for any other ulterior reason.

Several things happened at once.

Many lords dropped to their knees and removing their helmets bowed their heads. Some just stood there with mouths agape, some growled their disapproval or unbelief.

Sir Ector turned and stared at Merlin as if to demand, '*Why did you never say?*'

After several arguments Arthur, who had stared at the sword as if he had never seen one before, thrust it back into the stone. He swallowed quite a few times and licked lips that had gone quite dry before he was able to speak. It took several attempts before everyone was once again quiet.

'This isn't a trick. I never knew any of this before Merlin spoke. I am as surprised as you. But if it is God's will that I be king of

Britain, listen to me now.

'I have put the sword back into the stone. Please, come up, anyone who feels he has this right; take the sword and if it comes out I will serve him faithfully all my life. This I swear.'

He stepped back and came back down to the ground.

One by one several of the lords tried again and then, when the sword refused to budge, urged Arthur to try once again.

This time, when he raised the flashing sword high, everyone acclaimed him king and the sound must have reached the far side of the Thames as they shouted thrice, 'Long live Arthur, King of all the Britons.'

We rowed back across the Thames to the place where most of the men were encamped. News of the new king spread like wildfire and the cheering increased with it. Everyone made merry and many a man got drunk that night.

After placing the sword into the safekeeping of the scabbard that he was urged to belt around his waist (which caused the sword to hum within), we eventually all returned to our own tents.

No-one saw the malevolent eyes that watched them through the crystal. No-one saw the desire the witch had for that sword. No-one knew she had escaped from the ship so quickly. No-one had any idea what she had in store for all of them, and especially for Arthur and me.

THIRTY-SEVEN

There were so many quandaries back at the caer. Sir Ector was cornered on more than one occasion by those who wanted to know why he hadn't told them about Arthur Pendragon before now.

He eventually had to escape the Hall and leave it to the others to answer for him; no-one seemed to believe that he just did not know.

Gwen had taken herself off with her brothers to discuss whether or not her betrothal still stood. Did she really want to be a queen? Did Arthur think she would be fine enough for him now that he was to be crowned king? Perhaps he should choose someone else? Her brothers finally persuaded her to agree to be queen if Arthur still wanted her for his wife.

Thus it was, that as the celebrations for their victory reached their third day, Arthur presented to the whole company his future bride.

Suffice to say the celebrations then continued for the rest of the week, during which time the witch, disguised (extremely well) as a serving wench, penetrated the whole of Sir Ector's home. There were so many new faces rushing about here and there with bed linen, flagons of wine, tables of hogsheads and the like; who would have noticed her among all that throng? And who would have trusted that woman with food and drink if they had known she was there?

Merlin and Salazar, who had apparently relaxed their guard, certainly didn't notice her and even Cabby or Griff with their sharp sense of smell didn't detect her either.

Everyone just enjoyed all the fun and festivities. And Rhianne, fretting for her child as would any young mother who had been deprived of it, took no notice of the over-attentive maidservant as she fussed around her – plumping up cushions, dishing up the choicest meats and pouring the best wines; by the end of the week almost all that the wicked woman had set out to do was achieved.

Without any of us having the slightest inkling, she had got her revenge on me.

Now for Arthur and Merlin.

THIRTY-EIGHT

It had all been decided. The coronation of Arthur Pendragon would take place on 25th December at the Abbey of St Alban the Martyr.

There had been much argument as to where this ceremony was to take place, many believing it should be in London, several reckoned it should happen in the West Country and even some said Caernarfon. However, Merlin reckoned the Roman road led the way perfectly for each to get to London without too many problems and the abbey was situated almost due north of it. Again, if Merlin said it, it was generally done.

Gwen and her brothers returned to Wales soon after the festivities were over in order to prepare themselves for the coronation. Her father and most of the household would accompany her to St Albans where she would be the most honoured guest of the king as he would present her to the whole world as his future wife.

It was a mad time. No-one had time to talk! Merlin was busy with this and that and spent much time with Salazar. The women, including Rhianne and even Jasmine who, with sewing and stitching so many dresses, shirts, tabards, and more things than I can recall, didn't have time to talk and at night everyone just fell exhausted into bed.

I mean, there were three weeks before the ceremony. How long does it take to sew up a dress?

The look I got from Rhianne when I voiced my opinion in that regard would have withered a saint.

The only sensible time I had was with Cabal so we spent much of that walking among the now naked trees in the woods. Even the hare and deer had disappeared, so Cabby not having much joy in hunting was thus happy to spend his time with me.

'I think that witch has been around!' he told me on the first day after everyone had left the caer.

'What?'

'*Well, it was just a whiff! It wasn't even anything I could put my paw on! Just a short tickle to the nose late one evening. It wasn't windy or even breezy to bring something from a long way away, so it made me a little bit suspicious. But, because it was just a slight whiff I thought it might just be my imagination.'*

'Where did you smell it?'

'I was just outside the kitchen door; you know, waiting for anything Old Molly might toss out to me, when it just floated up my nostrils. It made me jump a bit but then I thought perhaps something had gone off in the food store. Then I thought that that was ridiculous because everything had been eaten for miles around to feed everyone – and there were hundreds. No, no food had gone off!

'I decided to check up and spent a couple of hours sniffing around here and there until I had covered the whole of the caer except the kitchens – you know Molly hates me being in there, but I found nothing else except a slight uneasiness in my bladder when I went into your bedroom.'

'You think the witch has been in our room? I don't feel any different. Oh, what about Rhianne?'

'She's all right. I saw her this morning and she was tucking into a good breakfast. It's a good job Kate isn't around, isn't it?'

I was happy and sad that Kate wasn't around but that was something I couldn't even start to think about with the present threat hanging over us. Mum was more than capable of looking after her. I had plenty to think about without worrying about her as well. I needed to get back to the caer and see for myself if Rhianne was OK. That witch was crafty and perhaps some of my training from Merlin would help me to detect anything that wasn't right. As far as Kate was concerned, I had always thought she'd had something to do with her sickness.

But Rhianne seemed fine, although naturally still pining for our daughter.

I had a word with Merlin about it when he was walking in the courtyard with Salazar. Both sorcerers had been unaware that anything untoward was happening during the celebrations but determined to check straight away.

So it was, that night, that I received the bad news that not only had Mab been here but that she had been here for almost a week.

'How could you tell?'

'I have this potion that is invisible to the naked eye but when sprayed lights up that which we are searching for. We had enchanted the potion to show up, in purple – but even that is invisible to the naked eye unless you have the magic within you – anywhere that Mab has been, if indeed she has been here. Come, Percy – I want to show you something.'

I followed him up the winding staircase to the battlements. He gave me the small pill that contains the magic for this particular activity and as it took effect I almost choked – there below me, all across the courtyard – into the stables, kitchens, up the side stairs into the sleeping quarters and almost everywhere were the purple footprints of the witch.

'Are you sure it's her?' I whispered.

'I'm afraid so! But she isn't here any more. Thank goodness that Cabby has such a strong sense of smell or we might never have known anything about this.'

'But how is it that he has only just smelled her?'

'She had probably used a powerful draught of some potion or other to disguise her own odour – not that she is ever aware of it I am sure, though how she doesn't I am at a loss to comprehend – just so that we and the dogs didn't discover her.'

'But what did she want? What has she done?'

'We will try to find out but we might never find out,' Salazar said in his deep and almost sad voice.

'But we will try,' Merlin added. 'She will not get the better of us!'

We hunted high and low. Merlin and Salazar went separate ways searching the kitchens and even into the darkest parts of the stables and outbuildings but she had been thorough; she had left no trace.

After approximately four days we all had to give up. Not only had we found nothing, but also Rhianne and the Lady Elise were beginning to get twitchy, especially when we put on those over-exuberant smiles, like you do, when you are trying to convince everyone that everything is fine.

It was the night before we were due to leave for St Albans and the coronation. Riders had been sent daily to the abbey whence they returned with the news that the priests had confirmed that all was in readiness for the coronation.

Then we were off. What a spectacle we made as we rode behind

Arthur who headed up our cavalcade with Merlin on his right hand side; for once Merlin could hardly keep the smile from his face. His long life had been for this moment alone – Arthur, the Once and Future King – King of all the Britons; how could he do aught else but smile? There would be peace at last throughout the land. Gwen, as his future bride, rode on his other side, straight backed and with her chin raised – she would be a queen to be reckoned with.

I rode beside Rhianne who, though still fretting for Kate, kept a calm, though pale, countenance and, dressed in the blue silk that became her so well, looked beautiful; we rode about tenth back from Arthur.

We spent the first day, once we were out on the open highway, trotting back and forth down the line of men, chatting and laughing. It was a merry time. Shake Spear drove everyone mad with his observations on everything from the sun in the morning to the moon and stars at night; from the smallest wren to the largest goose; every flower caused him to create an ode to it and as for the cavalcade itself, by the time we reached London he had almost written a play!

It took three days to get to St Albans where, with relief, we found everything in readiness.

As our journey had progressed we were joined by the lords and minor kings of the land, each one bowing and saluting Arthur; most had wide smiles, though one or two were obviously still jealous, as they'd always believed the crown was theirs.

Cabal reported every couple of hours; if that mad woman was anywhere around he would know it.

London, always a bustling place, with mean streets and filthy docks, was now crowded to bursting point. We stayed a mere night while the horses, tethered in the surrounding fields and farmlands, were fed and rested. Only two men were eventually left behind because they'd gone off and got so drunk that no-one could rouse them. They would be dealt with on the way back – that is, if anyone could find them! As it was, they were going to miss the highlight of their lives – Arthur's coronation.

Rhianne and I spent the evening with Merlin, Salazar and Jasmine. Our very small hostelry had three rooms, which Merlin had had the foresight to visit and reserve for us some few weeks ago. Cabby found us some time during the evening, though Griff had gone off somewhere else.

'I am going to send you and Rhianne back to Kate ...'

'No,' I interrupted him, 'I can't miss the coronation!'

'Neither can I,' Rhianne added more softly. 'Although I know now he is not my brother, I have known him all his life and have treated him as such and will continue to do so and to love him like a dear sister should and I just have to be here for this special time.'

I started to say something more when Merlin, who always commanded every situation, held up his hand and I couldn't speak.

'You will be back by morning, I promise.'

Merlin, wise as time itself, had seen how the separation of mother and child was having such a bad effect on Rhianne and thought that a short visit would help. We thanked him and spent the next half hour or so checking and double-checking the potions until we were sure we had it right.

And then the feathers hit the fan and it all went oh so wrong.

Merlin had made this blue potion – it was thicker than cream but not quite as thick as plasticine. It was a bit runny round the edges but chewy in the middle.

'When you want to come back,' Merlin added, 'all you need to do is think the word "return" and you will be here in no time.'

Not only did it not work – well it did work but not in the right way – but it would only work completely on one creature – Cabby!

Let me explain what happened.

Rhianne and I stood side by side holding hands and each lifting a phial of the blue liquid to our lips. Both of us had a picture of my family's kitchen in our minds and after a count of three swallowed the potion. It tasted a bit like strawberries but that isn't important. There was a humming in my ears, a slight pulling and then I literally appeared, alone, in the kitchen, where my mother almost dropped Kate onto the floor with fright.

I managed to step up to them and soothe mum whilst at the same time catching Kate (who thought this a delightful game) before noticing that Rhianne was not with me. Seconds later Cabby appeared in a flash at the same point that I had entered the room.

This time mum did scream. I mean, Cabby is not exactly small and the sneezes he made as he passed through time and space caused his top lips to lift and show some enormously dangerous teeth.

I managed to calm everything down and I think that it was right then and there that mum realised my stories were not made up at all.

But where was Rhianne?

I tried to reach back through time to find out what was happening but all I got was static.

'*Come outside,*' Cab said as he walked toward the back door.

'I think the dog needs to make a visit,' I explained as I walked out the back with him. 'Won't be long.'

'*What happened Cab?*'

Mayhem! When you both drank that potion, you disappeared but Rhianne just passed out.'

'*What do you mean?*'

'*It acted like a poison on her!*'

'*Poison? Oh no, oh no!*'

'*No! She's OK Percy! She came round in no time but Merlin has said, and he told me to come to you and tell you, 'that Rhianne will not be able to return to your time – er, this time – and that she will now not be able to see Kate, um, yet!*'

'No!'

I had said this so loud that my father, who'd been in the barn, came rushing out to find out what was going on.

I explained, though it took a lot of explaining because I knew he'd think me nuts if I said "the dog said" so I just said that I had brought that information back with me.

You have to remember that when I travelled back and forth in those days that even if I was away for months on end I would only have been away for minutes or hours at home so it wasn't unusual for dad, who'd been in the barn all morning, to have thought I hadn't been anywhere at all.

When he eventually went back to his work, Cab continued.

'*Merlin tried several things but nothing was going to work. "Well," he said to me, "Go after Percy and bring him and Kate back." Rhianne would hear nothing of it. She said that she could not be responsible for her death back there and though she would miss her more than life itself, if she could have life in the 20th Century, she would be happy; Kate would be too young to remember life back then and she might have a much better life now that she was away from the witch. After some reassurance from Merlin that you would be back in the morning, Rhianne left to go to her room. She was extremely distraught.*

'I'll stay with Kate for a bit longer and then we'll go back. We cannot miss Arthur's coronation. Anyway, how did you get here?' Percy added.

'Well, when Kate tried to drink the potion, only some of it went down her throat before she choked; the rest splashed onto my nose and the most natural reaction for any dog when something lands on its nose is to lick it off, so that's what I did. Merlin saw what had happened and quickly told me to come; it took seconds but I managed to hear what they had to say before I ended up here!'

'Well, let's hope you can return with me then!'

And he did. In fact, Cabby is the only one of all of us that has been able to come and go almost at will, as you will already have discovered.

We arrived back at the small inn in the wee small hours. Everyone was fast asleep, or at least I thought they were. I let Cabby out to go foraging then crept up the stairs to see how Rhianne was and wasn't at all surprised to find her awake; she had been staring out of the window at the sky to watch for dawn breaking and turned as I entered the room. The candle flame guttered as she jumped out of the bed and rushed toward me.

'How is she? How is Kate?' as if I didn't know who she was talking about but, then, she was missing her so much.

'She is very well and having a great time with her grandparents who, unless I take charge, will spoil her to bits.'

'What do you mean, "unless I take charge?" ' she asked me.

'Well, I hope to be able to go back and forth to make sure she is all right,' I explained.

'But she is well?'

'Yes, Rhianne – she is very well.'

'Though she can never come home?'

'No!' This said as a whisper.

'Oh why couldn't I go? I wanted to see her so much! Merlin tells me it was the witch; said she'd done something to me and I would now be separated from my beautiful daughter forever, though Arthur tells me it will not be forever.'

'Oh have you seen him?'

'Yes, he called to see Merlin who wanted to go over the ceremony with him.'

Collapsing onto the bed she fell into floods of tears. I put my arms around her and waited until she stopped.

'And how will the ceremony go?'

'It will go well, Percy.' She shook her head as if to clear it and then declared, 'I shall not let my sorrow spoil Arthur's day. I shall try and block it out until afterwards – sorrow forever waits round corners to pounce on us and try to destroy us – I shall try to ignore those corners and trust that she will always be safe. Who knows, maybe one day we might be together again. But I only want her to be well, Percy; I love her too much for it to be otherwise.'

'She will; I promise.'

THIRTY-NINE

The day arrived.

I reckon everyone had been up since the very early hours. Arthur was going to wear his wedding clothes for the coronation – they were rich enough; much ermine and velvet had been used and Smith had fashioned lots of leather for gloves and boots etc. He would be wearing the scabbard and the sword, though the sword would not be allowed into the Abbey. Salazar and Jasmine had said they would stand guard over it at the doors to the chapel where the ceremony would take place.

Then we were all on our way. I had never seen so many lords and ladies in one place at one time since I had begun my travels back in time. The common people lined the route at least three deep in places for the twenty mile ride to the abbey. It was a sunny but cold day with a soft breeze that made the flags flutter, and the cheers at times were deafening.

They were shouting 'Bless you sire, long live the king' and the like all the way along.

En route Merlin had leaned across and whispered to Arthur that where they had all once been afraid of marauding bands from some of the more unscrupulous lords and even from across the seas, he had now brought them hope – a Britain that was going to be strong under one ruler.

And so we took our places in the Abbey. There were no seats so we stood. A line of men from Sir Ector's workers, including Shake Spear, Tailor, Baker and almost all the others we'd met over the years – honest, trustworthy men who were brave and faithful – had been chosen for the occasion and stood facing each other across an expanse of six feet that stretched from the entrance to the altar. I don't think any of us forgot Wite – he was conspicuous by his absence and Brosc, even though he'd longed for this day, couldn't face coming, saying his sadness would overshadow their joy. The men were all dressed the same and stood (uncomfortably but proud in their new uniforms) shoulder to shoulder, each holding a staff (for the Abbot was insistent that there be no weapons in the house of the Lord, though he obviously hadn't seen the damage these men could do with a staff) and all the supporters and those who had been invited were to take their places behind them. There was the obvious jostling for the best positions and the building was soon bursting at the seams. Rhianne and I had found a great spot just inside the main doorway that had three steps leading to a small platform beside it. We managed to balance ourselves and thus had a great view over everyone else's heads.

Then the trumpets sounded the approach – a blast that shook us all to silence as effectively as a switch being thrown – and every head turned toward the door.

Sir Ector entered first and stood facing the left of the altar; Merlin then entered and stood to the right. Arthur stepped through, followed by everyone present's intake of breath. He looked magnificent – the tailors and seamstresses had done a magnificent job (and I did quickly look over at Smith who looked enormously proud at his additions to his lord's attire).

There were probably only about half a dozen of us present that knew Arthur very well and it was only we few that observed the nervousness of the future king. To everyone else he looked every inch a leader, with head held high and shoulders pulled back; his step toward the prepared throne was sure and his jaw was strong. He walked three steps in front of his two attendants until he reached the few steps that led up to the platform in front of the altar, where he stopped.

The Abbot had been waiting at the top of the steps and moved forward to invite Arthur to join him. The Abbot then stood with his back to the congregation so that all could see and more importantly hear the oaths that were about to be sworn by their future king; then began the ceremony.

It went on for quite a while – Arthur took several oaths to serve his country and his God, to look after his people and make fair laws, etc. Once he had made his vows he was led to the elaborately carved wooden throne where he sat and looked out at his new subjects.

It was a lot different to the coronation that had taken a few years before in the 20th Century in London when Queen Elizabeth II had been crowned. I had watched that on a small black and white television and it was a very long ceremony indeed with lords and ladies galore and bishops and clergy all doing their part.

Here it was a lot simpler and on a much smaller scale but for everyone there it was as though everything they had longed for all their lives was now happening. It was a joyful occasion indeed.

And then the crown was placed upon his head. It was a simple crown (not like the elaborate one in 1953) and was made up of a circlet of gold studded with rubies, sapphires and emeralds.

The Abbot then took two steps back and cried in a loud voice, 'God save the King,' to which the whole assembly responded in a joyous shout, 'God save the King.' We then heard all the people gathered outside crying out as well. Three massive shouts of 'God save the King.'

Arthur stepped down and began his walk back down the aisle. I know we should have been either bowing or curtseying but everyone was so excited that the room was filled with deafening cheers, whistles and laughter.

On stepping outside, the mid-winter's watery sun shone down upon the scene giving it an unearthly light. I shivered and thought it might not just be the cold weather but the thought was soon banished as we watched the people, so many of them that they seemed to vanish off into the distance, who were cheering and waving hankies and their hands at the newly crowned king.

I had never seen Arthur smile so much; always of a more serious nature in the past he seemed to radiate the warmth of those around him as he stood upon the steps of the Abbey and smiled and waved back at the people.

His people!

The thought must have seemed strange to him. One minute he was a minor son of a minor lord and the next the firstborn son of a major king. Then he was the only one able to pull a sword out of a stone and now he, too, was king.

I think at the time it was all a bit much for him but, well, you know Arthur – it wouldn't be long before you would think he'd been king all his life. He had a great head for strategy and he was as brave as the next man. He commanded and received respect from everyone he met; which was always tempered by the respect he held for all mankind.

He would be one of the greatest, if not the greatest king in all Christendom.

'*The Once and Future King!*'

I looked across at Merlin. We smiled.

Arthur got onto his horse and the procession headed into the meadows where tents and marquees had been erected, fires lit and whole hogs were roasting.

The celebrations were about to begin.

FORTY

We were laughing, drinking, eating, celebrating – many were going to feel the effects of all that wine the following morning.

Well, most were, I reckon, but Rhianne and I, who had hardly touched any of the banquet, had retired to our tent; she was still missing Kate and just couldn't keep smiling any more.

'What do you think we'll do?' she had asked.

I knew she meant Kate but didn't really have the words to say. Well, how could I? I mean, what was going to happen was that throughout our lives I would be to-ing and fro-ing back through the ages while my wife was in one place and my daughter in another. What should I say to my daughter as she was growing up? What could I say to my wife without hurting her? Little did I know that everything would be sorted out for me in that regard! Little did I know that I would have no choice! We could hardly shut out the noise of all that a campsite makes, especially when it is making merry, but eventually Rhianne drifted off into an uneasy slumber. I told Cabal to keep watch over her as I left to pay my respects to my friend, the new king.

I found him surrounded by lords and ladies whose daughters were fluttering their eyelashes at him outrageously. It was obvious that some of the lords had not thought it important to tell their wives (and thus their daughters) that Arthur had introduced his future wife to them, though it has in fairness to be said that not all of those lords were present when Arthur had introduced Gwen before. So, not being able to stand it any longer he stood up and waited until all the noise had died down before he spoke.

During the ceremony Gwen had kept a very low profile. Her mother and father and brothers, along with various other lords and ladies with their offspring, had lined the walls of the Abbey and watched but no-one had been given places of prominence; in those days it was a free-for-all, each lord elbowing his way to the best place, obviously believing he was better than his neighbour, and so no-one, except those in the know, knew of Arthur's betrothal. He had been getting really hot under the collar, even on this cold

December night, at the obvious declarations being thrown his way by the lovely and in some cases not so lovely daughters of the attending lords.

When all was still he held out his hand to Gwen who, now that she and Arthur had acknowledged their love for each other, rose to her feet and, stepping over the conglomeration of accumulating rubbish, eventually stood beside him, taking the proffered hand in hers.

I must say, though, they looked an astonishingly good-looking couple. Both had the taut skin of youth – one ruddy and the other pale though with softly glowing cheeks.

He was a little put off what he was about to say when one young woman, correctly discerning what was about to happen, started to sob quite loudly, but stopped when she was cuffed round the ear by a very large woman – obviously her mother – who was heard to say that if she had taken a bit more care of herself it might have been her up there! Mind you, once introduced to the mother, the daughter would not have stood a chance, Gwen or no Gwen!

But to get back to Arthur.

'My lords and ladies, my people …' His voice was firm and everyone was hanging on his words, but exploded into applause when called "his people". Once it quieted down he continued. 'Today you have made me your king. You have heard me make promises that I will keep, so help me God. Britain will be great and I hope to lead a people that will rise to be the finest in Christendom. With your help this will be achieved as no man can do this alone.'

At this there were more cheers and a tossing of hats into the air, followed by, 'Oi, that's not your 'at that's mine,' along with a lot of shhhhs, but only for a moment or two.

'With regard to being alone, God said, 'It is not good,' so he made woman so that they could help each other and find happiness. Therefore, I should like to introduce to you your future queen, Gwenhwyfar.'

Again there was silence for a few seconds and then the whole place erupted with cheers and 'bless you both' and 'wonderful' and more tears, most of which were of joy.

Arthur was eventually able to tell them that they were all invited to the wedding on St. Mark's Day next year where there would be celebrations unmatched in their lifetime.

'But she will only be able to prepare herself as a bride, never a wife!'

I was standing just behind Arthur as this declaration was made. We hadn't seen her coming; there hadn't even been a whiff that she was anywhere around but then she was there – standing in full view of everyone and no-one was able to move.

Arthur stood, almost blocking my view, holding Gwen's hand and everyone else was staring at whatever they had been staring at when she spoke.

I tried to pull my sword but my hand refused to budge.

I could just about swivel my eyes and looked across at Merlin. He, too, was rooted to the spot and his face was almost maroon with anger.

It was just like being at the movies when one reel finished and they had to put in another one, only they put in the wrong one – a different film and nothing was making sense. But this wasn't the movies!

What had she done? How had she done it?

Stepping across bodies and discarded hog bones and other litter, she walked up to the king and stared into his eyes for so long I wondered whether she was reading all that was in his head; that is something I don't think I ever found the answer to, but after a sharp laugh she turned and bent down to take Excalibur.

I tried to speak to Merlin but there was no connection; he still looked mad!

Lifting the sword high she swung it round over her head a couple of times before sticking the point into the ground and leaning on it.

'You know the prophecy, Arthur?

'Shall I sing it to you?'

Oh dear. I had never heard her sing, just whistle or hum and that was off-key, like Merlin. Did all sorcerers sing that way?

Then she chanted it:

'He will come
On a powerful charger with sword held high
He will come
Wearing the golden crown of the Once and Future King
He will come
Uniting all the kingdoms into one land
He will come
In the power of the Prince of Peace
He will come
He will rule in fairness and majesty
He will destroy every enemy
His most evil foe he must kill
And with the edge of Excalibur he will.

He will come.

But,'

And then she was silent for so long I thought she'd forgotten the rest, but no, it was all for effect –

'If he turns from the True Path
If he looks to his own glory
Then she will come
And him she will destroy.'

She stared at Arthur for a long minute before the laughter took over. It was the only sound for miles around; even the sparks stopped spitting from the fires and the fat stopped dripping from the roasting meats. It went on and on and on, bouncing from the trees and hills around until finally she stopped and all was once again still.

She took hold of the hilt of the sword and lifted it high. I was screaming inside my head as I am sure was everyone else. If that noise could have been let loose it would have lifted clouds but it was contained as my mind's eye let me see her plunging that sword deep into Arthur's heart and laughing as she did so. My fears reached a crescendo as she continued:

'You are now going to die young king. And how are you going to die?

'By your own sword, young sir!

'By your own sword!'

She stared hard into his eyes: there was no mercy in them. Hard, catlike, she stepped back from him and made herself ready.

It's funny how things change in the twinkling of an eye, isn't it? She was holding the sword high above her head with the point aimed at Arthur's chest when, what she should have done if she had had her wits about her she didn't do. Why?

Because she saw the scabbard. Mordred had brought back the information that it was powerfully magical; that the one who possessed it would not only be able to rule the land but no-one anywhere could stand against them. The sword and the scabbard together – she would be invincible!

'Oh yes,' she thought. 'I will not only destroy this king of not even one day, but I shall also have the bonus of ruling the world! And I certainly don't want this magical sheath being destroyed by his blood.'

She leaned forward and hitched the scabbard onto the point of the sword and, laughing, tossed it high into the air. As she caught it, with the largest grin on her gap-filled mouth, it all went wrong! But she was too far gone to realise it. One moment she was fantasising on the power that was about to drop into her hand and all she would do when she had killed the king, the next moment, as her fingers curled around the scabbard, her brain had ceased to function completely.

Then we were released.

Arthur jumped over to the sword and sheath and grabbing both made sure they were secure.

Merlin almost flew across the ground and standing over the woman who understood not one word he spoke declared, 'But you forgot one thing, Mab: the prophecy's last part! He has not turned from the true path!'

Mab lay on the ground with an inane look on her face; a few 'ag ags' escaped through her slack lips as rows of dribble followed one another down and off her chin.

The crisis well and truly over, Merlin told everyone to carry on with the celebrations; there would be no more wickedness this night.

He ordered Mab be pulled up from the ground – no easy task; it took four strong men to achieve this – and calling me to go with him led her away, noticing a skulking Mordred edging away into the trees.

Finally, when not even the echo of the festivities could be heard he called the dragon. Yes, he sang. I kept quiet!

Again my heart almost stopped in my chest as I watched her arrive, lighting up the sky with myriad colours as she and Merlin sang their song.

We hauled the senseless woman, now a dead weight, onto Moon Song's back and laid her between the dragon's wings. Then we were off, flying over the frozen countryside, west, ever west. It was beautiful. The land, covered in frost or snow looked asleep, covered with a crisp white blanket, while the stars, amazingly bright in the winter sky, gave so much light it seemed like day. I loved this time upon the dragon's back, flying high and clear over land, sometimes over sea. Would I have enjoyed it as much, though, if I had known it would be many a year before I would do this again.

But for now, in the eerie light of a winter's morning, we stood near a hill while Merlin called for the Lady.

We waited and waited but finally the mists crept around us and surrounded the island that seemed to grow from within its depths. Then she was there.

'Who is that with you, Merlin?' her voice tinkled the question.

'You know, Lady!' he replied.

'Why is she so dazed?'

'She has done wrong and it hurt her. Can you care for her?'

'Bring her to me.'

Merlin led the dazed woman to the edge of the lake where her sister stared sorrowfully at her for a few moments before, taking her hand, took her into those swirling, all-encompassing mists.

'Come, sister; I will care for you. We will get to know one another again and happiness will return.' Her voice was soothing as we watched and listened.

I heard her speaking to her sister as a loving mother would to a child who had been hurt and again wondered how two sisters could have led their lives so differently: one all goodness and the other the complete opposite.

I watched Mab's back as it disappeared into the haze and wondered if she would ever return. And, if she did, how long it would be before she did. And, more importantly, would she return like her sister or would the wickedness of aeons be unable to be washed away? I shivered as though someone had walked across my grave.

Shaking off these thoughts I turned and asked Merlin why he had let her go. Why had he not let the prophecy take its course? What was his reasoning?

He merely replied that it was not the right time and that blood should not be spilled on such an auspicious day – it didn't bode well. 'But the prophecy will come true, Percy; just remember that Arthur is the Once and Future King – he will have to return one day – will she also return?

'Just watch – a leader will emerge when Britain is in dire need of salvation. Who knows, he might even bear the same name as the Once and Future King!

I had to be content.

After days of festivities the various parties departed; before long, apart from the scorched ground where campfires had either lit up the area or cooked the food, you would never have known anyone had been there.

Merlin asked Salazar and me to return Androcles and the scabbard to his home and was only too pleased that he wanted the lion to accompany him. Goliath also demanded to go – and who would disagree with him? The Scribe wanted to stay with us and

Merlin was happy with that as he was completely intrigued with the magical chalk and needed to experiment with it.

Arthur was only too happy to hand over the scabbard. He had the sword! The sword was the sword of prophecy and using it in battle was something that was second nature to him, whereas the scabbard, with its humming and warmth scared him more than comforted him – he was not as happy with what he considered to be magic as either Merlin or I.

We arrived back in Jerusalem and eventually at Androcles' home. There was no sign of his grandfather; in fact the whole of the city, which appeared to be in ruins, and surrounding areas, seemed deserted. It looked as though years had gone by since we had first been in that place instead of the months that we had all spent together with Arthur.

And that was how we left them.

Androcles said he was determined to search for his grandfather and hoped he might still be alive but if he found out otherwise and he found him he wished to give him a decent burial. He was safe in the company of Goliath and the lion (which he had named Merlin) would keep everyone who had evil intentions at bay.

'I had wonderful talks with your new king; he, too, like me believes in the true God. Even if my grandfather is not alive in this world, because of his trust in the Lord, he will be fully alive in the next. I am content, and I have these wonderful new friends that I didn't have before.'

I looked at the lion and at Goliath and knew he would be safe.

Androcles smiled. 'Tell Arthur the scabbard is safe!'

Thus it was that we returned on 24th April, the day before Arthur's wedding. I never got used to the difference in days when travelling to and from the Dark Ages.

And all was in chaos to get ready in time.

FORTY-ONE

Rhianne heard that I'd arrived and ran to meet me.

'Where have you been? I've been so worried. Have you been to see Kate?'

'No. I have only been away two or three days – well, where I went anyway. But it seems I've been gone months here! It is just too weird.'

'Well all is in complete turmoil here. The Faerie have arrived and they are dressing the Hall – you've never seen anything like it. It's beautiful. Do you remember the fairy dust? Well, they have bucket loads of it and when Arthur and Gwen are pronounced husband and wife *and* King and Queen, well it will come down from the ceiling over everyone. Apparently it is magical and things might happen.

'Then Nell's son and Smith and countless woodsmen and others have been making a ship in the meadow just below the caer and …'

'A ship? But we're miles from the sea!'

'I know but it is where all the festivities will begin. It is not a real ship, of course, just the shell of one, but it will be dressed up in bunting and ribbons and, of course, the Faerie have had a hand in that too.

'Merlin has declared that Arthur is not just to be king over all the land but over the seas as well – hence the ship!'

'It seems that I've missed out on a lot of fun,' I grumbled.

'Oh no! Just a lot of hard work. But here comes Merlin. I'm sure he wants to find out what happened to Androcles.'

So I went off with the wizard and Salazar and told him about my short three-day trip to Jerusalem, giving great emphasis on the "three days" that I had been away. As usual he dismissed my grumps without even acknowledging them.

'… and Shake Spear has written a few sonnets which he and several others will lead during the festivities. Sir Ector and the Lady Elise have organised enough wine, mead and food that would satisfy even Goliath, if he were still here.' Merlin added as though I hadn't spoken.

'*And me; and Griff!*' Cabby added.

'And you two,' Merlin chuckled, patting the two wolfhounds on the head. There'll be plenty of bones for you!'

'Jasmine and I will be leaving these shores soon after the wedding,' Salazar spoke in his deep voice. 'We believe that the land will be strong under Arthur and we both need to see if we can find any of our families that might still be alive. It is important, as you may understand, to know where you came from.'

Merlin gripped his friend's shoulder and nodded his understanding.

'But not just you, my friend. I, too, shall be riding the dragon. I am flying away to a place unknown as yet to man and Nimue will be with me. It has been too long. Too many centuries have passed by with that terrible tearing loneliness that afflicts those kept apart. My work is now done and it will be centuries before I need to return again for Arthur. So, when I go I intend to enjoy my time with my beautiful Nimue.

'Moon Song, too, will return to her place and regardless of what might happen to her in the meantime, she, also, will return one day.'

He looked at me then, with such great sorrow that I was extremely afraid of what he was about to say.

'But it won't last forever; no-one who loves much can be denied so much. Remember that.

'So Nimue and I will at last be together but, and remember this in your hearts and then it will return to your heads, when you need me I will return – but only when you really need me. All you need do is say my name.

'Now, though,' and shaking off his melancholy he smiled as he jumped up. 'Rest my friends – tomorrow will be a wonderful day!'

We heard that the bride had arrived some time late the previous evening. Nell's son's mother – well, Nell, of course – had cleaned and scrubbed and cooked to provide a place for the bride and her maids and father; they couldn't possibly be seen by the groom before the wedding now, could they, and her hostelry was the nearest to the caer where the wedding was to take place.

Then the day finally arrived!

Last minute panics were over and the morning shone, freshly scrubbed as clean and bright as all the participants of the coming event.

The Faerie had not only decorated the Hall for the celebrations afterward but had also had free rein to do the same to the courtyard where the ceremony was to take place as well as the meadow and the ship.

At Arthur's command, though he called it a request, Brother Geraint was to conduct the ceremony and received special dispensation to carry out this important role. His smile was as wide as his heart when he heard he was to marry the newly crowned king and Gwenhwyfar.

The Faerie had constructed an arbour of willow, still with its new shoots flowing elegantly in the soft spring breeze and had intertwined it with primroses, crocuses and spring blossom of every hue. Silver dust had been liberally sprinkled over it and around the ground under it and millions of fairies, like fireflies, hovered all around; it was truly magical. Bunting and ribbons, flags and emblems flew high above from every window and along the parapets where soldiers holding cornets were ready to blow the fanfare as soon as the bridal party was seen approaching. It was amazing how everyone kept looking up at those men to see the exact moment they placed the trumpets to their lips but it eventually happened and everyone began craning their necks to see the bride arrive.

Arthur, dressed as he was for his coronation, was fidgeting until Merlin leaned across and told him to stop.

Kay, his best man, just stood grinning.

Brother Geraint looked so happy; his usual brown attire had been replaced this day with something a little less formal – he wore a grey linen outfit, still kept together by a white rope belt but he also wore a white chasuble around his neck that hung almost to the ground, which was decorated with golden halos and doves.

The bride arrived, resting a gentle, though slightly trembling, hand onto the arm of her father; her maids, dressed the same, were following.

In her other hand Gwen held a small bouquet of lily of the valley, which were held together with white silk flowing ribbons; both she and her maids were dressed in the palest of green silk.

There was such an intake of breath and then an eruption of cheering as they entered that even the trumpets were momentarily drowned out.

The ceremony began and I was taken back to the time I had married Rhianne. Taking her hand in mine I knew she was thinking the same. There was only one thing that marred the happiness of this day for us and that was Kate. What on earth were we going to do?

I eventually pulled myself back to the present to find that we had joined the procession out to the meadow where tables of wine, sherbet and small food awaited us.

At some time I remember Merlin standing on the foredeck of the wooden ship that had been gaily festooned and telling everyone to cheer their new king and queen who were standing alongside him, closely followed by Wirra who, holding Excalibur aloft, had now been given the honour of becoming the keeper of the sword for Arthur.

Other things happened but I was only really half there.

I was extremely pleased that Arthur and Gwen were now married and that Britain had a monarch that would rule well and I know that I laughed long and hard with everyone else that day but I couldn't help but see the sadness appearing now and then in one special pair of violet blue eyes.

As the light faded and the dew began to paint the grass a deeper green we all went back to the Hall. Again, I was reminded of my own wedding day – the glitter, the beauty and the joy of it all.

We had to wait until the bride and groom eventually left before we, too, could retire to our own room.

But before all had left Merlin came and took me by the arm. 'Now come, Percy, I need to speak with you alone.'

FORTY-TWO

'*Oh, surely there must be some other way.*'

'There is no other way, Percy. I've searched and I've tried but there is no other way.'

Salazar joined us and with a sadness to his proud demeanour added that he, too, had been unable to find a solution.

'Then that mad witch has won!' I groaned. 'She's not only done for me but now she's also done this to Rhianne and me!'

'She will never win!' Merlin almost shouted.

'I will keep searching,' Salazar promised.

'And so will I,' Merlin added.

'How can you do that if you are going away?' I almost spat at him.

'I will still search, my friend, even then.'

'Oh Merlin, forgive me; I didn't mean to hurt you. You have always been there; always done the best for me. It is her fault all this has happened. I am sorry I shouted at you.'

'Now, now, don't take on so. I know that! Don't you think I know you by now? We will overcome. **We will!**'

And so it was that Rhianne would stay here with her brother and parents and wait for a husband who might never see her again, while I would have to return to the 20th Century and bring up our daughter, perhaps never be able to return to see my wonderful, my beautiful wife ever again.

'I'm sorry, but we have nearly run out of the special powder that has taken you back and forth over the years.'

'But what about that blue stuff that Cabby licked up? Isn't there any more of that?' I begged him.

'I've tried it out a few times since – either on me or Salazar and on a couple of hare but it appears that it doesn't work on humans as they could not go; it worked on the hare but although they went they didn't come back.'

'So it's hopeless!'

'For the moment it would appear so. But there always has to be hope,' he said.

'How am I going to tell Rhianne?'

'Just tell her you might be some time but that you will try to come back. In the meantime I will see what I can do. However, you can always send Cabby – he can go back and forth at will.'

And that is what we have always done.

I can't, even now, tell you what happened when I spoke to Rhianne – it is still much too painful. But she is well; Cabby has always let me know that!'

At one point I didn't think I would be able to carry on without her but then, when I looked into my daughter's beautiful eyes and saw the trust in them, how could I leave her? No, I would carry on but there would always be that pain, mostly kept under control nowadays, in my heart.

Of course, you might think that when Cabal goes off into the woods he has just gone off to do his own business; sometimes he has gone to see Rhianne and even if he spends weeks with her, he is only gone from us for moments.

Yes Rhianne is well, though she has the worst part of this deal – at least I have our daughter.

'Granddad, you have to tell us now. Is it all a true story? Is our grandmother somewhere back in time?'

Jack laughed. 'Everyone's grandmother is back in time, Danny. Even the dead ones!'

'Oh, you know what I mean – in the Dark Ages.'

'Do you remember when you were very small; you always asked me to tell you a story and I would start it off something like, 'Once upon a time there were two little boys and one was called Danny and the other one Ben and one day …'"

'Of course I do. But what has that got to do with the other stories?'

'Well, they could be just like that – stories! Not real at all. But you liked being in those stories and I think that sometimes you even thought they were real. However, if you think they might have possibly been true, then I reckon they are good stories, don't you?'

'You're never going to get the truth out of him?' Ben laughed. 'I gave up trying a long time ago.'

'Well, I won't give up until I get to the bottom of all this!'

'Put a few more logs on the fire Ben,' Jack called over his shoulder at his oldest grandson. 'It's freezing in here.'

'The fire's blazing, granddad, but I must admit it is turning cold.'

And then she was there.

Cackling like the burning thorns on a fire, spitting and hacking as she fell about laughing, she eventually stopped and her face was as hard as flint.

'Thought you'd done away with me for good, didn't you?' Her voice was that of a very, very old woman. Not one tooth remained in her mouth and not one hair remained on her head. She had lost all the weight she once had trouble carrying around and was now stick thin; her once blue dress hung on her like something on a coat hanger.

She may have changed a lot in appearance but her smell was going to prove still as powerful as her magic.

They were almost knocked out by the smell but she had obviously cast some sort of enchantment because although they could move it was extremely slowly.

What had happened? How had she got to this state?

Jack looked at his two grandsons and was fearful of what she might do to them; would he be able to defend them in time? He tried so hard to keep his thoughts to himself so that she was unaware when he tried something. His magic had not been used now for so many years that he wondered if he could remember any of it.

Then Kate walked through the door.

Oh my! What was she going to do to her?

'*Merlin*,' Jack cried but would he be in time?

He quickly looked around. Ben was by the log pile; Danny beside the kitchen table and Mab was between the two of them; Kate had just come into the house and was still holding onto the door handle with Jack about three feet from her but to one side so she had a direct view of the witch; worse was that the witch had full view of her.

Although all their actions were sluggish anyway it was as though everything had been set to slow motion. Jack saw the witch delve into one of the pockets of her dress and start to pull something out; at the same time she was mouthing the word, 'Kate.'

Jack, pulling on the knowledge that had been imparted to him all those many years ago, found a spell that could be sent through his mind at the witch.

So it was that as the witch threw something at his daughter, Jack threw the spell at the witch, at the same time leaping – would he be in time – in front of Kate.

It was like fireworks night. Bangs, crashes, whizzes and flashes that filled the room with light, smoke and noise that seemed to go on and on.

It finally cleared and they could move.

'Oh dad!' Kate rushed over to her father who was lying spread-eagled on the floor.

Ben and Danny also ran across to him as Kate lifted his head onto her arm. They looked across the room to where the witch had been but all that remained was a crumpled almost blue dress that was disintegrating even as they watched; and was that also the shape of a sword that pinned the dress to the floor as it flashed a couple of times before also disappearing?

'So now you know!' Jack spoke with a faraway voice. 'Maybe it is all true. Maybe you will forget.'

'Oh granddad, what's wrong? I'll run for the doctor.'

'Too late, Danny. No-one can help me this time.'

'Come on dad. You'll be OK; you always are.' Kate was trying hard to stop herself from crying.

They watched as he relaxed and then within only a few more seconds he breathed his last. Cabby lay beside him licking his face.

'I'll help you with the funeral arrangements,' a soft voice spoke from the doorway.

'Mrs Ambrose,' Danny jumped up and ran to her. 'Can you do anything? You know, like you did for Cabby?'

'Not this time boy. But I will help you bury him.'

She was as good as her word. Before she went into town she took the wolfhound off into the woods to collect some bits of this and that. At the same time she told him to travel to and fro between the two time zones and keep an eye on everything.

Later she went off and bought Jack a fresh white shirt and a decent suit – nothing too fussy – and said it would be a good idea to make sure he had some of her special herbs that she had just collected in the woods packed around his body – to keep the wicked at bay.

'Oh do you think the witch will try to snatch his body?'

'No, of course not. It's an old tradition where I come from. And I think that old witch is no more. *Though I have often thought that before, but best not to worry the lad!* Your grandfather learned a lot, many years ago, and I believe it was for such a time as this. I understand that Merlin fought the witch many times but she always came back. I wonder if your grandfather was the one to pack her off forever.' The old woman paused a while as she thought about what she'd just said.

'Oh well, perhaps we'll never know.'

FORTY-THREE

They stood at the side of the grave.

Kate had an arm around each of her sons; all of them were weeping silently.

Four men, all dressed in clothes as black as everyone's spirits, were finally lowering the coffin down the six feet into the earth where only about two inches of rainwater now remained.

It had started raining the night before – hard at first but becoming softer and gentler as morning approached. The pump had been set up so that as much water as possible could be extracted before the burial itself commenced.

'I know he was old, mum,' Ben whispered, 'but he shouldn't have gone that way.'

'We all have to go some way or other, Ben,' she replied. 'But I know what you mean.'

It had seemed so pointless. Jack had everything to live for.

After the wake Mrs Ambrose asked Danny to walk back with her to old Mr Fellowes' cottage. Kate and the boys had said she could stay there while the funeral arrangements were being made and that she and the boys would stay in her father's cottage; however, this time she agreed that she was happy for Danny to spend the night with the old lady. Cabal followed them.

The old woman could see just how upset Danny was and determined that she would try and lift that burden from his young shoulders as quickly as she could.

They chatted for some ten minutes as they walked the serpentine lane down to the village.

Finally, Mrs Ambrose let them into the cottage and placed the kettle on the hob. 'We'll have a nice cup of tea and a cosy chat, Danny.'

The boy looked up, pale, with a wan smile on his face and just nodded.

'Now, how would you like to take a little trip with me? It won't be very far but it will be very different to wherever you have been before.'

Danny looked up at her. She had been speaking with her back to him as she prepared the tea.

'Where?' was all he could say.

The old woman turned and stared at him. *'Oh here and there, back and forth, fighting evil and the like.'*

He gaped. His mouth had dropped open – just like his granddad's bottom jaw used to do. He shut it.

'It's all true then?' he asked tentatively.

'Oh yes; it's always been true!'

'And I can do that too? Talk without speaking?'

'Of course!'

'But Cabal can't do it, can he? Not really? I mean – he's a dog!' He looked down at the hound who'd followed them home.

'So, I'm not all true then eh?' he grumbled.

Danny just stood and stared.

'Oh, there's something I must do before we go, though; that is, if you both want to go?' Merlin broke into the uncomfortable silence.

Danny looked down at Cabby who was looking a little happier, tail slowly swaying from side to side.

'I want to go,' Cabby added.

'Oh, yes, so do I! It's all true! It's all true!

'But will mum miss me? And what have you got to do Mrs Ambrose?'

'Like your grandfather, you could be away for a few days or a year, but you will only ever be away from here for moments. They will not miss you. And, who knows, somewhere back in time you might meet up with him again! Oh what stories you will be able to tell then, eh?'

And as she swirled, turning from an old woman to the tall magician of mystery that his grandfather had always described him to be, he watched as Merlin pulled a small device out of one of his pockets, pressed a switch and smiled.

'What was that?' Danny asked, intrigued.

'Oh, I shall tell you about that another time,' the wizard grinned, throwing some glittering dust over the three of them 'For now, Sir Niel, let's be away.'

Merlin had taken Cabal to one side while the family had been at the graveside and had sworn him to secrecy about Jack. The hound had looked so crestfallen that he felt he had to let out the secret for fear Cabal would pine right away.

So a happy trio disappeared; the kettle was almost to the boil and Merlin felt sure they would all return in time for tea.

Meanwhile, in the church graveyard some half a mile away a miniature explosion from within the single white rose in Jack's lapel sprinkled a small amount of grey dust over the person lying inside the coffin.

'Ah, you've come back at last!' Rhianne, now an old woman but as stunning as she was all those years ago stroked his brow as he lay, arms still folded in death, on the grassy bank near the river where Merlin had often allowed him to catch a glimpse of her as she ran a hand through the cool waters that flowed slowly by. Cabal, standing guard beside her, merely watched.

Opening his sleepy brown eyes Percy smiled up into her lovely pale violet ones and raising his arms to enfold her almost choked with emotion on his whispered words, 'And I will never ever leave you again, my wonderful, my beautiful, my beloved wife.'

EPILOGUE

And what of Merlin? Is it possible that he, too, can now take his ease with his loved one, Nimue? Well, maybe for a while – if all is right with the world. Who knows when the Once and Future King will return?

Sitting happily side by side in his sky tower, their contented faces lit by the last crimson rays of the evening's sun, they watch as it slips gracefully away before the beauty of the night sky begins her glorious display. The couple spend their time reminiscing and making plans whilst Merlin grinds some of his special, magical dust; dust that he has used since the beginning of all things to enable travel from here to there in the twinkling of an eye.

Danny, indoctrinated into the intricacies and mysteries of the Druid, was, like his grandfather before him, growing old and so someone else with the Gift of the Old Way has to be sought to one day take his place. There is no time like the present, Merlin thought, to start searching for that special person.

Lifting his eyes from his grinding, he stares out through the roof of his sky tower and watches as the stars come out one by one before, lowering his head, he turns his eyes and now looks out directly from this page.

Could you be the one?

ON THE DRAGON'S BREATH
...*A TALE OF MERLIN*

A tale about the greatest sorcerer of all time – Merlin the Magician, that embraces mystery, magic, mayhem and madness alongside dragons, druids and a dreadful witch.

JACK, our 20th Century hero, is taken back through the mists on the Dragon's Breath to a time of adventure in the Dark Ages of King Arthur, son of Uther Pendragon. He shares those adventures with the future king's wolfhound, Cabal, who is more than just a dog!

ISBN 978-0-9545423-0-6   327pp   £6.99

THE GLASTON GIANT
...*A TALE OF MERLIN*

MERLIN, drawing our 20th Century hero, Jack, back through the mists, plunges him once more into the intrigues and adventures of a time long forgotten – a time of wizards, dragons, giants and the faerie.

Their task, ultimately, is to find and dispose of the giant. So it is, that together with Arthur's faithful hound, Cabal, they set off... eventually to tangle with fabulous beasts and partake of frightening escapades before coming face to face with that fearful giant and his fanatical sidekick who is none other than that evil witch Mad Mab.

ISBN 978-0-9545423-1-3   392pp   £6.99

THE PLACE OF SHADES
...A TALE OF MERLIN

Percy – alone and friendless – finds himself below decks, in semi-darkness and manacled to an oar on a pirate ship. *'But there aren't any pirates like this anymore!'* The whip that cracks across his shoulders tells him otherwise.

Transported across time and space he soon discovers the madness of an otherworld where pirates – especially the Jackal (and is he all he makes out to be?) – run the show and other mysterious beings add to the insanity that runs riot in the Place of Shades (or should it be called by its proper name *The Place of the Dead!*).

ISBN 978-0-9545423-2-0   328pp   £7.99

THE MASQUE OF ALL MYSTERIES
...A TALE OF MERLIN

A trail of devastation, disappearances, destruction and death can only mean one thing – that the mad witch, Mab, has returned – and she's not only been able to escape the Place of Shades but has got her hands on a mask that once she can unlock its secrets could make her the most powerful sorcerer of all time. "Watch out Merlin!"

But where is Merlin? He's the only one that's ever been able to stand up to her and he's not been seen for nearly two years! In fact the word has gone out that he had gone completely mad and roams the forests unwashed, screaming and muttering. So if he didn't call Jack back, then who did?

ISBN 978-0-9545423-3-7   310pp   £7.99

www.jennyhall-talesofmerlin.co.uk